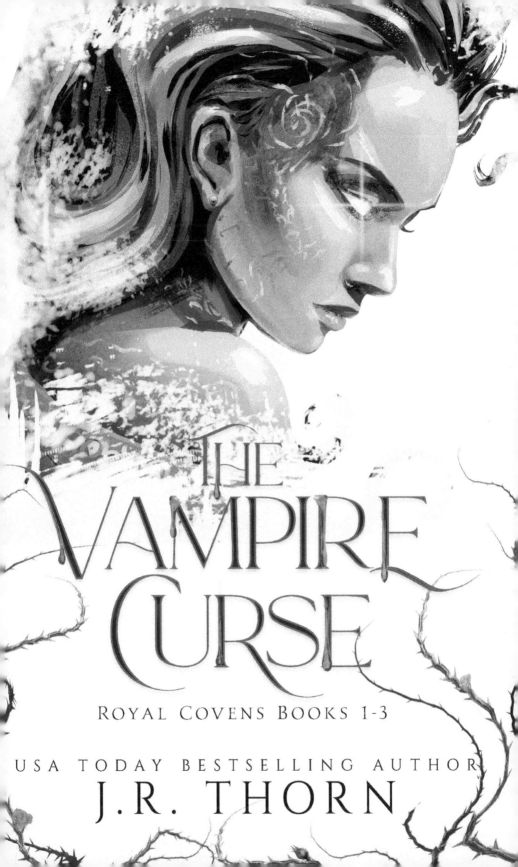

THE
VAMPIRE
CURSE

Royal Covens Books 1-3

USA TODAY BESTSELLING AUTHOR

J.R. THORN

RECOMMENDED READING ORDER

All Books are Standalone Series listed by their sequential order of events

Elemental Fae Universe Reading List

Elemental Fae Academy: Books 1-3 (Co-Authored)

Midnight Fae Academy (Lexi C. Foss)

Fortune Fae Academy (J.R. Thorn)

Blood Stone Series Universe Reading List

• *Chasing Fate (USA Today Bestselling Book)*

Seven Sins

• *Book 1: Succubus Sins*

• *Book 2: Siren Sins*

• *Book 3: Vampire Sins*

Royal Covens

• *Book 1: Captivated*

• *Book 2: Compelled*

• Book 3: Consumed

Fortune Academy

• Year One

• Year Two

• Year Three

Non-RH Books (J.R. Thorn writing as Jennifer Thorn)

Noir Reformatory Universe Reading List

Noir Reformatory: The Beginning

Noir Reformatory: First Offense

Sins of the Fae King Universe Reading List

(Book 1) Captured by the Fae King

Learn More at www.AuthorJRThorn.com

CAPTIVATED: BOOK 1

Four sexy vampires. One mortal-born witch. An ancient secret that will test them all.

I'm not a very good witch. It's not my fault. Being born a mortal sucks and my black cat familiar follows me around like a security blanket. All the other coven brats make fun of me.

My vampires don't seem to mind. They pose as my mentors and get Aunt Sandra off my back. My initiation into the Royal Covens is only three days away. They're supposed to teach me how to hide what I really am: a reincarnation of some ancient and powerful witch. I think they're just telling me that to get in my pants.

What my vampires don't hide is their hunger for me, both for my blood and my body. That dangerous kind of thrill is going to get me into serious trouble.

CHAPTER 1

I didn't want to be in a bad mood today, but an ominous sense of dread clung to my chest and wouldn't let go. Given that I was supposed to be initiated into the dark arts in just a few days, a little dread was to be expected. I scratched at the black lace of my bodice, which was actually my undershirt for the gown I was supposed to wear tonight. A black leather jacket and a pair of shorts pulled the outfit together, making me feel sexy and free—as long as I wasn't recognized.

I startled when a crow flapped to a nearby fencepost and squawked at me.

"Shoo!" I shouted.

It stared at me with beady, unreadable eyes.

Ignoring the bad omen, I gripped my sketchbook and wandered into one of my favorite places in the world. The graveyard that skirted around the old chapels on this side of my village wasn't frequented often, but that's why I liked it here. Witches didn't like places of death. Mortality frightened them more than anything else in the world, so they stayed far away from anything that reminded them of the finite length of our existence. Humans reluctantly accepted death as inevitable, but because witches had options, they seemed to fear it even more. Very few could boast true immortality, and those that could had likely paid far too high a price for that reward—in my opinion, anyway.

Sparkles, my midnight-colored cat and magical familiar, spun circles around my ankles, somehow managing not to trip me as I silently made my way past the cracked tombstones. Sparkles got his name because of the touch of magic that sparked on the edges of his fur. Every time he brushed my skin he donated a bit to me. He was a generous familiar, but I always felt like he did it out of pity. I was mortal. My parents weren't witches, and until I initiated into my coven officially, I didn't have much power of my own other than what others gave to me. I got doses at my adopted family dinners—I don't even want to know what was in our meals —some from breathing in the spelled herbs surrounding the estate I lived in, and a significant chunk of my magic was from my familiar when he was worried about me, which was all the time and especially when I was getting into trouble.

"Stop that, Sparkles," I chided him and bent down to scratch under his chin. He leaned into my touch and purred. His big emerald eyes blinked at me with feline smugness. "Just because I'm human doesn't mean I'm weak," I reminded him and I tugged a dagger from my frilly sock. He meowed at me, and even though no one else would understand him, I'd gotten pretty good at deciphering what he was trying to say.

"Yes, I have a story of where it came from," I answered him as I straightened.

I took a moment to admire the frosted swirl that ran along the edge before tucking it in my belt-loop. I liked daggers, especially unique, pretty ones. Since I was a witch, we were expected to have sharp, pointy objects at all times. Spells required blood, and getting an infection by cutting yourself with someone else's blade was quite embarrassing. For that reason I picked daggers that were easily recognizable. After I'd picked up this one from the human market, I'd fabricated a story of how I'd bumped into some old acquaintances from the Sapphire Coven and I'd bought it from them. Sadly, that was more acceptable than "I mingled with mortals."

Wandering deeper into the graveyard, I sought out my favorite spot, an ancient memorial with four spires, and settled myself into the middle of it. Sparkles joined me and curled up in a ball against my legs.

I opened my sketchbook and tugged a pencil from my pouch. I liked to draw whatever came to mind, but lately my sketches had started getting weird. I kept drawing the same rune over and over again—one that wasn't in any of the coven's books.

The first page of my sketchbook showed Sparkles, at least a cartoon version of him. That was before I'd started drawing the runes. I patted him as he sat at my feet. "What do you think, Sparkles? What will I draw today?"

He lifted his head and gave me a long yawn, which was as much appreciation as I was going to get for the portrait.

Sighing, I flipped through the pages, going past different things that spurred my creativity. I'd sketched out more daggers than I cared to admit, each one more elaborate than the last, and then I started adding runes to the blades. Finally, one particular rune started taking over my sketchbook until the last few pages were littered with them. I skipped past them, ignoring the sense of building dread. I was just nervous about my initiation, that's all.

When I stared at a fresh blank page, I pressed my pencil to it and frowned.

I closed my eyes and let my imagination take hold. Maybe I'd sketch the people I'd seen today, or a dream of a future where I wasn't destined to become a witch. I wasn't even sure what that might look like. It wasn't that I was ungrateful to my coven for taking me in. Some horrendous memory was a gaping black hole in my head. I assumed the darkness in the back of my mind was a repressed memory of what had happened to my parents. No one spoke of it. No one would talk to me about it as if they feared triggering a memory best left forgotten.

My pencil moved as the creativity in me sought an outlet. I did better with expressing myself through art than I did magic. Maybe it was the mortal side of me, just another flaw to my coven. My aunt—not my real aunt, just the woman who raised me—always told me it was a bad habit I'd have to drop when I was initiated as a full, respective member of the coven.

That day hadn't come yet. Soft scratching filled my ears as lead scraped over the paper and my fingers moved on their own. The sketches always seemed to represent what was most important to me, small things, big things. Today I hoped it would be a cool dagger or the hot guy I'd seen on the street. Not the damned rune…

When I opened my eyes, goosebumps spread across my skin. I'd drawn it again, but this time more elaborate than I'd ever sketched it before. It looked so real with hard, metallic edges as if it were engraved into my sketchbook.

I jerked when the crow squawked at me again and Sparkles lurched to his feet with a hiss. He growled low at the bird, and that's when I realized I'd misunderstood that this wasn't an ordinary crow.

While I'd been lost in a trance of my sketch, the four pillars surrounding me had come to life, and before I had a chance to scramble off the platform, a spell took me under.

I'D HAD my share of vision spells. Being a mortal-born witch put a giant target on my forehead. If I ever got on the bad side of a witch—which was often—I could look forward to a few very realistic living nightmares.

This vision, though, was all too real. The graveyard had taken on an eerie darkness that even managed to unsettle someone like me who loved all things Goth and tragic. Dead rose vines swept over the grounds and the distinct scent of ash tinged the air as if all life had been burned off the planet.

When I scrambled to my feet, I stilled when I realized that I wasn't alone. Sparkles hadn't made it through with me into the vision, but four dark figures stepped out from the pillars and gathered towards the center. They didn't seem to see me, so I swiftly stepped out of the way of the closest figure.

The vision solidified when they reached the middle and the darkness lifted just a shade. The figures took on coloring and shape until four gorgeous men stood before me. Each of them had glowing red eyes, the kind I'd only seen in powerful warlocks at the head of their covens. There was another possibility, though. There was another creature that had glowing red eyes.

Vampires.

I swallowed hard as I gathered the courage to drift closer. Their low voices hummed in conversation and I was dying to know what they were talking about.

"This is the stupidest idea you've ever had," the one with bright red hair said with a panty-melting Irish accent.

The man he was glowering at crossed his arms. He didn't look like any warlock I'd ever seen, not with two full tattoo sleeves and a lip piercing. "At least I *have* an idea, Quinn. What do you recommend we do? Let the covens kill us, just like they killed her?"

"That's precisely what we do," said the third male with a honey-sweet voice. I glanced at him, finding him the more refined of the four. Hard abs cut through a thin silk shirt and it was unbuttoned at the top, leaving enough skin to admire to make me blush. I drifted closer, but got the sense that they couldn't see me.

The fourth sighed and flipped out a switchblade, making my eyes go wide. He danced the blade over his fingers in a long-practiced trick, as if it helped him release his stress. "So, we're to become vampires, then, and add our own deaths to our grief."

My eyes about bugged out of my head. Instantly I knew who these four were, even if it was impossible.

They went silent as they seemed to accept the final male's

statement with only the swishing sound of the switchblade moving over expert knuckles.

"You're the founders of the lost vampire tribes," I breathed, amazed at what I was seeing, although I wasn't sure what woman they might be talking about. Regardless, this was a forgotten part of coven history—or perhaps it was a hidden part. The covens didn't like to dwell on their failures, which made me all the more interested in this vision.

As I settled in-between two of the guys, the refined-looking one and the Irish red-head named Quinn, I decided that I could get the lowdown of witchy secrets while admiring the perfect male specimens at the same time. Assuming, of course, this was actually a vision. It wouldn't have been the first time that warlocks pretended I didn't exist.

"Hey, you guys, I'm about to take my shirt off," I tested aloud, confirming that none of them could hear me when they didn't respond. Even if warlocks often ignored me, breasts always seemed to get their attention.

Satisfied that I was invisible to them, I leaned in closer to Quinn, grinning at him. "I bet girls take off their shirts for you all the time, huh?"

Quinn remained oblivious of me and watched the other warlock continue to toss his switchblade through the air. I got the impression that Quinn always thought his course of action through before making a decision. Whatever switch-blade warlock had decided, Quinn wasn't going to take it lightly.

Sighing, I tried the refined one. "What about you? What's your name?" My gaze dipped to the opening of his shirt and I sighed at the perfect lines that cut through the silk. "Maybe I should call you cut, because damn."

Before my tirade of inappropriate comments could continue, the ground rumbled and I buckled my knees out of reflex. The warlocks didn't seem to notice that the world was ending and had continued on in quiet conversation. "Uh, guys?" I said, suddenly wishing they could hear me. The ground shook again and the spires surrounding us began to glow. My sinking sense of dread flared into outright panic. Was this what my witchy senses had foreseen? That I'd die in the collapsed rubble of a faulty spell?

Whoever had cast it on me was dead... once I got out of here alive, that is.

Sparkles wasn't around to hit me with fresh magic, but I was deeply grateful he'd been rubbing against my ankles and had given me little doses all day. It buzzed in my veins and now that adrenaline spiked through my body, it sent the electric power into overdrive. Needles tingled over my arms and legs as I tried to calm my rapid breathing.

"You can do this," I told myself as I curled my trembling fingers into fists. "Just a simple grounding spell. You got this."

I closed my eyes and tried to ignore the sounds of the world around me shredding. The vision wasn't going to last much longer and if I was still inside it when it collapsed, my mind would break, which meant I was dead. If I didn't get back to my body in the next couple of seconds, my mind would be trapped here and broken into a thousand little pieces, leaving my corpse to rot while my mind lived on in insanity.

Man, who had it out for me that badly? What a way to go.

I couldn't go through my million-mile long list of enemies right now. It was time to focus on the one thing I sucked at the most.

Casting spells under pressure.

Okay... casting spells at all.

I drew my dagger, again grateful to have brought it with me, and sliced a clean cut along my palm, proud of myself that I didn't hesitate. Blood dripped to my feet and I chanted under my breath. At first, nothing happened as I fumbled over the Latin words and I cursed. How could I not even cast a Latin spell? It's not like I was trying to cast a native witch spell. Magic had its own language that full-fledged witches were fluent in. Latin was a poor man's medium of magic, and I couldn't even do that.

Pain shot up my right arm as the vision cracked in retaliation and I stumbled away from the breach. My eyes snapped open and I grit my teeth as frustration bloomed in my chest. I was going to die here, wasn't I?

I glanced back at the males who continued to act as if nothing was going on. Either they weren't really here, or...

The spires. I counted four of them and there also were four guys. That wasn't a coincidence. Their spirits were safe and sound in those spires which didn't show the slightest crack as the rest of the world tumbled to pieces. If I couldn't ground myself in my magic... I could ground myself in theirs.

Taking a chance, I bolted towards one of the pillars and smeared the blood from my cut hand over the stone. I winced as the rough surface snagged against my wound.

Turning back to the warlocks, I held my breath and waited.

Switchblade guy froze with his knife poised midair as his gaze snapped to me, pinning me to the spot. I sucked in a breath. Fuck yes. It was working.

Not wasting any time, I ran to the next pillar and sliced another cut on my palm, biting my lip down on a cry as I smeared fresh blood across the stone.

There was a distinct sensation of another set of eyes on me, as well as a refreshing solid feeling under my feet, so I hurried onto the next one. I was performing an unorthodox grounding spell, one that probably had some nasty side effects, but at least I wouldn't be dead.

By the time I bloodied the last pillar, the air around me cracked like a spiderweb and I knew I would have been dead by now had I not acted fast. Sweat gathered at my hairline and I held my bleeding, mangled hand to my chest, glad that even if I was no good at spells, I could at least be scrappy about using other people's magic. I was like the hoodlum of Wicca. That had a ring to it.

All of the warlocks were staring at me now in deadly silence. I glared right back at them. "What?" I snapped. "You think I'm just going to let whoever wants me dead win? Don't be a bunch of dumbasses."

The refined one raised a brow. Okay, so, they could hear me now.

Mr. Switchblade flashed his knife in an expert move, flicking the two handles so that they snapped into place and tucked the blade safely away. He marched up to me and my mouth went dry. My head came up to his chest and I had to arch my neck back to match his angry gaze. "Who are you?" he snapped as if I'd intruded on a private cocktail party.

I was about to retort something snarky like, "Your worst nightmare," with my best monster-voice, but dizziness swept through me as the vision finally crumbled. I grabbed my head and collapsed to the ground as blackness devoured me.

Maybe I was going to die after all.

RACE YOU HOME!

I woke up to Sparkles standing on my chest. He meowed bloody murder and nipped at my wounded hand. "Ow!" I cried and shot up, sending the cat launching into the air.

He landed deftly on his feet and glowered at me with green eyes that sparked with magic. So, I guess he'd managed to pull what was left of me out of the vision. I gave him a lopsided grin. "Thanks, Sparks. I'm okay now."

He growled with warning. I wasn't safe yet.

Then I saw why he was freaking out. Orange and pink hues bled over the horizon and my heart leapt into my throat. It was almost sundown. Shit!

Scrambling to my feet, I tried not to feel nauseated when I spotted fresh blood plastered on all four spires in sickly desperate streaks. I looked down at my hand to find it still mangled, which meant that even if I had been in a vision, my wounds and actions had carried over to the real world. That meant I'd been under an extremely powerful spell—Royal Covens kind of powerful.

Shit, what kind of enemy had I made now? I was trying to keep a low profile before my initiation, but one of the royals had it out for me bad and wanted me dead before the family magic made me too hard to kill.

A dusty wind tumbled through the graveyard and brought the scent of dirt and nature. It was oddly refreshing after my nightmarish vision, but it wasn't enough to calm my racing heart. I gave the sea of tombstones a once over, but the guys from the vision were nowhere to be found. I was on my own. I wasn't sure if I was disappointed or glad about that. Those guys had looked like trouble, and they hadn't been very happy when they'd noticed me.

"Get a grip, Evie," I chided myself. Surely those guys had just been magical conjurations of the vision and were long dead, right? There was no way that the founders of the lost vampiric tribes could still be alive. The Royal Covens had wiped them out eons ago. Witches and vampires might sometimes get along, but witches who turned themselves into vampires broke some kind of moral code and were outcasts.

Swallowing my opinion that I rather preferred outcasts to royals, I took in a deep breath before launching into a run to get home. Sparkles meowed and bolted ahead of me, leading the way down the twisted overgrown paths of the graveyard.

The castle wasn't far from here, but I was cutting it close. Anyone with supernatural blood, especially weak, young blood like mine, couldn't remain outdoors after nightfall; not since the breach.

The eerie howls carried on the wind and goosebumps

sprang up across my arms. Tossing open the squeaky gate to the graveyard, I banked a hard right and scampered down the cobbled street towards the castle.

A large field surrounded the estate and I could already spot the jasmine blooms starting to unfold. I had to make it inside before they activated. The jasmine fields were part of a spell. The best spells were grounded in nature and a jasmine field would make a barrier that no supernatural could cross— at least not without some seriously heavy magic. It was better to wait for the change of day. The spell was linked to the moon, just like the wolves that had been prowling the streets for the past few weeks.

Another warning howl sounded, this time much closer. I checked my hand and it was still bleeding. Shit, they could smell it!

I didn't have anything to wrap my wound to stem the flow of blood. I had to make sure I got home and then I'd deal with the ramifications later, even if Aunt Sandra would behead me thrice over. It was almost preferable to face demon-touched wolves than Aunt Sandra when she was angry... almost.

I reached the unguarded opening and the hum of the jasmine ward tingled along my skin. The sun hadn't fully set yet, but I was cutting it too close.

It was times like these when I was grateful for my pathetically weak mortal blood. The spell didn't hit me as hard as it would a full supernatural at dusk.

Sparkles mewled when he hit the wall. He was a little ball of magic and I plucked him up with my good hand. "Not leaving you behind," I assured him as I tucked him under my arm. He growled his disapproval for the undignified method of transport, but at least he didn't scratch me.

I ran as fast as my feet could take me across the long stretch of cobbled stones that led to the castle. Jasmine blooms scented the air and their amethyst magic sent delicate sparkles filtering across the field. I panted when the magic pulsed against me, warning me that I wasn't supposed to be there.

As I reached the end of the road and safely made it inside of the field, the spell snapped shut with a dull *thud* and I sucked in a breath. I'd almost been too late.

I set Sparkles down and offered him a nervous laugh, hoping he couldn't pick up how close we'd just been to certain death. He glowered up at me, his green eyes bright with magic. I winced. He'd been holding off the Jasmine spell.

"Thanks once again, Sparks," I whispered and turned to look back the way we'd come. Purple motes flung into the air, relentlessly spreading the field with the protective poison. Nothing supernatural could get in or out, not even a mortal-born witch like me.

I'm not sure what compelled me to stay there and keep looking. Maybe I expected to find a demon-touched wolf that had been hot on my heels. I squinted when I thought I spotted glowing red eyes in the sudden fog that had settled onto the streets, but then there was only the fog.

"I'm not your dinner tonight," I muttered. My heart thumped hard against my chest because I didn't want to admit how close I'd been to being a wolf's snack.

Sparkles wound around my ankles, reminding me that I had one more monster to face.

I laughed. "Right," I told him as I took my time going up the steps to the estate. I pressed my palm flat against the door, the magic in my blood sending the bindings to unlock with a soft *click*. "Let's go face Aunt Sandra."

TO MY SURPRISE, no one was waiting for me when I got inside. The low-hanging chandelier burned with its rich purple eternal flames and the two winding staircases that led up to the bedrooms were inviting as always with their pristine polished sheen. Everything was as it should be in the Amethyst Coven.

Irritation bubbled up inside of me. Had really no one realized I hadn't come home yet? How insulting.

Voices filtered in through the hall and I scampered away from them, recognizing Aunt Sandra's silky tones paired with her cousin's: the flippant Lady Isobel. I had no desire to run into either of them in my current state—or in any state, for that matter—so I ran.

I attempted not to bleed out over the expensive Italian carpets as I looked for Cassidy. She worked as my hand-maiden, but she was actually my best friend and partner in crime. It wouldn't have been the first time she'd stitched me up and got me to my bed without anyone noticing. Sleep sounded amazing. Narrowly escaping death was exhausting.

She should be downstairs in the servant's hall eating dinner at this hour. Nightfall was when servants finally got time for themselves. I used the familiar door that would take me to the underground network of the Amethyst

Coven. It was a mansion on its own down here and I slipped into the cool air, shutting the door behind me just as the two witches entered the room. I paused, waiting to find out if they'd seen me, but someone using the servant's door would go unnoticed to them. Servants were like ghosts to well-bred witches, better ignored until they became a nuisance.

I startled when Sparkles gave me a helpful meow. Shushing him, I assured him Cassidy would have cat food for him, but first I needed to make sure I didn't die of blood loss. Clearly he thought I was being overdramatic, but that's the downside of feline familiars. They thought far too fondly of food.

Encouraged by the thought of food, he tottered down the steep, short steps, tail high and whiskers flared as we searched for Cassidy together.

Purple flames glowed to life in the indentations of the walls as we descended. The Covens had as little electricity as possible and ran the household on magic. It kept the mortal servants in check, because if anyone broke the rules, magic would cease to function, and they'd be left in the dark. Frightening things came out in the dark... I knew that better than anyone.

I ran into a handful of servants on my way down, but Sparkles luckily had enough magic for me to work some camouflage. Outright invisibility would have been too powerful a spell, but he cloaked me in a mist of fine magic that worked as compulsion.

Two of the males carrying bundles of wine up from the cellar gave me curious glances, but I'd learned not to make too much of that. A petite servant girl wouldn't be out of place, but they were still men.

Offering them a shy smile as I clutched my hand to my chest, I nodded, and slipped past them. The spell wouldn't change my voice, so it was best to avoid conversation.

Once into the servant's hall I finally spotted Cassidy. She glanced at me, brows furrowing, as she fumbled with a broken shoe.

I was so glad to see her that I dumbly stormed my way past the tables and stopped by her side. "Oh, Cassidy, am I glad to see—"

Her eyes went wide when she recognized my voice and she slipped a hand to my thigh and pinched hard. I winced, but bit off my words. Right. No talking.

"Well, I'm glad to see you've finished your chores," she said, pitching her voice higher for the other servants who'd already started giving us more attention than Sparkle's spell could handle. The magic slipped over me in an extra layer as the black cat meowed at us pathetically. I could almost hear him. *Food, dammit!*

Cassidy grinned and stooped to give the cat a scratch behind his ear. "Heya Sparks. I saved some of the leftover fish for you."

That got his attention. He swarmed around her legs as Cassidy took me by the arm and guided me out of the servant's hall and towards her quarters. "First, let's fix up your mistress, shall we?"

He meowed his reluctant agreement, but only if there was plenty of fish for him when it was all said and done.

When we were out of earshot of the others, Cassidy hissed

at me under her breath. "What the hell is going on? I just left you in your room."

I halted outside her door as she held it open for me. No one was inside, so now was the time to sneak in before anyone saw us. Except, I couldn't shake the way Cassidy was looking at me. "What is it?"

She narrowed her eyes as if I'd irritated her, but then her gaze dipped to my hand. I looked down, only to feel dizzy as deep crimson blood overflowed onto the floor. I needed to close these wounds, and fast.

"Come inside," she said in a hushed voice. She glanced through the hall before closing it and flipping the lock.

I sat on her roommate's bed and tried to cup the blood into my good hand while Cassidy tossed open her lower dresser drawer and pulled out the emergency medical supplies. It wasn't common for a servant to have a drawer full of gauze, stitching thread, and alcohol but... like I said, Cassidy and I were besties and she patched me up a lot.

The small room came equipped with a miniature bathroom that would only be able to fit one tiny female body at a time. A microscopic shower nestled into the corner with a toilet unhygienically close to it. A small basin was wedged between the two, as if that was enough barrier to keep them apart, and Cassidy filled a bowl with water. She plucked a vial from the cabinet and put two drops.

Sparkles meowed his disapproval and Cassidy gave him a weak smile. "I have to stop the bleeding. I'll get another bonus in a few months' time."

I was starting to see black spots now, so I found it hard to feel guilty that I was using Cassidy's annual magic bonus. The liquid, eight drops to a bottle with a prescribed dose of two drops into water, could allow mortals to perform small works of magic. The servants typically used their vial in the first week, either for vomiting money, or for sexual prowess. The latter always made me laugh, because you could tell when the spell had worn off. There's a particular look in a man's face when his dick lost two sizes that weren't his to begin with.

Cassidy saved her bottle. This wouldn't have been the first time that she used a few drops on me.

I hissed when she pressed the cloth to my hand, but the magic took hold right away. My shoulders slumped when the pain lessened to a more manageable throb.

"What kind of spell were you doing in the past ten minutes?" she chided, not looking at me as she continued to dab at my mangled hand.

It made me dizzy to watch, but I needed to understand how magic worked. Cassidy and I weren't so different, except I was supposed to be trained in the magic arts and she was supposed to be trained in laundry. However, she worked the magic with such grace that I found myself mesmerized as the glimmering amethyst strands wove through my skin and closed the worst of the wounds.

"I just got home," I insisted. My voice had dropped to a husky growl of pain, and I hated to sound pathetic, but it'd been a rough day. "I ditched sword fighting and went into town instead." I grinned at her shocked face. "Got myself a new dagger."

She looked down at my hand again and turned it over. Blood clumped between my fingers and had already hardened under my fingernails. "I can see that. Was it sharper than you'd intended?" Before I could answer, she gripped my knees. "If you weren't who I put in your room, then who was it?"

All at once I seemed to register what she was telling me. Another witch or warlock had pretended to be me?

It actually wasn't that uncommon for witches my age to pull such a prank—just not on someone like me. I couldn't imagine anyone who would want to spend a day in my shoes. The kind of spell it took to take on someone else's appearance was a big one, especially to make it convincing.

I sighed and turned my hand over again, admiring Cassidy's work. My skin sparkled with tiny dust particles of Coven magic making my skin gleam with amethyst sprinkles. "It really could be anyone. I have no idea."

Cassidy nodded and straightened. She went to the dresser and gathered the thread and alcohol. "Well, let's get you stitched up and then we'll go tell Sandra."

My eyes went wide when she brought the glinting needle. "Aw, come on. I already cut my hand to all hell. I really don't want to get stabbed, too."

She pointed the tiny weapon at me. "My magic isn't like yours. It'll fade. That means I need to stitch you up with some good old-fashioned needle and thread so those wounds don't open up again." She glared at me until I sighed and offered my hand.

Sparkles reminded us of his presence with a soft trill. "Yes, Sparks," Cassidy said without looking up from her work. She carefully threaded the needle and I winced, but she was always surprisingly gentle. "I patch Evie up first, then you get dinner. If you want to try Jessie, go to the kitchens. She might give you some fish before I'll be ready."

Satisfied with that option, Sparks trotted to the small feline trap door that sat astride the locked opening. It glowed purple at his passing. No one would be able to get through it even if they were small enough. It was for feline familiars only.

For a moment I was jealous of my familiar. He was always welcome here and no one had to put a cloaking spell on him just so he could see his friend. Actually, it was even worse than that. He had friends—plural—and I only had Cassidy.

"What's on your mind?" she asked, always able to sense when I was about to have a pity party.

I gave her a reassuring smile, which probably wasn't very convincing. "I just, I had a long day." My heart twisted when she gave me a knowing look before going back to my hand again.

I couldn't tell her about what I'd seen. I couldn't tell her about anything that had to do with the witch world.

The reminder of that was at her thigh as the stark rune of the Amethyst Coven that glowed with harsh purple magic that bound Cassidy to this house. She was called a servant, but in all reality she was a slave. Just like all the other mortals here, her soul had been sold by her parents in exchange for a boon from the Coven.

When she caught me looking at it, she tugged her skirt lower. The mark had its own mind of where it might appear on the victim, but there was one rule in the Amethyst Coven. Servants displayed their marks, which forced Cassidy to wear unseemly outfits that were almost comical at times, but she managed to pull them off. Once, I caught her strutting around in some slacks with a giant hole cut out of the thigh. It was that sort of rebellious nature I liked about her and made me feel like we could have small victories.

"You don't have to pity me," she insisted. "We both know I don't have much longer anyway."

My heart twisted with a renewed pinch as the harsh words dragged me out of my thoughts. I glanced up at her and frowned. "It was one Sight spell done by another servant to just freak you out. You're not going to die."

She shrugged. "It's all right. I accepted it a long time ago. You'll go to your masquerade ball and that'll be the night that some wayward spell in this coven finally kills me." She gave me a weak smile. "At least I'll be free."

I shook my head and clamped my hand onto hers. "I will take you to the ball with me if I have to. Fate is not set in stone."

She chuckled. "You aren't a Fate Witch. Stop acting like one." She brushed me away. "I'm almost finished. Stop fussing."

When she was done, my hand felt like it was on fire between the alcohol and the thread, but it would do the job. I just needed to get to sleep so it could heal properly.

When I rose shakily to my feet, I sighed, because I remembered I had an imposter to kick out of my room, and then I had some explaining to do.

AN IMPOSTER

irst I had to go track down Sparkles who'd abandoned me sometime during Cassidy's treatment. I found him whiskers deep in bright orange salmon.

"Sparks!" I hissed, keeping my voice low enough so that servants getting ready for bed wouldn't notice me. "I need to go upstairs!"

Someone had given the cat enough food to make him sick, but he didn't seem to mind. Cassidy hadn't been kidding that there were leftovers. My coven loved to have giant feasts that would be impossible to eat all at once. I always found the extravagance wasteful.

I nudged Sparks with my shoe, but he just shifted out of my way and continued tearing at the soft fish. Unable to move the cat from his own little feast, I sighed and opted for a change of clothes as my disguise. Long black robes hung on pegs, perfect for cover if a servant got food on themselves cooking and then needed to go upstairs for a job. However, the robes were more for servants with tattoos on their hands or foreheads, given that the marks always had to be displayed.

I grabbed onto Sparks tail and swiped the soft fur across my brow as I chanted the familiar magic that gave me the needed rune to complete my disguise.

He gave me an irritated growl, but his fangs were too deep in fish to come at me.

"Okay, that's settled," Cassidy whispered. She wasn't able to hide her amusement and her lip ticked up on the side as she watched Sparks eat, but then she grew serious. "Are you sure you're going to be okay? You could stay down here for the night."

The very idea made me nauseous just thinking what my coven would do to Cassidy in retaliation. "No," I assured her. "I've given you enough shit for one night." I squeezed her arm. "I'll be fine."

She knew I was lying, because let's face it, I was a mortal-born witch who couldn't even perform enough magic to stitch myself up after casting a spell. Whoever was in my room pretending to be me had plenty of magic on hand, which made them dangerous.

"I could get Sandra?" Cassidy offered again.

I shook my head. "She can't know that I was almost stuck outside when the fields activated."

Her eyes went wide and the blood drained from her face. "What?"

I winced. Oops. "I can't talk about it, Cass, but I'm safe, so that's all that matters."

She snapped her jaw shut and wound her fingers around the hem of her skirt. "Right. Let's not tell the Coven's head witch that you nearly broke one of the most sacred laws. Good idea."

Now that I'd sufficiently worried Cassidy to death, my shitty day was complete. I gave her a quick hug and retreated before she could stop me.

SNEAKING upstairs was a lot easier with my servant disguise in place. Warlock Liam and his son Neil walked by, quietly discussing some offense the Sapphire Coven had enacted on our house, and completely ignored me other than Liam's trained glance that verified my servant's rune.

When they'd passed, I held my bandaged hand to my chest and slipped through the quiet halls.

I had to get back to the entrance where the spiral staircases went to my bedroom. It was the only way upstairs, even for servants, which meant that I had to put my disguise to the real test. Aunt Sandra had moved on to the sitting room with Isobel and they were already deep into the latest gossip. I paused at the doorway as I contemplated the best way to get past them.

"Did you hear about Warlock Roudan?" Isobel began as she crossed an exposed leg over her knee. She never wore anything remotely appropriate, even though she didn't have the excuse of a rune to display, and the slit of her dress ran up her sleek thigh. "I hear he's found himself a mortal hussy."

Aunt Sandra smirked, but buried her amusement into her teacup. After she'd composed herself, she set her cup down with a soft *clink*. "Wasn't your grandmother mortal-born?"

Aunt Sandra reminded her. She'd grown accustomed to hitting back racist punches with me in the house. To this day, I still didn't know why she defended mortal-born witches when it was such an unpopular opinion, much less why the coven had taken me in at all. That part of my past was a black spot in my memory.

Isobel didn't like being put in her place and she glowered. "My grandfather made many poor choices in his life, and I'm not too proud to admit that." She knocked her tea back, looking as if she wished it were whiskey when she frowned at the empty cup. "The covens are becoming diluted, which is unfortunate given the prophecy."

"Oh not with the prophecy again," Aunt Sandra chided.

That prophecy had been the blight on my existence. I knew it by heart.

When warlocks embrace vampirism and mortals weave their magic, darkness will claw across the skies and the Royal Covens will meet their downfall.

I took prophecies very seriously, as anyone in the magical community would. Seers were powerful and respected, as were their prophecies, but no one stopped to think about what they really meant. Could the downfall of the Royal Covens be prevented if the first half of the prophecy wasn't allowed to unfold?

My mouth went dry when I realized I'd met the warlocks turned vampires. Had I used their magic to escape the vision? Gods, I hoped not. I'd never hear the end of it if Lady Isobel was right.

Aunt Sandra's voice rang over the pounding of my heart and she stuck her nose up at Isobel. "We took in Evelyn because it was our duty. After her initiation, she will be just as much a witch as the rest of us. She will weave *our* magic, not the long-dead vampire warlocks. I really wish you'd drop it."

My cheeks burned. I never knew that Aunt Sandra defended me quite so openly. I was sure if she took the time to look over at the trembling servant in the doorway, she'd realize that Lady Isobel's accusations were right. She might be a bitch, but maybe she wasn't wrong...

Isobel scoffed and shot to her feet. "I've had enough for one day." She swiveled and then spotted me, making me suck in a breath as fear grappled around my throat like an invisible noose. I was grateful for the shadow of my hood and the glowing fake rune at my forehead that hopefully made me unrecognizable. "You!" she spat, making my blood run cold. "Go fetch my coat. I'm leaving."

I nodded emphatically, then scampered through the sitting room towards the foyer. Thank the gods she hadn't asked for more tea, or I would have had to go back to the servant's hall.

I glanced at the coats resting in the ornate closet by the door and grinned. She'd be pissed when I disobeyed her order. I didn't think Aunt Sandra would allow her to take it out on the servants when I didn't return.

Without any further time to contemplate the repercussions, I hurried up the steps and didn't stop until I reached the lone black door to my room.

THE IRISH BOOB-FONDLING BANDIT

I stared at my bedroom door as I waited for my heart to quit thundering in my ears, but when I realized my nerves weren't going to subside, I forced my fingers around the knob and twisted.

The door gave way without resistance. My imposter wasn't very smart. She hadn't even locked it. As it swung open, I stared face-to-face at my doppelgänger who was pushing her boobs up and admiring them in the mirror.

"Uh, sorry to interrupt," I began and peeled away the cowl of my hood. "If you could drop the act and put away my boobs, that'd be great."

The imposter brightened when she saw me. "Oh thank the gods," she said with a very suspicious Irish accent. "I'd love to have my body back, thank you very much." She swept her hands over herself as if I had been the one to cast the enchantment. "Now, if you'd dispel *this*, I'd love to have my penis back."

I blinked and my spine went rigid. My imposter was... male? And that accent... it couldn't be.

"Quinn?" I hissed and stepped inside, shutting the door softly behind me.

He brightened at his name, confirming the impossible. One of the lost vampiric tribe leaders, a warlock-turned-vampire creature of prophecy, was in my bedroom, and still had his hands on his—my—boobs.

He finally seemed to realize what he was doing and let go, then reached out and took my arm. Doppelgänger spells couldn't maintain the magic when the original caster touched the spelled body. Quinn transformed in a glimmering of Amethyst magic, a trademark of my coven. His form grew and soon I was staring at a very manly chest. I arched my head back and looked up at the red-eyed gleam of a vampire's excitement. He grinned and his fangs hinted at his lips, making him look devilishly sexy. "Fucking hell," I breathed, then heat swept over me as I realized that I'd said that out loud.

He laughed and the sound hit me like a delicious honeyed boom against my ears. "Thank you. Breasts are fun and all, but I prefer it when they aren't mine."

I stilled when he reached his thumb up to my brow and swiped along my fake servant rune I'd forgotten was there. "You're full of surprises, aren't you, lass?"

My blush deepened to scalding proportions and I slipped away from him. Removing the cloak, I went to the mirror and rubbed at the rune until it faded. "I had to get up here some-how, didn't I?" I whirled on him as I clutched my bandaged hand to my chest. "Would you care to tell me how all of this happened?" There was no way I'd been able to cast such a powerful spell on him. This had to be his doing... and those other vampire warlock lords.

Hot vampire warlock lords, my inner voice told me.

Quinn smirked, the impact devastating enough to make my knees shake and he waited for me to take a chair at my vanity. Not that I really used the vanity on my own, but I gratefully grabbed one of the bottles of water Cassidy had put there. I took a long gulp before Quinn started talking with that Irish lilt of his that had magic of its own over me. "You're the one who intruded on our resting grounds, I'll remind you. And you're the one who bound yourself to us, even if that was a stupid move."

Anger surged in me and I straightened. "I was just minding my own business. Someone else shoved me into that vision and I would have died had I not acted fast."

He glanced at my bandaged hand. "You must be mortal-born if that hasn't healed yet."

"Don't change the topic," I snapped, but the concern in his gaze made me want to like him.

Imposter, the little voice in my head reminded me, *who was fondling your imposter-boobs.*

Right. Quinn couldn't get away with stuff like that just because his wild red hair made me want to run my fingers through it, and his voice made my insides do little jumpy things. Nope. Not at all.

"Well, regardless of your intention—or lack of intention— I'm here, and I believe it safe to assume my allies have been yanked free of our prison as well." He gave me a slight bow.

"We owe you our thanks, Lady..." He gave me a raised brow as his voice trailed off.

"Evelyn," I told him, then wanted to kick myself. First of all, I wasn't a "Lady" as that was a title reserved for witches who'd passed their initiation as a member of the Royal Covens. I was simply the ward of the Amethyst Coven. And speaking of the Royal Covens, they couldn't find out about this. I should be figuring out how to lock him and the other warlocks back into their cursed resting ground. If anyone found out that I'd released them, there'd be hell to pay.

His smile made every thought fly out of my head. "Evelyn. That's a beautiful name." He tucked his hands behind his back and took his time pacing about the room. He seemed too big for my small chamber. I might be an official member of the Amethyst Coven, but I was still mortal-born, and until my initiation was complete, I was treated as such.

Quinn didn't seem to mind. He went to the window and looked out over the sea of jasmine that continued to sprinkle a glimmering hue of bright purple sequins through the night-time air. "Should I be worried for my allies?" he asked. "I haven't seen a Coven under siege like this in a long time. A Jasmine Field takes considerable magic. That sort of expense hasn't been used for ages. Not since—" He bit his lip, as if cutting himself off from saying too much. Although, that didn't work out very well, as he had sharp fangs, and he wiped away the droplet of blood. My eyes bugged out of my head when I saw that his blood actually fucking glittered. Then a brief whiff of sweetness hit me and my eyelids fluttered. He grimaced. "I'm sorry, Lady Evelyn. I'm a vampire. My blood has magical properties and I'm afraid a powerful witch such as yourself is highly affected by it. I did not mean to be rude."

I swallowed hard, then registered what he'd said. "Powerful?" I asked, then bit my lip hard enough I almost drew blood myself. If he thought me powerful, maybe that's why I was still alive right now. He wanted me to cast a spell to save his allies, or use me to take over the world, or whatever it was that the doomsday prophets went on about.

"Don't play coy with me. You have performed some impressive spells, Lady Evelyn," he continued as if explaining the obvious. He counted off each work of magic on his fingers. "You entered into a cursed realm where my allies and I relived the same night over and over again. You then broke us from that spell, and finally, you pulled us all out into the real world, neatly tidying up the matter by having me drop right at your Coven's front door in a mimic's disguise." He grinned again, making butterflies flutter to life in my stomach. "I'll tell you that it takes a lot to surprise me. Awaking from a century-long spell as a woman was most certainly one of them." He laughed and rolled his eyes. "Your Aunt bit my head off for dawdling, then shoved me into the dining hall." He grimaced. "Eating human food, even of the Royal Coven variety, when one is a vampire is most unappetizing." He held his stomach and covered his mouth as he hid a burp. "I tried to keep it to meats, thinking something with blood in it might help, but perhaps that was a poor choice."

My stomach grumbled at the talk of food and he laughed again. "I thought you might have been in too much of a rush to eat. I saved you some of the offensive meal."

I watched him, mesmerized, as he took a tray out from

under the bed neatly wrapped with plastic. "Did Cassidy fix that for you?" I asked, my eyes wide as I took the offering.

He nodded. "Quite the friendly handmaiden you have. I didn't have to fake feeling ill and told her I'd take my meal upstairs for later. She didn't make a fuss about it." He gave me a genuine smile. "It's good that you're kind to the slaves. They don't have much else to look forward to than a friendly face."

I winced at the term. "We don't call them that anymore," I told him as I peeled away the plastic and snatched up a fork. A tray of salted meats paired with cherry tomatoes and delights that would keep at room temperature made my mouth water.

He furrowed his brow. "But that's what they are, is it not?"

I managed to pretend to ignore him as I chewed my food. I closed my eyes and sighed. It had been such a crazy day and I didn't know how I was going to get out of the mess I'd put myself in, but at least I wasn't going to die of starvation.

"So," he offered after I'd had a chance to devour half my plate. I wasn't one of those girls who cared if a man saw her eat. If I was hungry, I was going to stuff my face just like any normal person would. He grinned when I glared up at him and dared him to make a comment on my appetite. "Are you going to take me up on my offer?"

He handed me my bottle of water and I sipped it thoughtfully. "What offer?"

He grinned, his fangs flashing and making him look far too mischievous. "It should be obvious. I am a powerful warlock, and immortal without selling my soul thanks to my vampirism, as are my allies. Assuming they survive the night from whatever is out there," he indicated the window with his chin, "then I propose we take our rightful place at the head of the Royal Covens."

The blood drained from my face and my fork clattered onto my plate. Of course, I shouldn't have been surprised the vampire would want to fulfill his role in the prophecy, but what about what came next? The end of the world... and all that?

"What would that have to do with me?" I asked.

He carefully took my tray away and set it aside. Kneeling, he took my hand and pressed my ring to his lips, his fangs softly brushing my skin and making me shiver. All Royal Coven members had jewelry that marked their status. Even if I was mortal-born, I still boasted an amethyst ring on my right hand, marking me as a member of this coven. "You broke us from our curse, Lady Evelyn, which means that we're stuck with one another."

My entire being focused on the place where his fingers met mine. His skin was both warm and cold, like ice that burned when you held onto it for too long. I wanted to run my fingers up into his red blazing hair that seemed so wild and out of place in my orderly world. "And what does that mean?" I found myself asking, my voice in a monotone of wonder.

His fangs flashed as he grinned. "It means that when we reclaim our place in the Royal Covens, you'll be right there with us."

TUTORS AND TRAINING

Surely the vampire was fucking with me. Even if he was somehow telling the truth, there was no way that his allies would be willing to share power, and I wouldn't know what to do anyway. I already had a place in the Royal Covens—a very low one. I could get through my initiation and then be free of scrutiny and finally blend into the shadows and be left alone. If I had any real station I'd be right back in the spotlight, and gods, what if I actually got in the middle of some revolution that started a thousand years ago? What if they succeeded and gave me power over the Royal Covens? I wouldn't even know what to do with it.

That's a lie, my inner voice insisted. *You could change everything.*

Rolling over, I put my back to the vampire who rested on the ground. He'd insisted on staying the night and said that he would climb out the window first thing in the morning once the jasmine fields dispelled. It still meant that he expected me to sleep with a creature that drank blood in the room—one that was probably starving.

"I can hear your heart racing from here," he complained. "If you're wondering if I'm hungry, yes, I am; but that's no reason to be afraid of me. I have control."

He'd said the last words as if it were uncommon for him to have control over his hunger. I wasn't going to take any chances and propped myself up on my elbow to glare at him over my shoulder. "Don't forget that I'm an all-powerful witch," I snapped, even though that was a lie if I'd ever heard one. "You get those fangs anywhere near me and I'll do worse than give you boobs."

His throaty chuckle made unfamiliar glimmers of excitement run up my thighs. I couldn't shake the fact that he'd been admiring the glamour of my boobs when I'd barged in on him. How much of my body had he seen?

My cheeks heated to a roaring flame as I flopped back onto the bed and pulled the sheet over my head. I didn't think that I could sleep, not with my hand throbbing now that the magic was starting to wear off. Sparks wouldn't find me until morning, which left me alone with my pain and a deadly vampire.

It was surprisingly the latter that helped me drift off. The vampire began to hum an Irish tune, and soon I fell into a dreamless sleep.

WHEN I WOKE, it felt like a fog had lifted over my eyes and I tried to swipe it away. The gesture sent my limp hand smacking into my face and I groaned.

Rolling over, I found that Quinn was gone and my window was neatly perched open. Sunlight streamed in and I yawned.

Then my bandaged hand caught against the sheets and I startled as all my memories came flooding back. I stared down at the bindings. Blood had seeped through the bandage during the night. Everything that had happened was real. I'd released the lost vampiric tribes and now they were out there plotting to take over the Royal Covens.

My first instinct was to rush down to speak to Aunt Sandra and tell her to warn the Covens, but then I hesitated and questioned my loyalty. The vampire hadn't done anything to hurt me. In fact, he'd been quite polite and made sure I'd had dinner, even if he'd gone hungry. What did I really know about the Royal Covens, other than they were snobby pricks?

My stomach growled, not caring that I was having a moral dilemma. I got out of bed, frowned at the bloodied outfit I was still wearing from yesterday, and peeled it off as best I could with one hand. Then I found some sewing scissors and cut away my bandage. My hand had healed a good bit, but it still looked gnarly with the puffy bruising around the stitching Cassidy had done. The wounds were sealed up enough though that I could take out the stitches, so I cut them away and plucked them out, grinding my teeth against the pain as I discarded each stitch into the bin.

That done, I opened the door to my private bath chamber and turned on the shower to scalding temperatures. I washed myself as best I could, cursing at my tangled hair, and then felt like a drowned rat by the time I got myself back to the vanity. I hadn't used my hand, but it throbbed with warning that my cuts would split open again if I pushed myself much harder. Great, and the day had only just begun.

A soft knock sounded at my door and I about melted with relief. "Cassidy, thank the gods, please come in."

The door eased open, revealing Aunt Sandra with an uncharacteristic smile tugging at her lips. "My dear, there are some new trainers here to see you and they—" Her smile slipped into a more familiar frown at my appearance. "By the gods, where is Cassidy? You need rescuing and fast before you'll be presentable."

I'd managed to hide my wounded hand into my towel before she could see it. I gave her a reassuring smile. "I'm sure she'll be here as soon as she can." I glanced at the window. The sun had only just risen. Birdsong drifted in and another day was starting as if nothing had changed. "It's still early."

Aunt Sandra swatted at me as if I were being ridiculous. "You must call on her instead of pretending you're a mortal, Evelyn. This odd behavior won't do when you're a full-fledged member of this Coven." She went about her usual tirade, chiding me for being exactly what I was—mortal, with mortal kindness and mortal mortality. Although, I wouldn't be mortal much longer. In a few days, the magic in my blood would convert me after my initiation. Living my whole life in this coven had changed me down to my DNA.

I sighed as she yanked on the lever that would ring the bell in the servant's hall. "But I am mortal," I reminded her. "Cassidy has other things to worry about."

"That's right," Aunt Sandra insisted. "She needs to find me

which servant left Lady Isobel waiting downstairs for her coat. We don't treat guests that way in this house."

I bit my lip, preventing a retort that would have given me away. I'd been the one to leave "Lady" Isobel waiting, and in spite of Aunt Sandra's complaining, I spotted the little smirk of satisfaction at the edge of her lips.

Aunt Sandra pulled up a stool and perched on the edge as if she were hovering. Even though it was early, she'd no doubt summoned her handmaiden hours ago. Her dark purple hair gleamed with a meticulous sheen and it tumbled over her pushed up breasts in a velvety wave. She was the picture of the perfect Amethyst Coven Witch; beautiful, elegant, and a little bit cruel. "Cassidy is a servant," she said with a tone that meant I'd better stop arguing.

"Cassidy isn't a servant," I retorted, unable to stop myself. "She's a slave."

I rarely made Aunt Sandra angry, but repeating Quinn's blunt honesty brought color to her cheeks. "Enough of that." She folded her hands and took in a deep breath as if to calm herself and redirect the conversation onto more "important" matters. "Now, with your initiation only days away, I had prayed that the Royal Covens would see fit to send you private tutors, but I hadn't dared hope that they actually would." She beamed with pride. "What a boon to this Coven that they have sent such blessings on us. You will surely be given a higher rank than we could have imagined."

I rolled my eyes. I'd rather liked the fact that the Royal Covens seemed to have forgotten my initiation was so soon. Let me get on with some simple trials and get a pitiful station off in the wilderness to be an herb witch. That sounded fantastic to me.

Cassidy hurried inside without knocking, as was protocol when summoned. I smiled at Sparkles who trotted at her feet and wound about her ankles. While the cat was oblivious to the tension in the room, Cassidy's eyes widened when she saw Aunt Sandra sitting next to me—the drowned rat—and tumbled into a bow. "I'm terribly sorry to have kept you waiting."

Aunt Sandra swept to her feet in a smooth, graceful motion. I always wondered if her grace was from years of practice, or if she cheated with magic. I wouldn't have put it past her. "Don't let it happen again," she said, adding a glower for good measure, before sweeping out of the room. She paused in the hall and brushed the edge of her dress that had touched Cassidy while Sparkles cleaned his paw. Aunt Sandra scoffed at the cat, but a familiar would do as he pleased and take his time no matter a witch's worries. She gave Cassidy a stern frown. "Make her presentable, but suitable for training. We don't want to keep her new tutors waiting."

Without waiting for a reply the door slammed in Cassidy's face.

I groaned. "Ugh, I'm sorry Cass. She's just all uppity about me placing a high station at my initiation now that I have tutors."

Cassidy gave me a raised brow. "Tutors? Only a few days before you go through the initiation?"

I shrugged. "If I tried to understand the Royal Covens, I'd waste all the years of my life and still get nowhere."

She smirked, and I was glad to help her forget my Aunt's

rudeness. At least we had one thing in common—we didn't much care for witch politics.

Cassidy worked quickly and efficiently, untangling my hair better than any witch could have done, and dried out the strands with a towel. She glanced down at our feet where Sparks was still cleaning his paws. "A little assistance?" she asked politely.

The feline looked up at us sleepily, his green eyes hooded with mild annoyance, but he obeyed and wrapped his tail around my ankle, shooting warmth and magic up my leg.

The air around me tinged with purple motes as I directed the first wave to my hand. Fuck my hair. I wanted to heal my slashed palm.

Cassidy laughed when my hand glowed. "I suppose that is a better use of Spark's magic." She shrugged and started braiding the strands. "That's just as well. I'll make a tight braided up-do suitable for training. Your Aunt can't be put off when I'm following orders."

DAILY POISON

I went downstairs with Sparkles winding around my ankles. It had taken years of practice not to trip over him when he did that—which was all the fucking time—and I was rewarded with small morning doses of magic. As my familiar, it was his job to recharge me until I was initiated and strong enough to have magic of my own. My heart did a little painful twist at the thought of parting with him, but I'd always known it would be coming.

As if sensing my dismay at breaking our bond in a few days, he offered me a comforting meow that said he'd never leave me. I grinned. "I'm sure you tell all young witches that, you little heartbreaker."

Aunt Sandra frowned when I entered the sitting room, seemingly annoyed with my practical hairstyle. She had been talking to my new tutors, ironically none of them sitting. It seemed Aunt Sandra's duty to entertain them while the rest of the Coven gathered in the breakfast hall for morning speeches and gossip.

I nearly died when I saw who my "tutors" were. Four of them… far too handsome for their own good and nothing like the old, shoddy tutors I'd expected.

Quinn grinned at me and gave me a tiny wave as he peered around Aunt Sandra. Somehow he'd managed to gather all his allies and spell them so they didn't have fangs or eyes that glowed like rubies. They looked as they had in the vision before their transformation as perfectly proper warlocks that would fit in when it came to places like the Amethyst Coven. Vampires most certainly would have triggered the alarms.

"Like the braids," said the tattooed warlock with blonde spiky hair. He crossed his arms, showing off his ink. "Glad you'll be ready for today's training." He gave the prim surroundings a look of disdain. I personally liked the library-feel the sitting room had with its shelves of old grimoires, records of family lineages, and historical tomes. However, this particular warlock couldn't have looked more uncomfortable with his surroundings. "After what I've seen of your coven so far, I was worried about what we'd be dealing with.

I gave him a raised brow, but Aunt Sandra managed to unhinge from her locked stance at the warlock's approval of my appearance. She laughed a bit too hard to be convincing and rested a light touch on his arm. "I assure you, Evelyn is full of surprises and as practical as they come."

Instead of laughing with her, he glowered until she removed her hand.

The refined one wearing a classy suit cleared his throat. "So, introductions are in order," he announced.

"Quinn," said the redhead with a smirk.

"Aaron," said the tattooed guy, then flicked his tongue over his lip piercing as if it were a habit.

The refined one gave me a graceful head-bow. "Marcus." He turned to the last warlock and cleared his throat again.

The final warlock seemed uncomfortable without his switchblade flying across his knuckles and his hand went to his pocket as he glanced at me. "Killian," he grumbled, as if giving up his name was some great sacrifice.

I resisted the urge to cross my arms and start bitching them out right here in front of my Aunt. I mean, were they *trying* to get me killed? If their deception slipped for just a second and she saw them for what they really were, we were all dead meat.

"Wonderful," Aunt Sandra said as she slapped her hands together. "If you could just show me your contract, I'll be happy to pay the training price."

All the warlocks froze at Aunt Sandra's request. Quinn was the first to recover. "Consider it on the house, Lady Sandra."

She blushed as his Irish accent played over her name. "Oh," she breathed as she brushed away a wave of her hair. "That is quite generous. Well," she motioned to the door to the breakfast hall, "surely I can interest you in some breakfast—"

"No," they all said in unison. I smothered a smile behind my hand as I feigned a cough.

"It's very kind of you," Quinn continued, leaning closer to her and a faint red hue glimmered over his green eyes, "but it's time to begin Evelyn's training. We'll take it from here."

Aunt Sandra swayed on her feet and I realized that Quinn

had fucking compelled her. She wasn't the most powerful witch in the Amethyst Coven, but I had imagined her at least immune to something as basic as compulsion. "Of course," she murmured as she wandered to the door. "I'll leave her in your capable hands." With a smile, she left us alone, and the warlocks relaxed.

When the clink of silverware resumed, I edged closer to them, comforted by Spark's warm fur a consistent against my ankles.

Sparkles meowed up at me, telling me that he trusted the warlocks.

I frowned. I wouldn't go so far to say that I trusted them, but I felt I was safe, for now. If they'd really been here to kill me, they would have done it by now. They wouldn't have faked their appearance and cast a glamour over themselves just to kill me quietly in the sitting room. Knowing that I was safe sent fresh rage and indignation through my chest. "Who do you think you are?" I hissed. "Pretending to be my tutors is a low blow. My Aunt will be devastated when she finds out you're just here to use me."

Marcus straightened. "Use you, Lady Evelyn?"

I growled. "Don't pretend you're here to help me. You're free of your curse and now you want what little power I can offer you."

Quinn knelt and took my hand. I wasn't sure why I let him, other than the curiosity to feel his skin again. Just as it had been last night, he was both cold and warm and magic tingled from his touch. There was so much energy and power in him that it made me give him my full attention. "I'm afraid you've gotten the wrong idea. We've been talking with your Aunt. You're mortal-born."

I couldn't help it. Shame wafted over me and I drooped. "Mortal-born" was a synonym to powerless.

Quinn lifted my chin. "Don't you know how special that is?" he asked, surprising me. "You're a mortal strong enough to survive daily poisoning of incredible magic." I startled at his choice of words. Poisoning? "With our guidance," he continued, "you'll be strong enough to help us overthrow the Royal Covens' modern rule, and then we can take our rightful place with you as our guide in this new world."

Aaron growled and bit at his piercing that ran through the side of his lower lip. "A thousand years," he whispered as his gaze unfocused. "The Royal Covens are still standing, but they don't even know what's going to come after them."

Dazed, I staggered away from Quinn's magnetizing touch. "Do you mean the demon-touched wolves?"

"That's just the beginning," Killian said. He brought out his switchblade, but didn't flip it open. Instead, he ran his fingers over the decorated edges. The motion was subtle and natural. The weapon wasn't meant to be threatening, but rather a comfort to him as the conversation grew dark. I found myself watching him just as intently as he watched me with those dark eyes of his. I guessed that his eyes had once been brown, but now as his magic slipped, the red hue threatened to take over. Fangs glinted at his lips, just for a moment, and then they were gone.

Sparks released a warning hiss.

"Control yourself," Marcus chided, then gave me an apologetic bow. "We've been busy fending off the wolves all night, so we haven't eaten yet."

My eyes grew wide. Four hungry vampires were alone with me in the middle of my coven. Wasn't that just dandy? "Well, shouldn't you go eat, or something?" I asked, sounding stupid the moment I said it. Maybe that's exactly why they'd come here. I took a step back as my heart skipped a beat.

Aaron's pupils dilated as he seemed to react to my increased heart rate. I probably was calling him to me like a human dinner bell, but that thought only made my heart race more.

Quinn reached out for me. "Calm down," he insisted and I didn't miss the note of panic in his voice.

Quinn telling me to calm down wasn't going to help anything. He and I had formed a fragile level of trust, seeing that he had been alone with me all night and hadn't tried to drink my blood. Still, he was a vampire and I wasn't going to forget that. I stifled a shocked gasp when Aaron rushed me, but Quinn was faster. Panic took hold and I drew my dagger from my thigh holster out of reflex.

The streak of crimson across Quinn's cheek betrayed how fast he was. That blow should have struck his jugular.

The vampires growled when a droplet of Quinn's glittering blood fell onto my face. Its heady sweet scent made me dizzy. "Hold onto me," Quinn commanded as Aaron made a threatening growl from somewhere behind Quinn's back.

I shouldn't trust a vampire, but the way he was looking at me was so confident. I glanced at the other guys, noting that their glamours had dropped. A lump formed in my throat. I wasn't sure what was worse; the fact that they all looked like they wanted to rip me to pieces, or that a member of my coven could come out at any moment and set the alarm.

An unfamiliar pull in my chest drew me closer to Quinn until he took me in his arms. He lifted me as if I were light as a feather. I was half his size, but I was still impressed with his supernatural speed and grace as he took us out of the coven.

"Sparkles!" I cried.

"Don't worry," Quinn assured me, "he'll find us when it's safe. He'll do some clean up and make your coven think you've gone off to training."

Sparkles would never agree to do something like that if he didn't trust these vampires, which said a lot. I'd almost forgotten that they were warlocks and could commune with my familiar—if Sparks allowed it.

Sparkles would never leave me in danger, and I sensed his magic retreating as Quinn moved. The world around us blurred as we fled the estate. The jasmine fields swayed in a blur of purple. When I looked over Quinn's shoulder, my stomach dropped. All the vampires pursued us with their fangs bared. The distinct personalities had been overtaken by a hunger that made all vampires eventually go mad.

"I'll send word to your Aunt when you're safe," he told me.

The wind nearly snatched his words away before they hit my ears, but he bent low and held me tight. I closed my eyes and clung to him. That tugging thread inside of me was only growing and it told me that Quinn would keep me safe better than my familiar or the covens ever could. Whatever magic had brought us together was old and powerful. For just this once, I wanted to believe that magic was on my side.

BLOODLUST

"The pasture," I shouted at Quinn as he ran the wrong way. The paved streets would take us into town and there was no way I wanted to bring trouble to innocent mortals.

There were three hungry vampires after me, and if they needed blood, perhaps they could feed on old Jordan's herd. I'd figure out how to repay him later, but I couldn't just let Quinn run with me trapped in his arms straight for a human feast.

He glanced down at me and fear washed through me. His fangs lengthened and his eyes burned with the same red haze that tinged with bloodlust that had overtaken the others.

"Are you okay?" I asked him as my voice trembled.

Instead of shrinking away from him, as would be the logical gesture when a vampire looked at me like that, my fingers wound through the opening of his shirt and made contact with his chest. The brush of my skin over his seemed to ground him and his body flexed as he continued to run at top speed.

He gave me a shaky nod. "Fine, for now." He glanced up again, as if dragging his eyes away from the thundering pulse at my throat. "Pasture. You mean livestock? That's a good idea. Where?"

I risked one finger out of my cocoon of warmth to point down an unpaved street. Quinn bolted for it, kicking up dust behind us.

The fencing rushed up at us and Quinn jumped over it. I screeched in his ear as we went airborne, expecting a hard landing. He buckled his knees when we hit, absorbing the impact, and then launched back into a smooth run.

The herd didn't see us coming. The poor creatures lazily soaked up the sun and munched on their grassy breakfast. Quinn zigzagged a path between them until we were on the other side and he spun.

The other vampires had stopped in their tracks. Finally, their gazes seemed to lose me among the sea of creatures with heartbeats and their eyes blazed with murky red power.

"What is that?" I asked softly, although I already knew the horrid truth, I just needed to hear it confirmed.

"Bloodlust," Quinn told me and set me down.

Barely able to stand on my shaky legs, I gratefully let him shove me behind him, blocking the others from my view.

I heard the carnage first. The cows bolted all at once as the vampires tore into them.

"Close your eyes," Quinn commanded.

The poor creatures were helpless and defenseless, but even I enjoyed a good hamburger, so I tried to keep things in perspective as the panicked sounds of the beasts took over the air, shortly followed by sounds of snapping bones and unnerving silence.

"They're being merciful," Quinn informed me, still holding me behind him.

I'd noticed that his hands had started shaking and I grabbed onto him. I wasn't sure if it was to comfort him, or to comfort myself. "What do you mean?" I asked.

"They're killing them clean before feeding. Even in the bloodlust, they are better than most who suffer the vampiric curse."

I risked peering around him. He cursed when I spotted Aaron and Killian latched onto their prey. They were covered in blood.

Even Marcus was trapped in the craze. His pristine suit didn't fool anyone as he tore into a carcass.

Managing to look up at Quinn's face, I saw that he was barely keeping it together. I didn't know why he was able to resist the bloodlust, but he was clearly starving. "Go," I insisted and gave him a gentle push. "Drink."

He glanced at me. It was hard to read the spiral of emotions that passed over his face so quickly I almost missed it. Perhaps it was shame. I'd known my share of powerful supernaturals, but they'd never been remorseful about the costs of their gifts.

Quinn gave me a curt nod and brushed the wild red hair from his face. "Alright, lass, but turn away. I don't like to be seen like this."

Stubborn, I crossed my arms. "Quinn. If you and I are going to be friends, there will be no secrets between us."

He'd just saved my life, so it seemed obvious that I was open to the idea of friendship. He brightened with surprise. "Very well," he conceded, then moved to join Killian and Aaron.

The vampires ignored him, but Marcus growled even though Quinn hadn't even gotten close to his kill.

I made a mental note that there was more viciousness to Marcus than met the eye, perhaps more than all of these vampires put together.

As I watched them feed, my stomach tied into knots with mixed reactions of morbid fascination and horror. I wondered if this was the cost of vampiric power. Uncontrollable hunger and madness was a steep price to pay, even for immortality and blood magic.

I found myself most interested in Quinn as he gave himself over to the bloodlust. His fangs grew impossibly large and he clamped down onto his prey. He drew in a long gulp and his eyes fluttered closed as his shoulders released their tension.

I knew it must be demeaning to feed on livestock, but Quinn didn't voice any complaints, and neither did the others. When he opened his eyes briefly and found me through the haze of red that swarmed over his irises, something in me snapped. Pain shot up my left arm and I cried out. It was the same side from which I'd cut myself the day before.

An unmistakable rune sliced over my forearm and I sucked in a breath. A rune marked in blood... Only the most powerful of witches were bestowed with runes, and even then they were the glowy magical kind, not ones that manifested on the physical realm.

My rune solidified in a kind of permanence that told me I was in deep shit. The spirals hardened and gleamed with power. As a member of the Amethyst Coven, I had been dosed with magic all my life. It was in my food, gifted to me from my familiar, and saturated the very air inside the coven walls. The magic was a part of me and mixed with the ancient bond that marked itself on my arm.

I looked up to find all the vampires watching me. The hunger had eased from their gazes and they slowly staggered to their feet, Quinn being the last to unlatch from the carcass. Blood ran down the soft arch of his neck.

Quinn approached me, stopping just out of reach as he stared down at the rune. "By the gods," he breathed, "the bond has taken hold."

"What bond?" I snapped, suddenly angry. I hadn't asked for this. There was no way I could expect to slip into the shadows and stay out of the Royal Covens radar when I had a fucking *blood rune.* How was I going to explain that one? A blood rune meant I'd performed blood magic and willingly linked my soul to someone else. I didn't know a lot about blood magic, except for what I'd read in the history books. The idea had stuck with me because a blood rune was commented as being the most powerful and dangerous of magics. I wasn't an amazing student, so I didn't remember any of the ways one could get a blood rune, or why it was powerful and dangerous. All I knew was that it was *bad.*

Quinn's lips ticked up on the side as he smirked at me. "I belong to you now, Evie."

My vision wavered. This wasn't like the servants' marks that bound them to the covens. If it had been, the vampires would have been marked, not me. I shook my bloodied arm at them. The pain was gone and a thrum of ancient magic crept up my elbow and frightened me. "Did you do this to me?" Was Quinn trying to fool me? I think he meant to say that *I* belonged to *him*. The bastard had somehow enslaved me!

Marcus cleared his throat and stepped up beside the Irishman. "Please, Lady Evelyn, accept our apologies for our inexcusable behavior. The bloodlust took us by surprise. Normally it's not so harsh." He gave a low bow. "We would never hurt you, and now that you've bonded to Quinn, you'll be better protected. I assure you, it's for the best."

"For the best?" I screeched. "You—"

"Who knew about the pasture?" Killian interrupted as he sulked his way up to the group. He looked the most shamed of the four. His eyes were still dark, but no longer swirled with danger.

"It was Evie's idea," Quinn said, brightening. He took note of me as I fumed and sighed. "The bond wouldn't have taken hold unless you'd decided to trust me. Do you trust me, Evie? I would never force you to do something you didn't want to do." His fingers balled into fists. "Never."

I believed him, but I was too pissed off to relent. Plus, I hated how he said my name, mostly because his accent made it sound far too erotic. "I don't fucking trust any of you," I snapped. My gaze dropped to the blood-soaked ground. Two cows had been slaughtered. What if that had been me?

No, I couldn't think about that. For now, I had to deal with the loss of two cows. I would have to talk to Jordan and make up a story about why his cows had been mauled. Could he tell the difference between vampire teeth marks and wolves?

Quinn stepped closer and the scent of fresh blood made my insides flip over. I held my nose and instantly backed away from him. He reeked of death.

He stopped and frowned at my reaction. "Evie. You were the one to free us from our prison. You were the one to initiate a bond by blooding each pillar that held us captive. If you didn't wish to free us, then why were you there?" Hurt tinged his expression. "Were you just after our magic? Immortality?"

I scoffed. "I have no interest in power or living on this wretched planet forever." My real parents were dead. One day, I would find them again in the afterlife, but only after I'd lived a full life on this planet. That's what they would have wanted for me and that's what I'd always intended to do.

Quinn's gaze dropped to the rune on my arm again and he frowned. "That's strange," he remarked.

That's when I realized the rune was still bleeding. Perhaps I hadn't accepted Quinn after all.

SECRETS

*L*uckily there was a stream nearby old man Jordan's place. Our village was a simple one on the outskirts of Belgium and safe from prying eyes. Jordan Styles supplied the majority of the butchers with cattle meat, and also kept our village stocked with fresh milk. He kept the two herds separated—those for butchering and those for milking —although I could never tell the difference between them. I hoped that it had been the butchering one that fell prey to the hungry vampires, as that cattle wouldn't be as sorely missed.

"I'm sorry to put so much on your shoulders just days before your initiation," Quinn offered as we approached the stream.

The others waded right in, clothes and all, and I imagined that no amount of water was going to wash away how much blood they were covered in. "Did you have a choice?" I asked him.

Quinn flinched. Now that I knew a soul bond was forming

between us, I decidedly didn't like him. Soul bonds were only for witches who made dark pacts, or for servants who didn't have any other choice.

Quinn eased closer to me and surprised me by taking my hand in his. He lifted it and examined the blood rune that glimmered with fresh crimson. "If you're not going to accept me, lass, would you at least allow me to bandage this?"

I glared into his eyes that swarmed with vampiric magic. He didn't hide who he was, and I begrudgingly liked that. "You're changing the subject," I complained, but motioned for him to get on with it. "Go on, then. Bandage first, then answer my question."

He smirked and gently released me. He worked at the hem of his sleeve as he reached over and tore a clean line with one of his fangs. He took my arm again and wrapped the fabric over the rune a few times before securing it. "I wasn't fully aware of my entrapment, not until you were there."

"You didn't know what was going on for a thousand years?" I asked. It seemed hard to believe. I had no doubt that Quinn and his allies were powerful. Whoever had trapped them in a prison strong enough to encase even their minds was impressive. "I suppose that is for the best."

He nodded. "I imagine I'd have gone insane if I really knew what was going on." He turned my hand over and ran a finger down the line across my palm. I shivered at the gentle contact. "But then you broke the spell on all of us. You did what no witch in a thousand years could do."

I raised an eyebrow. "Wrong. I was the only witch stupid enough to initiate a blood bond with four vampiric warlocks."

He grinned. "You're smarter than you look, lass."

I glowered at him, but I found myself unwilling to reclaim my hand as he continued to stroke down my palm. He turned his attention back to my fingers and took on a thoughtful look. "Your future is so uncertain."

Palm reading was actually an advanced skill that only manifested itself in witches and warlocks who would later turn into Seers. "What futures do you see?" I asked, curious. I'd never gone to a palm-reader before because I didn't trust a witch to give it to me straight. Quinn, though, was someone I could trust to be honest. Somehow I knew that deep in my core.

His silky skin hummed with magic and his fingers tickled across my hand. The sensation tugged at the bond inside of me. I tried to reject it now that I knew what it was. No matter how fascinating and intoxicating he was, no matter if every instinct said I could trust him, I could never allow my soul to belong to another. That was a mistake I'd seen made one too many times. The Royal Covens and the supernatural community might have taken everything from me, but my soul was my own.

"Your future depends on you," he said after a moment and reluctantly released me. His wild, red hair flung around his face as an uncharacteristic wind picked up, bringing with it the scent of honeysuckle and grassy fields. We were close to the pasture, but it typically smelled of dirt and livestock. I found myself drawing in a deep breath and relaxing as I wondered what secrets Quinn might be hiding from me. Seers were a rare segment of witches, even rarer among warlocks. Males inherently weren't able to contain the burden of power that came with the more intimate magics.

Seeing someone's future required empathy, curiosity, and sensitivity.

Quinn didn't flinch away as I tilted my head and appraised him. I thought I could see who he really was behind those vampiric eyes. There was sadness and hope inside of Quinn. Sadness because of something that had happened a long time ago, but the hope. The hope was new.

The flutter of emotions vanished as he gave me a coy grin and the scent of honeysuckle and grassy fields disappeared. "You're using my gift of Sight. I feel both violated and flattered."

I staggered away from him and shook my head to rid myself of the trance. Had I been using his magic? The rune under my bandage throbbed with a fresh spike of pain as if punishing me for letting go of the magic I'd been unwittingly using.

"Come on," he offered and tugged my arm. "Let's get washed up. It looks like the others are done."

I blinked as I watched Marcus, Aaron, and Killian step onto the pebbled bank. Their bodies steamed as their eyes glowed red. Their clothing clung to them as it dried, revealing hard lines that would make any girl blush. Killian winked at me and I glanced away, fighting the wave of heat that threatened to spread over my face.

"I don't need to wash off," I complained as Quinn dragged me down with him.

"Sure you do," he insisted and glanced at my bandage.

I followed his gaze and cursed. Blood seeped through the thin fabric. Wrenching myself free of my trance over Quinn had split the wound open again.

Hissing when the ice-cold water swept up my legs, I followed Quinn to the water that went waist-deep on him, but came up to my chest. My teeth chattered as Quinn laughed and splashed water over me. I was ready for it, but the cold still stole a breath from me anyway.

"N-No fair," I managed to say through my chattering teeth. "You're a vampire. You can't feel the cold."

Quinn eased lower into the water so that we were eye-level. "I feel it. The difference is that I like it."

I shivered. "Well I don't."

He moved closer to me, slowly as if he were approaching a skittish deer. When he wrapped his arms around me, I started to protest, but then my eyes went wide.

His skin radiated heat and I curled into his chest, greedily searching for warmth. "Is that your magic?" I asked, and in response, the faint scent of honeysuckle wafted over me.

He turned me around so that my back pressed against his chest, stealing away his warmth, as he worked at my bandage. I looked up at the bank to see if the other vampires were watching us, but they'd wandered further down the pasture and quietly talked amongst themselves.

"They'll respect our time to bond," he informed me, his voice low and alluring with his Irish accent that seemed to lull me into a false sense of security. "You're meant to bond with each of us. The magic can be slow, and sometimes ungraceful. It knows that you can only learn to trust one of us at a time."

I looked down at the blood rune that he now washed with care. I'd have never attributed Quinn with such gentleness. It'd stopped bleeding now that the sweet candy-scent of honeysuckle grew stronger. I rested my head against him as I watched his fingers dance over my skin. "You're strangers to me," I told him. He didn't respond, but waited patiently, continuing his mesmerizing strokes across my skin. The magic hummed around us as if building momentum. "The only ally I really have is Cassidy, and maybe my familiar." Big maybe on Sparkles. Damn cat might save my life, or abandon me for a can of tuna.

"You don't trust your coven?" he asked. His breath puffed against my ear and I shivered at how close we were now, but a part of me wanted to give in. I'd never trusted a supernatural in my life, not fully. Not in the way Quinn's words begged of me.

"No," I whispered as unshed tears stung my eyes. I never cried because it felt silly to mourn something I'd never had.

"Not even your Aunt Sandra?"

I shook my head. "Especially Aunt Sandra." The coven wouldn't have taken a mortal four-year-old child for selfless reasons. I was told that my father had killed my mother, and then he'd killed himself, leaving me alone and covered in the blood of my family. I had no memories of that night, only what Aunt Sandra had told me. I didn't feel like she had a reason to lie about it, and whenever I asked mortals if they remembered the incident, the stories always lined up.

That kind of blood sacrifice could be powerful to a coven and the horror of it had drenched into my very soul. Aunt Sandra had been honest with that, too, and told me that I would repay their kindness by taking a place among the Royal Covens and adding to the Amethyst's collective prestige.

"She just wants power," I told Quinn. I'd never been this

open with anyone except for Cassidy. "That's what all super-naturals want."

Quinn's gentle strokes paused. "Not all supernaturals," he assured me. His hands ran up my arms, making me shiver as he dispelled the cold from the stream. His fingers swept up my neck and then he began gently massaging my temples. "Let me show you, Evie. I'm not like them."

I was totally under some hot Irish-vampire spell, but for once, I decided to give him a chance. If he wanted to hurt me, he could have done it in my bedroom, or left me to be mauled in the coven when the others had succumbed to bloodlust. I wanted to understand this honeysuckle magic that teased me and promised things that made my toes curl into the river's soft bed.

"Okay," I whispered, and I could almost feel his smile as he pressed closer to me until his fangs grazed against my neck. I should have been terrified of a vampire doing that, but when it came to Quinn, I instinctually knew it to be an affectionate gesture.

A soft boom whispered out from us, sending the water rippling as the sweet candy-scent overwhelmed me, bringing a vision of an ancient field in Ireland with a sea of grass speckled with the distinctive wildflowers. The river and pasture swept away, replaced with a memory. Wind tangled through my hair and sunlight kissed my face. This was a place that was special to Quinn. The memory filled me with love and elation as I drew in a deep breath. It felt like home.

"This is what my soul looks like," Quinn whispered, his voice in the real world an echo of comfort against my senses.

A warm breeze picked up across the Irish fields and I relaxed. "It's beautiful."

His hands moved away from my temples and trailed down to my waist, pulling me closer to him. I was fully immersed into the vision now and I'd never seen anything so peaceful in all my life. If this was what Quinn was really like, then I wanted to know more about him. I wanted to know why he would give himself over to life as a warlock imbued with a vampire's curse. It must have been something terrible and important for him to do that.

"It was," he whispered, making me startle. He chuckled and the warm sound made my insides curl with a new kind of warmth. "You've opened yourself to me, Evie. I can hear your thoughts when we're close like this." His hands wrapped around me and flattened against my abdomen. "I can feel your desires."

I wasn't a virgin, but I'd never been excited by a simple touch like I was by Quinn's. There had been handsome warlocks that I'd been foolish enough to think cared for me more than just for a brief night of entertainment. Covens encouraged promiscuity, as sex could make a witch or warlock stronger, especially when mingling with other covens. But Quinn, he wanted to touch me because of something else. He had all the power he could ever need, which meant that his interest in me was genuine. If anything, by allowing the bond between us, I was the one taking magic from him and not the other way around. I swallowed hard as foreign excitement swept through me.

He turned me to him, bringing the hot red of his gaze into view over the endless field. I could see past the vampirism now. The sadness there was a distant memory, as if being near me buried it. "Quinn," I breathed and ran my fingers up his cheek. My thumb ran down one of his elongated fangs. "I need to know why you accepted vampirism." I wanted to trust him so badly. I could feel him down to his very soul. He wasn't a selfish monster like all the supernaturals I knew, but I had to know the answer to that question.

For the first time, his gaze darkened, as if that was the one thing he could never tell me. "No, lass," he said, breaking the contact as cold river water rushed in between us. "If you knew that, you'd never accept me."

My mind reeled from all the revelations Quinn had given me. He dosed me with enough magic to dry myself, and I was glad to see that the experience of seeing the reality of his soul had satisfied the blood rune on my arm. The skin had calmed down and the mark glowed with a pleasant purple glimmer of magic suited for my coven. No matter what magic Quinn worked on me, the magic in my blood was securely Amethyst.

"Here, wear this," Quinn said as he peeled off his jacket and draped it over me.

I peeked through the heavy fabric to fuss at him, then clamped my mouth shut when I saw why he'd covered me. Old man Jordan crested the hill to the riverbank and had just spotted us. "Oy!" he shouted with three sheepish-looking warlocks sulking behind him.

The warlocks had activated their glamour again, and this time they seemed in control after having fed. I was glad, because I didn't want to imagine poor Jordan fending off three hungry vampires.

He stumbled down to us and got up in Quinn's face. The mortal had to arch his neck to peer up at the Irishman, who I was glad to see had been smart enough to activate his glamour as well. "Care to tell me why two milking cattle are dead in my spelled field?" He grumbled under his breath about worthless magic peddled by Amethyst Coven punks.

Quinn grimaced, but I battled out of the coat—which was a sad excuse for a disguise—and shoved Quinn out of the way. I was the one who'd be coming to the rescue now. "Sorry, Mr. Styles. We tried to stop the wolves, but it looks like we were too late. You haven't seen any around, have you? I think they ran off."

The farmer brightened when he spotted me. I'd come to the farm ever since I was a little girl. He didn't know about my dark past, other than the rumors, but he did know that I was mortal-born, which was perhaps why he liked me so much. "Evie! Why didn't you say you were stopping by? Come on, now. I'll get the misses to make you some tea. There's been a cold-snap today."

I glanced down at the river, shivering. "Sounds good to me."

OLD MAN JORDAN was a lot less surprised than he was supposed to be, but after he'd told us how the demon-touched wolves were encroaching on his territory, I started to relax. The lie was at least believable if the wolves had already made a few attacks before. I felt bad that I hadn't been around often enough to hear about it. All my training for the upcoming initiation was taking all of my attention. Thinking about it made me cringe inwardly. How many days were left? Two, three at the most?

"They don't often attack in daylight, but it's just a sign that they're getting stronger," Marcus supplied, straightening as he held his teacup with one hand. I wondered if vampires liked tea, or if he was just being polite.

"Aye," Quinn agreed as he sank into old man Jordan's sofa, looking sleepy and content with the simple furniture. "Only going to be getting worse."

Aaron and Killian stood off to the side, peering out the window as if keeping an eye out for wolves. Of course it was just a cover-up, but I wondered if it could be true. The warlocks had said that the demon-touched wolves were only the beginning and things were going to get worse. Would the wolves start coming out in the daytime? If so, we were screwed.

Jordan sighed as he perched on his favorite stool. His wife worked on the dishes in the kitchen after having given me a crushing hug. She winked at me from the doorway, and then made glancing gestures at Quinn. I blushed. So, she'd already picked up on my interest in him. I folded my hands in my lap and made a mental note not to be so obvious about my attraction to the vampire. I wasn't sure if it was purely magical, or if there was something more. I had to admit that Quinn was unlike any supernatural I'd ever met, which was a good thing. Most of them had been assholes.

I felt someone watching me, and I looked up to see Killian.

He'd abandoned his mission to find the imaginary wolves wandering the pasture and instead seemed determined to figure out what was going on with me. He didn't flinch away when our gazes met. He didn't even go for his switchblade.

"So, what brings you out here?" Jordan asked, breaking the spell.

I shook my head and faced him. "I, uh, well you see—" Before I could make a fool of myself, Sparkles made his entrance through a cracked window and meowed, letting me know that he didn't appreciate how many memories he had to adjust so that I wouldn't be chased down by a panicked coven. A gentle glow of magic wafted off from him and I glanced at the humans, but they couldn't see it. Acting like he owned the place, Sparkles scampered down from the sill and jumped into my lap. I smiled and scratched behind his ear, to which he threw all his weight against my hand, making me chuckle.

"Lady Evelyn has her initiation in three days," Quinn said as he leaned his elbows on his knees and folded his hands. His wild red hair shone with health after the river bath and he gave me a coy grin. Gods, he was far too handsome for his own good.

Jordan brightened. "You're her tutors, then? By the gods. I'm glad the Royal Covens came to their senses and gave Miss Evelyn what she deserves."

Quinn gave the mortal a raised brow. Quinn had kept calling me "Lady," which was a term reserved for witches of considerable power and standing in the Royal Covens. Jordan knew what I was. I was a mortal-born outcast lucky to be taken in at all.

Jordan, seemingly oblivious to Quinn's distaste for the

title he'd given me, clapped his hands and stood up. "So, you're here for room and board? Of course you are. The covens wouldn't want someone so important being distracted by jealous witches or people from the village. Our guest cottage lies right on the edge of the cemetery, just how you witches like it." He motioned for us to get up. "Come on, we won't be forcing you to sit around and talk with the likes of us. Not if you say Evelyn only has three days until her initiation. My, does time fly."

Mrs. Styles came out of the kitchen, having finally finished the long duty of dishes. It was only the two of them, but she often complained to me in private of how her husband seemed to accrue dirty dishes just as fast as he did prized livestock. "You'll be staying, then?" she asked as a smile lit her face. "I'll make some meals and deliver them tonight. How exciting! We haven't hosted one of the coven in ages."

I glanced at the warlocks to see if they had a plan about where to take me. I didn't want to trouble the Styles unless we had no other choice. Quinn grinned at me while Aaron and Killian went back to window-watching again. Marcus seemed quite pleased with how things had turned out and straightened. "We are grateful for your generosity," was all he said.

So, guess it's a guest cottage and four powerful warlocks for me for the next three days.

Sparkles meowed his excitement.

"No, Sparks," I hissed my disagreement under my breath. "This isn't going to be fun."

TRAINING

Sparkles led the charge into the guest cottage, which was one of the older constructs on the property and hummed with protective magic. The Styles weren't kidding when they'd said they'd hosted witches before. The inside of the cottage contrasted starkly against their own simple home. On the outside, dark spires pierced the sky, making it look more like a miniature castle than a cottage. Once we stepped inside, familiar chandeliers with purple magical flames illuminated the silvered walls that would keep out any wolves or demon-touched predators. I'd never been inside the guest cottage. I wondered if my aunt had prohibited entry before. Had I known about it, I might have preferred it to the coven.

I noted that when each vampire stepped into the cottage they flinched as if magic had snapped harshly against them. Once we were all inside, however, they relaxed.

After Jordan left us, letting us know that his wife would be back in three hours with some meals, he shut the door without a moment's hesitation. I raised a brow with suspicion.

"I might have compelled him," Marcus admitted.

I glowered. "So you're making them feed us and house us for free?" I didn't appreciate Marcus using innocent mortals.

"Feed *you*," Quinn corrected and rested an arm around my shoulders. "We're good for a few days."

Ignoring the Irishman, I watched Aaron settle wood into the fireplace. He snapped his fingers, setting the logs alight.

Sparks mewled his delight and ran to it, curling up impossibly close to the flames until I thought he might risk catching fire.

Aaron chuckled and gave my familiar a quick scratch behind his ear. Normally, if anyone else besides Cassidy or maybe Aunt Sandra would touch him, he'd bite their finger right off, but the cat returned the caress with a head bump before curling up again and falling asleep.

"Traitor," I growled under my breath.

Quinn chuckled. "Come on. Let's get started on your training."

My eyes widened at that as I followed him away from the comfort of the living room and down a cool hallway. "You mean that wasn't just a lie to get me away from the coven?"

"Of course not," he said.

He opened doors as we walked, checking their contents before moving on. I peered around his shoulder to see what he might be looking for. The first room contained endless potions and empty glass jars. The second had scrying orbs.

And on and on it went until finally we reached the last room that only had two simple chairs.

"Ah, here we are," he said with approval before stepping inside.

Perplexed I followed him. He took the first seat and then motioned for me to take mine.

Swallowing, I obeyed as an ominous feeling swirled in my stomach.

"It's not a coincidence you've freed us just days before your initiation," Quinn informed me.

"It's not?" I squeaked.

He leaned forward in his chair, bridging the distance between us with a sense of familiarity. The room didn't have anything else in it to distract me, forcing me to put all my attention on him. He dropped his glamour, allowing the red haze of his vampirism to overtake his green eyes. "Tell me what you know of the initiation," he said.

Swallowing, I glanced once at the closed door before looking back at him. If I was in danger, Sparkles would come after me. Out of all the vampires, I felt safest with Quinn. I'd seen his soul. No matter what happened, I knew that I'd seen the real him, even if there was a darkness in his past he didn't want me to know about. I couldn't imagine what would be a strong enough reason to compel someone like Quinn to take vampirism's curse, but whatever it was, I was going to find out.

The best way to get someone to reveal their secrets was to get them to trust you, and to do that, I was going to have to be honest with him.

"The initiation will determine my standing in the Royal

Covens," I informed him, not sure how different the initiation rites might be from what he remembered from a thousand years ago. "I've been dosed by magic all my life. If I don't find a way to channel it, then I'll die." That was a truth that had been instilled in me since my first memory in the Coven.

Quinn frowned as he leaned forward a bit further. A wild tuft of his red hair brushed in front of his eyes, but he didn't move to push it away. "You mean poisoned," he corrected me for the second time.

"I was just a child," I snapped, surprised that I found the need to defend my coven. There was an innate loyalty there because if it hadn't been for Aunt Sandra, I would have been left to die. I couldn't expect anyone to take on such a burden as caring for a child, and I would always be grateful to her for bringing me in after everything that had happened. "The coven took me in," I admitted, finding it easier to talk to him about this than it should have been. It was like all the reasoning behind my existence needed to come out into the open just then. Someone had to hear my story and understand that I was just an inconvenience and I had only been a burden to anyone who's tried to care for me before. "I was an orphan. My father..." I drifted off, unable to speak the horror of what my father had done.

Quinn's expression softened. "Did your father hurt you?"

I shook my head. I didn't have any memories of my family. I couldn't even see their faces. I had been so young when I'd been brought to the coven that it was the only life that I'd ever known. "I don't think so, no. I just know what I've been told. My father, he, well, my mother died first, and then he died after."

Quinn's ruby gaze flared, as if angered by my words. "Did someone attack the village?"

I swallowed hard. He wasn't getting it. Somewhere deep in my soul I knew my father wasn't a bad man. I don't know what had compelled him that day, and even if I couldn't remember his face, I knew that he would have been just as kind as old man Jordan. "They were killed," I said, and that was as far as I was willing to go with it. "So when the coven took me in, it was a mercy. I have no other family—"

"That they've told you of," Quinn snapped. "I don't trust it, Evie. Covens don't just take in mortal-born children and raise them as their own. They know what you are."

My gaze snapped to him, stunned. "What I am?" I echoed. Was I something special? That was quite impossible. Surely he had me confused with someone else.

Tears pricked my eyes, because I wanted to be special. I wanted Quinn to like me and to respect me. It took all of my willpower and courage to pull up my sleeve and show him my blood rune. "This was a mistake," I insisted. "You have the wrong girl."

Quinn smirked, unimpeded by my stubbornness. "Magic doesn't make mistakes," he assured me, then nodded. "So the initiation. Tell me what you are expecting, and then we'll go from there."

I narrowed my eyes. "Well, as a mortal-born witch, I expect the trials will be simple. Potion brewing. A test of the history of the covens. An evaluation of which element I should be attuned with that'll determine my placement." I grimaced. "Hopefully there won't be any spellcasting or summoning. I can barely make it through a Latin spell, much less one in runes."

Quinn gave me a raised brow. "I saw a sketchbook of runes in your bedroom. Didn't you draw those?"

I sucked in a breath. "You went through my things?" Then I remembered he'd been ogling my boobs in the mirror when he'd been wearing the glamour that made him look like me. I wasn't sure which invasion was worse.

"You drew a rune I recognize," he said, ignoring my question completely. "You can't draw it again. Not until you are ready to know what and who you are."

I was tired of this. "If you know so much about me, then why not just tell me?"

"You have to survive the initiation, first, and you can't tell a secret you don't know. The Royal Covens don't need to know what you are, not yet, and neither do you." He held out both his hands, palm up, and waited. "Let's begin. This room is for Astral Projection, so let's start with that one."

I sighed. Astral Projection was a relatively advanced skill, and definitely one I'd never attempted. The idea of plucking my soul from my body didn't sound like my idea of fun.

"You seem to misunderstand," I said, "I don't want to score high on my initiation. I'd rather they think me weak and forget all about me."

Quinn's eyes hardened. "You don't know them like I do, Evie. If you fail them, they will try to kill you. You have to take this seriously."

My blood ran cold at the flat statement. No hedging around the truth. No assurances that the worst that could happen is I'd get placed as an herb witch and be sent to live alone on the outskirts of the village.

Now that I thought about it, I'd never met any of these herb witches that Aunt Sandra talked about. Was that her way of trying not to scare me? Well, shit.

Reluctantly, I rested my hands in his. The familiar hot and cold sensation of his skin still sent a thrill through me. "Fine," I conceded, and closed my eyes. "How do I Astral Project? Where's the target?"

I peeked one eye open when he didn't answer. He'd closed his eyes as well. "Focus," he chided without opening his eyes.

Sighing, I obeyed and waited for something to happen.

"You have to initiate the spell. I can't do it for you," he said.

I frowned. "Then why are we holding hands?" Not that I was really complaining. Now that I'd established that Quinn wasn't out to kill me, I liked the connection. The blood rune on my arm craved his magic, and something else inside of me craved his touch. I'd never had a real boyfriend, or a male who cared what happened to me. It was refreshing.

"You need my magic, for now," Quinn stated, as if that was obvious. "Until your initiation, your magic is dammed like a blocked river."

That was telling me more than he probably wanted to. If I was mortal-born, how would I have blocked magic?

Sighing, I buried the question under the thousand others I wanted to ask and focused on the task at hand.

I didn't really have a place I wanted to go, so I let my mind wander. At first that familiar rune popped into my head. Its hard edges with the one delicate swirl in the center looked like a mixture between Gaelic and Nordic writings, with a touch of something else. I'd always dismissed it as a real witch rune, but the way Quinn had talked about it said it actually was magic that I was writing down. Me, a mortal-born witch that could hardly mumble out a Latin-based spell. I traced the lines in my mind, over and over again, trying to understand what they could mean.

I flinched when a jolt of magic passed through Quinn to me and he grunted.

"I'm sorry!" I cried.

"Don't open your eyes!" he commanded and gripped my hands hard, then he relaxed. "Keep going. You're doing well, Evie."

The way he said my name made me smile and the panic dulled, leaving the soft thud of my heartbeat in my ears.

Honeysuckle filled the room as I drew on his magic again, this time slowly, and worked it around me until I could sense my soul.

"Good," Quinn approved. "Wrap the magic around your spirit, and then pull. You have to find a place that will draw you away from here."

Fear made my breaths come quicker. "How will I get back?" I'd started this exercise just to appease him, but now I realized that there was plenty of magic here to work with. I was actually going to go through with it.

His hands squeezed mine with reassurance. "Your natural state is with your soul inside your body. Once you let go, your soul will snap back into place. You can't get stuck."

I knew that wasn't necessarily true. We'd lost a witch to Astral Projection last year. She'd gone too far and pulled away from her body too hard, severing the connection. If the rumors were to be believed, her soul had floated away, leaving her to be a spectre that would roam the world forever and never find peace.

"I can't," I whispered. Fear made my palms sweat and I tried to slip away from Quinn, but he gripped me harder.

"You *can*," he insisted, and then he... shoved me. He didn't shove me physically, but pushed with a psychic power that surpassed anything I'd ever felt before.

My soul went tumbling out of my body and an instant cold came at me from all directions. I screamed as an insatiable void engulfed me.

ASTRAL PROJECTION

I reacted out of instinct, because the first place I went was the graveyard. That always gave me a sense of my family, somehow, and I didn't miss the connection. Some witches gained their magic through their ancestors. I always had this dream that I really came from some ancient, powerful family, and one day, their spirits would rise from their graves and give me a blessing that made the rest of my life have meaning.

When I opened my eyes, I found myself there among the gravestones. The four pillars still bore the faint bloody streaks from the day before. Had it really only been a day? It seemed so hard to believe.

I stepped onto the platform, frowning because it felt a little too real to be a dream.

I lifted my hand and my blood rune glowed with an angry red power.

Right, Astral Projection. I was here, in spirit, and I was using Quinn's magic to give my soul corporeal form. Yikes.

As usual, the graveyard was empty. No one seemed to mourn their dead in our village. It was like the moment their spirits left this world, the bodies were shoved away and forgotten as fast as possible. Better to forget than feel pain. That's what I'd learned of humanity and how they treated those who'd passed on. I didn't want it to be like that. I wanted to hold onto my family, what little I had of them, even if it was just a feeling that there had once been two people who'd loved me and had plans for my future that didn't involve personal gain.

One pillar hummed to life. A rune appeared, the same one that had carved itself into my arm, and I walked to it. My fingers grazed over the stone and it amazed me how I could feel the coarse rock.

That's when I realized that a piece of Quinn was still in there. Was this why he'd wanted me to do Astral Projection first? Did he know that he'd left a piece of himself behind?

I curled my fingers into fists and knocked, finding the pillar to be hollow. Backing up a few steps, I chewed on my lower lip. Either I was about to hurt myself, or I was about to help Quinn.

With a running start, I slammed my shoulder into the pillar and cried out as pain jolted through my ethereal body. I drew in more magic, feeling Quinn at my fingertips, and backed up again. A single crack had formed in the pillar. It was working.

I ran, bracing myself for impact and then slammed into the pillar. This time a crack sounded through the graveyard and a shockwave boomed after it as if I'd broken a seal. My eyes went wide as I peered into the opening, finding a pair of gorgeous earrings hanging suspended. A woman's earrings glinted with delicate gems in an intricate pattern.

Reaching in, I took the jewelry and frowned. They'd been talking about a woman during the vision. Someone who'd died.

Pain shot through my blood rune and I cried out as I buckled to my knees. A sharp tug insisted I head back to my body and I clung to the earrings, knowing I had to bring them back with me. This was a part of Quinn that he had left behind. I knew that without it, he'd be broken forever.

I FOLLOWED the tendril back to my body, although it was difficult as I brought the earrings with me. Quinn had left them on purpose, although I had no idea why. He didn't want to remember.

I would have given anything to remember my family before they were killed. If someone would have found that piece of me trapped in a pillar, I know that I would hope they'd bring it back to me.

I slammed back into my body and sucked in a desperate breath, hacking into a fit of coughs as the blast sent Quinn flying from me.

Knocking sounded at the door. Killian was shouting something. Was the door locked?

"Quinn!" I yelled. Smoke steamed off of him and it appeared that he'd slammed hard into the wall. His chair was now reduced to splinters and he groaned on the floor, hidden in the shadows. The room's only light was the small chandelier in the middle. It'd been cozy at first, but now I felt claustrophobic. "Quinn!"

He fumbled over onto his side and coughed up blood, rejecting the nourishment from the livestock he'd fed on earlier. I glanced down at the purple glimmer in his hands to see the purple earrings were there. I brightened. "I did it!"

Quinn didn't look excited. He didn't look like the Quinn I was growing to know at all. The red haze in his gaze took over and turned his irises into a deep ruby color as his fangs elongated and he growled with a deep, primal threat.

Shit.

"Evelyn!" Killian shouted as he beat against the door again. "It's magicked! You'll have to open the door from your side, quick!"

I'd been trained how to deal with predators. I didn't run for the door like every instinct in my body wanted me to. I treated this bloodlust-Quinn just as I would a demon-touched wolf. I moved slowly towards the door, not turning my back to him, and I didn't break eye contact.

He growled again as his fingers tightened around the earrings. Whatever piece of his soul I'd brought back to him, it'd thrown him right into bloodlust, and he looked like he was ready to rip my head off.

I tried to suppress the hurt I felt as I realized that I wasn't always safe with Quinn. Right now, he was the one who needed saving, but I had a feeling I wasn't strong enough to do that yet.

"Easy," I whispered as I reached for the doorknob. I

twisted it, thinking perhaps I could get it open without incident, but then the door latched and the sound broke whatever trance Quinn had been under. He launched for me and I tossed a hand up out of reflex to fend him off, what little good that might do against a vampire's strength and sharp fangs.

I braced myself for the pain that would come next. Instead, a sharp *ping* radiated through the small room as Quinn hit a translucent purple shield. I looked down at my hand, wondering if I'd cast the spell.

Sparkles meowed at me as he paced at my feet, making me release a short, hysterical laugh. "Right, Sparks. Thank you."

Killian blurred through the room and slammed into Quinn, sending them both flying into the wall. Another crack formed and Quinn roared in outrage.

"Get out and close the door!" Killian shouted over his shoulder at me.

I blinked at him. The warlock's switchblade had transformed into a proper sword and was now at Quinn's throat leaving a long, gruesome line of red. The pain and threat of death didn't seem to do much to deter the crazed vampire.

"Go!" Killian snapped, and I broke from my shock and did as he asked.

Sparkles kept right on my heel as I slammed the door closed. It magically locked the moment it shut and I swallowed hard. Right. If this really was a house for witches, a proper Astral Projection room wouldn't leave the body inside unprotected. The room sensed there were warlocks inside of it and it wouldn't open from this side. Whatever Killian was going to do to calm Quinn down, he was on his own.

Shame tugged at my shoulders as I staggered back to the

living room. I walked in to find Aaron and Marcus both near the fireplace watching the doorway.

"What the fuck happened?" Aaron snapped as he shoved away from the mantle.

Marcus glowered at him. "Don't talk to Lady Evelyn that way."

"No," Aaron snapped and I realized that the tattoos along his arms were actually moving. "What'd you do to Quinn?"

Anger wafted to life in my chest and I straightened. "I fixed him," I informed the rude vampire. Of course, it sounded ridiculous the moment I said it. Quinn was trapped in bloodlust because of something I'd done and now I'd be lucky if he didn't murder Killian in the process.

"Fixed him?" Aaron repeated. "Fixed him... how?"

"Aaron," Marcus warned.

Aaron lifted a hand to wave off the well-mannered vampire and took three purposeful steps towards me until he towered over me.

I arched my head back and glowered up at him. He wasn't going to intimidate me.

Sparkles growled at my feet, wholeheartedly agreeing that Aaron was being an ass right about now.

The tattooed vampire leaned in close until all I could see was the challenge in his eyes. "Quinn loved you, you know."

I tilted my head. "Loved? He only just met me yesterday." Even I had to admit there was something between Quinn and me, and now that Aaron was in such close proximity, I felt the faint tug of a bond there as well. Whatever I'd done at those pillars had initiated a connection between these four vampires, but that didn't make it love, did it?

"He's known you for a thousand years," Aaron whispered, lingering closer to me as if we were drawn to one another. "We all have."

"Aaron!" Marcus snapped. "That's quite enough."

A sound crashed down the hall and Aaron finally moved away from me. "I'll go see if Killian needs help," he growled, then stormed off.

"Don't mind him," Marcus said as he motioned for me to join him by the fire.

I sighed and slunk across the carpet, slipping into an extravagant chair that was perfectly angled to catch the warmth from the fire. "He seems to mind me," I complained.

Marcus chuckled, the sound so warm and enticing that I glanced up at him. His glamour was down, allowing me to see the red haze of his vampirism. His suit was too pristine and I knew that he must have used a good dose of magic to clean it after the carnage from this morning.

"He's just afraid of what he'll be like when you replace what he left behind." He continued to stare into the fire, not looking at me. "We're all afraid."

I sighed and Sparks meowed at my feet before jumping up into my lap. He wandered in a tight circle before settling into a ball. Soft waves of magic emanated from him, sinking into my skin even though I felt like I'd gorged on magic today. I stroked his fur and lowered my voice. "I don't understand."

"Have you ever heard of reincarnation?" Marcus asked, finally seeming to grow the courage to look at me.

I tilted my head. "Of course." When he didn't elaborate, I asked, "Are you suggesting that the woman Aaron was referring to was me?" If I had been alive a thousand years ago and in love with these men, I surely would have remembered that, past life or not.

Magical bonds in the supernatural community were more common than most realized. Only those training to be an official member of the Royal Coven would have access to the piles and piles of books that dive into history no one else knows. Witches don't live forever, and those that do go mad with power. Someone in the supernatural community needs to keep a record of things, and it was one of the studies that I enjoyed from my coven.

"That's precisely what I'm suggesting," Marcus said. The light from the flames danced across the graceful lines of his face. Where Quinn was wild, Marcus was reserved. He adjusted his stance so that he faced me. "You are no doubt the reincarnation of the Royal Queen." He smirked. "You earned a name for yourself near the end. Those opposed to your rightful rule called you the Rebel Queen."

My eyes went wide. There was no mention of any sort of Queen of the Royal Covens, much less a rebel one. The covens were all ruled by the respective houses with decisions being a group collaboration between those in control. There was no risk for a single individual to ascend to power. That might work for other supernatural races with immortal lifespans, but witches couldn't afford a power struggle every generation. Even the Amethyst Coven had three Royals, although Aunt Sandra made sure I rarely came into contact with them.

"I'm mortal-born," I reminded him. As much as I wanted to entertain the fantasy that I was a reborn Queen who had captured the hearts of these four intriguing men, I knew better. "I'm just a regular girl."

"No," Marcus said with such confidence that I snapped my gaze up to him. He looked as if he wanted to come closer, but he folded his hands behind his back and straightened as he regained his composure. "I mean, you're correct that if you had been initiated as a witch a thousand years ago, you would have been reborn as a witch. Alas, you were killed before your initiation could take place, which is precisely why we knew we'd find you again when your mortal soul was exposed to magic." He gave me a raised brow. "So you see, it is quite peculiar that the coven took you in, given your soul's past lives."

I scoffed, but I couldn't explain away his reasoning. It was... sound.

Sparkles trilled his agreement with Marcus. Even he thought that I was some reborn Queen. The cat blinked at me, indignant that he had to raise his head off his paws long enough to give me a glower.

I scratched behind his ear and he situated himself again. "Yes, Sparks. I get that you agree with him, but it all seems so... surreal."

Marcus smiled. "You had a familiar in your past life, too." He tilted his head, giving Sparkles an appraisal. "Perhaps it's the same one. That wouldn't be out of the ordinary."

I stopped petting Sparkles. "Is that true, Sparks? Did you know me in a past life?"

Sparkles conveniently pretended to be asleep.

Aaron came into the room, startling me with his heavy breathing. "Okay, we got Quinn tied up."

I twisted in the chair and Sparks complained as I dumped him on the floor. Ignoring him, I peered over the back of the chair to see a tattered-looking Aaron, soon joined by a bloodied Killian.

Killian wiped the back of his hand over his forehead. "Yeah. We just need to get him some food and get the bloodlust out of his system." He glanced at me. "What were you doing in there?" he asked.

"Quinn took me," I retorted. "He said he wanted to get me ready for the initiation."

Killian narrowed his eyes, then approached me. I flinched when he took my chin in his hands, but he was gentle. He turned my face as if searching for something.

"What is it?" I asked.

He turned my face the other way, then frowned. "You're moving quick. There's a hint of vampiric magic in your eyes. You drained enough power to compel Quinn."

"Compel him?" I could use compulsion? Seriously? If that was true, then I wanted to get back to the Amethyst Coven and try out a few things…

"You must have sensed something was missing and you wanted to fix him. It's okay. He'll thank you, once he snaps out of it." His finger flicked over my nose, the gesture affectionate. "Just be careful with us, sweetheart. We're not all as strong as we look when it comes to you."

It was true. I had used the Sight on Quinn. I'd seen the sadness in him. I'd seen the hole where a piece of his heart should have been, and then I'd seen the hope in his eyes when he looked at me. "Did I do all that?" I asked to no one in particular.

"You did good," Marcus said from behind me.

Aaron didn't seem to think so and stormed off again. "Going to sleep for twenty hours," he informed us, and then disappeared. A soft thud of a door closing sounded in the distance.

I turned and slumped back into my chair. Sparks had found a spot on the floor to curl as close to the fire as possible again. "Sleep sounds good to me," I admitted.

"Why don't you get some rest," Killian offered, moving into my peripheral vision. "Mrs. Styles should be over in a couple of hours to give you some food."

I closed my eyes. Food sounded amazing, but sleep first. "Nobody drink my blood while I sleep," I ordered, and then passed out.

BITE ME

*M*rs. Styles had come and gone by the time I woke up. I hadn't quite slept for twenty hours, but it sure felt like it.

Marcus had moved from his spot leaning against the mantle to the chair beside mine, angled so that he faced me enough to see me, but also so that he could catch the warmth from the fire.

I glanced over at the window and saw Killian sprawled out under it, catching the low rays. He'd cleaned up and it felt like I could have almost imagined the whole episode with Quinn.

"You're awake," Marcus remarked, then handed me a sandwich. "Hungry?"

My stomach chose that moment to rumble and I plucked the plump bread stuffed with goodies from his hand. "You have no idea." I'd missed breakfast, as well as lunch and dinner by the looks of how much of the day I'd slept through. If I was going to be hanging out with vampires, though, perhaps it would be better to get my schedule oriented to nighttime.

As I devoured my food, Marcus cleared his throat. "So, Quinn would be the best to train you, but I'm afraid he's still recovering. I know you meant well to reunite him with his memories of you, but out of the four of us, he was the one who handled it the worst."

I paused mid-bite as Marcus stretched out the Amethyst earrings I'd taken from the pillar. I swallowed my portion of dry bread and salted meat and wiped my hands on my pants legs before taking the jewelry. "What is this?" I asked. It felt so familiar and it hummed with power.

"It belonged to you," he said. "You were given a handful of Royal Jewels by the Amethyst Coven who was your prime supporter." He frowned as he steepled his fingers. "A thousand years has changed them, I'm afraid. I'm not so sure they wish to stand by a martyr and her bonded vampires."

"Of course they wouldn't," I agreed as I turned the earrings over in my hands. They glinted in the firelight and were the most stunning craftsmanship I'd ever seen. I wish I knew who'd made them.

Sparkles stretched and meowed, informing me that magical jewelry work was an old craft no longer in wide practice, but the craftswoman had been a powerful witch. He had quite liked her.

I gave my familiar a raised brow. "So, you're admitting that you *did* know I am a reincarnated queen?"

He ignored me, sauntering off into the hall.

Marcus laughed. "Killian caught some fish for your familiar. He set him a plate in the kitchen. I've never met a familiar who can eat quite so much."

I glanced at Killian again who was still sprawled by the window, but clearly awake as he watched me. "What were you doing out catching fish?" I asked him.

He sat up. "I had to get some blood for Quinn. Thought I'd get some fish for your cat while I was at it."

I grimaced, not wanting to know what species he'd attacked for the kind of blood that Quinn needed to recover from his episode. "Well, thanks, I guess."

He beamed at me. "Anytime."

"So," I said, turning back to Marcus. "Where's Aaron?" I felt like I needed to make amends with the tattooed vampire. He'd been upset that I'd compelled Quinn to help me learn Astral Projection, and that I'd used it to reunite him with a lost piece of his soul. I still couldn't believe that I'd actually done all of that, and mostly without knowing what I was doing. Hurray for past lives giving me an epic sense of instinct, I guess.

"He's resting," he reminded me in a way that said there would be no talking to Aaron right now.

"Of course," I muttered. "I didn't realize he'd been literal when he said he was going to sleep for twenty hours."

Marcus smirked. "Sleep helps recharge magic. Aaron's works a little differently than ours." When I gave him a raised brow, he threw up his hands in defense. "You'll have to ask him. His magic isn't my secret to tell."

"Very well," I groaned. "I'll just, uh…" I had a feeling that Marcus wouldn't approve of me checking on Quinn, but I needed to. I still held onto the earrings. I absentmindedly put them on, running my fingers over them.

"Suits you," Killian said, smiling.

A blush crept up my cheeks. "Right. Well, I'll just find a bathroom and see for myself before I settle on keeping them."

"You are who we say you are," Marcus insisted. "When you complete the blood rite, you'll remember."

I glanced down at the single blood rune on my arm. It wasn't bleeding, but the carving hadn't completely healed as if waiting for one last sliver of magic before it settled. I had a feeling if I could see Quinn again, I'd figure all this out.

"I'll be the judge of that," I said, and sauntered off into the hall, leaving the two vampires behind.

I STOPPED by the kitchens first, running into Sparks on the way. He was devouring a beheaded fish and worked his way carefully around the bones. Spoiled cat.

I grabbed a bottle of water from the fridge and took a few needed gulps, relishing the feeling of my thirst being quenched. The sensation made me think of Quinn. What did it feel like to be thirsty for blood and not have that thirst satisfied?

Shaking off the thought, I hurried to the end of the hall and knocked on the door. "Quinn?" I whispered. "Are you in there?"

I tested the doorknob, surprised when it gave way and the door opened. So, the magic room didn't work at night.

The room was darker than it had been before and I

covered my mouth to muffle a shocked gasp at seeing how much blood was thrown all over the place. It ran up the walls, had splattered over the beautiful chandelier, having put out a few of the flames, and covered a very disheveled Quinn who backed into the shadows.

Hurrying inside, I closed the door behind me. I had a feeling that this was the blood that Killian had gathered for the vampire. Quinn should be safe to approach, but if not, I had a new arsenal of magic to draw on, if I needed it. My fingers ran up to the earrings, testing the warm magic as it slipped a sliver of power into my skin. Okay, good, it worked.

"What are you doing here, lass?" Quinn croaked, his once velvety accent jagged on a throat gone hoarse. Had he been screaming? Killian must have soundproofed the room for my sake. Great. If I really got in trouble, hopefully Sparkles cared about me more than his fish.

"I'm checking on you," I said as I knelt just out of his reach.

Quinn slumped in the shadows. I couldn't see his face, but the red-hot magic in his eyes burned like two glimmering jewels. The faint illumination of his wild hair showed it stuck out at all ends.

"I don't want you seeing me like this," he complained and turned his face from me. "Full of lust for blood. This weakness has no business being in your presence."

My eyes stung with tears as my heart twisted. He was ashamed. He'd tried to kill me because the madness had taken him over. "I can't imagine what it's like," I offered, reaching out to touch his thigh.

He flinched when my fingers made contact. "Don't try to imagine it," he said. "You're better than us."

This wasn't the Quinn I'd seen with the Sight. This was a broken version of him lost in darkness. It was a good thing that I'd brought some light.

I held up my hand and purple glimmers came to life from my fingertips, illuminating his face. He hissed and flinched away from me, blocking my view, but I'd seen the blood splatters all over his cheeks and his fangs larger than they'd ever been before.

I shushed him and took his hand, lowering it. "Let me see your face."

There was so much pain in his gaze, but that's not what surprised me. It was the fear that didn't belong in those eyes that felt so familiar. Fear of losing control.

Easing closer, I ripped off my sleeve, just as he'd done for me, and began wiping at his face. The blood had hardened and stuck to his skin, so I wet the cloth from my bottle before working at the blood again.

"You don't have to do this," he said.

I grabbed his chin to keep him from moving as I scrubbed at a particularly stubborn spot. He closed his eyes at the contact as I shed my healing magic on him. It felt good to use magic—my magic.

I was sure that he could heal on his own, but the faint lashes where he'd fought with Killian hadn't closed up. It was as if he wanted to punish himself by remaining in pain. Reluctantly, the wounds closed as my magic swept over his skin.

"Eve," he whispered, making me freeze. That felt like a name from the past... something that once belonged to me.

"Listen, I'm not going anywhere."

"I'm dangerous," he protested.

I gave him a raised brow. "Are you going to bite me?"

He slumped. "No, lass. I'm not going to bite you."

"Good. Then I'm going to clean this blood off of you and then you're going to tell me what the hell is going on."

He chuckled, but obeyed and stayed still as I worked my way down his neck. My cheeks flared with heat when he peeled off his shirt for me. Gods he was beautiful. Blood had splattered all the way down his abdomen. A new glint was in his eyes now. "Will you help me with this, too?" he asked, indicating the blood that splattered low against his waistband.

I could have told him to go screw himself, but we were having a moment, so I wet my cloth again and wiped down the hard lines of his muscles. He flexed under my touch, and then flinched when I went past his bellybutton.

He grabbed my wrist and my gaze shot up to his. "Careful, lass. I might not bite you, but if you keep that up, there's something else I'll do to you."

I grinned. "Is that a threat, or a promise?"

His eyes widened, and I liked that I'd shocked him. The last thing I wanted to be was predictable.

His grip tightened, but only just barely. "I would never hurt you," he vowed. "Even in bloodlust, I have to believe that had I pinned you to the ground, I wouldn't have hurt you."

My smile faded. I wanted to believe that, and I know he did too. "You didn't hurt me," I stated.

Without warning, he pulled me into his chest. "Eve. I'm so sorry."

Instinctually I wrapped my arms around his neck and curled my knees up as I settled into his lap. The scent of honeysuckle and open fields hinted at the edges of my senses.

That was the real Quinn, the one from an ancient Ireland where he was free and happy. I wanted to be there with him and spread my fingers to play with the tendrils of the wind through his hair.

"I'm a monster now," he said and I'd never heard anyone so crushed and forlorn.

I shushed him and lifted my head from the curve of his neck. Our lips were just inches from each other now, and every fiber in me wanted to kiss him. If I was really the reincarnation of the Rebel Queen, then I knew Quinn better than I could even hope to imagine. He had been one of my guardians, and I suspected now why he'd turned into a vampire. He'd done it to protect me.

They all had.

I ran a finger over one of his fangs, wondering what kind of love might have been there for such a sacrifice, and if I could find it in myself again.

As if sensing my desire, he flinched away. "I can't retract them just yet. The bloodlust... it just takes a while for me to get over it when it's like this."

He thought I wouldn't kiss him, but he was wrong. I *knew* him, and if I could just open myself up to him, then he would know me too.

I turned his face back to mine and carefully pressed my lips to his. His cool fangs grazed against my skin, but he deepened the kiss without hurting me. His tongue danced with mine as if his thirst had been for me and I was the only thing that could quench it now.

His hands wound up my back and pulled me closer to him and the sweet scent of honeysuckle exploded around us. The blood rune on my arm burned hot, and I knew I was close to awakening something inside of me that was ancient and dangerous, but would bring me closer to Quinn. I decided in that moment that I wanted that. I wanted to bond with him.

When I broke the kiss, I looked into Quinn's eyes and searched for the lost memories of my past life. I knew I was using the Sight this time because I could see straight through to his soul. "Quinn," I whispered as my vision glowed with the golden aura of his magic, "you're so beautiful."

His smile took my breath away. "You always said that to me."

He was talking about when we were lovers, back a full thousand years ago when my guardians had sacrificed everything for me... yet I'd still died. It must have crushed him.

Straddling him, I unzipped his pants.

His eyes went wide. "Eve, I can't. It's not safe for you in here right now."

"You won't hurt me," I reminded him as my fingers slipped under his clothing and across hard, velvety skin.

He hissed at the contact and his entire body went rigid. He was holding himself back and I decided that I didn't like that. I rolled my hand down with one firm stroke.

He groaned and the sound was like music to my ears. I grinned, and then I did it again.

I would have thought that I was the one in control. The full length of Quinn's cock hard in my hands gave me power over him. He would do what I said, or that was the lie I told myself.

He moved with vampiric speed so fast that my world blurred as he flipped me onto my back. My head cracked against the hard stone and I winced. I drew power from my earrings and diverted my newfound healing magic to the throb, easing the pain.

When I looked up at Quinn again, he had a wild look in his eyes and the softness I'd seen of an old Ireland had retreated, replaced with a naked, hungry need. He bared his fangs at me, and I should have been afraid when he lowered the threat to my hip. He could bite me. He could shred me to pieces.

But he wouldn't.

His fangs caught at my pants and tore them open, not even nicking my skin. I sucked in a breath when cool air met my naked legs and he slipped his fingers over my thighs, going up, up, then pushing the delicate fabric away that had survived his rage to slip a finger inside of me.

He grinned when I moaned as he added another finger and twisted into my wetness. His thumb rode up and put pressure on my clit, making stars explode behind my eyelids.

"Your heart thunders," he growled, as if finally able to manage words again.

I didn't know how he was finding control, not until I saw the faint purple tendrils of magic slipping over my skin and into him. He lapped at it, giving me waves of ecstasy as he relaxed, trading me pleasure for magic.

"Quinn," I breathed. I wanted so much more. I wanted to bond with him. I wanted him inside of me.

When I looked back at him, I knew he could read the desire in my eyes. He moved his fingers faster, making me writhe. "Not yet," Quinn said. "Not with me."

It was something about the way he'd said that. *Not with me.*

If I slept with Quinn first, would I become overwhelmed by his magic? It swarmed around me now like a hurricane of sweetness and sex. I felt myself falling into it and I knew that if Quinn joined me, I could be lost in it forever. Quinn's danger wasn't just in his bite, but in the world he offered.

"What are you?" I asked as I moved further towards the peak. Every nerve inside of me lit up under his touch.

"I have incubus blood in my family line," he admitted. "When I took on vampirism, it… brought it out; enhanced it."

I gasped when he lowered his mouth onto me again, continuing to slide his fingers in and out of me with merciless thrusts. That was why he could feed on my magic like this. Sex with him could be dangerous if I didn't have some means to protect myself.

Not yet. Not with me.

I would have to bond with one of my other guardians first, before I could have Quinn.

The thought brought guilt and excitement thundering through me as I tipped over the cliff and my body tightened around Quinn's fingers as I screamed.

WALK OF SHAME

J'd never had to do the "walk of shame" as Cassidy put it when a girl left her lover's bedroom and tried to sneak back home without being too painfully obvious what she'd been up to. Except, I couldn't go back home, and I didn't even know where the bedrooms were in this place or which room would be mine.

"I'll go first," Quinn said, smirking as he raked his gaze over me after I'd tied the shreds of my outfit back together— my pants now more like a makeshift skirt.

Shit. I didn't even need a mirror to know what I looked like. I ran a hand up into my hair that frizzed out on the ends, as if in competition for Quinn's disheveled hot mess thing he always had going on, which was up a notch right about now. The spark of mischief in his gaze betrayed exactly what we'd been up to, and I sighed.

I tried to purse my lips, but they were still swollen from

kissing a vampire. Quinn had been careful with his fangs, but he'd still been rough—not that I was complaining.

Quinn gave my hand an encouraging squeeze before turning and venturing into the living room.

Sparkles peeked his head around the door to the kitchen and gave me a heavy-lidded look.

"Some help you are," I hissed at my familiar.

The cat meowed, surprising me by telling me that he wasn't going to be sticking around much longer. I didn't need him anymore now that I had new protectors.

"Aw, Sparkles. Are you jealous?"

He twitched his tail at me, which was as much reply as I was going to get before he followed Quinn into the living room.

I heard Killian's shout of surprise first. "Quinn! What the fuck you doing out here? Where's Evie? Fuck, man. If you—"

Before Killian could say something he'd regret, I hurried into the room. "Here!" I said, raising a hand as if I'd entered a classroom.

Killian relaxed and blew out a breath, as did Marcus who'd perked up by the fireplace.

"Fuck," Killian said, slumping down onto his perch at the window, only to snap his gaze up to me again, as if finally taking note of the evidence all over me.

I held my clothes together as much as I could without a boob popping out. Quinn had done a good job of slicing a clean cut so that I could hold the torn fabric in place. A little stitching, or magic, could fix it, but I was no good at either. "I was hoping for, uhm, assistance," I ventured.

Marcus was the first to take note of my meaning, and save

me from complete humiliation. "Lady Evelyn," he said, his tone light as he motioned to the hall I'd come from, "I believe I can assist you with that."

"WOULD you care to tell me what happened?" Marcus asked as he worked a fine layer of magic over my clothes.

Instead of answering him, I watched in fascination as his fingers moved back and forth as if threading a needle, but there was no needle, and there was no thread, just magic so delicate that I was afraid I would break it with a touch.

When I didn't respond, Marcus paused, lowering his hands until the faint hue of violet magic faded, leaving us in the soft glow of the bedroom's chandelier.

Each room had the same fixture as the Astral Projection chamber, except this bedroom had a small window. It gave me something to look at now that Marcus had stopped his work and I searched for the moon until it peeked from behind a layer of clouds. An entire day had passed by and the demon-touched wolves would be scouring the village looking for supernaturals who were dumb enough to be caught outside a protective field.

"They feed on magic," I told Marcus, needing to think about something other than Quinn and how the mere thought of him sent my blood racing. Marcus had only just recovered from his own bloodlust and I didn't want to make things worse by antagonizing him with a heartbeat that could rival a rabbit's.

"Who does?" Marcus, asked, his voice strained.

I blinked at him. "The wolves, of course."

He relaxed. "Oh. I see. Yes, of course."

I frowned. "But you already know about the wolves." His lack of response confirmed that. I shifted, wanting to cross my legs but then thought better of it before my clothing was properly mended. I narrowed my eyes at the refined vampire that seemed to hide one too many secrets. "Do you know what Quinn is?"

Marcus stood up and paced the small room. He fit right in when it came to a place of luxury like this. He ran his fingers over a polished dresser before sitting in a curved armchair. "He's a few things," Marcus admitted, his gaze flashing to mine, "but I suppose that could be said of all of us."

That didn't shock me. All the vampires were so distinctly unique that they had to be special. I found myself excited with the prospect of discovering who they were in a way no one else would ever know. "So, what are you, Marcus?" I asked. "Are you part incubus as well?"

His lip ticked up on the side ever so slightly. "No, I'm not."

Seeing that he wasn't going to reveal any secrets just yet, I motioned to my clothes he'd barely started mending. The torn seam had tried to stitch itself back together at my upper thigh. His magic still tickled there like a teasing memory. "Are you going to help me fix my clothes, or leave me a poor humiliated fool?"

His smirk turned into a full-fledged grin. "You have magic, dear. I was just showing you how it worked. Now it's your turn. Finish the process."

I glowered at him, but I was up for the challenge. I looked down at the work he'd started, noting how he'd commanded the magic to mend the fabric from the inside out, smoothing frayed edges before twining together. I stroked my earring as I concentrated and the small hum of honeysuckle magic filtered into me. Quinn's magic, and now my own.

When I'd finished the spell, I realized that I hadn't uttered a single chant. My clothes glowed at the torn edges until they fused back into place, as if never having been torn at all. I hadn't spoken Latin, or even a witch's spell. I'd simply... willed it, and it was done.

"Very good," Marcus whispered. I snapped my gaze to find him towering over me. I had been so focused I hadn't even heard him approach. He knelt and slipped his fingers over mine. When he tugged on my arm, I realized that another blood rune had appeared. The one that represented Quinn had turned solid like a tattooed mark, as natural as if it had always been there. The only evidence that I hadn't completed my bond with Quinn was the faint scab that ran around the edge, and one single pinhole mark that dolloped with blood. Above it a second rune appeared and blood trickled freely down my arm.

A new bond.

Horrified when I spotted the vampire's fangs elongated, I snatched away from Marcus. "I'm sorry," I said as I searched the room for a cloth or something I could use as a bandage. Panic filled me. I'd just survived one vampire with bloodlust. This must be making Marcus go insane.

He chuckled and caught my arm. He took a handkerchief from his vest pocket and applied pressure to the mark. How... chivalrous?

"I won't need to feed for quite some time," he assured me,

already guessing what had me so panicked. "I must admit, I thought Killian would have been second. What made you choose me?"

I swallowed hard. I'd nearly completed my bond with Quinn and I was still reeling from all the revelations and how he made me feel. I was a reborn queen... and these powerful men were my guardians.

"You seem to have the most secrets," I admitted honestly. I hated not knowing secrets. The one good thing about being mortal-born was that no one noticed me, and if they did, it was easy for me to slip into the background. People reveal a lot about themselves when they think they're alone. I knew everyone's secrets.

Marcus' eyes lit up with intrigue at my statement. "I suppose I do," he agreed. He offered me his hand. "Why don't we get to know each other a little better. You tell me one of your secrets," his tongue ran over one of his fangs, "and I'll tell you one of mine."

TIME TRAVEL IS A WITCH

J could tell that Marcus wanted to go outside for our talk, so the scrying tower was a good compromise. Its windows overlooked the farmland and we could see all the way to the Amethyst Coven where the soft purple glow of the jasmine fields kept the demon-touched wolves away.

Shivering when I spotted the magicked blooms, I wrapped my fingers around my elbows and leaned against the window frame. A chill breeze played with my hair. Scrying was always best done out in the open with no impediment to nature, not that I'd ever attempted it. The magic was another high-magic skill, just like Astral Projection, and had similar elements to the task.

I didn't need to scry to see supernatural danger whisper through my village. The wolves sauntered through the darkness with their red glowing eyes betraying their nature.

"They never go after the humans?" Marcus asked.

I shook my head. "Did they in your time?" A thousand

years was enough to change the entire world, but when it came to magic and supernaturals, I'd always been taught that some things never changed.

"Sometimes," Marcus admitted, "but in 'my time,' as you call it, there was more magic and less pure-blooded humans. Things have become more segregated now, and I'm glad for the humans. We always managed to mess up their lives."

I gave him a raised brow. I hadn't missed his slip. "You're older than the others, aren't you?" I asked.

He smirked. "You don't miss a thing, do you, Lady Evelyn?" He clasped his hands behind his back as he joined me at the window and looked out over the scenery. He seemed comfortable, even relaxed, but I didn't like the mask he wore in front of me.

"You don't have to wear your glamour with me," I told him, automatically reaching up to stroke his cheek with my thumb. His slick midnight hair curled elegantly behind his ear without my help. Even the wind couldn't disturb his perfection. His blue eyes matched mine and he dropped the glamour in a heart-breaking instant. His skin paled ever so slightly to the more delicate vampiric hue and the red glaze of magic glowed in the backs of his eyes. Now that I recognized its power, I found it fascinating. He was stunning.

"Vampirism is blood magic, obviously," I began, "but I'd never really thought about that connection. The Blood Stone gave many supernaturals their start in this world, isn't that correct?"

His eyes widened ever so slightly, betrayed he hadn't expected that bit of knowledge to be taught to a mortal-born witch, even one primed to be a member of the Royal Covens.

"Correct. Supernaturals such as shifters, Incubi and Succubi, and the witches and warlocks who respond to the darker elements can all thank the power of the Blood Stone for their birth. The stone comes from Hell. Only its Queen and those of the dark arts can ever master its power."

I nodded. "Would your secret have something to do with this dark power?"

That seemed to unsettle him, and Marcus didn't strike me as someone easily ruffled.

He sighed and looked out over the landscape again, narrowing his gaze as if deciding how much to tell me. "What if I said that I'd once been given a choice between this dark power, and love?"

I shifted closer to him as an invisible thread seemed to pull us together. I found my gaze wandering over his body, wondering what he looked like under that suit. Was he all hard edges and perfection, or grace like a marble statue masterpiece?

"Evelyn," he whispered, his tone chiding as if he'd sensed the improper places my mind had just gone.

I smiled and leaned back on the windowsill, propping myself up on my elbows as I threw my head back and looked up at the ceiling. "Power and love rarely go well together," I mused. I'd seen love. It was there between the farmer, old man Jordan Styles, and his wife. They'd loved young and grown old together, living a simple and peaceful life, but they weren't powerful. Now power, that I'd seen in plenty. It rested in the hands of people like my Aunt Sandra and I wasn't sure if she truly loved anything or anyone. She seemed to have a certain affection for me, but the more I was growing to learn about myself, the more I had to admit the covens could know who I was too, and Aunt Sandra just wanted the power I promised to herself.

"That was a lesson that took me a thousand years to learn," Marcus said with such weighty sorrow in his voice that I glanced at him.

Resisting the urge to touch him, I frowned. "What do you mean?"

He sighed, then indicated the scenery before us. "This is my home, Evelyn. I grew up here, but I wasn't born a thousand years ago. My original birth was planned, down to the second, by a clan of witches who specialize in time manipulation."

My eyes went wide. Such a powerful coven was often discussed as rumors when spells went wrong or worldly events were disrupted, but such things could often be explained away by the impressive power of the supernatural who policed our community. The three male muses towered over supernatural society with an iron fist, at least, until lately.

Marcus most certainly wasn't a muse. I would have figured that out by now. I leaned in closer until my arm brushed him. "Then how were you my guardian a thousand years ago?"

"You're asking the wrong question, Evelyn." His gaze challenged me. "You should be asking why I didn't stop your death."

I swallowed hard. A warlock who could control time itself would be all-powerful—or close to it, at least. He could have just gone through time and prevented my death all-together.

"Okay," I whispered, my voice wavering with a slight tremor, "tell me then."

He growled as his fangs elongated. "Your proximity has always been the only thing to break my composure."

"Because you're the most vicious of my four guardians," I responded instantly. I had already noticed that when he'd been the first to mercilessly maul one of old man Jordan's cows. I lifted my chin in defiance. "I'm not afraid."

He grabbed my chin and squeezed. "You should be."

"Answer the question," I spat. "Why didn't you save me?"

A darkness I'd never seen before clouded over his eyes and I recognized the fleeting emotion that swept through our connection. He was ashamed of what he had done. "I wanted this power," he growled and bared his fangs at me. "I wanted to become a vampire without becoming enslaved to a den or the Blood Stone itself. I needed a situation where I could be both a warlock... and..." His words drifted off as his gaze dipped to my neck.

Shit. My heart was definitely thundering. Aside from the naked hunger in his gaze, either for my blood or for something else, there was desperation, fear, and shame. Something was missing inside of him, just like Quinn, that was allowing him to spiral into this bleak pit of self-blame and depression. I knew there was more to the story. Magic didn't make mistakes. If he had been chosen as one of my guardians, then there was a reason. I only needed to get it out of him.

I went over what I knew of Marcus on a mental checklist. Pretended to be proper and refined, but he was totally vicious. He had a serious case of self-loathing going on. The best way to get to a guy who thought he deserved to be punished was to start by giving him exactly what he wanted.

"Some guardian you are," I spat, "you could have protected me but you let me die. And now? What will you do? Tear my throat out and let your vampirism control you? Sounds like you managed to find that monster you were so afraid of."

My provocation worked and he growled as red hazed over his eyes. "I loved you more than you'll ever know."

"Really?" I spat back, making sure I didn't sound intimidated as he slipped his arm around my waist and pulled me closer to him.

His fingers ran over my cheek. "I had to let you die, but I regret it now. It was my biggest failure. If the others knew, they'd never forgive me."

I placed my hand over his. The contact with his skin sent shivers through me and a new scent of Marcus' magic filtered into the air.

Roses and jasmine.

"But you want my forgiveness," I ventured. The raw hope in his eyes told me all I needed to know. I was back now, and even if I didn't have any memory of him, I knew there was history there. History I fully intended to explore.

He leaned down and pressed a gentle kiss against my lips. The magic around us hummed with anticipation. He pulled away and whispered soft words over my tongue that still tasted of him. "Yes, but I can never have your forgiveness. Not when you've seen what I've done for yourself."

"Marcus, I—" My protest was cut off short when the scent of roses and jasmine exploded and the world flashed with light.

I'd heard of time travel, but it seemed far too great and terrible a power to be real—yet, it was. Marcus yanked me out of the present and sent me flinging into the past.

A past where he and I were lovers and he'd lost all the will to live.

I WAS STILL IN BELGIUM. I could tell that much by the low streak of buildings on the horizon that marked the village and the recognizable spires of the Amethyst Coven. It had always been there, even a thousand years ago.

We were in the cemetery, but there weren't near as many gravestones or impressive sculptures. Only a simple row of ancestors were rooted in neat little lines with flat, engraved stones. I walked past them and the rich dirt with scattered pebbles crunched under my feet. The familiar scents of earth and history tinged my nose—but also roses and jasmine.

I saw why when I reached the four spires. The flowers made the ground bleed red with pure sprinkles of white mixed in. The sweet aroma wafted on a cool breeze and mixed into my hair. I hoped the perfume would stay with me forever.

Marcus knelt on the center of the platform. The spires didn't have runes or markings on them, which meant that this was before he'd turned into a vampire.

I approached him and he flinched. "Who's there?" he snapped.

"Marcus, it's me," I offered in my most gentle voice. I could feel his agony and torment from here. Something terrible had happened.

He whirled at the sound of my voice and his blue eyes went wide. "How did you…" His words drifted off when his gaze fell to my blood rune that had opened up again, sending crimson droplets trickling down my fingers before falling to the ground. The soil greedily soaked up my life-force and roses bloomed where the droplets fell.

"Oh," he murmured, as if that explained everything. His gaze flung to me again. "You're from the future."

He didn't seem surprised by that. I supposed that when a warlock was from a mythical time-traveling coven, it would be difficult to be surprised.

I approached him and stopped just out of reach. I crouched down and wrapped my arms around my knees as I appraised him. "You sent me here. I think you wanted to show me something." When he didn't respond, just kind of blankly stared at me with such hopelessness that I wanted to scream, I reached out and brushed his face. Electricity zapped between us and he flinched away.

"You can't touch me if I was the one who sent you here," he explained.

"Then talk," I said, letting irritation filter into my voice.

He sighed and struggled to his feet. That's when I noticed how thin he was. The Marcus I'd just left behind was lean, but muscular, and had an edge of power to him that could be frightening. This Marcus had sunken-in cheeks, dark circles under his eyes, and his clothes hung loosely from him in soft waves of the wind. "I'm supposed to be your guardian," he said, straightening. His black hair that was always smoothed back in perfect strands hung limply around his face with a lack-luster sheen. "Now you're dead and I won't see you again for a thousand years. I didn't stop it." His gaze flicked to the center of the pillars beneath our feet and my blood ran cold.

Was I buried here?

"There's only one way to ensure I will, in fact, see you again. Reincarnation isn't awarded to everyone." He swallowed and the muscles at his jaw ticked. "I have to talk the others into vampirism. It's been my plan all along." His gaze broke from mine as he looked at his feet. "But now that I'm living what I knew would happen, it's so much more... real."

Tears threatened at the edges of my eyes as his betrayal sank into me. "You counted on my death to bring them around," I said, keeping my voice low and steady. Marcus was right. I could never forgive him for this. "You knew I would die because you're from the future. You came back, wormed your way in as one of my guardians." I tilted my head. "How did you manage that?"

"I didn't change history," he said quietly. "I was always your guardian. It's the way of time-traveling magic. It knew that I would go back in time. History had already been written. I simply had to fulfill it. But, now that I have, I'm afraid that I made a mistake obeying it. I shouldn't have come here."

He curled his fingers into fists and his hands shook.

I glanced at the pillars. This was my grave and each pillar was my guardian who would forever watch over me. "When will you cast the spell?" No one had trapped them here.

Marcus was responsible. He'd wanted punishment.

"When we take vampirism," he admitted, "the others will know the cost. A thousand years of torment reliving our turn until you come to free us. When we're trapped here, we won't know you when we see you, but once we're freed, we'll resume our duties to protect you." His fists unfurled and he approached me, his hands hovering over my face, but he didn't touch me. Electricity crackled between us daring him to touch me. "I'll tell you the truth. I'll send you here so you can see my darkest secret, and then you will condemn me."

I tilted my head. "Is that what happens? I condemn you?"

He nodded and gave me a weak smile. "I'm a time-traveling warlock, my dear. I know my own future, and I know how gravely things will go wrong."

That didn't make sense. "Then why do this at all if you know I'll reject you?"

He stiffened. "Power? Immortality? There are a thousand reasons." His eyes went dark. "None of them are worthwhile without you in it. I know that now, but it's too late."

He swept his hands in a series of movements, sending the roses around us blooming and the jasmine's sweet scent spiking. A masquerade mask materialized and floated on the air, hanging there until I took it. "This was something I picked up in Venice that convinced me to pursue vampirism," he explained with a faint note of nostalgia in his voice. "It's from my clan in a realm where vampirism is considered royalty and the origin of our magic." His gaze met mine. "It's where I learned I would meet you, and when you accepted me, it became a medium for our magic we made together. Take it with you. I don't need it anymore."

The world around me spun as the warlock sent me home.

SCRY FOR ME

When I returned to the balcony overlooking a midnight pasture, Marcus was waiting for me in the shadows. All I could see was the ruby glow of his eyes.

"It's done," he whispered with such resignation that my insides twisted and I clutched the mask.

In my heart, I wanted to condemn him. He'd known everything. He'd known he'd become my guardian and failed in his promise to protect me.

Yet, he also knew that he would pay a steep price. He wanted to be punished and condemned because he believed he deserved it. He wasn't the same man he'd been before we'd met in my past life. The man now regretted his actions.

I smoothed the feathers from the mask. Its power hummed and resonated with a throb in my blood rune. If I could learn how to accept Marcus, I could change his fate. He might have seen a future where I rejected him, but I didn't believe in predetermined futures. I believed I could make my own fate. Marcus didn't have to be doomed to suffer for his mistakes.

"Now I know your darkest secret," I whispered. It was a dark one indeed. He'd allowed me to die, purposefully planned out the aftermath and convinced my guardians to embrace vampirism so that they could give me a second chance at life. What Marcus didn't know was that I had a secret of my own to tell.

"What if I told you that I was the one who trapped you? I was the one who planted this idea that you had to let me die, accept vampirism, and suffer like this?"

He breached the shadows and moonlight cascaded over his beautiful face. "What?"

My sketchbook. Inside of it there was a rune I'd drawn over and over again. No one could recognize it. My aunt had rifled through my sketchbook before and told me to stop pretending I was a witch. Now I knew better. The magic from my earrings and the mask awakened the truth in me. It was enough magic for me to remember who I'd been and how I'd planned this all out.

The rune was for fate and it was a spell even the Royal Covens didn't know about.

"It was me," I explained and eased closer to him as I wrapped my arms around his neck. He stiffened under me and his muscles flexed as I pressed myself to him. I needed him to know that it was I who needed forgiveness. "Every thousand years a cycle of death comes for this world. There are only a few who can stop it." I remembered the vision vividly. A Seer had come to visit me and told me that the cycle would be broken during this era and the echoes of calamity would spread out over the realms, breaking rules magic had put in place a long time ago. If calamity won, if *death* won, everything would end. Just, *blip*, gone, and nothing I ever would have accomplished would have had meaning.

"I know of the calamity," he said slowly as he accepted my warmth and wrapped his hands around my waist. "It's happening now. The demon-touched wolves are just the start. I know what's coming next. Vampires will be seduced by hell's power and will go mad."

I stroked my fingers up his chest and ran my touch over one of his fangs. He was so dangerous and powerful, but he was mine. He was my creation and my guardian. I'd broken him and I needed to mend that mistake. "You'll help me stop it," I promised, "but first, please stop asking for my forgiveness. I'm the one who did this to you."

Anger flashed in his eyes as if he'd finally accepted my truth. His grip on me tightened and vibrant reds and whites flashed to life around us as his magic mixed with mine. I licked my lips to taste its sweetness and his gaze dipped. "We start over tonight," he vowed as he slipped away the edge of my blouse, revealing my breast. My nipple pebbled as he rolled his thumb over it and I clamped my lower lip between my teeth. He didn't stop the torment and continued to tease me. He trapped me with his gaze and pinched, making me yelp. "Tonight, I punish you."

Gods, that sounded fucking amazing. "Yes," I whispered and pulled him in for a kiss, "don't hold back."

He thrust his tongue into my mouth and his fangs pressed against me. He moved down to my neck, tasting me as he grazed the sharp danger of his teeth over my rapid pulse. "You'll share your body?" he asked. "Your blood?"

"Bite," I commanded. It wouldn't be punishment without a little bit of pain. I trusted his bloodlust was sated, but his sexual lust raged hot enough to simmer the air around us. He deserved everything I could offer him.

He sank his fangs into me and pain spiked white flashes over my vision, and then the sensation swiftly turned to relentless tides of desire. My mouth opened in a shocked gasp.

His bite gave pleasure. Holy shit.

Heat ran down my neck as he fed, growling as he took what he needed from me. His hand moved down, opening my shirt and loosening my pants. He pulled my clothing down and out of the way and ran his fingers over my wetness.

When he released me and lapped at the wound at my neck, a tightness spread over my skin as the gash healed. I couldn't tell if it was his magic doing that or mine. I'd learned so much about myself in the past day. I was capable of so much more than I'd ever been told.

I was a Fate Witch.

Mortal-born or not, I had the most sought after incredible power in the world. I could change someone's fate. I'd changed my own. I'd plotted my own death and brought four incredible men into my plan, but I didn't know how deeply I'd fall in love with all of them. My memories were flimsy at best, but every moment I spent with my guys I unlocked a piece of my heart. Quinn and Marcus made my heart swell. I loved them so much that it hurt.

Marcus, refined and gentle on the surface, showed his true

self to me. Dangerous, violent, and a beast that had been uncaged groaned when I released his erection from his pants and stroked him. He pushed my hands away and flipped me around so that the top half of me dangled over the window's edge and the height made me dizzy.

He nudged at my entrance from behind and paused. Every muscle in my body was tight with anticipation. I'd never been taken like this. I'd never wanted anyone so badly as I wanted Marcus. His rage and passion burned with red-hot fury behind me and I licked my lips at the thought of him unleashing it on me.

"Are you sure?" he asked, even now as he was on the edge of losing control, he wouldn't hurt me. He'd never make that mistake again and I loved him for it.

I peered at him over my shoulder and grabbed his hand. "I'm yours, Marcus," I promised him. "Take me and know that I am yours."

I cried out when he entered me in one long, deliberate thrust. Pleasure wafted through me as he pressed me against the stone and worked his hips against me, pushing himself all the way into me before pulling all the way out.

Releasing him, I clutched at the stone as it scraped against my skin at the rough movements and Marcus took note of it, pulling out of me and flipping me again. He pulled me up and I wrapped my legs around his hips as he fucked me, bouncing me on top of him and cupping my bottom to keep me upright.

I wrapped my arms around his neck and held on as pleasure uncurled in me, bringing the cliff of my desire closer with every thrust. He pulled me closer to him and lessened his movements, keeping contact between his muscular abdomen and my clit, building the pressure as my eyes went wide.

A wicked grin erupted on his face, which was sexier than I thought it should be with my blood still on his fangs. He was a predator and he'd claimed me. I was his, and now he wanted me to claim him.

"Come for me," he commanded with a deep growl and grated me hard against him.

With the full length of him still inside me, he continued the constant rocking with his grip firmly on my behind as he kept me close. I didn't think that I could orgasm this way, but he expertly worked pressure and contact in all the right places, keeping my hips close to him as he rocked me against him.

The pressure and heat built until I thought I couldn't take it anymore. I threw my head back and allowed the tidal wave of pleasure to crash over me as I did exactly as he'd asked.

IN DESPERATE NEED OF A SHOWER, I rested on the floor of the scrying tower with my clothes in a pile next to me. Every part of me hurt with delicious soreness. Marcus had vampiric strength, which meant he'd inevitably bruised me. I sucked in a breath and winced. Maybe bruised a rib, too.

"Are you okay?" Marcus asked as he used his handkerchief to clean himself. I smothered a laugh. I sure did hope that he had more of those things.

"Fine," I whispered, then winced again. Okay, maybe more than just a bruised rib. "I think I'll just... lay here for a while."

He chuckled and the smooth sound was honey to my ears. He lay down next to me and curled his fingers behind his head as we stared up at the ceiling. I hadn't noticed before that small pinholes allowed moonlight in. Made sense. Scrying would feel a little suffocated if it had been solid rock above us. This at least kept most of the rain out, but allowed nature to come in. "My initiation is only three days away and I feel like there's so much left I have to learn," I complained. I'd concocted some desperate plan to rewrite fate and battle against the echoes of calamity. I wondered if I'd factored in the memory loss as well.

Or how distracting my guys might be.

Marcus absently reached out and took my hand with his. I shivered as a cold breeze swept over us, but I wasn't ready to put my clothes on yet. I glanced at him. "Do you happen to have any more of those handkerchiefs?"

He nodded and pulled a few more from his pants pocket. "It's an old magic trick I picked up when I was younger. I have an endless supply of them." He handed me the cloths. "All yours."

I smirked and used them to clean myself as well, then grimaced and crumpled them in a ball. After-sex wasn't like the movies where there was no cleanup and no mess. Sex was... messy. Luckily as a witch I didn't have to worry about diseases or pregnancy. A supernatural only got pregnant when she wanted to and I'd had my womb magically closed the moment I'd come of age, at my Aunt Sandra's insistence. I'd taken the spell gladly. Experimenting with sex was a part of growing up, and I couldn't imagine trying to raise a child in this crazy world. I certainly didn't have my shit together.

Magic also made clean-up a little easier. I flicked my wrist, smirking when the cotton I'd balled up erupted into flames. I'd seen a warlock do that trick before, but I'd never really had enough magic of my own to try it. It felt good, even just to be able to do simple things.

"You're remembering who you are," Marcus observed.

I nodded and lay back on the stone. My skin was hot, but cooling rapidly. Marcus still hadn't let go of my hand. "I'm a Fate Witch," I murmured.

He nodded. "You are."

I bit my lip before asking my next question. "Did you know that it would turn out like this?"

He squeezed my hand. "I wasn't sure, to be honest. When it comes to you, time isn't a straight line anymore. You're a Fate Witch. You can change what's meant to be, making my magic confused."

I smirked. It was why we were a good match. The last thing I wanted to be was predictable, and that thought took on a whole new meaning now that I knew what I was. "You never know what the future holds when you're with me?"

He turned to look at me and gave me a slow smile. His once perfect hair now draped over his face in attractive messy strands. "That's what I love about you."

His smile was contagious, infecting me with a giddy sort of delight that made me giggle. Normally, I'd say giggling should be reserved to dimwitted school girls much younger than me, but I was happy. I couldn't remember the last time I was really happy.

Marcus watched me, seeming to love this side of me. "You're going to change the world when your initiation comes. The Royal Covens will have no choice but to recognize who and what you are."

My laughter faded. "Is that why I was killed before my initiation in my last life?"

He nodded. "They figured out who you were. You were killed before you could have disrupted the order of things. The Royal Covens haven't had a Fate Witch ordained as their queen in thousands of years, not since the first cycles of death began." His gaze went distant as he looked out over the tendrils of the past. I ran my finger over the sharp curve of his cheekbone as his magic hinted its sweet musk around us. "I've tried to see who killed you, but I never learned who it was. It happened when I wasn't there. You'd run from us that night and faced your enemy alone. At the time, I thought allowing you to disappear was my sin, but you'd known you'd die all along." His eyes resumed their focus as he gazed at me. "My magic is limited. I can only travel through time when the magic permits it. Even then, I can see possible futures, but I can't always change them. Some things are destined by fate." He smirked. "That makes you stronger than me, little witch. You've always evaded my powers. I was a fool to think that I had any control over your actions. You knew exactly what you were doing." His hand went to my fingers that still stroked his face and he brushed his lips against my fingers. "You knew you'd come back to me."

I smiled, but didn't let Marcus know that my memories were still fragmented and faded. I had to face the very real truth that I'd never reclaim them.

I'd just have to make new memories with my guardians and fall in love with them all over again.

A NEW LIFE. A NEW ME

*a*fter finding the energy to get dressed, we actually did do some scrying that night. Marcus showed me how to work the long mirror laid out flat on the stones. He said bodies of water could work if I ever found myself in a jam, but I had to make sure the water remained as still as glass or the ripples would distort events.

We searched for my killer first. I'd been born a thousand years too early the first time around. If someone had killed me, then they had to have been powerful—probably powerful enough to still be alive. I couldn't allow them to kill me again.

A marbled building glowing with blue power illuminated across the mirror, revealing the Sapphire Coven, one of the neighboring royal houses that skirted the edges of France, making it the Amethyst Coven's closest neighbor.

I used to like the Sapphire Coven, before one of its warlocks had seduced me and then left me wanting. I didn't want to scry and see his stupid face again, but Marcus pushed me, insisting that the magic had taken us here for a reason. We were looking for my enemies, and even if my murderer could avoid my scrying attempts, anyone else she or he had talked to wouldn't be immune.

"Someone in that coven knows who you are," Marcus insisted, pointing at the image of the Sapphire Coven.

"Do you think they'll try and stop my initiation?" I asked.

Marcus shook his head. "They think you have lost who you are. Your magic was locked away with each of your guardians inside of your grave." He brushed his fingers over the mask I had clipped to my thigh and then over my earrings. "You shouldn't be strong enough as a mortal to reunite with such powerful magic. As long as they don't know you've awakened us, you will be safe."

I swallowed hard. "What if they're scrying, too?"

He shrugged. "As your guardians, we would have felt it. We have the element of surprise, for now."

For now... indeed. When the sun rose, my aunt would be checking in on us again. She was like a bloodhound when it came to magic. She'd smell it on me.

THE EVENING'S scrying came up with a big fat nothing. Tired and ready for bed, I left Marcus still hovering over the glass as he worked his magic in spite of my insistence that we wouldn't find anything tonight.

I pushed on the door at the end of the stairwell that returned to the main hall, but it wouldn't budge. That's when I realized it was because someone was blocking it. I shoved hard, sending the weight on the other side catapulting away from the door, resulting in a surprised manly grunt.

"Killian," I said, acknowledging the vampire who'd no doubt been standing guard at the door...

My cheeks flamed. Gods. I sure hoped his sense of hearing wasn't as good as rumor had it when it came to vampires.

Killian smirked, ignoring Marcus who'd sauntered over to us and placed his full attention on me. His gaze dipped to the blood rune that had solidified completely, more so than Quinn's.

"Making quick work of us, I see," he mused as his grin widened. He gave me a playful wink. "Am I next?"

My blush raged to epic proportions. "Not with that attitude you're not," I snipped and shoved past him. Even if my bond tied me to all four guardians, I was still in control. This was my new life. What if I didn't want to reawaken *everything*? That would mean Killian and Aaron had to remain strangers to me.

Very hot strangers, and one of them wouldn't stop giving me hooded looks.

"Stop antagonizing her," Marcus said. "She's remembering. Let's just be happy with that for now."

Killian barked a laugh. "Says the guy who just got laid."

I whirled on him. "Enough," I snapped. "I want a shower, warm bed, and time to think. Is that too much to ask?"

Killian gave me a raised brow. "How warm of a bed? I could—"

Marcus gave him a hard nudge in the ribs, making the vampire grunt under the blow.

"Thanks," I offered Marcus, then whirled on my heel and

went searching for the nearest bedroom I could claim for myself.

SPARKLES SEEMED to have been waiting for me as well, although I could never tell if he was particularly concerned.

He stretched when he spotted me and offered me a soft meow. He'd already claimed us a bedroom, apparently, and it had a nice view, according to him, anyway.

I followed him through the hallway, but he stopped at a crease in the wall. I tested it, revealing a hidden passageway not unlike the entrance to the servants' hall back home. We entered into another hall that had rows of doors. Sparkles led me to one at the end and I smiled. It was simple. A bed. Clean sheets. The best part was a giant window that looked out over a small garden entirely enclosed by the small estate. I wouldn't have even known about it without Sparkles.

"That's beautiful," I remarked as Sparks jumped up on the windowsill and flicked his tail, his gaze snapping to the night swallows diving from the trees. "I wonder if old man Jordan takes care of this?" The garden was in tip-top shape with even the blooms nestled into perfectly spaced clumps that let them still seem wild but they had enough room to breathe.

Then I spotted what kind of blooms.

Honeysuckle. Rose. Jasmine.

Sparkles turned and blinked his bright green eyes at me. This was once my home. This estate, the grounds, even this garden. It was my magic that kept it alive, and now that I was back, it would blossom again.

It felt right and I smiled, giving Sparks a quick scratch on the ear before going into the private bathroom.

The porcelain claw tub looked positively adorable and I opened the faucet, watching as it filled with steaming water. Once it was full, I slipped in and sighed as the scalding water soothed my aches. Sex with a time-bending vampire and my earlier escapades with a wild Irishman had me sore in sensual places.

A fresh bar of soap was waiting for me and I lathered, smirking when I realized the scent was jasmine. This estate was for witches and servants of the Amethyst Coven, but it was also a place where servants would be taken care of too. The herb provided magical protection and calming even without assistance. Even if I'd never been invited before now, it was quite the place of luxury and I could tell that the Styles put a lot of time into it. I'd thought them just simple farmers, but maybe there was more to them than I'd realized.

Sparks wandered into the bathroom, flicking his paws when he crossed a small puddle. He told me that the Styles were part of an ongoing generation of witch caretakers and they took their job very seriously.

"Why haven't you told me any of this before?" I complained as I sunk lower into the water. It was already starting to grow tepid. I still wore my earrings and drew power from it to make the water steam again. I grinned.

Sparks complained I was using my magic too flippantly instead of answering my question. I waved him away.

"You're one to talk," I grumbled. He'd used his magic to make fish jump out of old man Jordan's stream before.

"Instead of getting your princess paws wet, you used magic for a snack your fat ass didn't need."

Sparks narrowed his eyes at me and flicked his paw again, sending errant droplets flinging over my face and I giggled.

After relishing the feeling of being clean, drying my hair and finding some loose pajamas in the simple dresser drawers, I was thoroughly exhausted.

I scrambled into the cool, crisp sheets and tucked them under my chin. Sparks curled into a ball at my feet and fell asleep before I did.

My eyes heavy, I watched the trees outside sway as a soft glitter of power groomed the blossoms. This was my magic. This was where I was supposed to be.

This was my home.

OVERZEALOUS PROTECTORS

The faint sound of birdsong woke me from a deep and much needed sleep and the amount of sunlight told me it was well past noon. My brows furrowed together as I refused to open my eyes. I didn't remember opening a window.

The sensation of someone watching me made me give in to the need to pull myself out of sleep. My world blurred and then came into focus, revealing Quinn watching me from a chair.

I squeaked and shot up, pulling the sheets up with me. My pajamas were thin and didn't leave much to the imagination. "Quinn?" I asked hesitantly. "What're you doing here?"

He gave me a raised brow. "I should ask you the same, lass. We all about had heart failure when we couldn't find you."

"You don't have a heartbeat," I grumbled, making Quinn laugh.

"Aye, that's true."

Sighing, I slumped back into the bed. I was still sore all over my body from yesterday's events, especially in my more delicate places, and a blush crept up my cheeks as I replayed my memories with Quinn over in my mind. By the look he was giving me, he was doing the same.

"Stop that," I chided, and he laughed again.

"Sorry, lass. You're just a sight to look at in the morning."

I glowered. "And who said you could be here? I was tired and Killian was being all protective." I knew why he'd been waiting in the stairwell. Killian had already saved me from Quinn. Maybe he thought I'd need saving from Marcus next. Had I called out for help, I had no doubt that he would have been at my side in a flash.

"Killian worries for you, and for good reason," Quinn confirmed. "I had to put my glamour back on just to convince him I was fit to play protector again. Had I drawn the short stick, he would be sitting here and not me."

I rolled my eyes. "You drew straws to see who could leer at me while I slept? Gross." I was playing the pissed off lover who liked her privacy, but I secretly liked the guys fighting over me. Maybe they all were a bit too protective, but I had died once on them. I couldn't blame them for being cautious.

Quinn stood and stretched. "Well, time for your disgusting human breakfast, and then we have some preparations to do for tonight."

My stomach growled. Breakfast sounded wonderful, but I gave him a raised brow at the latter. "Tonight?"

"Yes, I—" He frowned and plucked my masquerade mask from the vanity, then ran his fingers over the earrings. It felt weird to go to sleep with them, so I'd set them down for the night. Now my body felt cold and empty without the boost of magic the artifacts offered. "You shouldn't part with these," Quinn said. Warning flashed in his gaze. "You're weaker now that your magic has been imbued with objects instead of resting in your soul. That's the downside of the spell we had to do in order to push your spirit into reincarnation." He thumbed the earrings thoughtfully. "We had to take your magic within ourselves so that it would be here when you got back. After your death, we each imbued your magic into an artifact that reminded us of you." He paused and a dark look crossed over his face. "I gave you these earrings after our first kiss." My heart twisted that I didn't have that memory. As if sensing my pain, he glanced at me. "You remember, don't you?"

I couldn't miss the naked hope in his voice. Since I'd come back into his life, he had hope again. I didn't want to hurt him, so I did what I did best: I lied. "Of course," I whispered, covering up my discomfort with a yawn. Maybe if I played it off as casual, he wouldn't ask me for details. "Awesome kiss. Best kiss of all kisses."

He smirked, and if he sensed I was lying, he let it go. "So, tonight. There will be a masquerade ball in honor of the initiates."

I squirmed at that. Of course there was always a masquerade ball the day before initiation. The initiates would go off to our witchy headquarters in England, appropriately named the Gem. I'd suspected I'd have to go through with the extravagant event, but that was before I'd learned I was a Fate Witch. I grimaced. "Won't I stand out?" It felt like it would be difficult to hide what I was now. I'd worked so hard to gather magic like a pauper would pennies, but now this pauper had struck gold and I didn't know what to do with it all.

"You'll be fine because I'm going to teach you how to cloak yourself."

I blew out a long sigh and slumped. Great, more advanced magic I never thought I'd have to learn. "When do we learn stuff like potion mixing or rune writing?" That sounded a lot safer to me. I could cackle over a cauldron and be all witchy. I'd be totally convincing.

Quinn tsked at me and then yanked the sheets off my body, making me squeak. "Are you going to get up, or do I have to convince you?"

I wrapped my arms around myself and shivered, but a smirk ticked my lips up on the side. "You can try," I said.

Taking the challenge, he crawled over me until his elbows rested into the pillow and he hovered over me. I would have thought him just messing around, but then he lowered his hips just enough so I could feel the hard length of him through our clothes. My painfully thin pajamas did little to protect me from the pressure as he ground his weight a little bit lower into me, making a moan escape my throat.

"Perhaps I'll let you stay in bed a little while longer," he mused, his eyes glinting with mischief as he rolled his hips again. He'd put his glamour back on to satisfy Killian's worry for me. It meant that Quinn was in control, but when the mirage slipped, revealing elongated fangs and ruby eyes, I shivered with excitement. What can I say. I like my guys dangerous.

He allowed me to undo the threads keeping his pants taut at his waist. His erection escaped and I shamelessly raked my gaze over him. He'd brought my earrings just close enough for me to reach and I snatched them up. Raw magic surged in my body, enough for me to push him over and wrap tendrils of power around his wrists.

I knew my Quinn. His vampiric side was dangerous, especially now when he pretended everything was all right. He starved for me. I could see the naked desire in his eyes. If I let him take control, he'd treat me nothing more than prey. I had to dominate him and show him that I was the one in power.

I drew down his pants enough to take him into my mouth. He bucked against me.

"Release me," he warned, then threw his head back when I gave his shaft a long lick.

"You won't take me," I told him. He wasn't like Marcus. I couldn't let him claim me or else this relationship would never work. I had to claim him and tame the wildness in him. "I will take you," I vowed.

Desire flared in his eyes as I licked and stroked him. Heat built between my thighs, wanting to feel him inside of me, but I would prolong his pleasure. I would make sure he knew what he meant to me.

I had never considered myself to be dominating in bed, but something about Quinn brought it out of me. I'd let him overpower me once, but now I knew how to play his game. He'd pleasured me when I'd wanted him, so now I'd do the same to him.

Taking off my shirt, I let Quinn feast his eyes on my breasts. Males were visual creatures. Seeing me made his cock throb hard in my hands and I grinned. I played my nipple over his soft flesh, drawing away the glimmering liquid of his arousal. I drew it up with my finger and licked, tasting the salty desire of him while keeping eye contact.

He tested the magical restraints, but I was ready for him. I poured my energy into keeping him where I wanted him, then stroked down, following with my mouth. He groaned and arched into my touch. I did it again, stroking, harder and quicker until Quinn panted, holding back his release. I wasn't going to let him do that. Mercilessly I worked him until he did what I wanted and exploded into my mouth as he cried out.

A man's cries are the most intoxicating sound, and Quinn's by far were the most erotic I'd ever heard. My under-things were completely liquified by the time Quinn came down from his high and he slumped into the bed. "Eve," he whispered, the nickname he used for me sweet music to my ears, "you have tamed me."

I grinned. Fuck yes I did.

TAME THE BEAST

S parkles was nowhere to be seen for the rest of the morning, likely disgusted with such "primal human activities" as he called it any time I did anything sexual. At least when it came to my guardians, he seemed to accept it. He'd always scratched any other suitors he'd come into contact with.

Quinn followed me into the bath and reached his arm over the tub while I soaked. We wouldn't have real sex yet, but he wasn't going to leave me wanting. Somehow both of us knew combining our bodies would unleash something inside of both of us that we just weren't ready for yet.

That didn't stop me from riding his hand as he whispered all the dirty things he wanted to do to me. He wanted to bite me, to ram into me until I screamed.

When he whispered how he wanted to take me together with one of my other guardians, my body clenched around his fingers. Fuck. Would that happen? Was that a thing with coven guardians?

Panting, Quinn chuckled and watched from a distance as I lathered and washed away as much evidence of my arousal as I could. He'd made me hit my peak, but that only seemed to make me want more of him and all that he offered.

"The masquerade," he reminded me with amusement in his voice. "We have some preparations to get you ready."

Right. Only my life was on the line. No big deal.

"If your enemies find you, then—" Quinn began.

"I know, I know," I snapped and snatched my earrings from him, shamelessly drawing power into myself to evaporate the water from my skin and hair. He frowned at my blatantly selfish use of the magic.

"You should be careful with that," he warned.

I rolled my eyes. "You sound like Sparkles."

He gave me a raised brow. "You mean your familiar?" He snorted. "You named your familiar 'Sparkles?'"

Glowering, I pushed past him into the bedroom and found myself clothes to wear. The dresser was fitted for a female servant, not stocked with clothing suited for a witch, but that's how I liked it. I found the pile intended for when servants had to go mingle with humans in town. Shorts and a tank. Perfect.

Quinn, still chuckling at having found out the name of my familiar, sighed when he saw my choice in clothing. "You never were one for extravagance." He glanced around the bedroom. "Then again, neither was I."

I didn't like how he spoke of us in the past tense. "I'm not dead anymore," I reminded him, "and neither are you."

He gave me a shrug. "Technically, that's not true." His gaze found mine. "Even if we did get a second chance, one of us is still dead."

I flinched. Right. Vampirism required death. It bound the spirit to the body and sustained it magically, giving the illusion of immortality when it was really just a never-ending limbo that could never be escaped.

Yet, now looking at my guardians, I could see both the downsides and the appeal of its magic. Had they not accepted the dark curse, I would still be dead, gone to wherever cursed witches go in their afterlife. There was no way my enemies would have allowed me to have found peace being a Fate Witch. Even in death, I would have been able to cause them trouble. No, my protectors gave up everything for me, accepted vampirism so that they could safeguard my magic and give it back to me in this life. I would love them forever for that.

"What?" Quinn asked, smirking. "You're looking at me funny."

I gave him a playful push. "Nothing, you big bad vamp. Let's go get some food. I'm starving."

AARON HADN'T BEEN KIDDING about his nap of the century. He found me eating in the living room with three spectators—four if I included Sparks glaring at me from the window—enjoying my late lunch. Between oversleeping and my adventures with Quinn, I'd missed over half of the day entirely.

Aaron stopped at the doorway and stared, as if stunned.

His nostrils flared and his eyes went wide. "The fuck?" he hissed. "Already?"

My cheeks flared. Damn. Vampires did have a good sense of smell.

Killian saved me from complete humiliation and slapped Aaron on the back. "Come on, I got you a cold bag of blood in the fridge. They sell it at the hospitals now. Isn't that incredible?"

Aaron gave Marcus and Quinn steady glares, then allowed Killian to guide him to the table.

My fork paused over a melt-worthy ham that Mrs. Styles had brought over. One of their own pigs, she'd proudly told Marcus when she'd dropped it off. I was sad to have missed her again, but also glad that I didn't have to explain the guilty look on my face. I didn't want her to get the wrong idea about me. The supernatural community embraced bondmate relationships. They were one of the most sacred forms of love in our world. Humans didn't have magic, so they couldn't understand what it meant to be connected to more than one soul. They did, of course, have soulmates. That was as close as it got between the races, though, and I didn't think Mrs. Styles would understand if I tried to tell her I had four soulmates.

Aaron ran his fingers over the table in an irritating series of thumps while he waited for Killian to return. He was clearly annoyed that I'd initiated my bond between Marcus and Quinn—or was that jealousy?

Marcus sat next to the vampire and settled a napkin into his lap as if he were about to have a proper meal. Killian returned with bags for all the guys and handed them out.

Each one had a cute little straw in it like they were going to enjoy slushies.

Aaron's fangs extended and he looked as if he wanted to rip the bag in half, but seemed to think better of it and took the straw into his mouth. He relaxed slightly when the bag was half empty.

Marcus sighed. "If you're going to pout, perhaps you should explain to Lady Evelyn why you're so upset," Marcus suggested, holding his bag daintily between two fingers.

Aaron glared at the vampire, the straw to his blood bag still sticking out the side of his mouth. "Isn't it obvious?" he growled around the mouthful. "After all we've done, she still died. I let you talk me into this shit and all it did was get my heart broken. The last thing I want is to get her killed again."

I rested a hand over Aaron's arm out of instinct. "I'm right here," I whispered. He couldn't talk about me as if I wasn't even in the room. I'd broken his heart? I think that's the sweetest thing I've ever heard.

Aaron glanced at me, straw still in his mouth, and then looked at where my hand rested on his arm until I finally pulled it away. He shrugged off a chill as if I'd just contaminated him. Okay, maybe he wasn't so sweet.

Since he wouldn't let me touch him, I appraised him with my gaze, trying to pick up anything that might trigger a memory. He was edgy and his bright spiky hair made him stand out. Then there were the tattoos and lip piercings... he looked too—modern. I furrowed my brow. "So, where are you from?" I asked Aaron, trying to sound casual. "Or I guess I should say, *when* are you from?"

That got him to spit out the straw to his blood bag and

Marcus flinched, his one tell. "All right. Who told her?" Aaron snapped.

Killian and Quinn swept up their hands in self-defense. Marcus shook his head.

"Your tattoos don't seem like they were made a thousand years ago," I supplied giving the burning skull on his left arm a raised brow, "they seem quite modern, in fact."

His shoulders unhinged from his ears. "Oh, yeah. I guess you'd notice that."

I tilted my head and forced the smile that wanted to spread over my face into a straight line. "Did Marcus pick you up from New York?" I guessed. "Or maybe Germany?" he didn't sound German, but some more modern Germans worked with American companies and lost their accents.

He straightened. "Germany. Good guess." He stuck the straw back into his mouth. "What tipped you off?"

I shrugged. "Just the look, I guess." I made a circle around my face, indicating his blonde spiky hair and lip ring. It suited him, but he stuck out from the group of vampires like a sore thumb. He probably felt out of place, but I knew that somehow, I had made him feel like he'd belonged.

Then I realized all of my vampires were originally warlocks, and there was only one coven in Germany. I sucked in a breath. "Are you from the Diamond Coven?" Laughter threatened to bubble out of me, even though Killian was making slicing motions over his throat at me to stop.

I couldn't help it. Laughter spilled out and I held my stomach. Marcus would have been better suited to the Diamond Coven. They were so proper and pristine. The very thought of one of their warlocks going off to get tats and piercings was beyond preposterous. No wonder he'd been willing to follow Marcus back in time. His family probably had a hundred assassins out to kill him just for the horror of it.

Aaron dropped his blood bag and crimson liquid seeped over the table.

"Shit," Killian muttered. "You've done it now, Eves."

Aaron shot to his feet and I'd never seen him so angry. His glamour dropped all at once, revealing fangs and red-hot magic that bled over his irises, but that wasn't what was so startling. His glamour hadn't just been hiding his vampirism.

It'd been hiding his tattoos and how they moved.

My eyes went wide. "You're a… shifter?"

The crack of the first bone was my answer and I flinched. The room exploded as Marcus, Killian, and Quinn jumped on Aaron as he transformed into the biggest wolf I'd ever seen. He kept his fangs and red eyes, but the beast that snapped its jaws gave the three vampires a run for their money. I backed away and pressed myself against the wall, scanning for Sparkles.

"Sparks!" I hissed.

My familiar gave me the faintest meow from underneath the couch. Yeah, no fucking way was he coming out. Cats and dogs did not get along. I was on my own.

"Evie!" Quinn shouted. "Lock yourself up in the scrying tower! He won't follow you there!"

I couldn't just let the three of them handle a shifter gone rabid. The wolf stalked down onto all fours and snapped out at the closest vampire, barely missing Killian who'd brought out his switchblade.

"Don't hurt him!" I shouted at Killian.

Killian froze, holding his switchblade at an angle as if he wasn't sure if he should attack the beast or back off.

Aaron answered for him and chomped down hard on his wrist, making Killian cry out as blood splattered onto the plush carpet.

Pushing the panic down into my chest, I bit the inside of my cheek and slipped the masquerade mask from my hip, securing it over my face. The magic clung to my skin and swept fresh power into me. Roses and jasmine sent sweetness lingering across my tongue.

I grazed my fingers over my earrings once, setting them alive with honeysuckle and the freeing breeze of Quinn's heart.

My power manifested as a long, sparkling purple whip and I grinned. Yeah, bitches. I'm going to tame this beast.

SHIFTERS AND SURPRISES

The image I had in my head was a whole lot cooler than what happened next. I launched my attack, aiming to capture the wolf around the neck and get him to calm down. Instead, my whip caught on the ceiling and brought down a cascade of rocks and I squeaked under the onslaught of destruction.

"Evie!" Quinn shouted and launched himself over me, taking the worst of the blow with a pained grunt as dust and rubble crashed all around us.

Aaron yipped as the rush of debris blocked him from my view. Fresh panic made adrenaline thunder through my veins. What if I killed him? He was a vampire, but he'd just shifted into a wolf. Didn't that cancel things out?

My head started to hurt, both from thinking too hard about supernatural rules and from the pebbles that still came down from the ceiling. Quinn shifted the rubble aside and gave me a chance to recuperate.

Killian and Marcus had shielded the wolf as best they could, confirming that Aaron was vulnerable in this form. "Come on, buddy. Snap out of it," Killian said, keeping his voice low and calm, but I could see his hand shaking.

That's when I saw the blood and my insides twisted. The wolf lay slumped on his side with a huge gash across the side of his head. Marcus immediately went to work with his healing magic.

Cursing, I dropped the magical whip and it disintegrated into ash the second it left my fingertips. I ran to the wolf's side and pushed my fingers through his warm fur. I added my magic to the scent of roses and jasmine as I poured my heart into the task. I hadn't meant to hurt Aaron. I was only supposed to have subdued him... not killed him.

"It's okay, lass," Quinn coaxed as he tugged at my arm, "Marcus can heal him. You don't have to—"

"I do have to!" I snapped as tears stung my eyes. I was too careless with my new power. I did this and I would help fix it.

My heart thundered in my ears until finally the wolf stirred, whimpering in a way that made my heart twist.

Marcus picked the beast up. "I'll take him to a bedroom to rest." When I stared at him, he explained, "He can't shift back until he's healed. It'll be all right. He'll be himself again by tonight."

I opened my mouth to speak, to offer to help or fetch some cold water from the stream or something other than sit here being useless, but Marcus turned and disappeared into the hall, leaving me alone with the rubble and destruction of the once pleasant living room.

Quinn tried to touch my arm to comfort me, but I flinched away.

Turns out I wasn't so good at this being in control thing.

MARCUS REFUSED to let me see the wolf, so I stayed back with the guys with the arduous task of repairing the living room.

"You did this with magic," Quinn complained. "Why can't you fix it with magic? It'd be a whole lot faster."

"No," I snapped. "I am not used to having power. I'm a mortal-born witch, remember? I don't have training for this." I kicked a pebble across the floor and winced. Yeah, rock versus toe does not have odds in my favor. "No magic," I hissed.

Killian gave Quinn a nudge in the ribs. "Back off her, Quinn. She's right."

Grumbling, the redheaded vampire grabbed an oversized stone and hauled it out of the room. He propped the door open, so Killian and I followed suit, carrying the worst of the debris out the old-fashioned way. While we worked, Sparkles meowed to let me know he was still alive.

"Some help you were," I snapped.

He picked his way through the dust and made sure I knew that he was none too happy about my misuse of magic. My power outstripped his by now and, as he put it, he "liked having all his fur."

"And you were worried about me using magic to dry my hair," I growled.

He flicked his tail, showing that he was irritated, before sauntering off.

Killian handed me a dustpan and broom. I quietly got to work sweeping up as much debris as I could, but the carpet clung to it with all its might.

"You were just protecting yourself," Killian offered.

I glared at him. "I could have killed us all."

He gave me an obnoxiously big smile. "Not all of us. We're immortal now, remember?"

"But not Aaron," I replied.

Killian's good mood faltered. "When he's in his wolf form, maybe, but that's not often."

Now I understood why Aaron was so bitter and full of anger. His family had rejected him because he had shifter blood. No matter if someone was born a witch or not, that kind of supernatural blood would eventually activate after a traumatic event. The individual's body takes on tattoos that represent their personality, and when it came to someone like Aaron, he was edgy and primal. His wolf needed to come out. Being denied a basic part of himself must have destroyed him. After taking on vampirism, his wolf became his weakness.

"He must resent me," I muttered as I continued to sweep the stubborn dust into the pan. I knelt and tried to shove the small, gravelly bits by hand, only managing to cut myself. I cursed and brought my stinging finger to my mouth.

Killian knelt and took my hand before I could clamp down on the wound. "Allow me," he said smoothly, then took my finger into his mouth. I swear his eyes fluttered closed for a minute.

Normally, I'd enjoy something like that, but right now, I

was in no fucking mood. Yanking my hand free, I glowered at Killian as all my rage crackled around me.

Quinn sighed and rested a hand on the vampire's shoulder. "You have terrible timing, Killian."

I couldn't take it anymore. My guardians had just accepted that Aaron was going to be stuck this way and they didn't seem to get how shitty this situation was.

"I'm going to go check on him," I spat and dropped the broom and pan, leaving a puff of dust behind me. "Marcus is going to have to tie me down in the tower if he thinks I'm going to stay away from Aaron."

Leaving behind a stunned Killian and a snickering Quinn, I marched down the hall and paused at the doorway as I built up my courage. I was sure that Marcus didn't want me to intrude right now, but I hated feeling helpless. I couldn't just hide from my mistakes. I had to fix this.

Easing the door open, I peered at Marcus as he stroked the animal. Now that I could get a better look at Aaron's wolf form, I saw how massive he was. His entire form slumped on the full length of the bed making it bow in the center. He was beautiful, too. He wasn't mangy or scraggly like the demon-touched wolves that hunted supernaturals. He was what a shifter was meant to be. Strong and powerful. His sleek white coat puffed out and I wanted to run my fingers through it and curl into his warmth, tell him how sorry I was and that I thought his wolf was beautiful.

Only, he wouldn't be able to hear me right now. He released soft whimpers as Marcus worked gentle magic through him. It was like when Marcus had stitched up my clothes. The fine magic layered over the broken skin at the wolf's head and the long gash at his snout before moving in a soft wave through the wolf's fur.

Without turning, Marcus said, "You can come in now, Lady Evelyn."

I flinched at the formal title. "Right." I slipped into the room before closing the door behind me.

Pulling up a chair, I perched on the end of it. I wasn't sure what to do with my hands, so I wrapped them around my knees. "Is he going to be okay?"

Marcus gave me a smirk, surprising me with the amusement in his eyes. "He'll be fine, Evelyn. It's you that I'm worried about." He glanced down at my mask that I'd secured on the belt loop at my hip. "Clearly you're advancing faster with your magic than we could have anticipated."

"I didn't mean to hurt him," I said as I ventured closer and brushed my fingers through the wolf's fur.

"Aaron is easily triggered," Marcus explained. "You didn't know."

I continued to stroke the wolf as Marcus expertly layered the healing magic over the wounds, both visible and hidden inside the wolf's body. The healing betrayed itself with the soft glimmering glow just underneath the wolf's coat.

"There," Marcus breathed, looking only slightly paler after his expenditure, "he'll heal quite rapidly now. Perhaps a few hours. The damage wasn't as bad as I'd initially thought."

I winced. I'd damaged Aaron. I was an ass.

Marcus rested a heavy hand on my shoulder and I slumped under the weight. "Would you like to stay with him until he wakes up?"

I gave him a skeptical look. "Is that such a good idea?"

Marcus pinched my chin before standing and leaving me with the wolf. "He loves you, Evelyn. That's why you can trigger him so quickly. Just be kind and gentle with him and he'll show you nothing but loyalty and adoration."

"What about the masquerade ball? The cloaking spell I'm supposed to learn?"

Marcus smiled. "You'll be no good to anyone if you leave things like this with Aaron. I'll prepare your dress and a spell for you. Your job is to mend things with Aaron."

I sighed. "Right. Okay." I grabbed his hand when he moved to leave. "Thank you, Marcus."

He gave me a respectful nod. "Of course."

Then he was gone and I was left with a massive wolf hanging off a very expensive bed. I blew out a long breath. "Fuck, Evie. What have you gotten yourself into now?"

A STUBBORN WOLF

I'd nodded off by the time Aaron shifted back. The cracking of bones made me startle awake and I watched with morbid fascination as he transformed. First the fur disappeared, sucking back into his body until it left tiny black dots behind that swirled and morphed as Aaron's human body took shape. His snout retreated into his face, then his human features poked through. His ears were the last to change, making him look like an elf for a minute. I reached out and touched them until all that was left was Aaron's cute human ears.

He flinched and opened his eyes and I snatched my hand away. "Oh, hey," I offered. "How're you feeling?"

He sank back into the pillow and groaned. "Like I've been hit by a boulder." He touched the bruise at his temple and winced.

My hands had gone back to fumbling over my knees. I was so bad at shit like this. "I didn't know," I said, feeling that the words were about to vomit out of me but I couldn't stop them when I got nervous like this. "When it comes to Quinn or Marcus, it's not hard for me, you know?" I admitted. "The bond just clicked into place, well, Quinn almost, we're not a hundred percent the way there yet because, uh…" Aaron was staring at me now like I'd grown a third eye. A blush crept over my cheeks. "I mean, anyway, you're a shifter. I didn't know that. And your blood rune," I shoved my arm in front of his face that definitely only had two runes on it, "it's not on my skin yet. I don't know you, not even a little bit. I know we have this epic history, and I'm a douchenozzle, but I didn't mean to hurt you, I fucking swear to the gods."

He eased up onto his elbows. "…Douchenozzle?"

I blinked at him. "Yeah. You know. Idiot. Moron. Jerk."

He held up a hand to stop the onslaught of douchenozzle synonyms. "Yeah, I get it. I just mean—you're, uh, not exactly the same as the Evelyn I once knew."

I brightened. Okay, good. I could work with that. "Right, because you know, that whole nature versus nurture thing. I had a different upbringing than a thousand years ago, so I'm bound to be different, right?"

He narrowed his eyes. "Right. I guess."

I bit my lip and my hands started writhing again. Now that I'd stopped my babbling, I felt even more like a douchenozzle.

When I opened my mouth to say something that would probably make me sound even more idiotic than I already was, he rested a warm hand over my thigh. "Stop," Aaron commanded and I snapped my mouth shut. "Look, I'm not mad at you, okay?"

My head bounced. "Okay, that's good. But you should be."

He gave me a wicked grin. "Why? Because you brought a house down on my head? I was the one who shifted and scared you. You were just acting in self-defense."

I blushed again. His hand was still on my thigh and I stared at it. "I was careless. I said things that hurt you and you had every right to shift and try to tear my throat out."

His hand slipped up higher on my leg and warm tingles sparked in my body, finally recognizing the glimmer of the bond that existed between Aaron and me. "No one deserves that, especially not you. You didn't know. It's my fault." His hand slipped up around my hip and he brought me closer to him, turning me so that my back pressed against his chest. When I squirmed, he blew softly on my ear, making goosebumps explode across my skin. "I'm a wolf. I cuddle. You'll get over it."

Snorting a laugh, I relaxed. "Very well. Just for a little while. I do have to get ready for some stupid masquerade ball or whatever."

He hummed against my throat, having settled there and he seemed to have no intention of moving. The closeness seemed natural with Aaron. His hands wandered my body, but he didn't move to do anything inappropriate. I felt safe, comfortable, and inevitably relaxed into his warmth. Unlike the other vampires, he'd retained body heat. It must be a side-effect of being a shifter.

"You nervous?" he asked, his voice low, gravelly, and sleepy.

I tugged one of his arms under my chin. "Yes. I have magic now, a lot more than my coven thinks I'm supposed to have.

Quinn was going to teach me a cloaking spell so I could lay low, but I think I'll have to leave my artifacts behind instead. It's the only way."

His hold on me tightened. "You should never leave your magic behind. It's what got you killed last time."

I stiffened. I knew that I'd died once before, but I had no memory of it. This whole time it felt like my past life was a different personality. Another Evie that wasn't me, but to hear Aaron's warning sparked fresh fear inside of me. I'd made mistakes before that cost me my life and tormented my guardians for a thousand years. I had to be careful, which meant I had to know what mistakes I made before so that I could avoid them.

"Really?" I asked, venturing into a conversation that made my blood run cold.

"You don't remember?" he asked.

I shook my head. "Quinn doesn't know I can't remember," I admitted. "This is just between us, okay?"

He turned me to face him and stroked my cheek. He'd put his glamour back on, but it didn't make him look any less edgy. He'd been a bad-boy warlock before his turn, so the red eyes and fangs kind of completed the ensemble.

"Why won't you let the others know?" he asked, continuing to stroke my face.

My fingers wound over his arm, exploring his tattoos that swirled under my touch. I'd never been up close to a shifter before. I could feel the faint hum of his magic. "Because it would hurt the others. It would hurt Quinn."

Aaron scoffed. "Quinn is too sensitive for his own good. You're too gentle with him."

That's when I realized that I understood each of my guys better than they even understood each other. I smiled, my touch running over his collarbone and up to his cute ears. "Not everyone is a big, bad shifter."

He pulled me closer to him, and this time there was definitely something hard pressing against my hip. A blush crept over my cheeks. I'd thought him just playful like a wolf might be, but I'd forgotten something important about wolves. They were predators and they claimed their prey.

A glimmer of fight sparked in his eyes. "I've been keeping my distance from you for that reason," he growled. "You bring out the beast in me. It's dangerous."

My mouth parted as he brought me closer. His arms trembled as if he was fighting the instinct to claim me and that thought made tingles gather between my thighs. "I like dangerous," I whispered, feeling as if I was about to taste something forbidden.

Aaron moved so fast that he blurred as his hand went to my throat. A low, rumbling growl warned me that I'd crossed a line. "No," he said and his chest vibrated against mine, only serving to painfully harden my nipples against my bra. A smile spread across my lips as his grip on me squeezed. "Why are you smiling?" he asked, sounding irritated that I wasn't more afraid of him.

"Because," I began, inhaling the lingering new scents hinting around me as the barrier between Aaron and me cracked, "you hold a secret that belongs to me. I'm quite determined to get it." I wasn't someone who often got what I wanted, but when it came to my guardians, I had a feeling I was very rarely left wanting.

His hand worked down my throat, as if to intensify his warning, but the heat between us was tangible. His soft magic of burning wood and the distinct smells of a forest tinged my nose, making my nostrils flare. A sharp pain spread over my arm, telling me that a new rune had broken my skin.

Whether he thought I was ready or not, Aaron would be mine.

HELLO AUNTIE

We had to get the place ready for my Aunt Sandra's arrival, but it was impossible. I was a wreck and my magic sizzled underneath the surface threatening to break out. I'd tasted it, and it'd tasted me. With my guardians turning into vampires the bond between us had become something new and different. Their magic was endless just as their lives would be and gave me everything I could ever need to become the most powerful witch this world had ever seen.

"If they find you out, it won't matter how powerful you are," Killian warned. He'd resumed flicking his switchblade over his knuckles in a blurred display of his skill.

"Would you put that thing away?" I snapped, crossing my arms and sinking lower into the one couch we'd managed to clean off the worst of the debris. "You're making me nervous. I think I've seen enough weapons for today."

"Killian's right," Quinn insisted, leaning against the

mantle and looking far too attractive with his wild red hair strewn over his face. He didn't move to brush it away and instead watched me between the silky strands. His red eyes burned with passion and heat. Our bond was so close to being set in place that the tension between us felt like it would snap. My rune burned, telling me that nothing else mattered and I needed to take him right here, right now, in the dirt and my other protectors watching. The fantasy made a blush creep over my cheeks and I pressed my thighs together to try and stem the ache.

Quinn noticed my cravings because he smirked, but did me the mercy of not commenting on it.

Marcus was thankfully not watching any of us. Instead he peered out the window at the pastures that swayed with a slight breeze as if nothing of importance was going on. There was no masquerade ball, no visiting Aunt Sandra, no need to impress the Amethyst Coven—or hide who I was from them. When I looked at the freedom of the long stretch of grass, I thought of my guardians and how all I wanted to do was to explore my connection with them and live as a family together. That hadn't happened in my last life. If I did things right this time around, maybe it was a dream that could come true.

Sparkles meowed and jumped up into my lap, nudging at me until I unwrapped my arms and scratched him behind his ears. He didn't want me to forget about him, but the connection between us was already thinning. My guardians were taking all of me, bit by bit, and I had no room for a familiar anymore.

"You're looking thoughtful," Killian commented. "Do you have an idea for how to deal with your aunt?"

I grinned, still stroking Sparkles who purred on my lap. "Yes, actually. I do."

A WITCH's connection with her familiar isn't intended to be permanent. Think of it as a security blanket when a witch doesn't have enough magic of her own. There had always been some teasing when Sparkles entered with me into a room of other witches and warlocks my age, but as a mortal-born witch, a familiar was necessary.

If that connection was prematurely broken, however, a witch received a surge of power, like a farewell dose of magic from the familiar. It would be enough to explain the devastation in the guesthouse, as well as any jump in ability of magic that I displayed. The only thing I would have to hide were my blood runes.

Marcus made quick work of that. He was the only one of my guardians who'd completed a bond with me and his magic came easily, flooding the room with the sweet pungent scents of roses and jasmine.

His touch grazed over my arm, the runes slowly fading until only smooth skin remained behind. I could still feel the burn and the cravings the runes gave me, but they were diluted under Marcus' magic.

"There," he said, satisfied. "No one will be able to see your runes until midnight."

I winced. "Midnight? The witching hour is when all the

exciting shit happens. No way the ball will end before midnight." I gave him a steady glare. "You're a warlock. You should know that."

He shrugged. "It's the best I can do. Most spells expire at midnight. I'll just reapply it once it wears off. It'll be fine."

My eyes widened. "You're going to be there? No fucking way."

He smirked, looking devilishly handsome as he straightened his suit. "Does that mean you don't want a date?"

I'd never had a date to anything in my life. I gave Marcus a raised brow. "One, wouldn't that be suspicious? And two, who's to say that you're going to be my date? What about Quinn, Aaron, or even Killian?"

Marcus beamed with pride. "I'm the only mate you've bonded with so far. I claim that honor, for now, until you've bonded with the rest."

"No," I said flatly, then stalked to the other side of the room just to get out of his reach—and away from the intoxicating scent of his magic. I was a helpless puddle around my guys when they turned the charm on, Marcus especially.

He shrugged again, seemingly unperturbed by my rejection. "You don't have much choice in the matter. As your mentors, we'll all be there. I don't have to go as your date, but it would make it easier to explain why I'd be touching you at midnight."

I sank my teeth into my lower lip to prevent all the retorts that wanted to come out at that. He was just trying to make an excuse to be close to me, not that being close to me was necessarily a bad thing, but I couldn't put him in the spotlight like that. I couldn't put any of my guys anywhere near the coven's attention. If they figured out who they were, then I would lose them forever. My heart pinched at just the thought of it. I would never do anything to put them in harm's way. "This is something I have to do on my own," I insisted.

Marcus opened his mouth to retort, but a knock at the door caught our attention.

Great, Aunt Sandra was already here.

"Well," I said with a sigh and hung my arms limply at my sides, "looks like it's showtime."

Sparkles wound around my ankles, meowing profusely as he declared breaking my bond with him was unacceptable. I wasn't anywhere near ready and with only one blood rune locked into place, I could lose control over the excess of magic and die.

"Stop being so dramatic," I chided him as I tried to untangle him from my feet so that I could go get the door. "You just don't want to go back to the astral plane."

Marcus gave me a raised brow. "Are you talking to your familiar?"

I hesitated, then yipped when Sparkles bit me. I stuck my hand in my mouth and glared at the unruly cat. "Yeah," I said after taking my throbbing thumb out of my mouth, "doesn't everyone?"

Having waited long enough, Aunt Sandra tested the door and it swung open. She gave us a beaming smile, then her eyes dropped to the destruction of the living room and her smile faded. "What in the seven circles of hell has happened here?"

SPARKLES HAS A SECRET

I sat Aunt Sandra down on one of the cleared sofas while Marcus went to get her some tea from the kitchen. I wished that all my guys could be here to help me face her, but Quinn and Killian were with Aaron making sure he didn't lose his shit. Apparently after shifting his decision-making skills were a bit lackluster. His wolf acted by instinct and had more of an "ask questions later" sort of attitude. Not the best approach when it came to a powerful witch of the Amethyst Coven who needed to be fooled.

Sparkles refused to leave my side and clung to my lap when I'd settled in front of the fire onto the floor. I'd opted out of one of the dusty chairs, regretting my choice as I shifted my leg that had instantly gone numb and Sparkles complained by sinking claws into my leg to keep from falling.

"I don't understand," Aunt Sandra repeated as she straightened. Her eyes always went dark when she was upset. Her magic was strong and it hummed around her, coming to the surface when she spoke and giving her words an edge to them that was inherently unnatural. It always made me nervous when she got like this. "Why would you try to break your connection with your familiar?" She glanced at the kitchen. Marcus was taking far too long to get us tea, the bastard. He was leaving me to deal with her alone. "Was this your mentors' idea?"

I put on a rigid smile and nodded. "That's right. Won't there be an assessment period at the ball? I need to be at my most powerful for the best placement."

Aunt Sandra nodded, relieving a small weight on my shoulders that she might buy my lies. "Correct. If you display enough power, you'll be placed at a higher level for your initiation." She gave me a raised brow. "You've always made it very clear to me that you have no desire to be noticed. What brought on this change of heart?"

This was the moment I had to convince my aunt that I'd done a complete one-eighty when it came to my goals as a witch. We both knew that a higher placement meant a more dangerous initiation. Now that I had magic I couldn't explain, I had to do it for the sake of my guys. My assessment would come back much higher than it should be, and I needed an excuse to explain the magic my guardians had awakened in me. I didn't think that my guardians knew that about the terms of a witch's initiation. Perhaps things had changed in the last thousand years.

I stroked Sparkles as I contemplated my answer. When forced to lie, it was best to wrap it in as much truth as possible. "My mentors have convinced me that higher placement in the Royal Covens would give me more options for my future,"

I admitted. It was true. If I placed high enough in the Royal Covens, I could change the laws that made vampirism illegal, as well as lift the stigma and fear against Fate Witches. It was a lofty goal, probably more like an illogical dream, but if I really was a Fate Witch, then I was capable of incredible things. I could build a future where my guys could be safe and happy and if that meant striving for a high enough placement in the Royal Covens to overturn centuries-old laws, then that's what I would strive for.

Aunt Sandra nodded, then appraised the damage again. "So, what went wrong? Obviously you're still bound to your familiar. Did the separation fail?"

I suppressed a grin. "Something like that."

Thankfully Marcus finally made his entrance with a tray in hand. He set it down on the only cleared space on the table and began pouring our cups. "Your ward is an impressive young woman," he began, giving Aunt Sandra one of his charming smiles.

As he glided over the floor, barely stirring up dust, I realized that Marcus was the perfect member of my guardians to make an impression on Aunt Sandra. She respected refined men like Marcus. It meant that they came from a background of nobility recognizable in the higher estates managed by the Royal Covens. His air of wealth and prestige gave Marcus a bit of leeway when it came to my Aunt Sandra.

She beamed when he handed her a steaming porcelain cup and she took a graceful sip before codling the cup in its saucer. "Is that so?" she asked, not giving me a second glance. Marcus had her full attention.

He handed me my cup. Sparkles still refused to budge and

181

was softly snoring in my lap, but I knew if I tried to move him his claws would come out and he'd stick to me like Velcro. I sighed and held my cup aloft and took a sip, wincing at the bitterness. No sugar, of course. That was only proper. Witches were supposed to taste all the herbs and gain power from their origins.

He nodded, then glanced at me. "Why don't you show us how much you've learned, Lady Evelyn. What powers have I put into your tea?"

I glowered and my fingers pinched hard around the porcelain handle until I felt a slight crack under my grip. Luckily for him my original goals had always been to be a recluse herb witch, which meant I knew my herbs—especially his. "Rose and jasmine," I declared, "magic from your homeland."

He gave me gentle applause. "Very good." He gave Aunt Sandra a proud smile. "Confirm for yourself, Lady Sandra."

She furrowed her brow as she tasted the tea again. She smacked her lips together and the lightest of ruby magic glimmered around her features. "Yes, I do believe I sense it." She gave me a relieved smile. "Very good, Evie, very good indeed. Even I can barely sense your mentor's magic."

Thanks to my bond that burned hot under Marcus' illusion, I had no difficulty at all sensing my guardian's magic. I took another sip of the tea, this time relishing in the power now that I knew what it was. Strength and love swelled in me. Marcus could protect me this way. If he could come to the masquerade ball, I wouldn't have to worry about what trial or assessment the Royal Covens would throw my way. I'd be ready for it.

Yet, there was still the slight matter of breaking my bond with my familiar to get Aunt Sandra to believe it.

"We could use your help," Marcus admitted, his gaze going to Sparkles sleeping soundly in my lap. "The familiar has given her a dose of power, but if she's to be ready for the ball, we need to break the bond tonight and he's not ready to let go."

There was an edge to Marcus' voice that I almost would have missed had I not been dosed with his own magic. I studied him, noting how his cup had started shaking before he set it down on the table a little too deliberately. Marcus wanted me to break my bond with my familiar, but not just because he wanted Aunt Sandra out of our hair. He had personal reasons.

"Very well," Aunt Sandra said, rising from her chair. "I can help with that." She snapped her fingers and motioned for me to give her the cat. "Let's get on with it then. Your mentor has convinced me you can survive the parting and you'll be better off for it. The assessment will be in your favor if you don't have a familiar bond in place."

My stomach twisted and my fingers ran through Spark's fur. I'd never tried to communicate to him mentally as he did with me, but I knew something was wrong. I pushed my fear and concern to him in a mental wave and he stirred, his green eyes snapping open as he startled.

"Right then, Sparks, it's for the best, okay?" I offered, even as I pushed every mental wave of power to him to tell him that this was not okay. Something was wrong. There was something Marcus wasn't telling me and I couldn't break the familiar bond until I knew what it was.

He meowed, as if agreeing, but his mental reply was to tell me not to be afraid. He had one last trick up his sleeve he'd been saving for the right moment, and now that moment had finally arrived.

Curious, but too unsure to feel relieved, I managed to unlatch Sparkles from my lap and set him on the ground. He trotted over the dusty carpet, tail high, and stopped mid-way between the circle made up of Marcus, Aunt Sandra, and myself. I swallowed hard. I couldn't shake that ominous feeling I'd had ever since that day in the graveyard when all this had begun. Something big was about to happen... but I had no idea what.

Aunt Sandra reached out towards Marcus and me. "Join hands. This will be over quickly."

I did as commanded, taking Aunt Sandra's silky hand, followed by Marcus' strong grip in my other. Closing my eyes, I let the link of magic run through me.

Aunt Sandra began chanting in witch's tongue, making me nervous that the spell was stronger than I might have initially imagined. Many powerful spells worked on Latin, but witch's tongue was reserved for only the most delicate of spells. One wrong syllable and it could all go wrong. I'd never seen a familiar and a witch forcefully unbound. She'd been the one to give him to me, so it made sense that she could be the one to take him away.

I squinted one eye open and glanced down at Sparkles whose tail twitched as if he was waiting for the right moment to pounce.

"Focus," Aunt Sandra hissed, biting her nails into my skin.

I squeaked at the pain, then squeezed my eyes shut.

Marcus held on tight, continuing to funnel me with a dose of his magic and my blood rune burned so badly I feared it'd sear right through the cloaking spell Marcus had placed on it.

The tension built and an invisible hot breeze wafted through the small room, tickling my nose as it kicked up dust. A sneeze threatened to take me, and the moment I gave into it, the room exploded.

A bright flash streaked across the ground and engulfed my familiar. Aunt Sandra cursed and yelled something, but I couldn't hear it as another shockwave hit us and sent us all flying away from each other. My back slammed against the wall, thankfully missing the mantle that probably would have snapped my spine. Embers from the extinguished fire went flying and I covered my ears as another boom came again, and then again until the light throbbed over my familiar like a strobe on steroids.

"Sparks!" I shouted, but the glow had engulfed him. All I could see was his small silhouette—then it changed, became bigger, unfurling until it took on the form of... a man?

Marcus came out of nowhere and dove over me, shielding me from the worst of the blast when the magic solidified, sending out heat and power streaking across the room.

Underneath the vampire's heaving body, I clung to his battered suit and found his muscular chest. Managing to peer around him, I saw the result of the spell had not only failed to break my bond with my familiar... it'd failed to contain him in his diminished form.

"Hey, Evie," he said shyly, now a completely naked man standing in the middle of the living room covered in dust. A fine tabby pattern wound over his body and his eyes still had the eerie slits of a feline, and slightest points of his teeth poked at his lips.

My jaw dropped open. Not only was Sparks a man now... he was fucking hot.

AUNT SANDRA SHOULD HAVE BEEN hysterical, instead she seemed livid. Her eyes had gone completely black as she crossed her arms and glowered at the human familiar.

"You should not be here!" she snapped.

At that moment, all three of my remaining guardians came spilling into the room. Quinn with his wild red hair around his face, Killian with a switchblade poised at the ready, and Aaron with clenched fists that made his knuckles white all said they were ready to battle anything that threatened me to the death. When they spotted the naked man, however, they all stopped in their tracks completely stunned.

"Bast?" Quinn said first as shock and recognition swept over his face.

"What?" Aunt Sandra breathed. "What did you just call him?"

My familiar ignored everyone and approached me, staring down at Marcus who still shielded me. "She doesn't belong to you," he warned. There was a note of a lie in his voice, meaning that his words were for Aunt Sandra's benefit.

Marcus swallowed hard, then nodded and stepped aside, leaving me to drop my gaze over the full unadulterated beauty of the man before me. His feline features were distinct, but only served to make him more stunning. His ears, slightly pointed, twitched before he reached out and offered his hand. His fingers were elegant and his tabby pattern wound around them, disappearing under the stark points of his fingernails. I stared down at them in slight horror and he chuckled, retracting the claws until only smooth human nails were left.

"I'm sorry I didn't tell you sooner," he said, and there was no hint of a lie in that statement.

I blinked up at his fascinating eyes. To anyone else, they might have seemed frightening or odd, but to me they seemed so familiar that it was easy to slip my fingers into his grasp and something inside me locked into place, completing a connection I hadn't known had been unhinged all my life. "Tell me what?" I marveled. That he wasn't a normal familiar? That much was clear. Or that he was more sentient than he'd led me to believe? Or that he was a man... wait. He was a man. My eyes widened and I yanked my hand free of him. "You pervert!" I shrieked, making him startle.

"What?" he asked, backing up a step as if he was afraid of me. It was ridiculous. Bast was a god of ancient witch legend and powerful enough to snuff me out of existence if he wanted to.

"You always showered with me!" I shouted and covered my arms over my chest.

Aunt Saundra laughed on the verge of hysteria. "Who cares! This is Bast." She fell to her knees and clapped her hands together. "This is a god who has chosen to bless our coven. Blessed be."

Bast rolled his eyes, startling me from my indignation. *No one* ever rolled their eyes at Aunt Sandra. "I have not come to bless your coven, witch," Bast snarled, his irises shrinking until the emerald green of his eyes stood out starkly against his pale skin. "I've come to protect Evie." He turned his anger on me. "Which means that our bond shall not be broken." He opened his hand to me again. "Forgive me, Evelyn. I did not mean to offend you."

A blush crept up my cheeks, and I took his hand again.

Fucking hell. Four warlock-vampires and a god of Ancient Egypt were claiming their right to protect me, but who was going to protect me from them?

MAGIC RUNS THICKER THAN BLOOD

*A*unt Sandra forced a bracelet on me before we left for the Amethyst Coven, insisting that I wear it. Its cold magic snapped over my arm like a vice and wouldn't budge when I tried to remove it.

"Gods aren't to be trusted," she warned me with a harsh whisper under her breath as she cast glances over my shoulder, "and neither are mentors with that kind of magic."

She'd tasted Marcus' power in the tea, which was supposed to make her trust him. He was powerful and worthy of her respect, but my Aunt Sandra wasn't a moron. She only suspected him even more now that she knew he wasn't a member of the Sapphire Coven. If they hadn't sent the mentors... who had? And why? I knew those questions were burning in her head right now, but she kept her cool, letting us all believe that she'd accepted the lies we were giving her.

She shook my wrist, making sure I was paying full attention to her. "I know you don't trust me, Evelyn, but I promise you, I'm the only one in this coven who has your best interests at heart. No matter what happens, I'm on your side, do you understand?"

I wanted to believe her. She'd been like a mother to me, albeit a cranky, strict, and harsh one, but she was all I had when it came to family. *Magic runs thicker than blood,* the mantra she'd always told me ran through my mind. Whether I wanted to admit it or not, a reluctant kind of love for her rested in my chest, so I nodded and allowed her to give me a quick embrace.

My mentors gathered at my back, all of them keeping a respectable distance from Bast who'd they'd manage to fit with some of the more respectable guest clothes. He'd left the upper set of buttons undone on his silk shirt, leaving him with a feral look. When he noticed me watching him, he grinned.

Frowning, I turned and nodded at Aunt Sandra. "Let's hurry. Sunset is almost here." The orange blaze of the sun diving into the horizon put me on edge now that being trapped outside the jasmine field meant facing off with demon-touched wolves. My guardians had survived them, but they wouldn't be able to use the full extent of their powers while also maintaining their glamour that made sure Aunt Sandra didn't sense they were actually vampires. No matter her claims of her love for me, she'd report vampires to the Royal Covens in two seconds flat even if it meant my downfall. Some rules weren't broken when it came to the Royal Covens... and I hoped to change those rules from the inside out.

We scurried along the dusty road, leaving behind the

guesthouse. I wanted to go say goodbye to Jordan and his wife, thank them for all the food and apologize for the damage they'd no doubt have to fix, but a part of me thought it was for the best when we silently marched past their simple home. To witches like Sandra, the farmers who knew of the witches' existence and kept the secret, served, and behaved, were rewarded enough with protection from supernatural attack. There didn't need to be mindless chitchat in there as well.

I stifled a sniffle that threatened to betray my raging emotions as we left the human household behind. I wasn't very good at goodbyes, so it was just as well. That ominous feeling in my gut had returned, telling me that my life was about to look very different after my initiation. I just hoped that I survived what came next.

THE JASMINE FIELDS locked into place once we crossed the threshold, spiking the air with its sickly sweet and pungent scent.

"Inside," Aunt Sandra commanded and hurried us all in.

Bast stalked until he was beside me and twined his fingers through mine. The motion was so natural and effortless that I found myself relaxing. I had so many questions. He and I shared a bond. I could feel it burning inside of me. It didn't dismantle what I had with my guardians, but supplemented that magic with his own protective power. Who was he, really? I didn't believe in gods. Sure, there were powerful supernatural creatures, but they'd simply become so powerful that they'd learned how to force their own reincarnation, or live without a corporal body entirely. I wanted to know where he'd come from and why he'd chosen me.

There was no time for such questions now. The entire coven was waiting in the summoning hall for my arrival. Well, not just my arrival, but the tributes attending the masquerade ball this evening. I nearly choked, realizing I was still covered in dust and dirt and not at all prepared for a ball.

As if sensing my panic, Aunt Sandra chuckled and rested her hand on the bracelet she'd given me. "Relax, child. I wouldn't allow you to be humiliated." She whispered a word of power under her breath and then the bracelet fucking bit me.

I opened my mouth to screech as the spikes from the bracelet speared into my skin. Blood gathered in a red line around the bite of metal over my wrist, but didn't fall. The bracelet sucked it up and then glowed. Magic funneled through me like a thousand tiny needles pricking my skin and a soft glow illuminated my clothes until they transformed into an elaborate dress.

Bast's grip on me tightened, but relaxed as the magic dissipated having completed its work.

I still had my masquerade mask, as well as my earrings, and the magic hissed away from them, leaving the artifacts untouched. Aunt Sandra frowned at that. "Your mentors gave you gifts as well, I see."

I nodded and forced myself to smile. A quick glance over my shoulder made me want to groan. All my protectors looked livid. I widened my eyes at them and hoped they got the message. *Do not fucking intervene.* No one could know what they were. If they insisted on attending the ball with me, then they had to play it cool. I had a feeling this night wasn't going to go very well, given their level of self-restraint.

Luckily Bast was getting all of the stares right now and no one noticed the four guardians hovering behind us.

"It's the god of familiars!" shouted a witch who recognized Bast. Thanks to his distinct features, it wasn't too hard to see who and what he was.

The crowd hushed in stunned agreement, some even going to their knees.

Bast didn't release his hold on me. "I am here for Evelyn," he announced. "She is my charge and I am her familiar. I will accompany her to the masquerade ball and assist in her placement."

I didn't even know if that was allowed. It sort of felt like cheating, but having a god on my side certainly would help me place high for my initiation without having to explain where I was getting the boost from.

As if hearing my thoughts, Bast gave me a wry grin, which was devastatingly handsome and made one of my knees buckle. Damn. If he could make me literally weak in the knees with a look, I was in trouble. Glowering, I straightened, determined not to let his supernaturally charming looks get the best of me.

Murmurs of stunned agreement echoed through the chamber. Even if I was the least favorite among them, I was still *one* of them. Bast could have chosen a member of any of the other covens, yet he'd chosen me.

A long row of filled seats were lined up to watch the initiates travel through the portal that would take us to England for the ball. A few of my rivals stood on stage already ready to go through, but now were staring as stunned as the rest of the gathering of witches and warlocks at our arrival.

I tugged Bast towards the stage. I didn't want my coven to change its mind of accepting that a god had chosen to protect a mortal-born witch. "Come on," I hissed, and my dress rustled as we moved.

"Be careful," Aunt Sandra called and I gave her a nod.

There was one face I wanted to see before I left. I scanned the crowd, sweeping over the ever youthful faces of my coven and searched those in shadows and cloaks, easily spotting Cassidy who stood out with her painfully short skirt that displayed her servant's mark. I grinned at her and waved.

She went deathly pale as she scooped her hood closer around her face and shook her head. I wasn't supposed to be friends with a servant, but just now I didn't care. In fact, I was going to break one of the coven's rules just to test how much I could get away with when it came to having a god on my side.

"I want Cassidy to come with us," I declared loud enough for the gathering to hear.

Aunt Sandra shuffled through the crowd and hissed at me from the foot of the platform. "What are you doing?"

I straightened, determined in my resolve. I didn't need an excuse. If I wanted my best friend to come with me to a party —even if it was a prestigious witchy party—she was going to come with me. "Cassidy is my friend, Aunt Sandra. She's coming with."

My aunt paled, then chuckled and turned to the crowd. "Evelyn is feeling shy. She's mortal-born and not used to all this attention," she explained, then beckoned Cassidy

194

forward. "A servant will make her feel confident. You'll attend to her every need during the ball, won't you dear?"

Cassidy seemed frozen to the spot, then a warlock behind her gave her a strong shove, sending her stumbling forward. "Go, then. Serve your coven," he barked.

I resisted the urge to strike him down with all of my new powers. Bast gripped my hand as if sensing my anger flaring.

Cassidy yelped when Aunt Sandra pricked her finger with a dagger she'd flashed out of nowhere. Every witch had a weapon on them somewhere, but Aunt Sandra seemed to be the best at making her weapon appear and disappear without a trace. I never knew where she kept it, and I was pretty sure I didn't want to know.

As blood trickled over Cassidy's finger, Aunt Sandra used the small pain as fuel for her magic, sending a flurry of glimmering power cascading over Cassidy until her depressing cloak turned into a dress fit for the masquerade ball just like a sexy Cinderella.

The frilly amethyst-hued lace fit her perfectly, but kept short in a cute bob that flared at her hips so her servant's mark was still visible. "Off you go," Aunt Sandra snapped, then shoved Cassidy toward me.

Cassidy stumbled up the steps and I gave her arm an encouraging squeeze. "Kept my promise," I said, my chest puffing with pride.

My best friend was too stunned to supply me with one of her witty comebacks, and then the real event of the evening began.

Warlock Nero, a tall man with a trimmed goatee, clapped once to get our attention. "Enough excitement," he declared, then gave Bast a bow, "I assume His Lordship is quite ready?"

Bast nodded, glancing once over the crowd that hadn't stopped staring at him. "You'd do well to remember I reward the covens that please me," he said, his words sounding more like a threat than encouragement, "and the witch I choose to bond with will always be the best of you." He glanced at me. "The choice was easy this time."

Heat burned in my cheeks. I sent him a mental wave, *Are you trying to get the entire coven to hate me?*

He grinned, which unnerved me even more. We couldn't really communicate telepathically... right?

We've been doing it as long as we've been bonded, a husky voice said inside my head. I'd never heard his actual voice in my head before, but the sensation was all too familiar. Shit, he'd just said that we were bonded, didn't he? By the way he was looking at me, it wasn't just a simple, platonic familiar-witch bond, it was—

Warlock Nero clapped his hands again and began the chant that would open the portal to the realm known as the Gem, the heart of the Royal Covens that resided in England in an alternate dimension.

The collective reluctantly joined in on the chant, each of them pricking their fingers to supply the pain and blood required of teleportation magic. A purple light swirled on stage as a magical wind kicked up my dress and flung my hair over my shoulders. Cassidy shifted closer to my side, boxing me in between her and Bast.

There were four other coven members staring at us who were dressed to the nines and ready for the masquerade ball.

By the look on their faces, they hadn't expected to compete with a mortal-born witch with a god for a familiar.

I always kept my distance, never making friends or connections within my own coven. Cassidy and Sparks—I mean, Bast—were all the friends I needed.

Three witches—Penny, Julia, and Lauren—all sneered at me. I'd been invisible to their little clique all my life except to poke fun at the "mortal-born." Penny crossed her arms and glowered at me while Julia and Lauren hung on Ian's arm, a handsome initiate who seemed more interested at staring at Lauren's pushed-up cleavage than anything else. He finally caught me staring and grinned at me, giving me a lewd wink.

Right, now that I had a god for a familiar, I was going to get all the unwanted male attention.

"Pay them no mind," Bast purred at me—yes he fucking purred.

We were still holding hands, which should have felt awkward, but it didn't. I gave his fingers a light squeeze and forced myself to look away from the coven brats, focusing instead on the portal that sputtered to life. As if readying myself for battle, I slipped my masquerade mask from my hip and secured it over my face.

I wasn't sure what to imagine when walking through that haze of purple. I'd avoided thinking about this moment as much as possible. Of course I'd seen a conjuring of the portal to the House of Gems before, but I guess on some subliminal level I thought that as a mortal-born witch, I wouldn't get to go to anything fancy or see the house where the highest level witches lived. My initiation was supposed to be quiet and unhindered.

I reached my free hand behind me, blindly searching for one of my guys. A comforting touch found mine and a body pressed up from behind me while everyone was distracted by the portal.

"We've all got your back, lass," said Quinn, his delicious accent making me purr a little.

My other guys hummed their agreement, Marcus, Aaron, even Killian, were all close enough that my runes warmed on my skin.

No matter what happened next, I wasn't going to have to do it alone.

A DINNER TO DIE FOR

My foot found solid ground on the other side of the portal, but the air felt wrong. An icy breeze threaded unwanted fingers through my hair and my breath hitched. The feathers on the edges of my mask frosted over as the foreign magic ripped through me. My first instinct was to rip the relic off my face, but Bast held my hand in an iron grip and widened his eyes until I could see all the way to the edges of his sliced irises. He didn't speak to me, but I sensed an unspoken urgency that I couldn't betray the effect the magic was having on me. Something was definitely wrong, but his grip said that something would pass.

Cassidy inched closer to me and rubbed my arm as if to fuel life back into it. "You're freezing," she whispered.

"Let her adjust," Bast replied, his voice low and edged with warning that we shouldn't speak further on it.

I trusted him. I have never really trusted my familiar farther than I could toss his little cat form. He'd only been as trustworthy as his next meal and as finicky as a mood attached to an autumn breeze. However, in his human form, I sensed a deeper connection and understanding. He cared what happened to me. Giving up his primal body in exchange for a human one changed him on a fundamental level, including how he perceived me. I was important to him now and he wasn't going to let anything happen to me. I felt that conviction in the strength of his gaze and the warm grip he held around my fingers.

A deep breath filled my lungs as Marcus stepped through the portal, bringing with him warmth and a sensation of relief that I wasn't going to die. The mask on my face warmed instantly, and then dread wrapped around my heart.

The runes. The bond. I'd become dependent on my protectors. By the slick sheen of sweat across Marcus' face, the connection went both ways. This must be why they'd insisted on coming.

My rune blazed with scalding heat that melted the icy invasion and I winced as the jolt of sensation ran up my arm, but the glamour held.

Marcus donned his own mask, a flurry of deep purple feathers that fanned around his face. He grinned at me, but I could see through the fake sense of calm he tried to lace around his demeanor. His shoulders slackened once he finally brushed his fingers over my skin.

Quinn stepped through next and another constricting lock on my soul loosened its grip. It hadn't hurt to be apart from him as much as it had with Marcus. I hadn't yet bonded to him, not completely, and I chewed my lip as I thought of the consequences of that. If I didn't bond with all my protectors, would they be safe? My biggest fear sprouted its ugly head in my mind: What if something happened to me? I couldn't put them through more heartbreak or put them into danger. The magic that had allowed my soul to reincarnate was gone, consumed when I'd been born. They'd already made their sacrifice. They didn't deserve to be bound to my weak, mortal body. One day, I would die, and I had a feeling that they'd die right along with me.

I opened my mouth to ask Marcus what he'd done and why he hadn't told me before I'd completed our bond, but trumpets sounded with obnoxious blaring through a crowded courtyard.

I blinked as awareness came back to me and I finally had the strength to take in the scene.

A cascade of a flurry of colors filled a massive courtyard and framed what could only be described as the House of Gems. Towering spires glittered in the low moonlight and the pulse of power that emanated from it made me suck in a breath.

One of the most beautiful women I'd ever seen approached us along the crisp reflective path and offered a smile. She stood out with her short bob of blazing red hair and massive emerald earrings that hung from her lobes. "Hello," she said, her voice as smooth as honey, "I'm Rebecca, Anointed of the Emerald Coven."

I hadn't expected one of the Anointed to greet the initiates, but no matter how far down on the totem pole we were, we were all witches of the Royal Covens.

Lauren giggled and brushed her friends aside to greet the

witch first. "We are thrilled to be here," she said, offering herself in a low curtsey.

Rebecca smiled at her, but seemed unimpressed and scanned the rest of us as if looking for someone. Her gaze rested on Bast, recognizable with his wild coloring that stood out with distinct magical glows in this realm, then she noted how he still gripped my hand.

"We were not told you would be joining us, Your Divinity," Rebecca said with a friendly smile. For someone greeting a god, she didn't seem to be overly thrilled, but kept a polite demeanor as she waited for Bast's reply.

My familiar finally released me, only to wrap an arm around my shoulders and bring me to his hard chest. The musk of him wrapped around me and I held in the sound of contentment that wanted to escape me. "My chosen witch is finally ready for her initiation," he said, presenting me with a squeeze. "I hope you'll give Evelyn all the consideration she deserves to have earned the attention of a god."

Rebecca noted me with a twitch of her gaze. Something dark and wrong flickered in the backs of her eyes, but it was gone before I had a chance to study her. She flicked her wrist and lights blared across the walkway, leading us towards the glimmering mansion. "Of course," she said, offering Bast one more slow smile, then turned on her heel. "This way, everyone. We have a feast prepared and we don't want it getting cold."

A FEAST WAS AN UNDERSTATEMENT. Once we'd wandered into

the mansion and passed through glimmering halls that trapped the light and twisted it into miraculous colors, we arrived at the main dining hall where a mass of witches and warlocks waited for our arrival.

"Finally, the Amethyst Coven graces us with their presence," a young witch complained, flicking her napkin over her lap as she sat in front of an empty plate. She held up a fluted glass. "Wouldn't even serve us drinks until you were here for the toast."

Penny, Lauren's evil little servant of a witch, stepped forward at the chance to throw me under the bus. "Evelyn insisted on bringing all of her mentors, her familiar, and even her handmaiden. I'm sure she's very sorry for the delay."

All eyes turned on me, giving my entourage far more attention than I had hoped. All of the covens were here and designated by a speckle of color that glowed over masks. Sapphire, Emerald, Diamond, Pearl, and even Amber.

Self-consciously I swiped my fingers over the feathers of my mask that held Marcus' power. It held a deep purple hue of my own coven, but I didn't feel like my coven had my back, not even a little bit.

Cassidy straightened at my side, hardly looking like a handmaiden with her gorgeous dress and curled hair. I'd never seen her so elegant and she fit the role with ease, enough to make my heart pang that this would likely be the only time she would be dressed how she deserved. "You delay us further with your complaints," Cassidy snapped at the witch, making a gasp fall over the table.

A chuckle rumbled in Bast's throat, and when a god laughed, so did you. Everyone joined in, releasing the tension in the room until I was sure that the witch at the center of the joke had it out for me for good. Her gaze burned with hatred and her fingers turned white as she pinched her empty glass until I was sure it would break.

The room quieted when the grand doors overlooking the long dining table opened and the most powerful witches in the world glided into view.

Rebecca, no longer needing to be our guide, walked down the pathway and rested her hand along the railing as she climbed the steps to the platform and took her seat. A green, glimmering power swept over her as she settled into the throne and I made a mental note that the witches anointed by the power of the Royal Covens rested their magic primarily in their thrones. It seemed a cumbersome place to put magic, but I supposed they had enough of it to go around.

The rest of the witches took their seats and a disembodied male voice introduced them as they took their seats.

I recognized Lenora, the Anointed of the Amethyst Coven. She made all the decisions for our house and had personally approved my adoption, which made me feel a fondness for her I didn't know if she really deserved. Early on in my life she'd been kind to me and made sure that my coven took care of me and accepted me as one of their own—at least as much as the coven brats would accept a mortal-born. It didn't matter. I'd been saved from a life on the streets, or death without someone to watch over me, because Lenora had ordered the coven to take me in and tasked Aunt Sandra with my well-being.

The powerful witch glanced at me and my stomach dropped. I wasn't sure what I expected. I wasn't naive enough to expect her to run down the steps and gather me into her arms like a long lost daughter. I figured a smile wasn't too much to ask. Even on that, she failed. Lenora gave me a nod of recognition as the introductions went down the line. I balled my fingers into fists under the table.

The Sapphire Coven was represented by Iris, a beautiful woman of African American descent who surprised us all with her Australian accent. "I am pleased to see my coven represented well," she said as the blue magic of her house swept over her, leaving sparks of blue across her ebony skin.

The Sapphire coven straightened, only three girls but I sensed their power even from here. All of them batted their eyelashes at the witch and giggled as if starstruck.

Next was the Diamond Coven, represented by a tall and elegant blonde with a gown that glimmered with her movements. I wondered if it was really entirely woven with diamonds. "The Germans are still at this table," the witch named Sarina announced proudly, noting the warlock and two females who'd taken the diamond seats. I found myself curious and I wished that we were sitting closer to them. Instead, servants prepared our chairs, four for my coven bratmates, then another four for my "mentors," and finally one for Bast followed by two more, one for Cassidy and one for myself. I noted the one on the end was for Cassidy because it was a simple wooden chair without a cushion. She frowned at it, but didn't comment.

We took our seats after the last two covens' Anointed had been introduced. Willa, a soft-spoken witch with elegant glasses represented the Amber Coven and finally Heather, a proud Brit, played the part of the Pearl Coven with her jewelry dripping with the white baubles.

Servants brought in our meals and glasses of champagne that soon had everyone smiling.

"A toast!" Rebecca announced as she stood with her glass in hand. We all followed suit and held up our drinks. "To the new initiates, may you make your covens proud."

"Blessed be," we all said in unison, then downed the sweet liquid. Heat slipped down my throat with a delicious burn.

Quiet conversation carried through the feast as servants brought entree after entree. It was a guilty pleasure to fill my plate and dig in. I wouldn't obsessively exercise to burn off the excess calories, but I would indulge myself once in a while when it was offered. The Masquerade Ball wasn't a feast one turned down.

My fellow initiates took that mentality to heart and shoved so much food into their faces that I realized I was outmatched when it came to indulging. That's when my nose twitched as I scented the familiar metallic tang of blood. I leaned to peer past Bast and my guardians, glimpsing Lauren with her finger pinched under the table against a blade to give herself a boost of magic. The coven brats took eating disorders to a whole new level.

No one here was overweight or aged. Magic could do incredible things, but I knew there was a consequence of using magic so frivolously. I glanced at Bast and he gave me a knowing nod. Whenever magic was used for personal gain there would be consequences.

Other than that lingering moment of understanding, Bast didn't seem perturbed by the excess and filled his plate with an entire helping of gleaming orange fish eggs. If I hadn't guessed what they were, I would have thought the decadence was almost pretty, until the smell hit me and I wrinkled my nose. Bast's sliced irises shrank with delight as he inspected his plate. Even if he had taken on a human form, there was still a little bit of the feline in him.

Rebecca wandered down from her perch while the row of initiates ate. She smiled when she spotted Bast opting out of the silverware, instead extending his claws and digging into the pile of eggs as he shoved them into his mouth.

"Our guest deity is pleased," she said, raising her voice over the soft clamor. Voices quieted as she surveyed the room. "I encourage everyone to follow suit and indulge tonight. This is your Masquerade Ball. Enjoy it!"

Soft applause followed her words. I used the distraction to glance over and see how my protectors were faring. They said they could eat, but could they keep up with a feast like this? One glance at Marcus made me relax. He filled his plate with lightly seared beef and flashed me a grin before biting off a slab of meat and swallowing it. I was impressed that he kept his fangs sheathed and his grimace hidden underneath the relaxed facade.

I had my own modest plate that I was nervously picking at, which soon awarded me a frown from Rebecca. I wasn't interested in gaining the attention of an Anointed, so I smiled at her and shoved a forkful of peppered steak into my mouth. It melted on my tongue and I tried to hold in a moan, not fully succeeding.

Bast eased closer to me, only smelling slightly of fish. "I like it when you enjoy your food," he purred.

I waved my hand in front of my face. "And I like it when you don't smell like a raw mackerel."

He chuckled. "It's salmon eggs. Very big difference."

Rolling my eyes, I was readying another retort about the utter lack of importance fish species had in my life when a scream made every nerve inside of me light up in high alert.

The quiet excitement in the room turned to frozen horror as one of the girls from the Diamond Coven collapsed onto her plate and violently convulsed, blood and foam pooling from her mouth and making my stomach heave. While I managed to keep the contents of my stomach in place, not all the initiates succeeded and a few doubled over under the table.

"You've passed the first test," Iris announced, poised as if one of us hadn't just died on her dinner table. She straightened and twirled one of her sapphire earrings. "Well, all of you except for one." She smirked. "Diamond Coven, minus one point."

Sarina crossed her leg and flashed more skin than I needed to see as her glimmering dress of diamonds battled with the room's candlelight. She pouted—fucking pouted!—and crossed her arms. "The games have only just begun," she retorted and stuck her nose in the air as if unperturbed by the loss of a life from her very own coven.

Nausea wound my stomach into knots and I fumbled my hands under the table, finding both Cassidy and Bast reaching out for me. My runes burned as my protectors growled and their bodies went tense.

I had allies on my side, but I had a feeling that we were outmatched.

TRAITOR

*B*ast sprang from his seat and snarled at the Anointed who blinked at him with incomprehension. "How dare you poison the food," he snapped. His hand went to his throat and rubbed over his tabby-patterned skin. "Was all the food tainted? Do you dare harm a god?"

Iris stood and her sapphire gems glittered with her movements. A layer of deep blue power washed over her features and I knew it was an intimidation tactic. "Of course not, Bast. We enchanted the food to kill any outcast bloodlines from our initiates." She splayed open her fingers, as if helpless as she raised her eyebrows with an air of innocence. "You can't expect us to proceed with an initiation without confirming the bloodlines are pure?"

Oh gods. The nausea wasn't just from my mortification. I dabbed my finger under my nose, only to find it blotted with blood. Black spots sizzled over my vision as panic took hold.

I was a Fate Witch. I was an Outcast.

"My magic is not considered Outcast magic?" he snarled, using his body to shield me from the Anointed's view. By the stiffness of his body, he knew I was in trouble and was just buying me time.

Cassidy grabbed my arm. "Take what you need," she demanded and offered her arm.

I stared at her arm and the delicate blue vein that ran up her fair skin. When she gave me an exasperated sigh and started fumbling through my dress, I hissed. "Hey! Don't try to feel me up!"

She snickered. "Where's your knife, dumbass? Cut me and work some magic. Seriously."

Oh, right.

Her gaze flicked to my nose, following a drop of blood that ran down my chin and I swiped it away. "Okay, fine." I was glad I hadn't eaten much of the feast. It was the only reason I wasn't dead right now. The poison must have been slight, and my Fate Coven magic hadn't been fully activated, so perhaps with a little healing spell I could survive it.

Bast continued to argue that his body was mortal and if he showed any signs of illness he'd have all their heads, to which the crowd turned sheet white. Apparently Bast had a bad track record when it came to his mercy.

I plucked my knife from a strap at my thigh—hey, where else is a girl going to hide a knife in a dress?—and readied the blade over Cassidy's arm.

"Why are you hesitating?" she hissed.

Wincing, I made a slight cut, hating that I had to hurt my friend. I'd cut myself in a flash, but Cassidy's blood would make this go quicker. I was already weakened and Cassidy's blood was strong. I chanted over the droplet, watching it steam into the air. I took a long, deep inhale and let the magic fill me.

Sighing as relief washed over me, I slumped back into my chair and wiped the blade clean on my napkin.

"Evelyn, House of the Amethyst Coven!" Rebecca snapped, startling me.

I shoved the blade at Cassidy just in time for Bast to step aside so that the Anointed all had a clear view of me. They glared down at me. Gods. Did they see me healing myself?

"Tell your familiar to get in line," Rebecca said, her words cool and dangerous.

I blinked at her in surprise. She'd been treating Bast with the utmost respect, but now she glowered down as if he were my responsibility. With a glance at Bast, whose face had turned beet red with fury, I decided to take a gamble. "Bast is a god. I can't tell him what to do."

Rebecca's eyes narrowed impossibly further and her emerald earrings flashed with a sickly green magic. "Even gods have their limits. This is the House of Gem and we are permitted to our rituals and traditions. Not even a god has a place to question them."

Bast's claws extended a fraction further and he lifted his lip in a snarl. Before I had a chance to reach out and stop him, he flashed over the table with his claws aimed at Rebecca's throat.

The Royal Covens acted in unison, their magic an instantaneous flash that sent the crowd of initiates screaming and covering their eyes. When I recovered, Bast laid out on the table and held his chest as he gasped for air.

"You said it yourself," Rebecca sneered down at my familiar, "you are weakened now that you're in mortal form. You should have remained a cat. Now that you've offended the Anointed, you will be our prisoner until you've paid your penance."

My mouth went dry and I glanced at my guys to see if there was anything they could do. By the look on Marcus' face as he gripped Killian—likely keeping the vampire from retrieving his switchblade—I knew that Bast was on his own on this one.

My familiar glanced back at me as an invisible magic dragged him over plates and overturned glasses. His sliced irises held a certain calm and relief.

Don't let them know what you are, his voice permeated the wild panic of my mind.

Don't let them win.

THE MASQUERADE BALL proceeded as if a member of the Diamond Coven hadn't just been murdered and one of the gods of old hadn't been dragged out by his scruff.

Marcus took my hand and guided me onto the dance floor. My mask perked at his presence. The purple feathers puffed awake as Marcus filtered his magic into me. The rune on my arm burned with heat at his proximity as he pulled me into his chest and swept me in a skilled twirl, soon mingling us with a dozen other initiates and guests of the ball.

I couldn't see beyond the sea of feathers and masks and was thankful to press my cheek against Marcus' chest as we danced. I didn't want to dance, not when my stomach was tying into knots and Bast was gods knew where with Rebecca doing gods knew what to him.

"Bast can take care of himself," Marcus assured me. The soft rumble of his voice vibrated against my cheek and I curled even closer to him, inhaling the sweet rose and jasmine scents of his soft magic.

"Are you sure?" I asked. I didn't believe in the gods as the covens knew them. Such creatures like Bast weren't gods. They were powerful beings that had both strengths and weaknesses—including Bast. While he was more aware in his human form, I sensed it weakened him in ways he wouldn't admit. He'd lost the selfishness of his feline form, trading it for a willingness to protect me even when it put himself in danger.

"The night isn't over," Marcus warned, diverting the subject with a taut snap of his tone. I glanced up at him only to find him scanning the crowd.

"What is it?" My fingers clutched possessively around his arms. If the Anointed thought they were taking any more of my guys I'd rip out their throats.

"This is another test. I sense a spell being formed." He flicked his gaze to the upper corridors that gave spectators a view of the dance floor. Pristine gems lined the pillars that hid the masked spectators under a canopy of shadows as if this were a theater and we were dancing puppets on display.

"Is it the Anointed?" I asked, hating the tremor in my voice. My heart wanted to stand up to them, but my body screamed I was still mortal-born, still weak and powerless. A lifetime of being taught my place wasn't easy to overcome.

Marcus' hands went to my waist as he twirled us around so that he could get a look at the other side. He scanned the upper balconies again. With his vampiric sight, he'd be able to spot anyone even if they tried to hide in the dark. "None of the Anointed are here."

That made me even more nervous. Were they doing something to Bast? My hands gripped tighter onto Marcus until I left soft semi-circles against his skin as my nails dug into him. "We have to go get him."

When I flinched to move away from him and do... something, anything, he gripped onto me... hard. "The spell is coming from someone in this room. It's not one of the Anointed. They aren't here." His eyes flashed red, snapping me rigid by his attention and holding me captive. "The spell is targeting you."

I cursed under my breath. It could be any of the witches or warlocks here. I had little to no friends in the Amethyst Coven, even less among the other houses. In particular the Sapphire Coven brats seemed to hate me the most. One of their houses was situated in France, a close enough neighbor that they'd heard about the mortal-born Amethyst brat and made their judgments.

Searching the crowd for familiar faces, I found the investigation hopeless. "I can't recognize anyone with these damned masks."

Marcus nodded, but not at me. Killian, Aaron, and Quinn stood with Cassidy. Even with the masks it was easy to recognize them. None of the warlocks were quite as bulky or muscular. They each took turns surveying the room while one of them kept an eye on me and the other on the exit.

A strange tingle swept over me then and I knew that the mysterious spell had found me and was starting to dig its spurs into my skin. "Marcus?" I asked in a hushed plea. If I was found out... if they were taken from me like Bast, then I'd lose my shit.

"Don't move," he said and stilled me against his chest as the music faded away into silence.

A single pair of elegant shoes clicked across the marble floors and I followed the sound to find Lauren slinking towards me. She pinched a bloodied napkin between her fingers and wrinkled her nose at it. "So, I did a little spell. It seems this napkin is yours." Her perfectly plucked brow raised beyond the scope of her mask that barely covered her features. Lauren was way too prideful to hide her magically-enhanced good looks. She shook the fabric at me. "Care to explain why there's blood on it?"

The Anointed made their entrance then, filling up the upper banister with their judgmental stares. I gasped when the main doors opened and a pair of warlocks sent Bast falling to his knees that cracked hard against the unforgiving floor.

"What spell did you weave, Evelyn, that required blood?" Sarina asked, her nose in the air as she twirled a perfect blonde curl around her finger. Her diamond earrings caught the light as she smirked. "Was it a healing spell, perhaps?"

My stomach dropped. Marcus hadn't released his hold around my waist and I sensed the rest of my protectors easing closer to me. I wanted to whirl on them and remind them to stay out of this. If I was going down, so be it, but they were

215

not going to be captured and their magic sucked dry on my account. No fucking way.

Lauren obscenely sniffed the evidence, then frowned at me. "Correction. One drop is yours, the rest is your hand-maiden's, but my nose doesn't lie. Your blood is tainted."

A gasp swept out through the crowd and Rebecca waved them into silence. "Is this true, Evelyn? Did the poison affect you and you attempted to hide it?"

As if hiding the fact that I'd almost died was a traitorous act, the Anointed standing behind her shook their heads in disapproval. Oh, my bad. Sorry I didn't keel over on your dining table.

"I have Outcast magic," I admitted, straightening my spine as I proclaimed the one thing that could get me killed. The crowd released another collective gasp before I quickly added, "Magic that the Amethyst Coven poisoned me with."

Lenora twirled an amethyst ring around her delicate finger, but the expression she wore was anything but gentle. "That is a dire accusation."

"What are you doing?" Marcus whisper-yelled into my ear, making me flinch.

"Just trust me," I shot back. I spared a glance over my shoulder to find that my protectors had stopped their approach and now looked at me with varying degrees of rage. I glared back. It wasn't their job to protect me all the time. Sometimes it was me who needed to protect them.

Untangling myself from Marcus' death-grip, I propped my hands on my hips and glowered at Lauren. "Yes, that is my napkin. I cut my handmaiden to use her blood and pain to heal myself." I hated that I'd done that, but it would be an action that other witches would find natural. I turned my glare up to the Anointed who stared down at me. They hadn't ordered that I be dragged out of the room, and they'd brought a beaten-up Bast here to intimidate me. That meant that they feared what I was. I would use that to my advantage. "I think you know what I am," I tested, seeing how much of me they really knew.

The Anointed of the Amber Coven surprised me by hauling her leg over the railing and launching herself over with a soft grunt. Gold magic swarmed around her, helping her float down to the ground.

Fuck. Could have just used the stairs. But no, gotta show all the witches in the room who has the most power.

Willa, a soft-spoken witch with elegant glasses that I'd underestimated, snapped her fingers and summoned a blade that hovered inches from her reach. "You'll submit to a test," she ordered and beckoned for me to approach. "We've been waiting for you for a long time, but we must be sure."

I could almost feel my protectors going taut behind me when I took my first step towards the witch. Was Willa the one who'd killed me? Were all of the Anointed actually ancient thousand-year-old witches that reveled in my death?

Bast growled as I held out my arm. *You take that knife and you cut me with it,* he ordered. *Use the magic that I have to offer you to fight.*

I went rigid at Bast's words that pushed relentlessly into my skull. Sparing a glance at him, I slightly shook my head rejecting his demand. Fighting the Royal Covens wasn't how change happened. That's how death happened, and I had no interest in watching everyone I cared about killed before my eyes.

The room held its breath as Willa made a clean slice across my arm. The blade was so sharp that I didn't even feel it at first. A soft sting radiated from the place she'd cut as blood seeped to the surface. She grabbed me by the wrist and magic plucked at my skin, sending the blood floating up into the air in front of us until there was enough for her to work with. When she released me, I hissed and slapped my hand over the wound. I needed to convince her I wasn't a threat.

The blood swirled in the air as magic threaded through it, separating the droplets until it was a mist that swarmed like bees. Finally, the magic *popped*, and the mist turned purple.

Willa frowned. "Unconfirmed. The Amethyst Coven influence is too strong." She glanced at me, as if annoyed that my blood wasn't cooperating. "Save us all the hassle and tell us what you are, *witch*." She sneered the last word as if I didn't deserve the title.

Do not tell her you are a Fate Witch, Bast demanded.

I caught his gaze from across the room. It felt like something was building and I didn't know what to do or how to protect those I loved. I closed my eyes and drew in a deep breath as I focused.

Concentrating on the sensations, I tried to separate the barrage of magic and influences in the room. Marcus' rose and jasmine scented-fear still clung to me, while the perfume of Willa's amber magic plucked at me with metallic, slow movements. Then there was the spell Lauren had cast, a simple investigation to link me to the bloodied napkin. She wanted to win affections from the Anointed, no doubt, by revealing a traitor, even if it was from her own coven.

There was something else, though, something that hummed low in the background that I almost would have missed it. A heartbeat. Something that thrummed through the room with slow, steady confidence—and it was growing louder.

My eyes snapped open, searching who might be casting such a forbidden spell. Instinctually I knew what it was.

Blood magic. Forbidden summoning that would bring about creatures from the pits of hell.

"You think I wouldn't recognize you?" Sarina's silky voice boomed through the chamber. She'd barely whispered her words, but magic writhed around her. Her eyes lit up with ruby power that could only come from blood magic. Her diamonds reflected the eerie light until it looked as if she glittered with red.

I spun to find Aaron's mask ripped off as a magical wind tore at him, taking chunks of his suit with it until hard exposed muscles flexed as he growled, teeth elongating and glamour slipping.

Right, Diamond Coven, Aaron's old stomping grounds.

The crowd eased away from him, all except for Killian, Quinn, and Cassidy. She'd actually snatched someone's blade and now held it backwards in her grip—all badass style.

"Sarina?" Heather asked, her pearls trembling at her earlobes as she stepped away from her Anointed sister.

Sarina turned her attention to me. "I've been waiting for you," Sarina said as a wild grin overtook her face. The air crackled around me and I froze, waiting to see what would happen next. I had two of my powers unlocked, but not all of them. I wasn't ready for this fight.

"You can't kill me yet," I guessed, jerking my chin up. "It's not time." I hadn't just been randomly killed a thousand years ago. If Sarina really was a Blood Witch, then she was immortal as long as she dealt in blood sacrifices. The sacrifice of a Fate Witch would make sure she lived forever.

I could see the slightest of wrinkles around her eyes as her wild grin grew. She was starting to age, which meant she needed another boost of magic.

She needed my death to avert her own.

She slowly nodded. "Impressive. The Fate Witch remembers her place."

The entire collective of Anointed turned their attention from Sarina to me, their jaws dropping open. "Fate Witch?" Willa asked, stepping away from me.

A surge of pride swelled in my chest the way that Willa said that with sudden fear making her voice tremble. Apparently I was a bad-ass. Damn right I was.

I was also Sarina's battery. Details.

Sarina reacted first, sending the air splitting and deep, terrifying growls sounded through the new caverns that exploded all around the ballroom. The witches and warlocks finally reacted, shrieking and sending the whole place erupting into chaos.

My guys took advantage of the moment. Bast, who'd been pretending to be beaten and weak a moment before, broke his chains as if they were toys and launched himself at Willa, clamping down on her neck like a wild animal. Blood spurt all over me as she cried out in surprise and pain. She worked her jaw to start a spell, but Bast held on tight and no words came out.

Aaron growled, bones snapping as he shifted into wolf form, leaving Marcus and Aaron to guard me on either side. Their masks gone and glamour dropped, their fangs and red eyes made them intimidating.

"There's no way out of here," I shouted over the chaos as warlocks and witches cast offensive and defensive spells that sent the air trembling. They knew just as well as I did that there was no way out. We'd been sent in by a portal opened by a coven collective. The only way to get out again was if the Anointed sent us out... or one hell of a powerful spell.

"You've done it before, lass," Quinn assured me, brushing his body against mine. He wrapped his arms around me as his chest pressed against my back, exposing his wrists. "Still have that knife of yours? Take what you need. Vampire blood is powerful." He lowered, his lips against my ear as he grinned. "Especially mine."

Before I could contemplate doing anything of the sort, another kind of shriek made my blood crawl.

Demons.

They poured into the ballroom through the caverns that Sarina had opened. Red mist wafted around them and engulfed their victims, making witches and warlocks spasm until their eyes turned red and they stilled. The affected moved like zombies as they turned their attention on me.

"Don't have much time, lass. Looks like diamond bitch has unleashed hell on us."

I swallowed the hard lump in my throat. I wasn't prepared for this, but I tried anyway. Bringing out my knife I sliced a long line up Quinn's arm. Blood gushed out and I reminded myself that he was immortal. I couldn't hurt him, but my heart still twisted in my chest.

Marcus joined us, embracing me from the front so that both Quinn and Marcus surrounded me. I heard the fighting start in the background. Aaron's wolf growled and snapped, tearing into demon flesh. Likewise Bast had disabled Willa who now lay unconscious on the ground. He moved with impressive speed as he climbed the column to the bannister where the Anointed had gathered around Sarina to cast a spell of their own. I didn't know what they were doing, and I didn't much care. They weren't coming after me.

But Sarina, her red eyes trained on me and ignored everything else, making me shiver with an ancient memory that threatened to bubble to the surface.

Blood. Hellfire. Magic. Sarina had been the one to kill me before... and I had no doubt that she was going to do it again.

I SNAPPED my eyes shut and tried to shut out all of the chaos. I had to open a portal out of here or I would lose everything. My protectors. My familiar. My best friend, and then my life.

A low hum sounded in my throat. This sort of magic wouldn't need latin phrases or ancient witch chants. I needed to reach through time and space and grab onto my goal and rip it through. That was how fate worked when manipulated. It was distant, ambiguous, but it could be controlled. Instinct from who I used to be tugged at me from another life and then my eyes snapped open, but I wasn't in the ballroom anymore. My spirit sped through time and space... searching.

Just before I started to gain my bearings I was snapped back again with both my guys sprawled out on the ground held down by snarling demons and Sarina was in my face, her smug grin making me want to claw her eyes out.

"None of that, dear. You are under my control now." She flicked her wrist and bulky iron chains clamped around my wrists, making me whimper as pain shot up my elbows and a sensation of heaviness weight down on me. She was grounding my spirit to my body and preventing me from working Fate magic.

"Evie!" Cassidy shouted.

My attention swerved to the source of the sound, only to see a couple of red-eyed zombie warlocks drag off my best friend.

A helpless cry escaped me and my heart sank.

Don't you give up, Bast's voice thundered in my mind.

I found him up on the banister decked out and this time he wasn't faking his injuries. Burn marks scalded his right cheek in a gruesome line of blisters and bite marks lined his arms where he'd gotten into a scuffle with some demons. At least by the looks of it, he'd won the fight over the demons, but the Anointed now held him down with varied ropes of colored magic that sizzled against his skin. Red glows illuminated their eyes, revealing that they were all Sarina's puppets now.

Sarina let me take in the scene, until finally I got to my

protectors. Aaron's wolf was badly injured and blood matted in his fur. Marcus, Quinn, and Killian all had their arms bound behind their backs and were pinned down by the same weighty chains that Sarina had put on me.

She straightened and folded her arms as a satisfied smirk tugged at her lips. "Take them to the dungeons, and give her the one with good manners as a cellmate. She'll need to regain her strength for what I have planned."

FORTITUDE

*A*ll of my energy drained out of me just moments after being placed into the cell. Whatever magic had bound me through the chains was ten-fold wrapped around the iron bars that made me feel like an elephant was sitting on my chest.

"Don't hurt them!" I shrieked as Sarina had the demons shove the rest of my protectors into nearby cells.

She waved her hand at me in dismissal. "They'll be fine. The shifter gets his own doggy bed," she said with a grin. "He did always complain we never let him be a beast. He can be one as much as he wants around here."

I growled and moved to launch myself at her, but Marcus caught my wrist. The chains were gone, but deep bruises marked where they'd been and I winced at the contact. "Regain your strength," he whispered so only I could hear. "We will try again."

I wanted to believe we *could* try again, but we were found out. Sarina watched me with morbid fascination as Marcus' touch awakened his magic in me. My wilted mask hung on a hook at my waist. I lifted my hands to run my touch over my earrings to try and build my power, but flinched when I found they were gone.

She dangled them from her grip. "Looking for these?" She turned them in her hand and stroked the dull gems. "Fascinating work, little witch. You will have to teach me how you hid your powers into artifacts. I'd thought such an art long lost." She grinned at me. "I'll let you keep the mask. I need you alive a while longer."

She sauntered off then, her hips swinging as she hummed a low tune. "You come back here!" I snapped. "Don't leave us like this!"

She ignored me and the demons snickered at my panic, giving me one wayward glance before shutting the door to the Royal Coven's dungeons with a final *thud.*

My vision wavered as panic threatened to take me under. It was Marcus' touch that brought me back. His hand wound around my waist, pulling me close to him.

I turned and buried my face into his neck and choked on a sob. "I'm so sorry," I whispered. "This is all my fault."

He shushed me and stroked my hair. "No, Evelyn. You are not to blame. I should have taken you far away from this place. I was a fool to think you could go through the masquerade ball undetected."

Sniffling, I blinked up at him. "Why didn't you?" It wasn't an accusation, but a genuine question.

His pained grin made my heart ache as he brushed hair away from my tear-streaked face. "You are the most powerful and coveted of witches. You aren't meant to hide in the shadows." He pressed a light kiss to my lips. "You're meant to rule them all."

We sank down together as he stroked my arm, his thumb automatically going to my rune that marked me with his soul, as if to reassure himself that we were still bound together and I hadn't rejected him.

As his thumb traced slow circles around my rune, sleep threatened to take me, but I resisted it, too worried about how the others were doing.

Then Marcus began to sing a foreign song, one that was low, melancholy, and magical. The air hummed with weak power even against the weight of the bars.

Aaron's wolf howled, joining in, then Killian and Quinn added their lyrical voices, supplying new flavors to the melody. Finally, when Bast and Cassidy began to sing, my heart unclenched.

No matter what happened, we were all in this together, and I would never stop fighting.

Sarina might have killed me in my past lives and used my magic for her own gain, but she wasn't prepared for what I brought with me in this life. A fierceness for those I loved and a will to protect them that would challenge fate itself.

TO BE CONTINUED...

Oh yeah, this is a boxed set, so turn the page to keep reading!

COMPELLED: BOOK 2

There will be a sacrifice at the witching hour—me.

Okay, so throwing a shoe and casting my laxative spell didn't do me much good. Time to go to Plan B.

I'm a reincarnated Fate Witch and rightful Queen of the Royal Covens. None of that is why I'm going to get out of this, though. I'm a mortal-born witch in this lifetime, which means I'm scrappy as hell. I'll use my strengths against their pride and get the Royal Covens to turn on each other. While they're cat-fighting it out, I'll use the opportunity to work together with my guys and make an epic escape.

To everyone's surprise, Plan B worked! (Yeah, even I was surprised, I'll admit it.) We head on over to an underground retreat for vampires who royally pissed off the Royal Covens (see what I did there?). Anyway, they're all really nice and accepting except for this super hot vampire named Tiros. His first reaction when he sees me is to give me the bird. Yeah, he's awesome like that.

Behind all that brooding and crudeness, Tiros is hiding something. Well, he's a master thief, so he's always hiding something, but I think he knows something about my past. I'll charm it out of him. Because yeah, I'm charming. Totally.

IMPRISONED

*F*uck.

"You can say that again," Marcus agreed with a low grunt as he shifted my slight weight on his lap. Normally I'd get all hot and bothered being this close to him, but I couldn't feel much of anything right now. Even his typical rose and jasmine scented magic couldn't overcome the heavy weight of iron that left a metallic taste in my mouth. The Diamond Coven Blood Bitch (her official title, according to me) had placed us in a cell imbued with dampening magic. It felt like an elephant was constantly sitting on my chest and I figured out real fast why she let Marcus in here with me. If the ancient warlock turned vampire hadn't been here to hold me together, I would have been crushed into a thousand little Evelyn-shaped pieces. There were times when being a mortal-born sucked, and this was definitely one of them.

Marcus chuckled. "Why don't you tell me how you really feel?"

I hadn't realized that I'd been murmuring profanity out loud. Even just a few hours in this cell was driving me insane. "We have to get out of here," I wheezed, barely able to form the words with the amount of weight pushing down on me from all directions. It felt like I was a million miles beneath the ocean and all the weight of the world was crushing down onto me.

Marcus wrapped his arms tighter around my chest and his fingers brushed the masquerade mask hanging loosely at my hip. The air pulsed with his magic, giving me a stronger dose than the steady current he was feeding me. For just a brief moment I was able to suck in a lung-full of air before the weight came down on me again.

"The others?" I asked, breathless. If I was having this hard a time, were they doing okay? Oh gods, what about Cassidy?

Marcus brushed away a strand of hair from my sweat-slick face. "The others are keeping the human alive. Bast is in a cage on his own, but he's a cat, he's got nine lives."

I glowered up at him, then didn't have the energy to stay mad. "Don't pick on Bast," I chided as I snuggled closer into his chest. Burying my nose into his neck I inhaled as deeply as I could until I got the faintest whiff of his magic.

I didn't get time to try and get comfortable. The main doors to this level of the dungeons creaked open and heels clicked against the uneven stone floors. I expected it to be a return visit from Sarina, but when I spotted Aunt Sandra's familiar furrowed brow, I sucked in a breath. "Auntie?"

She didn't look very pleased with my predicament, but she wasn't trying to get me out, either. Instead she sighed dejectedly at the bars. "Are you still wearing that bracelet I gave you?"

I blinked at her, the weight pressing down on me making it hard to think. "Who cares about a fucking bracelet?" I snapped. "Get me out of here!"

She continued to frown down at me, unimpressed by my outburst. Her gaze shifted to the vampire who held me in a tight embrace. "I should be surprised that your 'mentors' are actually vampires. You have always attracted trouble, though, so I can't say it's a huge shock."

I growled and unwrapped myself enough from Marcus to stand. It would have looked badass had my knees not buckled. Marcus managed to hold me upright while I tried to kill my aunt with my eyes. If hatred were a magic, then I'd be winning the shit out of this staring contest right now. "You know what I am, don't you? That's the only reason you took me into the coven."

Her frown deepened. "I was told that you were a rare bloodline, but not what. I was also told that your uniqueness could remain dormant, so I never truly had my hopes up that you'd be anything but a mortal-born witch who would serve us best as a healer on the outskirts of our town."

Not that long ago, that sort of existence sounded wonderful. Now that I knew I was born for something greater, though, I realized the insult that it was. I was meant to rule, to change fate itself and make the world a better place. "You used me!" I shouted, launching myself at the bars and not even caring when the magic in the iron sizzled against my skin.

"Evelyn," Marcus chided, grabbing my wrists and trying to wrench me free.

I growled, twisting my fists around the bars even tighter as I leaned in. Aunt Sandra actually backed off a step, horror on her face. "I will never be used again," I assured her.

Aunt Sandra swallowed and her fingers absently went to the gem at her chest. The long chain held one of her prized possessions, an artifact that held a portion of her power. My gaze went to it and I snarled. "We're not so different, you know. The only difference is that you happily play the part of their little puppet, doing whatever you're told."

She bristled, but straightened and looked down her nose at me. "I'm sorry that you feel that way, child. This is not easy for me, which is why I came to tell you to use the power I bestowed into the bracelet when the Anointed try to sacrifice you. It might just be enough to set you free."

My eyes widened. "I can't trust you," I said. "If you really wanted to help me, you'd use all the power in the amethyst around your neck and undo these bars right now, right here."

She shook her head and a loose curl flapped around her face. She was always so put-together and perfect. Even that little imperfection told me how upset she was right now, whether I wanted to trust her or not. "I can't," she insisted, her voice lowering to a harsh whisper. "Even if I set you free, I couldn't open a portal to get you out of here. But at the ceremony there will be enough power for you to channel it into a portal and then you could escape." Her gaze snapped to Marcus again. "If you've befriended these vampires, they can get you to a stronghold where you'll be safe."

I wanted to trust my aunt so badly, but how could I? She was the reason I was here at all.

"We don't have a choice," Marcus said as he sagged against my back.

I stiffened, realizing that this was tiring him out. He'd been keeping us both alive in the weight of the cell and I hadn't stopped to think how it might be draining him.

Allowing him to pull me back to the corner where the wall could support our weight, I glowered at my Aunt. "Fine, just tell me what to do."

WHEN MAGIC FAILS, TRY INSULTS

*A*unt Sandra made me draw the runes in the dust over and over again until I was able to draw them by memory.

"Recite the words when you draw them," she said, having told me the words separately.

I'd never performed a real spell. The ones I'd managed were with clumsy Latin or this one gag where I'd made Lauren shit for a week. I'd framed one of the Sapphire brats and it was an easy sell. No one believed me capable of magic, so I'd gotten away with it.

"I'm going to make Sarina have the shits," I declared once Aunt Sandra was gone and I was alone with Marcus.

To my surprise it was Bast's voice that carried through the damp air. "That's my girl," he murmured, then there was a shuffling sound as if he'd turned over and gone back to sleep.

I lifted an eyebrow, glancing up to see Marcus completely passed out. Even in his sleep one of his hands was still latched onto me and fed me power. I felt a special kind of love from him then that even unconscious he wouldn't let anything happen to me.

I didn't want to wake him, but my nerves were getting the best of me. "Cassidy? Guys? Are all of you there?"

Cassidy whimpered in the distance. "Yeah, here," she said, sounding horrible as if she'd been crying for hours. "I think they lowered the oppression spell."

I realized that while it still felt heavy, she was right, the weight had lifted enough for me to take a full breath. I'd thought Marcus had just gotten a better hold of his magic. "Yeah," I agreed. "Is that a good sign?"

"Don't count on it," Bast offered. "Get some rest. We're going to need it."

Shuffling uncomfortably, I tried to find another position where one of my legs wouldn't be asleep. Needles stung up my calf as I shifted, and I grunted with discomfort.

Marcus moaned something about damned cat gods, then fell back to sleep again, making me grin.

Settling my cheek against his chest, I brought one hand up to stroke along his collarbone. Soft scents of roses and jasmine wafted over me as I petted him and his skin grew warmer.

He was so pale, even more so than a vampire should be. "Are you growing weaker?" I asked.

Marcus knit his brows together as if I was bothering him. "Hm?"

I shook him, an irrational fear taking hold of me. "Maybe you shouldn't fall asleep. What if the spell crushes us both?"

He shook his head. "I'm fine, I just..." He licked his lips and I noticed how cracked and dry they were.

My eyes went wide. "Do you need blood?"

He flinched away from me, but I kept myself pinned to his chest. "I'm fine," he repeated.

That was all I needed to hear. My vampire was keeping me alive and he was running on fumes. I grabbed his chin and wrenched him back to me, then held my wrist over his mouth. "You bite and take what you need right now or I'm going to kick you in the balls."

He chuckled, finally slitting his eyes open so that the ruby irises glittered at me. "You're such a charmer, aren't you?"

"Damn right," I replied. "Totally charming." I ran my skin over his lip and his mouth parted as his gaze grew hooded. "Now stop talking and drink. You'll feel better."

His free hand ran up my arm, sending goosebumps exploding over my skin. "Maybe just a little bit," he ventured, then opened his mouth and grazed a fang over the skin without breaking it.

I tried not to suck in a breath as my lady bits grew instantly wet. Damn. How was that so sexy?

"Go on," I insisted. "Just a little bit."

He glanced at me, the lust and desire clouding his gaze and making me bite my own lip in return. He growled at the motion, then bit, sending pain followed by the most intense pleasure through my system.

"Oh," I moaned in surprise.

"Hey, what are you two doing over there?" Bast complained. "You're waking me up."

"Nothing!" I shouted back, only to be cut off when I

moaned again as Marcus ran his touch between my thighs with his mouth still on my wrist.

When he unlatched from me, he grinned, blood red on his fangs, as he gave my cunt a squeeze before pulling away.

"I feel better," he said. "Thank you."

My world swarmed and a small whimper of need escaped me. "I don't," I complained.

He chuckled and settled me onto his chest again. "There will be plenty of what you desire once we are free," he promised. His gaze flicked to the other cells in the darkness. "It wouldn't be fair to take you now when we could all die tomorrow. I will abstain and use that drive to make sure you live to ride my cock when I'm at full strength and can do your body justice."

Heat flushed at my core at his words. "That sounds nice," I said, my voice wavering, then I chuckled. "No sex before battle, huh? You're a true warrior."

SEVERAL HOURS later our jailer returned with an impressive gathering of zombified coven members. I recognized Ian, one of the Amethyst warlocks who was supposed to be a part of the initiation, and frowned.

"Sleep well?" Sarina chimed, looking somehow even better than yesterday. She must have feasted on the blood of a virgin or something—not that it would be anyone from my coven, so I didn't have much to worry about. Definitely no virgins there.

"Delightfully," I replied with fake charm. Staggering to my

feet, I kept one hand linked with Marcus who had a strong grip on me. He was right. Abstaining seemed to bring us closer together. We both had decided to ride this storm out and make it on the other side alive.

The only evidence that my cheerfulness set Sarina off was the slight twitch of her smile. Her eyes flickered with malice as if she wanted to rip my head off right here, but then she was her charming self again as she flipped a lock of perfectly straight blonde hair over her shoulder. "Wonderful."

The "guards" unlatched the cell doors and brought us out. I gulped in a delicious full breath of air that came without any effort or strain and had a sudden appreciation for the simple things. Breathing. I like breathing.

A warlock secured iron chains over my arms that brought that heavy feeling back, although it wasn't as intense. Instead of glaring at him, I watched down the dank halls as the rest of my protectors were brought out, followed by a very tired looking Cassidy. She was as white as a sheet and her lips were blue. I flinched. Aaron, Killian, and Quinn all looked exhausted. Marcus had managed to keep me alive, but I still had magic in my veins and two awakened artifacts with my power. Cassidy didn't have anything at all. It had taken almost too much of a toll on my guys to keep her alive and my heart swelled that they'd sacrificed their strength to make sure she didn't succumb to the weight of the spell.

Bast came out behind them and stretched as if he were a cat waking up after a long nap. Sarina rolled her eyes at him. "I'm glad you all had a good rest, because that was your last." She turned on her heel and waltzed towards the door, flicking her wrist and sending the spelled warlocks lurching into action.

My stomach dropped as a warlock yanked me to follow her.

WE WERE ESCORTED through the back halls of the sweeping mansion. Once we were spat out onto a courtyard filled with dying flowers, I knew exactly where we were.

These grounds were reserved for sacrifices.

An entire day had passed and it was close to midnight again—the witching hour—when spells would be at their strongest.

The moonlight filtered differently here. Once we passed through the invisible veil where the living flowers trans-formed into dead, I saw all the way through to her soul. Glancing around, no one else seemed to react to Sarina and instead they were looking up at the eerie blood moon.

My gaze moved back to the woman in the Diamond dress and I tilted my head as the magic of this space revealed the swarming red flickers of power inside her chest. She'd fully given herself over to Blood Magic. Even vampires still had a soul, but witches like Sarina had given all of that up, trading their soul in exchange for immortal life.

I'd never paid too much attention to the different kinds of Blood Witches, the matter seeming too grotesque to learn about. I never planned on giving up my soul, and the practice was outlawed by the Royal Covens, so I'd thought it about as useful as a dead language.

Wrong.

Sarina's heels clicked as she glided up the steps of the long slab of stone. Dark splotches marred its otherwise onyx sheen where the blood from previous sacrifices hadn't quite dried.

She turned, her skeletal face grinning at me. "Still going to pretend to be better than me?" she asked. "I know what you are, Evelyn. A Fate Witch, and your power is nothing more to me than a battery to feed my eternal life."

Quinn was the first to wrench free of his guards and lunge at her. With a flick of her wrist his chains seemed to gain a hundred pounds, sending Quinn crashing to his knees. "You bitch!" he cried.

Sarina flicked her wrist again, sending a streak of blood across Quinn's face. He grit his teeth together and growled at her. "Down boy," she said, her words smoother than honey. She glided around him and swept her fingers over his shoulder before running her touch through his wild red hair that I loved so much.

I don't know what it was that really did me in, but no bitch was allowed to touch my guys. I slammed to my knees and started chanting the spell.

That's right, *the* fucking spell.

Sarina's grin twitched as a peculiar expression went over her face. She zoomed in on me as surprise made her ghostly brows shoot up. "Are you trying to cast a spell on me?" Her lips curled over her teeth in a sneer.

My plan included distracting Sarina with the shits, which would have been both hilarious and effective. I hadn't factored in that she wasn't as corporeal as I would have liked for that particular spell. The inky purple magic that I'd woven into existence slipped right through her stomach and hit the first unsuspecting warlock who immediately jerked to attention and grabbed his ass. He grunted in urgent tones. I wasn't sure if zombified warlocks could talk, but he certainly made an effort of it.

Sarina rolled her eyes. "Yes, fine. Go." When he broke out in a run down the path, she shouted after him, "But don't shit on the flowers! This is a sacred space!"

Bast was near hysterical by this point. He threw his head back and laughed. "Oh my gods, that is hilarious! I haven't seen anyone cast a shitting spell in ages."

Sarina glowered at him. "You're all ruining the ambiance." She flicked her wrist and our chains lifted us towards the sacrificial slab. "No matter. Your antics will die with you."

I struggled against the pull, craning my neck to peer over my shoulder at everyone I loved being dragged after me. I couldn't let them die. I'd only just met my guys, was just getting to understand their complex hearts and desires. And Cassidy, she was my only friend, my best friend. Her once poofy dress now sagged around her in sad little wrinkled folds. Her hair matched her dress, and her eyes just looked tired. She tried to offer me a smile when our gazes met, but then Sarina sent me crashing into the slab, the corner of it digging into my ribs and knocking the breath out of me.

"I want to thank you, Evelyn," she began, her freezing fingers running an icy touch over my skin. I tried to flinch away from her, but my chains kept me bound with my arms stretched over the slab. She grinned, seeming to enjoy making me uncomfortable and prone. "I have sacrificed you more than once and you give me another thousand years of life. My trade to the Blood Coven was a risk, of course. Many choose to bind themselves to an archdemon or a blood stone, but I wanted to have control over my fate." Her fingernail grazed a painful line across my cheek, drawing blood. "What better way to do that than by sacrificing a Fate Witch?"

I refused to flinch from the pain. Instead, I glared at her and tested the theory that hate could generate magic again. I wanted to burn a hole through her creepy face. Even if it didn't work, it was fun to visualize it. "What if I'm not reincarnated this time?" I asked. It was a risky game, but if I was going down, I could take her down with me.

She shrugged, seeming unperturbed by the idea. "That would be a hassle for me, yes. Finding another Fate Witch would be challenging, even with a thousand years to do it." She glanced at the four growling vampires now on their knees. "However, that's why I will make your mates watch. When I offer them a chance to save you again, they will take the deal, just like they did last time." She left me, taking her icy presence with her. I strained to watch her as she went to Marcus. "You were the most amenable last time. You'll work with me, won't you? You don't want to live a thousand years with the memory of Evelyn's severed head all you see in your nightmares."

I gulped. Marcus' face turned grim. He refused to look at me and kept his gaze trained on the Blood Witch. "Perhaps that should be my punishment. I fell for your promises last time, and look where they got us?" Finally his gaze drifted to mine and warmth flooded back into the sparkling red of his irises. "I failed Evelyn once. I won't do it again."

Sarina dismissed him with a wave of her hand as if he was

just being stubborn. "You're all talk, Marcus, just as you were last time. Once I break you, you'll come around."

As Sarina went on with her confidence and threats, I watched as shadows drifted in the distance, finally revealing themselves to be the mind-controlled Anointed members.

I pursed my lips in thought. All of them were ancient, powerful witches. Even blood magic shouldn't be enough to control them for long. Perhaps they just needed a little push.

With a yelp, pain erupted in my wrists as the chains yanked me up until I was dangling, then I was slammed on my back on the sacrificial slab. A starry night sky greeted me, looking peaceful and eternal just as the sky always did. The blood moon wasn't quite in position. I felt its rays awakening my magic, just as it would any other witch.

Except I wasn't just "any other" witch, I was a Fate Witch bound to four immortal protectors and a god.

A flaming red scythe interrupted my view, summoned by Sarina and suspended in midair. She began the low chants of the ceremony and I caught a few of the witch words that began the spell that would transfer the energy of my death to fuel the Blood Witch for another thousand years of life.

I strained against the magic weighing me down to see the Anointed flinching under Sarina's control. She was working another spell, which meant that she couldn't control them one-hundred percent. If I just gave them a push...

"Hey! Iris!" I shouted at the leader of the Sapphire Coven. She flinched, her white gaze jerky and uncertain. "You know I framed one of your coven brats for the shitting spell on Lauren? Yeah, that's right, that was me, and the retaliation Lauren gave back ten-fold was all my fault." Iris' left hand twitched at my revelation, making me grin. Lauren had rained terror on that coven for weeks, bringing out all sorts of hellish pranks. There'd never been any evidence that had pointed back to her, naturally, so there had been nothing that the Sapphire Coven could do.

"And you! Willa!" The Anointed of the Amber Coven turned to me when I said her name. "You're going to let Sarina destroy me and have my power all to herself? I thought you were the historian of the Royal Covens. You're just going to let all this fascinating history go to waste? I have past lives and shit you could study. Sarina is making a fool of you!"

Sarina growled and the scythe lowered until its heat made me sweat. "Shut it or I'll kill you now!"

Ignoring her, I continued on my tirade, insulting Rebecca that emeralds were the puke gems of the Royal Covens and that Pearls were for primpy bitches to Heather. Finally, when I told Lenora that Aunt Sandra said her ass looked fat in that dress, something in the air broke.

All of the Anointed came out of their spell at once and turned on Sarina, wasted no time as they raised their voices in a low hum and magic sliced through the air like a hundred daggers.

Sarina, distracted by her own spell, was caught off guard and cuts erupted all over her ghostly skin, sending a sickly dark pool of blood splashing around her feet. She swerved her scythe as a makeshift shield to block the worst of the onslaught.

Strong hands were snapping off my chains before I had a chance to even sit up and Bast had me in his arms, sweeping me off the slick onyx of the sacrificial slab. "Good work," he praised under his breath before sweeping me further into the shadows. Instead of going towards the path back to the Royal Covens, we slipped into the black dead blooms, brown leaves crunching under our feet and soft soil welcoming our footsteps.

The rest of the guys followed us, making quick work to evade the invisible blades that slid through the air. The vampires seemed to sense them and dodged with supernatural speed before getting close enough to us that they could rip off their own chains.

When Aaron presented Cassidy tucked in his arm passed out, but alive, I breathed a sigh of relief.

Marcus stroked my cheek, swiping away a lost streak of blood before popping his finger into his mouth. His red eyes flashed with the fresh dose of power. "You can draw from Quinn and me," Marcus informed me, indicating my artifacts. "However since our bond is secure, you'll need to take most of your power from me. Don't hold back."

With a shaky nod, I turned from them all, feeling suddenly shy with an audience.

I needed to open the portal back to Berlin and get us out of here. The first place I envisioned was the guest house where I'd started to get to know my guys. It was the first place in my life that had started to feel like home—a place where I felt safe.

With that image and sensation in my mind, I began the runes that Aunt Sandra had taught me as I muttered the witch words in time with each stroke of my finger through the soil. Power built in me, and when my bracelet bit into my wrist, I winced, but I didn't stop.

I took my free hand and stroked the fluffing feathers of my masquerade mask, then ran my touch over my earrings. Roses and Jasmine bloomed at my feet, filling in the lines where I'd just drawn the first rune. The ground rumbled and the air shimmered with glimmering purple motes.

A shout came from the sacrificial platform and I was tempted to see what was going on. Was Sarina winning? Or maybe the Anointed had already put her down? There were a lot of them and I bet they were pissed off. Even if the blood moon gave Sarina power, she's lost her element of surprise.

"Keep going," Cassidy said with a scratchy voice that made my insides twist. "I want to get out of here."

Right. Focus.

I drew the second rune, but when I went to touch my earrings they felt cold. Marcus was immediately beside me, pressing his lips to my ear and whispering how much he loved me. I closed my eyes and let the power funnel into me as I finished the rune.

One more. I already felt so drained and stuck my finger in the ground next to the two glowing runes. "I don't know if I can do it," I protested. I'd never cast a spell like this before.

Marcus cupped a finger under my chin and turned me to face him. His fangs were out, his once perfectly slick-back hair now tousled around his eyes that burned with emotion. "You are not going to die here," he promised before planting a kiss on my lips. His tongue speared into my mouth without permission, making a surprised moan escape my lips.

Then I tasted blood.

It wasn't mine. Marcus had bit himself and now fed me his blood. I'd never had blood before, much less vampire blood, but it wasn't what I expected. It tasted sweet and came with a powerful dose of magic that gave me the boost I needed. When Marcus parted from me, he grinned, looking weakened, but alive. "The rune," he reminded me.

"Shit, right," I said, turning my attention back to the ground and drawing the last long strokes that completed the spell.

The portal burst open just inches in front of my face, making my hair fling back and my ears pop with the change of pressure. It was an unstable portal, messy and amateur, but it was there.

"Come on!" Quinn shouted and grabbed me by my arm, yanking me up with him.

Bast hooked his arm around Marcus who looked like he was fading fast, his eyelids fluttering and his eyes rolling back into his head.

"Marcus!" I shouted. He'd better not die on me or I'd kill him. Don't ask me how that works. But that's what was going to happen.

Aaron hurried towards the portal with Cassidy as shouts came from behind and the ground shook as a new spell built under our feet.

Whoever had won the battle was no longer distracted and coming after us.

Without turning around to see who the victor was, I followed Quinn's shadow into the portal, and then everything went black.

FOUR HORSEMEN

*B*eing yanked through an unstable portal is about as much fun as it sounds. My insides heaved and everything went black when my brain refused to process the world where physics stopped making sense.

I was way too human for this shit.

Being a mortal-born witch means that my parents weren't magical. They were as human as human can get, which isn't surprising given my past life's events. I'd been killed by that sadistic Blood Coven bitch and my soul probably wanted nothing to do with magic anymore.

Yet, when the Amethyst Coven took me in and started feeding me magic, I changed on a fundamental level. Most mortals didn't survive the process, especially when the magic was fed later in life. I couldn't remember much of it other than the sensation of constantly wanting to heave up my guts until there was nothing left.

When I spilled out onto soft grass, I held my stomach and

relived memories from my childhood. The portal had been fueled by my magic, but passing through it without the skilled protection provided by a trained coven was like going through the inside of an electric wire. There was no way I wasn't going to get burned.

I blinked my bleary eyes at the lopsided building before us. It looked so black and crooked. Man, I really was out of it.

Quinn had been the one to drag me through the portal and his grip was still on my arm. He squeezed even tighter as he followed my gaze. "We can't stay here," he said. When I didn't respond, he gave me a light shake. "Lass, I know you're tired, but I need you to stay focused for just a little while longer. Can you do that for me?"

I couldn't tear my gaze away from the smoke billowing out of the building. I'd envisioned the place I wanted the portal to take us: the guesthouse where Mr. and Mrs. Styles had made us feel welcome and safe. My blood ran cold with worry.

"What?" The single question escaped me. What was I seeing? This was some kind of nightmare, right?

Cassidy pried Quinn's iron grip off of me and wrapped her arms around me. The sobs came then when I realized that this wasn't a dream. "Hey," she whispered, stroking my hair from my face. "The vampire is right. We can't stay here, Evie."

I blinked at her and tears stung where Sarina had cut my cheek. "Why would they kill them?" I asked her, even though I knew she didn't have any answers.

Her lower lip quivered, but she sucked it into her mouth before it could betray that she was about to fall apart and straightened. That was my Cassidy. No matter what was going on she would always be the strong one. "We'll find out the who's and the why's later," she assured me, giving me a squeeze. "We can't do any of that if whoever did this finds us too."

Giving her a shaky nod, she finally released me. I glanced when a strange far-away sound trilled in my ears and I noticed Quinn sticking two fingers in his mouth and blowing. I squinted, realizing that he was whistling, but I couldn't quite hear the sound.

I could *feel* it.

The response to his summons came as a gallop of hooves that dug into the soft earth. Horses blacker than night parted from the shadows and startled me with the bright ruby glimmer of their eyes. Their sleek coats shone like midnight made flesh.

"Don't be afraid of them," Marcus said, rubbing my arm. "They're our mounts."

Four of them approached us, one of them with a white streak across his left eye going to Aaron and giving him a friendly nuzzle.

I blinked. "Wow. You guys aren't the four horsemen, right? Because I can't handle that shit right now."

Quinn snickered and patted his own horse fondly on its rump. "Maybe we are in some parallel dimension, lass, but in this life, nay, we are just ordinary warlocks turned vampires who had their familiars turned into horses."

I gave them a raised brow. "Yeah, normal. And you still have your familiars?"

They laughed together as if I'd said the most hilarious thing. "Only witches worth their salt keep their familiars,"

Marcus told me with a wink. "The covens don't want you to know that."

I gave Bast a quick glance and he only lewdly licked his lips at me, making me shiver. "Right."

We mounted the horses with Bast and Cassidy sharing Aaron's mount since he was the hardiest. Marcus and I shared his, and Quinn took his own mount which had a tint of wild red to his hooves, leaving Killian and Aaron to share the final mount who seemed about just as pleased as his master at the prospect of the two males riding together.

Marcus wrapped his arm around my waist and pulled me closer to him than was really necessary. "We ride!" he shouted and the others cheered. He chuckled in my ear. "I've always wanted to say that."

I rolled my eyes.

Men.

THE HORSES WERE INDEED familiars and had impressive magic of their own. Just as Bast had always fed me slivers of magic through our points of contact, the mounts exuded raw power and didn't seem interested in keeping it all to themselves. The air shimmered as we slipped into an in-between veil where their hooves glided effortlessly inches above the ground, floating through buildings and trees as if they were nothing at all.

The sensation was disconcerting, but I still felt corporeal, as did Marcus behind me. The more the mount bucked beneath us the more friction grinned between Marcus' hips and my butt, which seemed to encase his growing cock far too perfectly.

"I think I can enjoy this," he growled into my ear, his hand inching up to my breast.

Horrified, I glanced to see if the others could see us, but a ghostly film made it impossible to see. "No fair," I protested half-heartedly, "no one can save me from being molested." I was pretty sure if I jumped off the horse during this peculiar spell I would not be pleased with the results.

There was no danger of that, however, because Marcus held me tight against him, his cock growing even harder behind me. "When we're safe and alone, I'm going to do all the things you've been fantasizing about."

I swallowed the lump in my throat, this time not protesting when his hand went from my breast to caress low across my stomach, stopping just above the apex of my throbbing need for him. "What if I've been fantasizing about Quinn?" I countered, hoping to make the vampire jealous.

I realized my error when his hand slipped lower to possessively claim me for himself. "Then he will join us, because I'm not waiting to take you."

My cheeks flushed at the images that fluttered into my head. "Oh," I said pathetically.

Marcus chuckled. "Look, we're almost there."

Managing to focus through the haze, I watched as the other horses flanked us, Quinn on the left and the others on the right, as we rode into a gaping hole that glimmered with red around the edges.

It reminded me of blood magic, which made fear send my heart into a gallop that matched our pace.

Marcus squeezed me. "Nothing to be afraid of, Evelyn. This is a vampire stronghold. You'll be safe here."

I wanted to believe him, but not all vampires could be trusted. In fact, none of them could as far as I was concerned. My guys were my guardians and had once been warlocks, making them an exception. The rest? They'd traded their lives for immortality, bound themselves to blood magic, and not so different than witches who joined the Blood Coven.

"I trust you," I muttered, knowing that I didn't sound very convincing.

When the mists parted and the horses dropped the veil of magic, the scent of blood and the impact of prying eyes hit me, making me flinch.

Yeah, this couldn't go well.

UNDERGROUND

"Welcome to the Underground," a vampire said cheerfully. He might have looked friendly had he not had blood dripping down the side of his chin.

Quinn cleared his throat and indicated the same spot on his face to the vampire. "Uh, got something, on your, yeah, right there."

The vampire squinted at him, running his fingers over his own face, only managing to smear the blood hopelessly further. "Get it?" he asked.

Quinn grimaced. "Uh, yeah, sure."

The vampire beamed. "It's not often we get non-vampiric guests," he said, directing his attention to me. His ruby eyes lit up with more excitement than I was comfortable with. When his gaze dipped to the thudding pulse in my neck, Marcus snapped his fingers.

"Hey, eyes up here Jeff," Marcus snapped.

The vampire flinched, snapping his gaze up to Marcus.

"Right, sorry boss! Glad you're back. We'll get the rooms ready." He bowed low, sweeping his arms towards the billowing drapes that hung from a two-story column. "Right this way."

We'd landed in a shadowy chamber with columns that went high into darkness. "Where are we?" I asked, half-terrified, half-mesmerized, as I kept close to Marcus and followed him to the drapes.

"This is the entrance chamber to one of our underground strongholds." He gave me a wink. "You helped us create them."

"Oh," I said, then brightened, "of course I did."

I wasn't prepared for the sight that greeted me beyond the drapes. When I imagined a vampire underground stronghold, dank caverns and drifting corpses came to mind. Instead, I was greeted with such luxury that even the Royal Covens could be put to shame.

Long, sweeping banisters framed walkways with timeless masterpieces. Each painting was framed with swirling gold and crystal. Plush carpet gave way to marble halls and I felt dizzy following all the different trails and doors.

Jeff ushered us to hurry. "This way, please."

We followed him as a beat-up and tired crew of misfits. Hundreds of vampires conversed, stopping when they spotted us. Many had attractive human men or women on their arms who didn't seem to be under any sort of spell at all. They shyly watched us with curiosity as Jeff barked at everyone to stop gawking and mind their manners. The masters had returned home.

I gave Marcus' fingers a squeeze. "You guys are big shots around here?"

The corner of his mouth lifted in the slightest of grins. "You could say that."

We walked on in a strange silence with only our footsteps to proceed us in the echoing halls. We didn't climb any of the stairs, but followed the white marble until we reached decorated double doors.

Jeff grinned at me. "Been a long time since we had some humans to feed. The cook will be delighted."

I gave him a raised brow, hoping he meant I'd get fed and not *be* the food, but he clapped excitedly and burst open both doors, sending a series of lights flickering to life in the room that held one long table that could easily sit my entire coven. Jeff skipped—yes, skipped—to the end of the room and rang the bell.

In a puff of purple smoke a small woman appeared looking rather annoyed. "I told you Jeff, I can't make you blood smoothies!"

Biting his lip, Jeff grimaced at Marcus' glare. "We have guests, Falina."

The tiny woman planted her hands on her hips and swerved to glower up at us, but when her rage landed on my guys, her eyebrows shot up with her hands. "Masters! You're alive." She scampered, giving each of them a hug and making me blink in surprise.

All the guys seemed happy to see her and gave her a friendly squeeze, stooping to accommodate her short stature.

Quinn even gave her a quick kiss on the top of her head. Before jealousy could rip into me, I made note of how the gesture seemed familiar, as if they were brother and sister and nothing more. "Sorry to have worried you, Fal." He grinned, then indicated me with a wave of his hand. "We have two human guests for you to feed."

She clasped her hands together and her eyes sparkled with renewed excitement. "I haven't had real guests to feed in ages!" She ushered Cassidy and me to a table immediately. "Go on, make yourselves comfortable. I can sense that you're absolutely famished."

I gave Marcus a worried glance, but he only grinned wider. "I'll leave you to Falina's wonderful care."

When he turned, I scoffed at him. "Where do you think you're going?"

Quinn slipped around him to give me a quick kiss on my cheek. It was a lot more sensual as he formed his lips to my skin than he had been with Falina, so I relaxed. "We used to run this place, lass. We have a lot to catch up on." His ruby eyes sparkled with delight. "I've been dying to bring you home. We'll be safe here and you can trust the others."

I gave him a dubious look, but was soon worn down when delicious smells came from the kitchen. Falina was already cooking something with garlic, butter, and herbs and it was making the air itself taste delicious. My mouth instantly filled with water.

Quinn laughed. "That smell is like sewage to me, but you seem to enjoy it. Have a nice time." He elbowed Bast in the ribs. "Falina will whip something up for you too, kitty cat."

Bast gave him a glare. "You are not permitted to call me 'kitty cat.'"

Ignoring the familiar, Quinn sauntered off to join my other protectors as they left us alone in the hall that seemed empty with only three of us in it.

I brushed Bast's arm, but flinched when a weird static shock made me jump back. His trained sliced irises latched onto me. "What was that for?" he asked.

I rubbed my fingers where the zap had gotten me. "I was just wanting to comfort you. I guess this place has some static."

When I turned to the table, I saw that Cassidy had already taken her seat. She shivered, settling her hands in her lap as she faced her empty plate. I'd never seen her look so tired.

"Are you doing okay?" I asked, which was probably an extremely stupid question. She'd almost died last night. She'd been dragged into an impossible situation all because of me.

Cassidy's faraway look eased into a smile as she reached out for my hand. "Two days in a row I get a fine meal. I'd say things are going pretty well."

I didn't correct her that we'd been in the dungeons for longer than a day. Instead I smiled back and patted her hand. "You deserve it."

When Bast moved as if to sit beside me, I inched closer to Cassidy to give him room. Instead, he straddled me and pulled me into his crotch so that his arms wound on either side of me. I scoffed, trying to sound indignant when his unashamed hardness rubbed up against me from behind. "Do you mind? I can't eat like this when Falina comes out."

He nuzzled into my neck, the fine hairs along his chin tickling me. "You'll manage. I was worried about you." A low vibration rumbled from his core. Was he... purring? "Plus, I think you're in heat. You can't blame me for reacting to you."

A blush erupted over my face. "What? I'm not in heat. What's the matter with you?" Cassidy giggled, earning a glare from me. "You're supposed to be mortified and beat him off of me," I informed her.

She shrugged and took her napkin, unfolding it with care. "I think it's sweet." She gave me a smug grin. "Plus, I don't think he's wrong. I can smell you from here and I'm human."

I straightened. "Smell? What the fuck do you smell?"

She laughed. "It's not bad. It's like roses and jasmine, and there's something else too I can't put my finger on. Whatever it is, I only just started smelling it a few moments ago when Bast touched you. I guess it's a next level familiar bond thing." She grinned, turning her attention back to her napkin and pretending to be fascinated. "Good luck. I don't think Bast is going to last long if you keep that up."

I sniffed under my armpits, and maybe I could smell some faint magic coming from me. Bast didn't hide his interest, pressing himself harder against me and wandering his fingers over my arms, scratching lightly. When we heard sounds from the kitchen, I elbowed him in the ribs and demanded he get off of me. He finally let me be and took a seat at his own plate, adjusting his pants and looking irritated, making me grin.

Falina finally came out with a plate balanced on each hand, as well as an additional tray on each arm that she held tucked in by her chin.

"Do you... need help?" I offered, my eyes already going to the steaming treats.

Falina glided over to us, her grace and balance betraying that maybe she wasn't quite human after all. I could have sworn a little bit of pink glitter drifted from her fingertips when she set down the plates. "Nonsense. I'm here to serve you. *You* are guests of the Palace."

I gave her a raised brow. "The Palace?"

She nodded, her concentration focused on setting out the delectables in a neat row. "That's the name of the vampire stronghold you're sitting in, my dear." Taking our plates, she piled on the delights, ranging from stuffed ham, skewered fruit, to little cheese puffs that I wanted to gulp down by the dozen.

No longer caring about the thousand questions I had bubbling up in my chest, I grabbed a fork and dug in.

After I'd gulped down at least four massive bites, I stole a glance at Bast's plate. Falina had even made the same little salmon egg treats he'd enjoyed so much at the Masquerade Ball's feast.

"Don't those give you a bad taste now?" I asked around a mouthful of food.

He shoved another handful into his mouth and chewed thoughtfully. "No," he said after swallowing, "they're still delicious. I think these are even better."

Falina beamed at the compliment, having come out of the kitchen with more dishes for us to sample. "I only have familiars to cook for these days, even if they are horses. I figured a cat familiar would favor fish delights, even in his human form."

Cassidy had been devouring her food without taking a breath to speak, but she paused and put her fork down. "How could you tell he was a familiar?"

Bast puffed his chest out. "I'm the god of familiars, I'll have you know."

Falina patted him on the head, making my eyes go wide. I watched Bast to see what he'd do, but when she scratched behind his ear, his eyelids lowered and the tension swept out of him. "Of course you are, dear. I can tell."

Satisfied, Bast returned to his feast, as did the rest of us. Only when we felt sick did we finally stop and hold our stomachs in indulgent satisfaction.

Falina started clearing the table and this time I most definitely spotted the pink glittery motes coming from her fingertips. "What is that?" I asked, pointing to the drifting speck that floated through the air.

She waved it away as if it irritated her. "Since I'm half-fae, I leak sometimes. Don't pay me any mind."

My eyes went wide and Cassidy snorted on her drink. "Fae?" I asked, stunned. I knew there were a lot of supernatural creatures in the world, but some of them were myths and —pun intended—fairy tales.

Falina didn't seem proud of her heritage as she brushed away the offending pink glitter from her dress. "Yes, from my mother's side. Never met her, of course. She seduced my warlock father and then pawned me off on him." She sighed as she scooped up a handful of plates. "Oh well. That was over two thousand years ago. I really shouldn't be vexed about it now."

We all stared at her as she started humming under her breath and swept out of the room.

I gave Cassidy a knowing look and she nodded in agreement.

We were in over our heads.

IS IT HOT IN HERE?

*A*fter the plates had been cleared, Jeff appeared in the doorway, looking both nervous and excited, although I got the feeling that he always looked that way. He seemed to play the role of butler, but his half-open shirt that revealed perfect abs and the smoky makeup around his eyes gave him more of a bad-boy drunk rockstar look.

He grinned at me as I appraised him. "If her lady is satisfied with the meal, shall I show you and your guests to the bedrooms?"

I gave him a leveled glare. "Where are the others?" Marcus had told me that I would be safe here, but asking me to trust strangers was a hard pill to swallow.

Jeff licked his fingers and started straightening his hair. "They're with Tiros. Lots of handover to be done." He grinned, his fangs flashing. "Tiros isn't as happy they're back as I am. But that's okay. The masters can handle Tiros."

My fingers curled into fists. So, not everyone here was as

trustworthy as Marcus wanted me to believe. "When will they return?"

Jeff swirled his hands in the air, as if getting impatient with me. "They have lots to do. Lots to discuss. Most vampires don't sleep, but though the masters do here and there. Little humans always need their rest, don't they? High maintenance creatures." When I glared at him, he faltered. "I mean, witches too. Even more high maintenance, of course."

Rolling my eyes, I brushed past him. "Whatever. Let's go." I wouldn't admit it, but with a meal like that I was ready to turn into a puddle and sleep for a week.

Cassidy slipped her fingers through mine as we walked. I squeezed her hand with reassurance. This place was beautiful, but it was overwhelming. I got the sense that she didn't want to lose me in the winding halls and I didn't blame her. I didn't want to be by myself either.

I tried to pick up bits of conversation as we made our way through the halls. Banisters railed the upper levels and voices trickled down like rain, splashing me with just enough information to drive me insane.

"Did you see who they brought with them?"

"All this time, and now they come back?"

"Who do they think they are?"

None of it sounded good to me and I put an imaginary notch on my "do not trust" quota for any vampire in this place, Jeff included.

As if he could sense I'd decided not to trust him, he skipped around me and shoved open a door. "Best room in the house!" he declared.

Bast shoved him out of the way. "Come on, Evelyn," he said with a gruff bossy tone.

Jeff's fangs lengthened and he hissed, bringing his fingers up in faux-claw motions like Dracula, which was actually kind of adorable on him and made me giggle. He glowered at me. "This room is for the lady guest. Not for stinky cat gods."

I waved my hand at him. "It's all right, Jeff. Bast is my familiar. He's slept in my chambers all my life."

Jeff lowered his guard, but still gave us wary glares. I didn't mention that Bast had never been in his human form when we'd shared a bedroom.

"And me?" Cassidy asking, clasping her hands on her hips. "I won't be too far from Evie. I don't trust you fanged bastards, even if you are hot as hell." Her cheeks flushed as her gaze dipped to the opening at his shirt.

That made me burst out into an obnoxious laugh which I promptly covered up with both hands, then frowned when I realized they smelled of intense roses and some faint herb I didn't recognize. My eyes went wide with horror. I'd been holding Cassidy's hand, which meant...

Jeff seemed unperturbed by her interest and opened a door on the other side of the hall directly opposite my room. "The Masters instructed that you be given the second best room in the house. Please feel free to make use of all amenities."

Cassidy peered into the room, then turned and gave me a raised brow. "The bed is huge!" she declared in a whisper-yell. Then she gave Jeff a raised brow. "You don't, uh, happen to be tired?"

Jeff frowned, not catching her drift. "Like I said, most

vampires don't sleep. I couldn't sleep if I wanted to. I'm like the energizer bunny with fangs."

Cassidy giggled and ran her fingers over his collarbone. "I like bunnies," she said, her voice going low.

Finally seeming to pick up what she was putting out, he brightened. "Oh, do you? Well, let me tell you all about the bunny things I can do."

I watched them with fascination as they disappeared into Cassidy's bedroom and the door shut behind them.

Bast chuckled, taking my wrist and guided me into our room. "Look what you've done."

A FAMILIAR BOND

*M*y heat magic was definitely getting worse. The second I got close to Bast his nostrils flared and he flinched away. "If you don't want me to blow in my pants, you better not get too close to me smelling like that."

Bristling, I took a step back. "What the hell, Bast? What's wrong with me?"

Eyes dilated, he appraised me as his tongue ran across his lips. I'd never felt more like a morsel to be devoured. "Well, when I became human, it was because you'd rejected severing our bond. I'd hoped that you would want to strengthen what was already between us." His gaze grew distant. "When you met your protectors, I wasn't sure you'd have me."

Without thinking, I went to him and ran my touch up his chest. His hard muscles flexed under my care and I knew that the scent of my magic was hitting him hard, but I couldn't let him think that I ever wanted to break our bond. "You never told me what you were," I protested. "I just thought you were my friend, my familiar, when I bonded to the others."

His nostrils flared and his fingers wound through the roots of my hair, pulling my head back and exposing my neck. His lips grazed my skin and he started to purr again. With so much of his body pressed against me it was an intoxicating feeling. "I'm jealous of them, but you have gone into heat. You are reacting to our bond. Your body wants to solidify it." He grinned, testing my neck with his teeth. "It's instinct that's driving you. If you don't want this, just tell me to stop. I can leave you to your protectors if that's what you really want."

The hard need of him pressed against my hip and I did just as he said, reacted on my instincts. My hands went to his waistband, my fingers slipping under it until I met supple skin. He hissed as I found the hard length of him and gave him a confident stroke. "I will never leave you, Bast, only if you promise never to leave me."

His gaze turned hooded as he allowed me to stroke and pet him. His fingers went to my shirt as he slipped one edge over my shoulder, exposing bare skin. He leaned down and gave my shoulder a bite as if he wanted to taste every inch of me. "I am not like your protectors, Evelyn. I will be jealous when you spend time with them."

Thinking of what Marcus said to me, I smirked. "Then maybe they should join us so you don't have to part from me."

His eyes widened, then a feral grin took over his face. "You surprise me, little witch." Curling his hands over the roundness of my ass, he hoisted me onto his hips, making me let go of him to wrap my arms around his neck. He ground his hips into me, the layers of our clothes making me whimper and writhe in frustration. I could sense something in me making me impossibly horny. Literal heat wafted over my skin followed by whiffs of roses and that particular herb.

I threw my head back when Bast ground harder into me, giving me just enough pleasure to make me go crazy. "Gods, what is that smell that I'm giving off?"

He chuckled. "Do you really want to know?"

My heart thundered in my ears, but I made myself focus. "Yes," I said, looking him in the eyes. "What is it?"

With a grunt he flopped me onto the bed and pulled my dress over my head with one move. His fingers went to my underwear, one claw extending and running a line down my stomach without cutting me. He slashed the thin fabric so that it fell off of me, making me gasp as cool air hit my throbbing folds. "It's delicious," he told me, retracting his claw and running a circle around my clit, making me whimper. "It's something that drives me crazy." His irises were impossibly dilated now, his eyes dark and filled with lust. He speared one finger into me, making me cry out.

He placed another finger inside of me, burying them up to his knuckles. As he pumped me, he used his free hand to lower the zipper of his pants so that his impressive erection escaped. My mouth watered at the sight of it.

With a growl he pulled out of me, grabbed me by the hips and flipped us so that he was lying on the bed. Somehow my ass was in his face and the fullness of his dick was in mine. I stared at it, mesmerized, then moaned when his coarse tongue ran across my wet skin, awakening nerves and pleasure I hadn't felt before.

"Wow," I breathed, "your tongue." It felt amazing as he

lapped at me. He jutted his hips up, pushing his cock into my face. I took the hint and wrapped my lips around the head. I was rewarded with a groan and his cock pulsed in my mouth.

Feeling renewed confidence at the sounds of pleasure coming from him, I suckled him and tried to keep myself in one piece as he ravished me between my thighs. When I approached the cliff, I took him out of my mouth. "Bast, stop, you're going to make me—" He clamped down on my clit, making me buck in a powerful orgasm as his tongue swirled on just the right spot.

A pleasure so intense it almost hurt forced me to arch my back into the sensations. I let it jolt electricity all the way up my body before I collapsed into a useless panting heap.

Bast's cock twitched next to my face, but I was too spent to give it the care it needed. So he flipped me over, wrapped my legs around his waist and lined up his cock to my throbbing core. He grinned at me, his lips swollen and slick with my wetness. "Do you accept our bond?" he asked seriously. He ran the head of his cock over my pulsing clit, making me shiver.

"Only if you tell me what the hell that scent is," I demanded, not forgetting what we'd been originally talking about.

His grin widened. "It's catnip."

I balked at him. "Catnip?" I nearly shrieked. "Gods, I'm, oh—" When he started to push himself into me I rolled my eyes into the back of my head and no longer cared what kind of magical scent I was exuding, as long as it made him do things like that to me.

He paused just before the full width of his head could spread me open. "Tell me you want this."

The bastard wanted me to beg for it. "Yes," I said, knowing I sounded pathetic, but I didn't care. "I want you to fuck me. I want to be bonded with you."

He grinned. "As you wish, my little witch." He rewarded me by sheathing himself fully into me, making my back arch with the overwhelming girth and length of him.

"Gods!" I cried out. He was big. Too big. When he started to move I clenched my fingers into the sheets.

He lifted my hips, making his cock hit me at the perfect angle, and then his thumb ran over my clit as he moved. "Come for me," he commanded, his voice low and husky with an inhuman growl.

I opened my eyes to see his teeth sharpened and his tabby pattern starker than it was before. He moved with a steady rhythm in and out of me, never pulling all the way out as his thumb gave my nub careful attention. "I can't," I protested. He'd already made me climax too hard with his tongue. I felt both overwhelmed and numbed, but he continued rolling his touch over me as his cock slid in and out over and over again with agonizingly slow movements.

When he increased speed, he started to pant, but his gaze was relentless on me. "I will not have release until you come around my cock," he said, his dirty words making me blush.

I wanted him to come in me, I realized, which only made me blush harder. Arching into his touch, I felt the cliff approach far more rapidly than I was ready for. He moved faster, and then faster still, until his thumb was flicking over my clit with relentless lashes and his cock pummeled into me and his thighs slapped against my ass. The orgasm hit hard from his constant attention and I cried out as my whole body went rigid with the bolt of pleasure.

Bast growled with his own release, his hot seed spilling into me and making my muscles clench hard around him.

When we were both spent, we collapsed onto the bed, Bast still inside of me, and welcomed a much-needed sleep.

BAST MUST HAVE WOKEN before I did, for I had a pillow under my head and a blanket over my body. I lifted it, finding that I was still naked, but I'd been cleaned.

Then I frowned at a weird smudge over my chest. I rubbed at it, but it wouldn't come off.

Flinging off the blanket, I gasped when I realized it wasn't a smudge at all. It was definitely a tabby pattern that covered me from my neckline to my thighs.

Bast decided to come in at that moment with a towel wrapped low around his hips. He still looked a little more feral than usual, his ears extra pointed and his hair puffed out in spikes. He grinned when he saw I was awake. The grin widened as his gaze lowered. "Hi there, little witch."

Scoffing, I launched off of the bed. "Don't 'little witch' me!" I declared and stabbed a finger into his chest. "What the hell is this? Did you tattoo me in my sleep? What the fuck, Bast?" Never mind "how" he would tattoo me in my sleep. He was sneaky. I wouldn't put it past him.

He threw both hands up in surrender, which of course

sent his towel falling to his feet. His cock was already hard. "I swear, I didn't do anything. It's a result of the bond."

I frowned down at his rigid appendage. "Put that away."

He chuckled and leaned down to grab his towel. "Sorry, but you are naked, and you're my bonded mate now. If you don't want me ready for you then *you* need to put *that* away," he said, indicating my tabby-patterned breasts with a swirl of his hand.

Scoffing at him, I turned on my heel and marched to the dresser. I started rummaging through the pile of fine clothes. There were all colors and sizes, but I dug until I found cotton panties, a pair of shorts, and a tank at the bottom. Pulling those on, I gave Bast a raised brow.

He'd hooked his towel over his waist again, but there was still an unmistakable bulge between his massive thighs. He had so many muscles winding around his torso that were all rigid at once as his nostrils flared.

"I'm not giving off the scent still, am I?" I protested.

He grinned, revealing his pointed teeth that only made him look even sexier and more dangerous. "It's not as potent, but it's still there. Your inner animal isn't sated." He patted his junk lightly. "Would you like some more?"

I put up a hand in front of my face to block the obscene view, even though wetness was already building between my thighs, making me feel heated and uncomfortable. "No. No more. We are going to get out of this bedroom and go find Marcus."

Bast sneered. "You said you wouldn't leave me for them."

"I'm not!" I yelled at him, knowing that I was starting to

sound bratty but not caring. He wasn't listening to me. "You know I can't undo my bond."

"You don't have to bond to Killian or Aaron," he offered, his gaze finally going to the runes on my arm that he'd avoided bringing up until now. "At least that's two less that I have to compete with."

The blood runes that displayed my connection to Marcus and Quinn had burned through the glamour when I'd opened the portal back to Earth.

"No," I said flatly, then marched up to him and glared. I had to throw my head back to glare at him, so I'm sure I wasn't very intimidating, but I tried anyway. "Tell me, is this really about jealousy?" I'd known Bast all my life and he'd never liked my suitors, but I didn't get the sense that he really cared that I'd bonded to Marcus or that I'd started the bond with Quinn. There was something he was hiding from me.

He frowned, his arms going over his chest. The gesture made his towel fall again and I refused to look down. "It's dangerous."

I snapped a finger in his face. "Ah! There is it. You're worried about me. Why is that? What happens when I bond to all four of them?"

His frown deepened. "You'll remember who you are." His gaze dropped, raking over my body as if he could see through my clothes. "You will cast me aside when that happens. I can't compete with that kind of power." An expression crossed his face that I couldn't quite recognize until I finally realized it was self-consciousness. He scratched the back of his ear. "The covens call me a god, but you always saw right through the title."

"You think you aren't good enough for me," I said with a gasp. Grinning, I wrapped my arms around his neck and pulled him down to me, planting a kiss on his lips. "Bast. You've been there for me when no one else was. I would never cast you aside."

Even though he didn't seem entirely convinced, he dug his fingers into my hips and kissed me again, grazing his coarse tongue over mine and making sensations zing over my body. When he pulled back, his sliced irises watched me with affection. "I'll hold you to that, little witch."

COVEN'S LOSS

hen I knocked on Cassidy's door, a little voice in my head fussed at me for letting her go with Jeffery last night. What if I opened this door and found her sprawled on the ground torn open like a piñata?

There was no answer and I swallowed the lump in my throat before I tried knocking again. "Cass? You going to answer or what? I'm starting to get worried."

Finally there was a groan from the other side of the door. I couldn't make out the words, but it sounded like my best friend being very irritated for waking her up. The corners of my lips lifted.

When the door creaked open, I stifled a laugh when Cassidy answered, hair sprawled in all directions, clothes torn, and a very sleepy but satisfied look on her face. "Evie. Gods. Do I have a story to tell."

Bast snickered from behind my shoulder and I whirled on him. "You're supposed to be minding your own business!" I reminded him and he shot up his hands in defense. This time he was fully clothed so there was no danger of the gesture assaulting me with a full view of his cock.

"Hey, I just heard a lot of banging out here and was making sure my witch was okay."

Cassidy didn't seem to mind that Bast could tell what she'd been up to. She just grinned at him as if proud. "Hell yeah there was a lot of banging."

Ignoring my clearly inebriated friend—on what, I don't know—I leaned around her and shouted. "Jeff! You have some explaining to do!"

The energetic vampire peeked his head around the corner, looking even worse for wear than Cassidy. He had nail marks all over what I could see of his chest as he gripped the wall, making sure I couldn't get a look at the rest of him. "That human is crazy!" he insisted, then grinned. "So am I, so it works out." When he spotted Bast, he gestured wildly. "Dude, get over here and find me something to wear!"

Bast rolled his eyes, but brushed past us to assist the vampire.

As I ushered Cassidy to the bathroom, she blew a kiss at Jeff, giggled, and then leaned heavily against me.

Once inside the bathroom, I grabbed a hairbrush and started tackling the knots in her hair. She didn't seem to mind when the brush pulled at her scalp. "So... how're you feeling?" I asked.

Cassidy swayed slightly back and forth, leaning her head back and making a low throaty sound as I worked. "Feel amazing."

I stopped brushing. "No, really Cass, I'm worried. You're

not acting like yourself. I think I did something to you last night by accident." I bit my lip. "Remember I was in… heat?"

Her eyes blinked open and then she snort laughed. "What? Are you saying that it rubbed off on me?"

I grimaced. "That's exactly what I'm saying."

She held her stomach and laughed even harder. "Oh my gods! That's amazing." When she wiped the tears forming at her eyes, she added, "You need to go into heat more often. I just had the best sex of my life last night." She perked up. "Oh, does that mean that you and Bast…" When I didn't answer she squealed. "Gods! You had the best sex, didn't you? Details!"

Rolling my eyes I grabbed her head and forced her to look straight so I could continue working on her hair again. "Nope. Not happening." She simply gave me that goofy grin in the mirror until I finally buckled. "Okay, fine. Yes. Sex. It was… yes. The best."

The brightened. "So like, comparing to all the other times you've had sex, scale one to ten."

"Cass!" I shrieked.

She shrugged. "Hey, I want to know! Not every day I get to hear about a sex god."

I rolled my eyes. "He's a familiar god. Not a sex god. He's a god who had sex. But he's not really a god. Stop calling him that or he'll get a big head."

She wagged her brows at me. "I bet he's got a big head."

"Oh my gods, Cass, will you stop?"

She laughed, but now that I'd pulled her away from Jeff she seemed to be sobering up. She sighed and leaned back as I continued to brush her hair. I'd gotten the knots out a while ago, but it felt like she just needed the attention.

"Aren't we a sight?" she murmured as I worked. "A Royal Covens witch brushing a slave's hair."

I smirked. "Pretty sure I'm not part of the Amethyst Coven anymore." That thought gave me a lot of feelings I wasn't ready to process. On the one hand, I hated the covens. They were full of power-grabby witches who only cared about themselves. On the other hand, there were conundrums like Aunt Sandra. She'd given me a chance to escape when Sarina tried to sacrifice me. Even if a part of me still believed she had a selfish motivation for keeping me alive, she was the only family I'd ever known.

As if sensing my despair, Cassidy reached out and grabbed my wrist. Her thumb ran over the blood rune that marked my bond to Marcus. When she touched the rune that represented Quinn, a small dab of red came away. "You have a new family now and that bond is still growing," she reminded me. "Don't think I didn't notice the blood runes."

I slapped her hand away, but was grateful for her encouragement. She was right. I had people who actually did care about me and had already risked their lives for mine. I didn't have to worry about being alone anymore. "Yeah," I agreed. "Who'd have thought I would get blood runes?"

She smirked. "Are you going to get more?" She jumped up and shoved me into the chair, working on my unruly hair like she had a hundred times. "If so, I better pretty you up. Bast did some damage here."

Giggling, I let her work. Her expert fingers unwound the knots without hurting me and soon she was working the strands into delicate braids. "They're all so amazing," I mused, thinking of my protectors. "Marcus is so refined on the surface, but on the inside he's more savage than any of them. I don't think many people know that about him." I grimaced. "Unless they got on his bad side, then I guess they didn't get to live long enough to figure it out."

She smirked, seeming amused with the oxymoron that was Marcus. "I can see why you would bond to him first. He sounds interesting."

I hummed in agreement. "Yes, but I was actually attracted to Quinn first."

She laughed. "Ah, right! Who could resist an Irish accent? It's so hot."

Grinning, I enjoyed watching her laugh. We'd done this a hundred times, talking about boys while she did my hair, but this time it was different. Her laughter didn't have the bitter undertone that usually came with it and my jokes weren't just intended to make a bad situation seem less terrible. I could feel the new sensation in the air and I instantly knew what it was.

Freedom.

AFTER CASSIDY AND I had our fill of talking about boys, and she'd told me all the kinky details about her night with Jeff that I totally didn't need to know, we got dressed and met the others down in the dining hall for breakfast.

Bast had already scarfed down his meal and stood next to

me while I ate. I appreciated his protectiveness, but he did leer quite a bit.

My tabby marks were still underneath my shirt when I checked, but they had faded, which had me relieved. Maybe they only showed up when I was in heat. I wanted to ask Bast how often that might be, but I wasn't sure if I would get a serious answer. Being mated to a black cat familiar god of witches was complicated business.

Jeff escorted us to a new room, only stealing a few glances at Cassidy that included entirely inappropriate hand gestures. "You had your fun," I warned him. "Cassidy was under the influence last night. Don't think you are all *that* charming."

He actually looked hurt when I told him that it wasn't all him that had won Cassidy's affections.

Feeling sorry for him, she patted him on the arm. "I had a good time, Jeff. Maybe we'll do it again, but I don't think it'll be anytime soon."

Slumping in defeat, Jeff cracked the door open and gave Cassidy a weak smile. "If you ever want to see me again, just call out my name."

Before we could ask him what he meant, he'd disappeared using his vampiric speed.

I shivered. "Creepy. Does that mean he's going to be stalking you now in case you call his name?"

Bast grinned and Cassidy looked a little bit sick. "Probably," my familiar agreed.

Having had enough of this conversation, Cassidy scoffed and shoved the door the rest of the way open, barreling into what was apparently an intense meeting that included all of my protectors, a line of elderly wrinkled women, and a very pissed off vampire that had his fangs at Aaron's throat.

"Get off him!" I shouted, nearly sending Cassidy tumbling to the ground as I launched past her.

The vampire growled and snapped at me, then accentuated his distaste of my presence by shooting me the bird. "Don't know who the fuck you are, but you're not welcome here."

Killian unfurled his switchblade and pointed it at the vampire's eye. "Don't talk to her like that if you want to keep your pretty face."

"It is a pretty face," Bast agreed, taking a protective stance in front of me. "I could add a few scratches to it, if you like."

I promptly shoved Bast out of the way and gave him a glare. I didn't need anyone threatening someone's life just because there was testosterone in the air.

The vampire in question actually did have a very pretty face that was only marred by a small tattooed "X" beneath his right eye. The vampire growled, but backed off.

Marcus, ever the peacemaker, cleared his throat. "This is my bond-mate, Evelyn of the Amethyst Coven, as well as her familiar, Bast, and finally her human companion, Cassidy."

The vampire appraised each of us with a calculating glare. "Need to give her a new title. Perhaps Evelyn of the no-coven now that the Amethyst Coven's been wiped out."

My eyes went wide and my stomach immediately dropped at his casual statement. "What?"

Quinn cursed. "Damn it, Tiros. We needed to break it to her gently. Why do you have to be such an arse all the damn time?"

Tiros. The name sounded familiar, some vampire who'd been running things while my guys had been gone. How did he know anything about the covens? Why would the Amethyst Coven be simply wiped out overnight? That wasn't even possible… was it?

Aaron led me to a chair and helped me sit down. "She's in shock." He growled at Tiros, the sound coming from his shifter side. "Go make yourself useful and get her some water."

Tiros cursed something about not being a damned servant, but marched off anyway.

All my guys surrounded me, Bast included, as if sensing I needed their proximity just now. I relaxed, breathing in the roses and jasmine of Marcus, filling our link with strengthened magic. Even a hint of honeysuckle tinged my nose as Quinn leaned in close and massaged his fingers into the knots in my shoulders. "There, lass," he whispered, his words gentle, "we know it's a shock. We'll explain everything."

My stomach flipped. It was true. My coven was gone. "How?" That was the only word I could croak out, which showed me how much I actually cared about my coven. No matter how ready I was to move on to a new family, that had been my only home for so long that I couldn't imagine it not being there.

Marcus was the one who answered, his voice soothing me. "Do you understand the power that comes with being Anointed?"

I knew to an extent. The Anointed were the leaders of our covens, each imbued with the core of our power and in turn fed the rest of us with continued strength. It was a cycle of give and take. The link between coven members and the Anointed was strong on purpose and only severed on rare occasion. Anointed members rarely died suddenly. They all had access to witches with the Sight and knew when it would be time to undo the link. If an Anointed Witch suddenly died while the link was intact, the entire coven would feel the shockwave, but even if that happened, it shouldn't be enough to kill everyone. "They're linked," I replied numbly. "But I don't understand. Everyone is dead? Why am I still alive?" If anything had happened to Lenora, I should have felt it.

"Lenora is dead," Marcus confirmed. I went still. The leader of my coven was dead. "Sarina was able to take her down. She targeted Lenora on purpose to try and take you down with her. The sacrificial ritual had already started and she believed that if she killed everyone in the Amethyst Coven then it would be enough to finish it."

I shivered. "So she killed Lenora. It was enough to take the whole coven with her?"

Marcus shifted uncomfortably, glancing at the elderly women who had been watching the exchange quietly all this time. "We were able to save you, thanks to these rebel witches, but we couldn't save anyone else, so I'm afraid even if Sarina didn't satisfy her Blood Bond with the death of a Fate Witch, the death of an entire coven was likely enough to keep her alive for another thousand years."

The most ancient woman of the group took her cane and shakily stood to her feet. I'd just assumed these to be human women. I'd never seen an elderly witch before and my eyes went wide. "Witches?"

She chuckled. "Never met a rebel witch before? We don't

use magic for personal gain. While magic may sustain our lives into longer lifespans on its own, we don't work spells to keep our youth. When we die, we die because our time has come, not because we've been fighting it."

Cassidy seemed to be fascinated. "Not even to ease pain?" she asked, glancing down at the witch's knobby knuckles. Her entire body looked like it hurt the way she creaked around.

The witch gave her a stern look. "I will use magic to ease the pain of others, but I will not use it for natural things such as the pain that comes with age. Magic has better things it could do with its time."

Aaron grunted his approval. "A true witch worth her magic. I respect the rebels."

The witch gave Aaron a nod. She didn't seem the type to smile often, but I could tell she liked Aaron. She steadied herself on her cane and cleared her throat. "We used our magic to shield you from the shockwave, child. Sarina has committed blasphemy and the entire Diamond Coven has fallen in line with her wicked ways. If we don't stop her soon, the other covens will soon follow, or perish to feed her magic. She is a Blood Witch and has corrupted her people out of fear, likewise sacrificing those who resist her. If we don't do something soon, the rest of the covens will soon bow to her and for the first time in millennia, the Royal Covens will have a queen."

Sarina, Queen of the Royal Covens? Yeah, that sounded like a terrible idea to me.

RABBIT HOLE

"I have to see it for myself," I said. My words were stern and strong, which was a good thing. If I sounded at all how I felt then no-one would be taking me seriously. I wanted to curl up into a ball and sleep away a hundred years, but that wasn't going to solve anything. There was no more time to be the shy mortal-born witch anymore. It was time to take charge of my fate, which started with getting a grip on my situation. I needed to see the end of my coven for myself.

"I don't know if that's such a good idea," Marcus warned.

"I disagree," said the eldest witch named Phoebe, who was quickly starting to become my favorite. "Lady Evelyn deserves closure on her old life."

"She's not ready," Marcus pressed, leaning on his knee as his other hand braced on the chair, his knuckles turning white. What was he so afraid of?

His lack of confidence in me made me self-conscious and

it bothered me how much I knew Marcus could hurt me if he wanted to. He was the first of my guys that I'd really bonded to and he was also the first male who had the ability to get under my skin.

He didn't need to know that, so in a display of indifference I crossed my arms and looked down my nose at him. "I really don't care what you think," I said, trying to sound stern, but it only made me sound a little bit like a coven brat. Unfurling my arms, I sighed. "I've lived my whole adult life in that coven. If it's really gone, I need to see it with my own eyes. I hope you can understand that."

Phoebe stood up for me, literally, rising with the help of her knobby knees as she wobbled onto her cane. I knew better than to tell her not to strain herself. There was no telling how old she actually was. The fire of life burned in her eyes and I had no doubt that this elderly witch could take care of herself if push came to shove. "The young woman is right," she said, forcing her hunched back to straighten slightly. "We must all understand our past, as well as our present, in order to build a path for the future." Her wrinkled eyes shifted, taking me in with both pride and wonder across her dark irises. "I knew you in your past life. You were strong then, just as you are strong now." The side of her lips hinted at a smile. "Yet, you're different in this life. There's a light in you now that wasn't there before. I would like to see it ignited into its full potential." She turned to Marcus, her hint of a smile fading into a stern frown. "I support Lady Evelyn's decision. If you won't help her, then the rogue witches will." The women behind her murmured in agreement as soft light flashed in their eyes.

Marcus sighed and slapped his hand on his knee. "Fine. I will escort her." His ruby eyes glinted with anger and frustration. "But if she reverts, then you are the first witch I'll be coming after."

"WHAT DID YOU MEAN BY 'REVERT?'" I demanded.

Marcus refused to look at me as he stormed through the halls of the vampire stronghold. We'd left behind the others to bicker on about the future. Even Bast seemed interested to partake in the conversation. When Marcus sped out to show me the way to... whatever he was going to show me, the others had encouraged us to go alone.

The idea of being alone with Marcus both terrified and thrilled me after all we'd been through. I was grateful to him for saving my life in the dungeons, but I was also wary to tell him of my bond with Bast. No matter what he'd said, surely he wouldn't want to share me with a god.

Marcus seemed to be unconcerned with anything I might want to tell him. Gold and luxury surrounded us in a blur as we sped onwards, but Marcus was as cold as iron.

"Marcus!" I snapped, trying to snag his clothes to get him to stop. "Tell me what you meant by revert!"

He snorted. "That is none of your concern."

I finally grabbed his arm, forcing him to stop and look at me. He twisted, glared, and then ripped out of my grasp and kept going.

Stunned, I stared after him. Rage bubbled up inside of me. "Marcus! Don't you walk away from me!"

"I'm not walking away," he growled, not stopping. "You just aren't doing a very good job of keeping up."

Normally when someone talked to me that way, I was able to brush it off, but this was Marcus. Anger like I'd never felt before surged in me and I swear my vision turned red.

Stumbling to keep up with him, I growled my next question, not caring that anger made my voice tremor. "Where the fuck are we going then?"

"Scrying chamber," he said without missing a beat. I could tell that I was getting to him, though, because his fingers curled into fists. His refined visage was cracking under the pressure.

I grabbed his arm again, this time determined not to let him ignore me. Rose and jasmine scents tinged the air as I pulled from the magic at the mask on my hip. Heat burned through my arms and curled into my fingers as I gripped onto Marcus—hard.

He grunted as he tried to drag me along with him, but I dug my heels in and yanked him backwards until he was forced to my height.

"I need to go there in person," I demanded through clenched teeth. "Scrying is not what I had in mind."

Marcus stared down at where my grip held him tight. I finally let go when I realized I was probably hurting him. He readjusted his jacket and rolled his arm as if I'd nearly yanked it out of his socket. When there was a small pop and he grunted, I winced. Shit.

"This is proof of why I can't take you *anywhere* just now," he said, hissing through his teeth where very dangerous looking fangs extended. "Your magic is only growing and that'll make you a beacon for those who want to use you."

I narrowed my eyes at him. "Wasn't the whole point in bonding with you to give me my magic back? Won't that make me safer when I can protect myself?"

"No. Not until you are in full control of your powers. Right now the magic is running off your emotions. I pissed you off, right? What happens when you're afraid? Your magic will flee from you and you'll be helpless." He moved in closer, his hand going to the small of my back as he bought me close.

My mouth bobbed open to retort, but I realized he was right just as the anger flooded out of me. His touch calmed me, and the thought of being taken prisoner again had me terrified, even if I wouldn't admit it. That cell had made me feel so helpless—just as he's said, and the very thought of it made my stomach twist into knots.

"Evelyn," he said, breathing my name.

My eyelashes fluttered up to him and I almost forgot why I'd been so mad at him in the first place.

Almost.

"I can't just hide here and pretend I'm safe," I said. A flicker of power tingled around my body, surging through my core and coming to the surface in visible red wisps. I felt pretty badass until the power went straight to where I wanted Marcus to touch me—across my lips.

He grinned down at me and his thumb ran over the flickers of magic, sending it dissipating into the air like smoldering embers. "I know. This is only temporary." He took my face with both hands. "I promise you, Evelyn, that you will find out the truth. You will understand everything, in time.

For now, I will show you the truth of your coven, even if it is only by scrying. That is the most I can give you right now without putting you in danger." He came even closer until his scent threatened to overwhelm me. His breath puffed against my lips. "I also promise that I will remind you of our bond the moment I know I've done everything I can to keep you safe."

He'd been apart from me all night, which had given Bast an opportunity to claim me. A flicker of guilt tugged at my heartstrings.

"I mean to tell you... Bast and I," I began.

Marcus silenced me with his mouth. It wasn't the passionate, possessive kiss I expected, but sweet and tender. His fangs pressed against my mouth and then his smooth tongue grazed mine, a contrast to Bast's roughness.

Marcus stroked my cheek with his thumb as his eyes fluttered open. "I know." His grin widened, then he tapped his nose.

I cursed. Damn vampiric sense of smell.

"That's no damn fair!" I said, only to find Marcus shifting away from me, leaving cold air to rush in and take his place. Instinctually I crossed my arms as if to embrace the sweetness of him, which was now surely gone as he smirked at me over his shoulder. He looked far too damn sexy and mischievous for his own good.

"We'll discuss the arrangements with your familiar later," he said. His eyes dropped to my chest and I looked down, finding the tabby markings had strengthened. Damn it.

What a mess.

MARCUS BROUGHT me to a far more impressive scrying chamber than had been at the guest house on old man Styles' farm. Like everything else in the stronghold it remained underground, however sunlight and the sound of waves, even the salty taste in the air invaded the open space.

I looked up at what seemed like water with visions of the outside world just on the other side. Ripples fanned out, separated only by thin columns of silver bands that seemed to hold the infrastructure in place. When I reached out to touch the shimmering surface, Marcus pulled my hand away.

"Wouldn't touch it," he warned, then gave me a smirk. "This is a more advanced scrying chamber. The walls are spelled. Their magic is constantly surveying the best the world has to offer when it comes to the elements." He strode to the far side of the room, waving his arms wide at the broad bands of sunlight beaming down on him. He closed his eyes and sighed as he soaked in the warmth.

I gave him a raised brow. "I guess that confirms that sunlight turning you into flames is a myth."

He chuckled. "Running with you through the streets in broad daylight wasn't proof enough?"

I shrugged. "Berlin is pretty overcast. I wasn't entirely convinced yet."

He flashed his white teeth at me in a smile, his fangs having regressed. Even without his fangs he managed to look inhuman. His deceptively refined look was complete with slicked back hair and a suit. For the first time I noticed his handkerchief had now turned purple and was poking out of the vest pocket. Following my gaze, he took it out and unfurled it. "I fancied a new look," he said, as if the color of his handkerchief was a vital accessory to his appearance.

Rolling my eyes, I turned my attention back to the scenes before me. The long spanning waves that sent mist into the air intrigued me the most. "What is this place?" I asked. It seemed like something important, something I should know.

Marcus joined me and tucked his arms behind his back as he admired the view. "It's Killian's home. He refuses to go there, but I catch him here from time to time, just staring at it with a faraway look."

Sea foam lapped over itself at the shore and a sense of freedom came on a cool breeze that managed to catch a lock of my hair and send it fluttering. I smoothed the silky strands. There was so much to all of my guys that I needed to know, needed to explore. One day, I would ask Killian what this place meant to him and why he refused to return to it in person.

Marcus clapped his hands together, startling me. "Okay. Let's get this over with before I change my mind."

I glanced around the chamber. Only a wide open space greeted me beyond the illumination of the scenery displayed through the walls. "Uh, how?"

Marcus grinned, his ruby eyes flashing with power as he whispered under his breath. I recognized the witch language as he thrust his hands out, sending a wave of red power flushing through the air. It settled like fine dust and drifted to the ground.

The floor shimmered, and then it was gone, replaced with a pedestal that lifted into place. A series of lengthwise mirrors surrounded a glowing stone, all the mirrors facing outward with the closest one reflecting my shocked face.

I knew that Marcus was inherently a warlock, but it was so easy to forget that about him. His vampirism stood out with its lethality and danger. Underneath all of that instinct and hint of bloodlust was a time-witch who had more secrets than he likely cared to tell.

Marcus stalked the mirrors and I didn't miss the fact that his reflection wasn't the same as mine. It faded in and out, sometimes disappearing altogether. I paced with him until he finally settled on one. He nodded at it. "Place your finger on the glass."

Out of all the mirrors, this was the only one that didn't show his reflection at all, not even a hint or a shadow. However I stood out perfectly and I swallowed hard. "Is it safe?"

He smirked. "Having second thoughts? I can take you back to your chambers instead." He growled at the idea, invading my space with his body heat and lingering scents of roses and jasmine that made my head spin.

I cleared my throat and purposefully stuck my finger onto the glass. "Let's just get on with it."

Now that he was close to me, he didn't seem interested in backing away. He wrapped one arm around my waist, steadying me against his hip, and then extended the other over my shoulder until his hand rested atop mine. He leaned into me, pressing his weight until the glass bowed with our weight.

"That hurts," I complained.

"Patience," he whispered into my ear, the effect of his

breath on my neck sending goosebumps down my arms. He only seemed encouraged by the response and he twisted, settling what was definitely an erection between my butt cheeks.

Flustered, I wanted to tell him to lay off, but then I felt the magic.

Heat coursed through my veins as Marcus encouraged the spell, muttering words under his breath that even I, a trained witch of the Royal Covens, couldn't understand.

I ground my teeth together when the mirror shifted and an image started to come through. Marcus continued to press my finger into the glass, then forced my entire palm to lay flat. "Marcus?" I asked, my voice a plea to stop whatever he was doing. I wanted to see what had happened to my coven, but if he kept this up, he'd push me straight through the damn thing.

When the mirror rippled like water, I sucked in a deep breath before my entire body fell into it.

Holy shit balls. Did I just fall down a fucking rabbit hole?

QUEEN OF HELL

*H*ot ash burned my eyes and I tried to rub it away, but both my hands were pinned to my chest, covered by Marcus' arms that wrapped me tight.

"Don't move," he instructed, his lips right against my ear so that I could hear his nearly imperceptible whispers.

The air cleared enough for me to see the destruction—as well as the few survivors who stumbled across the debris.

No, not survivors. Sarina and the Anointed, as well as a few demon-touched wolves who somehow weren't ripping their heads off.

Sarina seemed to have no trouble getting her hands dirty as she stabbed her heels into broken planks and climbed the giant mountain of rubble. Her hair flew around her face like angry vipers and her eyes blazed with fury. "Where is she?" she demanded. "She must be here. She has nowhere else to go!"

Willa, the Anointed of the Amber Coven, scrambled over

the debris and snapped a finger at the witch as if she were an unruly child. "I told you that killing Lenora wouldn't get you what you wanted, you bitch!"

Sarina seemed to be in no mood for opposition and smacked the petite girl across the face, sending her elegant glasses flying and cracking hard over the rubble. "Don't speak to me like that unless you want to join her coven!"

The other witches flinched at the blow, but didn't move to take Sarina down. Rebecca seemed the most defeated of all as she slumped into herself. Even her emerald earrings had lost their luster and glinted nearly black in the dull moonlight.

Iris straightened and smoothed her leathers that stuck to her curves. "We've had a great loss," she reminded Sarina. It seemed to soothe the witch, although I was sure it helped that she had an Australian accent. Who doesn't love accents?

Sarina glowered. "I've lived for a long time and loss is just a part of life. They'll get used to it."

"Why do you want Evelyn so badly?" Heather asked as she swiped frizzy strands of hair away from her face. Her pearl earrings glowed defiantly and I was glad to see that not all of the Anointed had lost their nerve.

Sarina lifted her lip in a sneer. She grazed her touch over the stolen amethyst earrings hanging at her lobes that belonged to me. "Because she is *mine*."

Willa picked up her glasses and wiped them on her blouse. She winced when they cracked further. Defiantly, she settled them on her nose and peered at Sarina. "You already destroyed an entire coven. Is that not enough sacrifice to satiate your needs?"

Sarina rolled her eyes and dug into the debris, tossing

away rocks and planks with far more ease than I would have given her credit for. Apparently the death of my coven gave her some serious mojo. "You wouldn't understand. She is part of a contract. I might have sacrificed enough witches to stay alive, but my master will be expecting her soul soon."

I flinched at that, as did the other Anointed. So, Sarina served a master. The Blood Coven ran off of sacrifices and encouraged witches to serve a master, be it an archdemon or a blood stone. Something warned me that Sarina served a master worse than those two combined. It was almost like a memory tugging at the back of my mind that had my whole body shaking.

Marcus held me and I'd never been so grateful in all my life. If he hadn't been there, I might have shattered into a thousand pieces. Sarina rummaged through the remains of my home and when she overturned a pillar to reveal a broken Aunt Sandra, I nearly lost it. Her legs twisted at wrong angles and only her face seemed unharmed. It was her lifeless eyes that stared up at the sky in shock that really brought the reality of the situation home for me.

They were really dead.

Everyone I had ever known.

The tears came, hot and ugly. Marcus tugged at me to bring me back to the vampire stronghold and away from all of this horror, but I struggled against him. "She can't get away with this!" I cried as tears streamed freely down my face.

Sarina flinched at my shout, her gaze locking onto the place we were standing, but not quite focusing on us.

"This is an immersive kind of scrying," Marcus warned, "close to astral projection. She'll be able to detect you if—"

I ripped out of his grasp. "I don't care!" Rage burned inside of me, wafting fires anew that I didn't even know had been a part of my soul.

Sarina was responsible for death, and death is what had always taken everything from me. If I hadn't gotten away from her, she would have killed me too. Now she was looking for me and my guys would put their lives on the line to stop her. I saw that look of raw determination in Marcus' eyes when he should have abandoned me, but instead marched to my side and gripped my arm. Magic seared through me uncontrolled and wild, flinging electricity into the air and causing a storm to swirl above the broken remains of my home.

The other witches all started talking at once, but Sarina silenced them. A crazed grin spread across her face.

"She's here."

ALERTING Sarina to my presence was probably one of my top ten most dumbest moves ever, sitting next to that one time when I thought about stepping on Sparkles' tail to get his attention when he'd been ignoring me. I still had a small scar up my left thigh from the bastard.

Sarina didn't waste any time and shot out a blast of magic zig-zagging through the air. It had a sickly redness to it, like blood turned electrified, and it was heading straight for me.

Marcus slammed into me and sent us both crashing to the ground just in time to miss the blast of the freaking blood ray. "The fuck was that!" I screeched.

"That's what happens when you don't listen to me!" he spouted back, grabbing me and hauling me back towards the shimmer that reflected the scrying chamber on the other side of a small veil.

We swept towards it, but Sarina was already on our trail. "I can smell you, little witch!" She was almost ecstatic as she sent out another blast, this time nicking my shin and I yelped in pain as red hot embers burrowed into my skin.

Growling, Marcus extended his fangs and hissed, but I doubted there was much damage we could do to the witch when we were scrying. Speaking of, since when was scrying painful?

Marcus went for her, eyes wild and hands outstretched. Bloodlust lingered in his gaze and I knew that he'd lost himself to the vampire in his soul. And he said I had problems controlling my emotions.

I watched in horror as Marcus slipped right through Sarina. As I suspected, we weren't really here, and even though she somehow seemed to be able to hurt me, there was nothing we could do to her.

"Willa!" Sarina shouted. "I need more blood!"

The Amber witch glowered at her and crossed her arms. "You're standing on a pile of rubble and corpses. Get it from the ground. Don't expect me to cut my wrist so you can attack ghosts."

Sarina stared at her, then grinned. "Right, of course. What a brilliant idea."

Rolling her eyes into the back of her head, Sarina made a low hum and the ground rumbled.

"Marcus!" I shouted. "We have to get back!"

He'd clearly gone off the deep end. Marcus lashed out at the witch, going for her throat, but his hands and fangs only slipped through her. He gnashed his teeth in frustration.

Cursing under my breath, I abandoned the ground I'd gained back towards the veil and ran to Marcus. My blood rune lit up when I touched him and Sarina spun on me.

"I smell you," she said, her grey eyes taking on a ruby hue as she crooked her fingers and brought up a thousand droplets of blood from the ground.

This was the blood of my coven, all of it swirling in the air and forming long pointed daggers that now hurled towards my face.

I ducked, but not fast enough. One caught me on the shoulder and sent me flying. I cried out as fresh pain swept through my body.

"Marcus!" I cried.

He seemed to snap out of it when the hint of hysteria tinged my voice. His eyes cleared and he launched after me. Wrapping his fingers around the makeshift spear that had impaled my shoulder, he grunted as his skin seared against the heat.

"Get through the veil!" I commanded him. Pain tore through me when he yanked again and by the faint smell of burnt flesh, Marcus wasn't doing so well either.

"Not without you," he growled through clenched teeth. I'd never seen him like this. His once sleek hair was now tousled around his face and splattered of blood marred his otherwise perfect complexion. His whole body shook as he tried to get the spear out of my shoulder, but it had pinned me to the ground.

Sarina cackled as she danced over the remains of my coven, sending dust and particles drifting into the air. "You fool!" she cried. "You are trying to spy on me and thought I wouldn't notice you?" She swept her fingers through the air until she zoomed in on the location of the veil. "Ah, there it is. Time to sever your link home."

My blood drained from my face as she sent a perfectly aimed blood spear hurdling towards the faint shimmer that reflected the scrying chamber inside of the vampire stronghold. Once the weapon pierced through the air, the veil cracked and disintegrated into a thousand pieces.

Well, shit.

No FUCKING WAY was I going to die here, helpless and pinned to the rubble of my destroyed coven. Aunt Sandra had raised me better than this and there was one last thing she was going to do for me before she found peace.

Crooking my fingers, I commanded the wild powers that rested in the earrings at Sarina's lobes. The artifact reacted to me and tore off of her, making her release a shriek of pain that gave me a delightful moment of satisfaction.

My earrings flew through the air and closed the distance between us, landing in my hands and shimmering as they moved into the astral plane.

Putting them on, I summoned the wild powers that Quinn had awakened in me. I sensed its weakness compared to what it should have been. I would have to bond with Quinn completely to gain full control over his power, but the surge was enough to jumpstart what came next.

All of the blood still remaining in Sandra's body slipped through her pores like sweat, beading until it drifted into the air like mist, mimicking what I'd seen Sarina do.

Marcus' eyes went wide when he spotted the spell. "Evelyn, no. You cannot work this kind of magic."

"Shut the fuck up and let me concentrate," I barked at him, then I gripped the spear still embedded into my shoulder.

I was a Fate Witch, which meant that I could manipulate any magic that I came into contact with. All magic was bound up in fate, good or bad.

What I could do in theory was something entirely different in reality. I ground my teeth together as I channeled Sarina's fate. She'd stolen from me for thousands of years, using my power to divert the inevitable fate that came to all beings: death.

Aunt Sandra's sacrifice worked to my advantage as I took that untimely death that had derailed her fate, infusing its power into her blood. The droplets glowed and I grinned.

Sarina's grin had wiped off her face and now she started hurling more blood spears at Aunt Sandra's corpse. Her weapons sliced through the air, harmlessly passing through the droplets as I worked the spell as it built momentum. A low hum sang through the ground, growing louder until my teeth chattered against the unseen drums of a heartbeat.

Marcus' eyes went wide. "What the hell is that?"

What the hell indeed.

I didn't fully know what I was doing. It was the memories of my past life and instinct that drove me. When the ground finally opened up and creatures poured out into the open, I balked. I'd actually summoned demons.

I hadn't expected a woman to walk out with them who wore the most breathtaking gold glittering crown atop her head. She found me instantly, seeming to have no trouble spotting my incorporeal form. Her tight fitting blouse stopped at her midriff, revealing tattoos that swirled around her navel and glowed to life. She gave me a curt nod, and then snapped her fingers.

All of the Anointed burst into action at once, screaming different curses about "the Queen of Hell" and "damned Succubi."

When four men joined the woman from the flames, I nearly passed out. A man with swirling black tattoos that marked him as a shifter, another vampire who reminded me of Marcus, a male with a sexy smirk followed next, and finally a blonde with an internal ethereal glow that marked him as something holy. He shook the flames from his fingertips as if he still wasn't quite used to them yet.

"Let's go!" Marcus hissed, breaking my attention from the mesmerizing group.

I scrambled to my feet, almost passing out when black dots sprinkled across my vision. Marcus grabbed me before I fell.

Stumbling, Marcus guided me back towards where the veil should have been, but it was gone.

"She destroyed it," I said, trying not to get hysterical as a fight broke out behind us. I didn't even want to turn around. Somehow I'd summoned someone named the Queen of Hell who had some serious badass bodyguards. She might be my ally while Sarina was alive, but I didn't want to stick around and find out if that alliance was temporary. I'd used blood magic to open a portal to hell. What if she expected me to join the blood coven with her as my new master?

Marcus pulled a stone out of his pocket and held it to his lips as he whispered a word of power. Roses and jasmine flooded my senses, making the air shimmer and faintly revealing the stronghold once again. Marcus shoved me in without a moment's hesitation.

I landed hard as my elbows cracked against the ground. Trying to suck in a breath, I twisted onto my back only to see the mirror foggy and bent as if it was about to curl into a ball and die. All the mirrors around it had already shattered and their pieces of glass reflected the otherwise cheery scenery that surrounded the chamber.

"Marcus!" I reached for him, every fibre of my being terrified at the thought of losing him. There was so much that had been left unsaid. There was a connection between us that we'd only just reignited with a thousand years of history left buried like a divide between us. Not having the chance to understand him like he deserved gave me a deep-seated fear that left me frozen.

Just as Marcus said it would.

I had no magic when I was afraid. I'd been royally pissed off when I'd twisted fate to summon the Queen of Hell, even if it was kind of an accident. Now that I was safe and Marcus was not, I wasn't angry anymore; I was afraid.

His face shimmered in what remained of the mirror. I sucked in a breath when the woman with a glowing crown came up from behind him. She raised her hand and grinned at me. I didn't know what she was going to do. Was she going to suck out his soul? Was I going to watch Marcus die right before my eyes?

To my shock, she pushed him—hard. Flames erupted around him with a red haze of power that hit me in the chest, and then he came barreling through the mirror before it finally folded in on itself and glass shattered all around us.

"Marcus!" I shouted as I dove onto him, not caring that glass dug into my palms as I scrambled across the floor. He grunted when I pulled him up and wrapped my arms around him as tightly as I could. "Praise all the gods. You're okay, aren't you?"

He coughed. "I will be." He untangled our arms, not seeming phased by the amount of blood that covered both of us.

Sarina's spell, as well as mine, had done some serious damage and we were hopelessly drenched. Marcus didn't even have his fangs out, which gave me chills. Did he really care for me so much that he could overcome his bloodlust?

"Hey," he said, taking my face with both hands and forcing me to look at him. "We're okay now."

A sob mixed with a laugh escaped me. Fear had been choking the life out of me and I finally let it go. Without its strings to keep me up, I tumbled into his chest. "Don't ever do that to me again," I murmured against him as I dug my fingers into the tattered remains of his suit.

He chuckled. "Next time when I tell you something is a bad idea, will you listen to me?"

I punched him, although it was like hitting a brick wall. "Douchebag! I couldn't have known that Sarina would be there." My whole body shivered at the sound of her name. There was power in names and I didn't want her magic to find us here, so I pressed my lips into a thin line and vowed not to say her name again.

Marcus shushed me and wrapped his arms around me until I felt like I was in a soft cocoon of his protection. I was a strong woman when I needed to be, but just now, I needed to fall apart while Marcus held me together.

"Why could she see us?" I asked finally when my fear had subsided enough for me to speak. "And who the fuck did I summon?"

He chuckled again, this time untangling me and brushing away hair that had stuck to my face with slick blood. "Sarina is a powerful witch. I didn't know that she would be there." He paused, then sighed. I was glad that he didn't point out that we might have remained hidden had I not lost my cool. She hadn't noticed us until I started screaming. "The woman you summoned," he continued, surprising me as his chin puffed out with pride, "is an ally against the Echoes of Calamity. In fact, she's responsible for stopping the first wave, if the prophecies are to be believed."

My eyes nearly bugged out of my head. "The *first* wave? You mean the world almost ended and I didn't even know about it?"

He ran his thumb across my lower lip, still smiling at me, but now a flicker of desire burned in his gaze. I wasn't sure if he was getting worked up because I was sitting on his lap, or because the scent of blood clung around us, leaving a metallic tang in the air. "Why don't we get you cleaned up, first, and then I can answer your questions with a clear mind."

Feeling slightly disappointed that it was the blood that had piqued his interest, I pushed away from him, but he grabbed my wrists and hoisted me up with him, keeping me close to his body.

"I mean, let's get cleaned up, together." When he bent down and licked across my lower lip where he'd been staring, it sent heat gathering between my thighs.

"Okay," I said, hoping I didn't sound too eager. I bit my lip. If Bast saw me like this he'd lose his shit and blame Marcus for almost getting me killed when it was really all my fault. I was the one who'd demanded he take me scrying. "You got a room yet? Mine is kind of far away."

Marcus grinned, seeming to know my real reason for not wanting to go back to my room, but he nodded anyway. "My chambers are just this way."

A BOND TO REMEMBER

I hadn't expected Quinn to be waiting for us when we arrived. He didn't seem the type to sit and read, but just as Marcus opened the door for me, I caught Quinn sitting by a roaring fireplace with a glass of wine—that wasn't wine—and his nose buried in a book. He glanced up at us, then stood so abruptly that his chair flipped behind him. "By the gods, lass, what happened? Are you all right?"

Marcus chuckled and his torso brushed my chest as he squeezed past me. When I gave him a dirty look, he shrugged. "Okay, so this isn't my room. I brought you to Quinn's."

"Why would you..." My voice trailed off as Marcus gave me a knowing look.

He stroked my earrings and offered me a weak smile. "Because you are weak without all of your magic returned to you. I underestimated you, Evelyn, and I won't do it again." He brushed his lips across mine before taking my hand. "Your bond with Quinn is close to completion. If you accept him, trust him, then you will have everything he's safeguarded for you."

When Marcus marched us into the room and placed my hand in Quinn's, I shivered.

Quinn looked between the two of us with his eyebrows shot all the way up. "Marcus?"

Marcus had already shut the door and peeled off what remained of his jacket. His muscles cut through his silk shirt, leaving little to the imagination. "You're cementing your bond, tonight." Normally I didn't take well to orders, but perhaps this one I could get behind.

Quinn looked as if he was trying not to smile, but the side of his lips ticked up. He looked down at where we were still holding hands. "Was that your request, lass?"

My vision wavered and I found myself stumbling closer to Quinn. He caught me with ease, holding me up by my elbows and tucking me into the crook of his arm. "Quinn," I said, my voice breaking. I'd seen the utter destruction of my coven, my life, and I'd nearly lost Marcus all because of my foolishness. The tears came when I thought how close I'd been to losing everything. If Sarina had won, if she'd managed to kill me, my guys would have been left alone all because I hadn't listened.

He shushed me, stroking strong fingers through my hair as he pulled me close. When I sniffled and looked up at him, I saw that his fangs had extended. My gaze lingered on them. "The blood?" I asked. I knew I was still covered with it and probably looked like a victim from a horror movie.

He chuckled, the low sound sending a thrill through me. "Nay, lass." His fingers ran down my arm, brushing a circle around the rune that bound us together. "This."

A blush crept over my face. He meant that he was excited about the idea of fulfilling our bond. When he lifted my chin and took my mouth with his, I breathed in his magic of honeysuckle and grassy fields. He was always so wild and free and as his tongue danced with mine, I felt my sadness slipping away.

When another set of hands found my waist, I stiffened. I broke the kiss with Quinn to find Marcus behind me, fangs extended and eyes hooded. "Ready for a bath?" he asked, but I didn't miss the mischievous grin that came with his innocent question.

"With... both of you?"

Quinn answered by nipping at my neck and I squeaked. "We used to share you together," Quinn whispered, his voice husky. "Do you think you'd be okay with that?" He glanced at Marcus, grinning. "You've already bonded with this bastard. Being together will make your bonding with me... smoother."

My mouth bobbed open and closed like a fish and no sound came out. Marcus saved me by taking my hand and guiding me to the bath. The sweet scent of his magic hit me like an invisible wall when I stepped inside. The luxurious room was garnished by rose petals and soft eternal purple flames danced in the air. The testament to the Amethyst Coven brought a smile to my lips.

The steaming waters looked so welcoming that I didn't even feel shy when Marcus and Quinn peeled away my clothes, first lifting my shirt over my head and then pulling my pants over my hips. When I was left naked, I turned, my eyes dipping to the barriers that kept their bodies from my gaze.

They were both too engrossed in devouring me with their eyes to notice my silent request. Quinn's gaze raked over me with fresh hunger, and Marcus finally licked his lips as if I was a morsel he was ready to savor.

I cleared my throat as a blush finally found its way over my face. A part of me felt that this was all going way too fast, but I tried to listen to the deeper, ancient part of me that craved to reunite with the vampires. Marcus and Quinn *knew* me, cared for me, and would die for me. Fuck, they actually *had* died for me. Taking on vampirism was not something to take lightly and I appreciated their sacrifice more than they could know.

Marcus stayed back while Quinn came to me first. I wasn't fooled by Marcus' refined appearance. He could be vicious and dangerous, which both frightened and thrilled me.

Quinn, however, had a sense of freedom that made me feel carefree, as if I hadn't just almost died by the hands of Sarina —again.

"We'll go at your pace," he told me, taking my hand and placing it on his chest. His taut muscles were hard under my touch and I felt for a heartbeat, but there was none. Only the small quiver and his breath that told me what I was doing to him.

Glancing up at him once, I met his gleaming ruby eyes and smiled. "Can I take this off?" I asked, tugging at his shirt.

He grinned. "Only if you want to see what's underneath."

My fingers seemed to move of their own accord as my fingers trailed down his chest and curled around his shirt, lifting it up to expose the tight V that delved into his pants. It was the hottest thing I think I'd ever seen and I paused as I leaned in to admire him.

I didn't realize my mistake until it was too late. By leaning in, Quinn had gotten the wrong idea, and a sudden hardness pushed against his pants. I don't know why I did it, but my instincts seemed to know what to do as my fingers abandoned his shirt and moved down to stroke the bulge.

Quinn hissed and closed his eyes. "Lass, that's the opposite of taking off my clothes."

I grinned because I realized he was holding himself back from touching me, as was Marcus who was out of arm's reach watching my exploration. All of his attention was on my lips and I grinned, knowing what I had to do next. These were dangerous vampires and if I wanted to be in control, I needed to show them I had power over them.

Lifting Quinn's shirt again, I ran my tongue down one of the sharp lines of his abdomen, making him buck against me. I was ready for it and slipped my fingers into his waistband, holding him in place as best I could without magic.

My mask was still attached to my pants and out of reach, but I had my earrings. With one finger I stroked the delicate gems and extracted a sliver of magic. As if it wanted me to bond with Quinn, the magic came easily, making the air around us dance with vibrant amethyst hues. With one swift motion I sent the magic through the clothing, disintegrating Quinn's clothing into purple glimmers that left him suddenly naked before me and my mouth dropped open.

Marcus chuckled. "There's our girl, Quinn. She's remembering."

I knew Quinn wanted to believe that my memories of my

317

past life were coming back. Perhaps my instincts were there of who I used to be, but I didn't have any memories. Even so, the look on Quinn's face when he finally opened his eyes made my heart race. There was hunger there, yes, but also relief. He slipped his fingers through my hair, gripping at the roots to tilt my head back, and then took me in the most passionate kiss I'd ever had. His tongue grazed mine and his body came flush against me. His erection pressed into my abdomen, but Quinn didn't seem to mind or to be shy about it.

When my hands lowered, trying to stroke him, he released me and grabbed my wrists. "I will be inside of you soon," he promised, then looked to Marcus, "but if I take you first, Marcus might explode in his pants."

Marcus gave Quinn a glare. "That only happened once."

Snickering, I crooked a finger at Marcus. He'd been making dirty promises to me ever since we'd arrived and I had a feeling he would have no issue delivering.

He adjusted himself before obeying and coming within my reach. My magic still hummed in the air, now growing stronger with Marcus under my fingertips. My eyes widened when I realized that I didn't need my masquerade mask to access its magic if I touched Marcus. Testing it, I called on the roses and jasmine that played in the air. Magic whispered, throwing my hair back and obeying my command as Marcus' clothes transformed into rose petals landing in a soft pile at our feet.

Marcus grinned, his hand gripping me by the roots of my hair just as Quinn had before he took me with a kiss. Unlike

Quinn, Marcus' kiss was claiming, devouring, and left me breathless when he finally pulled away.

It felt right with my guys, easy and natural. Taking both their hands I guided them to the steaming waters. The cool air on my skin was making me shiver and slipping into the warm embrace of the bath made me sigh.

Quinn guided my hips and settled me onto a stone bench hidden by the water murky with oils and a slight glimmer of magic. My blood runes hummed across my arm, the one that represented Marcus alight with power, and the one that represented Quinn hungry to be completed. I lifted my arm above the water to look at it, finding a single droplet of blood escaping the rune in protest of the delay.

Quinn was quick to lap the blood up, his tongue grazing over my arm and making me shiver. His fangs grazed my skin with their cool danger, but he didn't bite down.

When Quinn moved his kiss to my neck, I arched to give him access and my eyelids fluttered as sensations swarmed through me.

Marcus joined me on my other side and his hands disappeared under the water, moving to stroke and play with my breasts.

It was so hard to believe that this was actually happening. I lowered my hands into the water and reached out for both of them as if to assure myself this was real. I found their cocks, Quinn in my left and Marcus my right, and when I squeezed their moans elicited a new shiver through my body.

Quinn's fingers found me first while Marcus continued to work my breasts. He kissed me, but I gasped because Quinn had already found my clit and ran his fingers around it in enticing circles.

When his fingers slipped inside of me, I hissed in a breath and went still.

"Relax," Marcus instructed, nipping the bottom of my lip. "We are here to pleasure you."

I still had ahold of their cocks and I made a determined stroke down with both, making them groan. "What of your pleasure?" I asked. The desire to taste them was making me dizzy.

Marcus shared a knowing glance with Quinn. "Is that what you want of us?" he asked.

I nodded as heat gathered between my thighs. They both stood so that their balls just crested the water, bearing themselves to me and I licked my lips. They eased closer so that I could keep hold of both of them.

Licking up Marcus' shaft, his thighs bulged, but he didn't move. Moving to Quinn next, I tasted him, and he seemed to have lost his patience. He angled his cock down and moved his hips forward, testing the head across my lips. Indulging him, I took as much of his length as I could.

"Fuck the gods," Quinn groaned, then hoisted me up, making me squeak. He flipped me over and growled in my ear. "You know better than to tease me."

His cock nudged at my entrance and my blood rushed between my thighs in anticipation. "I'll do as I please," I told him as I struggled to turn around, but he wasn't having it and he pushed a fraction inside of me, making me collapse onto the wet tiles as the first wave of pleasure swept through me. It was both torment and relief as the pressure spread me open, but he hadn't moved in any further, not how I wanted.

When I angled my hips back to take more of him, he held me still and waited as Marcus got out of the water and sat on the tiles, holding his cock in front of my mouth. Distracted by the beauty of him, I admired the long veins that wound about his shaft before tasting him.

Quinn thrust in the moment Marcus tilted his head back in pleasure, making me scream. With all of Marcus in my mouth, it only came out as a strangled gurgle. He grinned, seeming to enjoy it.

Quinn stilled, completely buried inside of me and my body burned for him to move, to fuck me and to complete our bond. I felt it on the brink like a thread ready to snap. "Do you trust me?" he asked.

Through the haze of desire I almost missed the fear and doubt in his voice, the lasting pain of whatever had happened between us in my past life a barrier that needed to come down. I wished I could remember what it was that had all my guys so terrified. Marcus had said he was afraid that I would "revert," and whatever that meant, I only knew that there was no one else in my life that I had come to trust more than my protectors.

Marcus shifted backwards so that I could speak and he lifted my chin up so that I could match his gaze. "Answer him, sweet witch," he said, his voice a throaty growl that demanded I be quick about it.

I wiggled against Quinn even as he tried to hold me still. "I trust you, now fuck me before I lose my mind."

His fingers tightened on my hips and I felt him harden

impossibly more inside of me. "As you wish, my witch," he said, and then began slow, torturous thrusts that made my eyes roll in the back of my head.

Marcus moved to my side and his fingers found my clit, working me into a tingling, heightened sense of pleasure. I reached out and found his cock, somehow finding the strength to stroke him as he pleasured me.

"Come for us," Marcus whispered in my ear, making me attempt to push my thighs together, but Quinn used his knee to push my legs apart, giving Marcus more access to ruthlessly stroke my clit. "You have accepted us," he said, a devilish grin in his words, "and now you'll give Quinn your pleasure."

I had almost forgotten that Quinn was part incubus. A tingle of his magic sent little bites all over my body, giving me pain and pleasure at my nipples and around the sensitive skin where Marcus stroked me, circling my clit and never easing up on the merciless pleasure. My vision started to sprinkle with stars as the cliff came closer. An orgasm so powerful was on the other side and it frightened me. If I fell so hard, could I ever get back up again?

Quinn pulled out of me just long enough to flip me over. He spread my legs and pushed inside. With my clit so exposed, Marcus was able to touch me, not seeming to care if he grazed Quinn's cock that never stopped pounding into me. As Quinn increased his movements, his low pants and groans making me go crazy, I realized he was just as close to the edge as I was. The bond between us had become impossibly taut and was ready to snap into place.

Something inside of me unhinged and I stopped trying to close my legs. I arched into Marcus' touch, let Quinn's cock slide a little bit deeper into me and I embraced all of the sensations they were giving me. These were my protectors, my lovers, and they deserved all of me.

When the climax came, my entire body went taut and I spasmed around Quinn's cock as I cried out, forcing him over the edge, sending his hot seed inside of me. Marcus took over where my hand had stilled and pumped himself until his seed covered my breasts.

A sharp pain radiated up my arm and I knew my blood rune had locked into place.

Quinn's hands stroked my quivering thighs as he rested, still inside of me. I realized that I was covered with Marcus' mark, and inside I had accepted Quinn's.

"Evie," Quinn breathed, "you're so beautiful."

Marcus smiled, his eyes saying how much he agreed.

I blushed, because I had never felt more beautiful and wanted in all my life.

AFTER I COULD FEEL my limbs again, I took another bath and indulged in the oils that rested at the edge of the tub. I hummed with raw pleasure when Quinn washed my hair and Marcus took a cloth and cleaned my body where he'd made a mess. It felt so good to be taken care of.

After toweling dry, I tested my control over Quinn's magic. I didn't even have to touch the earrings as his power slipped through me. I hadn't realized that before I'd completed our bond, there'd been a slight zing of pain that came with the flush of honeysuckle and cut grass, but now I only felt a sense of freedom and warmth. I used the magic to dry myself just enough that I wouldn't have to deal with the cold chill of the air when I left the steamy bath.

Quinn seemed pleased as he wound his fingers through my hair. "How does it feel?"

I leaned into his touch. "Natural," I admitted.

Marcus pressed a kiss to my cheek. "As it should be. We carried your magic for a thousand years, but it has always belonged to you."

A frown tugged at my lips. "Isn't it your magic as well?" I countered. "There are scents that come with it every time I use your magic." I brushed my fingers over Marcus' broad chest. "Roses and jasmine," I told him, then leaned into Quinn's neck to take in a deep breath through my nose, "honeysuckle and freshly cut grass."

They both looked at me like I was crazy. "You sure I didn't hurt you, lass?" he asked, genuinely worried. "Was I too rough?"

I chuckled. Sure, very sensitive parts of me were already sore, but I loved it. "You really can't smell it?"

They shook their heads.

With a shrug, I dismissed their inability to smell magic. Maybe it was a Fate Witch thing.

The bed was so enticing when I went into the dimly lit room. It was big enough for six people—which sent a scene through my perverted brain before I could stop it. I'd bonded with Bast, Marcus, and Quinn, but there was still Aaron and Killian to explore. This bed could fit all of us.

"I may not be able to smell magic," Quinn said, his voice dropping lower as his hands slipped around my waist, "but I can smell when your thoughts turn dirty. Your arousal gives you away, lass."

Blushing, I tried to swipe him away. "Stop smelling my arousal!" I commanded, eliciting a growl from him as he lunged for me. I twisted, but only managed to send both of us tumbling into the bedsheets as I squealed.

Marcus chuckled. "Round two? This one's mine, Irish bastard."

Quinn clutched me around the waist and bit down on my neck in response. His fangs didn't break my skin, but I suddenly felt very... claimed. He growled at Marcus in warning, but I sensed the playful competition between the two.

Marcus only seemed turned on by the challenge and climbed into the bed.

If sleep had been what I'd been going for that night, then I sorely failed.

INFILTRATION

I was one hundred percent passed out by the time morning came. Someone beat against our door and I groaned, throwing a pillow over my head. I'd had so much sex and magic that I felt hung over. "Too loud!" I complained.

Quinn chuckled. "Yes, you were far too loud when Marcus made you come all over his cock last night," he said, making my thighs clench in remembrance. "It was almost as hot to watch as when I came inside of you."

"Just get the door," Marcus said with a laugh. "Poor Evelyn needs a break." Even as he said this, he slipped his hand under the covers and pinched my nipple, making me throw a pillow at his face.

Quinn gave me one more lasting smirk, then opened the door. Killian barreled into the room, eyes wild. "We have a problem," he began, "there's..." His words drifted off as he spotted me and a long silence settled into the air.

"Can it wait?" Marcus asked.

Frowning, I pushed away from him, which was to no avail given his vampiric strength pitted against my sex-satisfied noodle limbs. Why did Marcus always have to be so competitive?

Killian recovered from his surprise and glowered at Marcus, as if sensing the claim the vampire was already making over me. He might have been willing—even glad—to share me with Quinn, but I sensed he didn't share such a benevolent relationship with Killian.

Killian's fingers went to his pocket where he kept his switchblade. Not a good sign. "No, this can't wait," he said, his words ground out through gritted teeth. There was an extra slur to his words and I noticed that his fangs had sprouted as well. "We've had a breach," he added with a sense of dread and finality.

Instantly serious, Marcus shot up, sending the blankets unfurling off of my body. Since I wasn't wearing any clothes, and I still barely knew Killian whether he was my protector or not, I squeaked and pulled the sheets up to my chin.

"West Wing?" Quinn asked, ignoring my dilemma.

Killian wasn't so oblivious of my apparent nakedness and instead of staring, pointedly kept his gaze averted, pretending to be fascinated with a spot on the wall. "East Wing," he corrected Quinn, his fingers slipping his switchblade free from his pocket.

"Shit," Quinn muttered. He rushed to the dresser and rummaged through it until he found an undershirt, then tossed it to me. Since my hands were still gripping the sheets to protect my irrational modesty, the cloth hit me right in the face and tumbled onto the bed.

Marcus, ever the gentleman, eased out of bed and held one of the larger blankets up, blocking me from Killian's view. I spotted my underwear and pants crumpled on the floor well out of reach, so I slipped the shirt over my head, grateful it was long enough to tug over my thighs, as I awkwardly got out of bed and picked up my things before bolting to the bathroom.

Pressing my back to the door, I released a heavy sigh. A drone of male voices kicked up on the other side and I cursed my mortal-born hearing. They would take advantage of my absence to bicker—most likely about things that had to do with me—and I wanted to know what Killian had meant by a breach, and why it was important which Wing he was talking about. I had no idea how large the stronghold was, or which Wing we were currently in, but I had a feeling my protectors would want to keep me out of it. They were good at that.

Glancing around the bathroom, I opted for the logical course of action. Eavesdropping. Yep. Totally mature in this situation.

My gaze landed on a razor and I didn't hesitate, slamming it on the ground and plucking up the blade that popped free. The drone kept going on the other side of the door, the guys likely too preoccupied to pick up what I was about to do. Before I could change my mind, I nicked my finger and winced at the ice-cool pain that throbbed at the wound; a pain unique to razor cuts. I much preferred regular blades.

Audiunt, I whispered the Latin word for hearing and the

spell leapt into action. Taking hold much faster than I'd anticipated, magic sent a sharp ringing through my ears. I grabbed onto the sides of my head and tried to adjust to the flooding of sensations and heat. Instinct made me draw from Quinn's magic in my earrings. It fueled the power of my spell and I altered the flow into a more manageable trickle, sending the roar of my surroundings into a dull ache until I could pinpoint the voices outside.

"I thought we agreed that we wouldn't bond with her, not yet," Killian's voice growled low and was barely perceivable even with my magically enhanced hearing.

A moment of silence passed and I wondered if my spell had stopped working. It gave me time to question what Killian really thought of me. He and I hadn't gotten a chance to really get to know one another, but maybe I'd made assumptions where I shouldn't have. He was one of my protectors, but maybe he didn't see me in the same way the others did. Just as that doubt started creeping over me, it was instantly smashed into a thousand pieces as another growl sounded, this time possessive and threatening. "You know how I crave her, yet I've kept my distance and kept my dick in my pants because I *care* what happens to her. Can you assholes say the same?"

I expected Marcus to play the peacemaker, but then a punch landed and the scent of roses lingered in the air. Marcus was losing control. "Never tell me that I don't care about her. I love her more than I love time itself. Who do you think put the loophole in our punishment for Evelyn to reconnect with us when she reincarnated? I couldn't imagine a life without her, especially an immortal one."

"Then why did you bury yourself in her?" Killian whisper-shrieked, likely thinking he was keeping his voice low enough that I couldn't hear from the bathroom and a slight pang of guilt spread through my chest, but I kept listening. "Why would you bring her to Quinn? Now she's in danger of..."

Marcus cut him off just when Killian was about to reveal something important about me. "That's precisely why I bonded with her and why I requested Quinn to finish what he'd started. Starving the bond only weakens her. I see that now. She almost died twice because we've been trying to keep the truth from her, keep her magic from her. Sarina won't stop and she almost won because we were too dumb to see that Evelyn is stronger in this life. Much stronger than any of us has given her credit for."

"You see what you want to see," Killian growled, seeming unmoved by Marcus' sincerity.

"All we've been doing is depriving her of what she needs," Marcus countered. "Of what *we* need." A shuffle of feet sounded and I knew that Marcus had gotten close to Killian as tension made the air go taut. "I fucked her, then I fucked her again, and watched Quinn bury his dick in her. I'm glad you weren't here to stop it, because now I see what you are. You're a coward."

Killian roared, the sound blistering into my amplified senses as he slammed into Marcus and they went crashing into the furniture. Something fell, sending a sharp ring stabbing into my eardrums and warmth trickled down my neck before I managed to disperse the spell. I dabbed at my skin, my fingertips coming away stained with red.

I washed off the blood as quickly as I could—no way was I

going to enter a room with enraged vampires with blood on me—before I opened the door. Marcus and Killian tumbled over the floor trading blows with each other's bloodied faces. Quinn watched them, arms crossed, with an amused grin on his face.

When I moved to stop the testosterone-fueled fight, Quinn shook his head. "This has been building up for quite some time, lass. Let them duke it out."

My jaw dropped open as fangs flashed and blood splattered across the carpet as Marcus and Killian upgraded from punches to vicious bites.

Just when I thought they were going to shred each other to pieces, a low, feral growl filled the room, making everyone turn to stare at a very pissed off wolf in the doorway. Aaron snapped his maw, growling until Marcus and Killian finally untangled themselves, chests heaving and red eyes aglow with murder.

All the vampires seemed ready to strangle one another, although I wasn't entirely sure if it was for the same reasons. Marcus was protecting my virtue, or some shit like that. Killian thought Marcus was putting me into danger, although I wasn't entirely sure why. Then Quinn just had this sadistic kind of look about him that said he'd thoroughly enjoy watching them all tear each other apart, and finally, Aaron shifted back into his vampire form, standing naked and looked ready to take a bite out of each of us for wasting his time.

I tried not to let my gaze dip, but I was worse than a guy, I swear. I couldn't help but take in all of the perfect lines and hard muscle that made up Aaron's body. He looked like a roman statue come to life, athletic but dangerous. He had the scars to prove it. His wild eyes found mine and he lifted a lip in a primal snarl. Marcus rushed between us. "Get your beast on a leash," he commanded, his voice strong and authoritative and more in line with the Marcus that I was familiar with.

Unimpressed, Aaron rummaged through the dresser and found some pants and slipped them on. "You're one to talk," he said, jerking his chin at me. "Didn't Killian tell you we had a breach? Or were you all too busy fighting over a girl?"

"Excuse me!" I shouted, pushing Marcus aside. He could have stopped me, but he chose to move, making my indignation much more satisfying. "This *girl* is right here."

Aaron rolled his eyes at me. "I can see that, cub."

Did he just fucking call me a cub? No, he did not...

"Who's been taken?" Marcus asked, oblivious to the insult. "Was it Sarina?"

Aaron's anger seemed to seep out of him and his gaze fell onto me again, this time somber and pained. "Yes, and they only took one person."

Quinn straightened and crossed his arms. "All that trouble just to take one vampire? Seems like a waste."

Aaron rubbed the back of his neck. "Not a vampire—a human."

My eyes went wide. There was only one human they could possibly be talking about.

Cassidy.

THE EVIL WITCH that had killed me in one lifetime now had my best friend in the whole world. She'd already destroyed my entire coven and now she'd found a way to burrow into the one place I thought I was safe and snatch the last connection I had to family. My guys might be building a new family, but Cassidy and I were like sisters. I couldn't imagine anything happening to her and my heart pumped a million miles a minute just thinking about what Sarina might be doing to her right now.

"You need to calm down, lass," Quinn soothed, rubbing my arms as if trying to bring life back into my shivering body.

A deep cold had settled into me when they'd told me the news and I couldn't seem to shake it. My body succumbed to relentless tremors and even my teeth chattered. I clenched my jaw trying to stop the evidence of my terror that was running rampant through my body. My knuckles went white as I gripped the sides of my chair and tried to ignore the growing pressure in my chest.

Marcus had retrieved Bast sometime after Aaron had dropped the bomb on me that Cassidy was in the enemy's clutches. My familiar wrapped his arms around my shoulders and purred against my neck. His attempt to comfort me made tears burn in my eyes, as well as push the shame I was feeling to the surface. I should be jumping up to my feet and running after Cassidy, not sitting here cowering in overwhelming fear, but I couldn't move if I wanted to. I could hardly breathe.

"You're having a panic attack," Bast whispered in my ear without any judgment in his voice. Just a matter-of-fact statement of what I was experiencing. "You can't stop it. All you can do is let the fear run its course. A panic attack isn't about forcing it or controlling it, but surviving it. That's all you need to do, Evie. Survive."

I released a shaky breath, not realizing that I'd been holding it. Without realizing it I had been trying to stop the fear from crushing me, but Bast was right. Fighting it was pointless, so I let it wash over me in a single crushing wave. Instead of panicking when my chest went tight, I pretended I was inside a dream where I was drowning, forcing myself to take a deep breath even though every instinct told me that I would sputter and succumb to death. I didn't die. The breath came and filled my lungs and I breathed through the tidal wave that tried to drown me.

"How did you do that?" Quinn asked with a raised brow. He'd been watching us this whole time looking as if he wanted to push Bast away and comfort me himself, but had stayed back.

Bast stroked my arms, up and down, then again, soothing me to the rhythm of the waves that crashed over me as if he could sense them. "She's always had panic attacks, but I was able to stem the worst of them when I was her familiar. Now..." he frowned, looking down at me and the tabby-cat lines around his face seemed even starker against his features. "In some ways I can offer her more power, but in others, I cannot access her thoughts and emotions like I could in my feline form. This is the best that I can do."

I blinked at him, wide-eyed, amazed that he'd done so much for me all my life and I hadn't even known. Thinking back to those times when Aunt Sandra cornered me, or

Sapphire Coven brats tried to make me feel like shit, I'd felt a pang of fear that was quickly swept away. Until now, I'd never realized that it had been Bast who'd taken that fear from me.

Feeling vulnerable, I tried to shrug off his arms and he immediately responded, shifting away from me and giving me space. His warmth and musky scent lingered on my skin in spite of his sudden absence. "I think I'm okay now," I said, my breath still shaky. I matched the gaze of each of my guys who'd been watching me. Marcus leaned against the dresser wearing a simple t-shirt and slacks, his hair still tousled after the night's events. Quinn knelt at my feet and rested one hand on my thigh, gazing up at me with fascination and adoration. "Are you sure, lass?"

I nodded. "Yes." Standing, I tried not to wobble as black spots sprinkled over my vision. "We have to go after Cassidy." That was the right thing to do. She would do the same for me in a heartbeat.

Killian flicked out his switchblade. Silver metal flashed in a fantastic display as he danced it over his knuckles. "That's exactly what Sarina wants. We'd be walking right into a trap."

I hadn't missed the slip that Killian had said "we," but I didn't comment on it. Wherever I went, my protectors would follow.

"I agree," Aaron said, having shifted back into his vampire form. He wore a borrowed pair of trousers and every beautiful muscle was display as he crossed his arms over his naked chest. He narrowed his eyes and his arms bulged, sending his tattoos rippling with his movements. "There's no way you're going to let Sarina get you just because she nabbed your slave. It's too dangerous."

Before I could correct him that Cassidy wasn't a slave, Bast surprised me by releasing a growl that could match a shifter's impressive warning. He loved Cassidy just as much as I did. She was family. "You don't get to make decisions for Evelyn. If she wants to rescue her friend, then we are to do our best to make sure she survives it, not question her choices."

I wondered what kind of arrangement the vampires had made with me in my past life. We had clearly formed a bond and they had all vowed to protect me with their lives. Now, though, things felt different. I was mortal-born and I had a familiar to contend with as well. I didn't see any of them blindly following me anywhere, much less into Sarina's trap, but what other choice did I have? I couldn't just leave Cass in Sarina's clutches.

Killian slapped the ends of his blade in place and pointed the sharp end at Bast. "You are her familiar, which makes you just as much her slave as the girl." He straightened. "We are her protectors, and sometimes that means protecting her from herself."

My eyes went wide and I made a mental effort to unclench my fists. "Marcus?" I asked, pointedly looking at him to get his input on the matter. "Do you agree with Aaron and Killian?" I was hoping it was just a matter of the effect my blood runes had on my bondmates. Aaron and Killian just hadn't reconnected with me yet. By the distance they kept from me, I wondered if we'd ever reconnect. There had been stolen moments between Aaron and me when I'd learned that he was a shifter, but now he seemed to be on the same wavelength as Killian and glared at me as if I was being a bratty child.

Marcus sighed and ran his fingers through his tousled hair. Gods, I loved it when he did that. "I don't know, Evie, they have a point. Sarina wants you to come out to where she can grab you." He glanced at Quinn. "If you hadn't been with us, she might have gotten to you instead of the human."

"Her name is Cassidy," I snapped and my fingers bunched into fists again. I didn't try to unfurl them this time. "Quinn?" I snapped, just daring him to side against me. "Do you think Cassidy isn't worth saving, too?"

He winced at the venom in my voice, but he shrugged. I gave him credit for looking me in the eyes instead of cowering away from my rage like I sensed he wanted to do. The thrum of power between our bond hummed with energy and my blood runes burned on my arm, a testament to the anger it had for them to go against me even in this. "I can't say I agree or disagree, lass. I do think that we should make a move against Sarina, but I don't think this is how we should do it."

Growling, I backed into Bast's chest and relaxed when he wrapped his arms around me. "Okay, so two of us wants to save Cassidy, two don't, and two are undecided."

"A tie," Bast agreed, his voice rumbling through my body in ways that made heat go to my core.

I didn't like the idea of a tie. I snapped my attention to Quinn. We'd only just cemented our bond and his power coursed through me. His magic tasted of honeysuckle and filled my senses with the wet taste of grassy fields. Yet now that we had bonded, there was so much more. I sensed his other powers that filled me like a bottle that had been empty my whole life suddenly filled to the brim with fizzy champagne. He had been a Seer and had the power of foresight here and again, but there was another power that intrigued me even more. His latent powers of his lineage from a relative of the Succubus family extended through our bond. Sexual excitement was native to my connection with my guys and I already used our emotions and our desire to carve a path for my magic to find its way to me, but could I also use that trait to make them see my way of things? I leaned further into Bast's hard chest, closing my eyes and inhaling the sweet musk of him. I was short compared to him with my head just barely hitting his sternum, but he sensed the change in the air and shifted to allow his hips to grind against me. My mouth parted when I realized that I'd managed to arouse him with just a thought. He was a different part of my bond, maybe even closer to me than the others because he'd been inside of my mind long before he'd ever been inside of my body.

The guys sensed the change instantly. I opened my eyes to see them all straightened and their nostrils flaring as if they could sense the new magic that enticed, stroked, and commanded.

Quinn reacted first, being the origin of the magic I pulled from him and the earrings that hung on either side of my head. I didn't have to touch the gems to bring out the power that smelled like him, had been bathed in him for so long that it had taken on his Incubus traits.

His eyelids were heavy as he stepped closer, each movement seeming to be a struggle against approaching me.

"Lass?" he asked, the word both a question and a warning. "What are you doing?"

Taking his worry as a sign of encouragement, I splayed both hands out beside me so that I could grip Bast's thighs. I pulled him closer so that his hips ground against me again until I could feel the strength of his erection between my butt cheeks. Since I only had thin shorts on, there wasn't much of a barrier between us. My mouth parted when Bast groaned behind me.

When Quinn reached me, he looked so unsure, but his gaze dipped to my lips, then my breasts. My nipples hardened instantly and I craved for him to touch them like he had done last night.

As if he could read my thoughts, he reached out, doing just as I wanted, making me release a sigh.

The other guys all shifted uncomfortably at the sound, seeming affected by it. Only Aaron was able to bite out a retort. "Quinn. She's using your Incubus powers."

I was proud of him that he could sense it so quickly, and at the same time, I was thrilled that I could use supernatural gifts that weren't a natural part of my bloodline.

Quinn didn't seem to register what Aaron had said as his fingers ran lower and hooked on my shorts, tugging them down. My breath hitched when he knelt, shifted the fabric just far enough to expose my folds, and gave my heated cravings release as his tongue grazed over my sensitive skin. I shivered against Bast's hard chest. He helped my shorts along, baring my ass to him and he wasted no time rubbing his dick between my butt cheeks. I could tell that he wanted inside of me and my thighs clenched when I realized that all of my guys were here, Marcus, Aaron, and Killian watching as their hands went to their erections, while Quinn pleasured me and Bast rubbed himself against me.

Power swarmed between all of us, even though I hadn't formed a bond between Killian and Aaron, I could taste their magic mixing with desire in the air. Killian's power tasted metallic, but also salty with a touch of the sea. Aaron's magic was primal and smelled of burning wood and a lush forest. Even though he'd figured out what I was doing to them, he allowed his magic to slip to me and I sighed as the desire ramped up even further and Quinn's tongue threatened to push me over the edge.

Power. I needed more of it. This is exactly how I could save Cassidy. Maybe there was a way to get it from my guys without pushing them like this, but with Quinn's magic I could sense a long-seated desire that had always been there. I couldn't force them to feel things they weren't already open to. I wasn't really a succubus, but could only borrow the whisper of Quinn's power to mimic the process of desire acting as a medium to transfer power. My mouth parted and I shifted my hips back, allowing Bast to slip inside of me. When he was buried in me to the hilt I cried out and Quinn used his fingers to rub against my folds, stimulating while Bast rocked against me, his thighs slapping my ass as he pumped again and again. Magic unfurled like a faucet had been open and heat crawled under my skin that built with the power of my approaching orgasm. I tried to hold it at bay. I needed more of this. Each sensation brought a sliver of strength that I would be able to use. I used my magic to call to the guys that were still out of my reach. I needed all of them right now.

Marcus finally succumbed to my call and pulled his dick out, giving it a long stroke before letting me lean down and take him into my mouth. Quinn stood, holding his own cock out for me and I took it in my hand, stroking in rhythm with Bast's thrusts that were growing more frantic.

Only Killian and Aaron seemed to be able to resist me. Their cocks were out and I raked my gaze over them while Marcus was still in my mouth, moving his hips to thrust deeper down my throat.

Aaron was just as impressive as I imagined a shifter might be. He stroked himself, his eyelids heavy and his breath coming in ragged deep gasps.

Killian wasn't faring much better and I was fascinated to see the beautiful length of his cock that was nearly as large as Aaron's, but more graceful and pink. He stroked himself as he leaned against the wall, seeming defeated as desire rolled over him. Just like fear, he allowed it to wash over him and he didn't try to fight it, but he still wouldn't come to me, not yet. He'd mentioned before that bonding with me meant that he would hurt me, and even now when I had him in the grip of lust-driven power, he wouldn't risk anything that could put me in harm's way. Instead he suffered silently as he watched me with hunger in his eyes that I'd never seen before.

I took Marcus deeper into my mouth, making him groan, and then I pumped Quinn hard with my other hand. Quinn kept rubbing my clit, bringing me closer and closer to the edge. When he joined his own Incubus powers with the magic I was extracting from him, heat flooded my core, and Bast growled out as he thrust against me, hard, raw, deep. He came inside of me, making the hairs along my arms stand on end as

I succumbed to my own release. Quinn took over my strokes, releasing his seed over me and Marcus exploded into my mouth.

I collapsed to my knees, because three men had just cum in and on my body, and with it, the full force of the magic they'd been holding back flooded into my soul and burned like hellfire.

KINDRED SPIRIT

*S*oft applause filled the room and I shifted to look over my shoulder. I'd fallen to my knees, bringing Bast and the others with me. My eyes went wide when I spotted the woman from my vision at the door.

"Impressive," she mused as she adjusted the gleaming gold crown that pressed down on her brow. She frowned at it, as if burdened by its weight, and finally flicked her fingers. The crown burst into a brilliant flame that was so hot that I feared she'd set her hair on fire, except then it vanished, leaving a perfect crown of hair atop one of the most beautiful women I'd ever seen in my life.

All of us were still in compromising positions and the room smelled of sex and magic. The woman seemed to enjoy it, though, and licked her lips as she raked her gaze over the scene. Finally coming to my senses, I untangled myself from my guys, grimacing at the stickiness between my thighs and fingers, and snatched up my clothes. I covered myself as best I could, ignoring the sensation of semen running down my leg.

"Who are you?" I demanded. She'd come barging into Quinn's room and I doubted that she was a vampire. She'd stopped Sarina from taking my life, but that just meant we had a common enemy. I knew better than to assume we could be instant friends.

She rolled her eyes as if that was obvious. "I'm the Queen of Hell and you summoned me, Fate Witch. I stopped the first Echo of Calamity and you're trying to stop the second, right? I don't mind offering some tips, but not if you're going to give me an attitude." She pointed at the guys who'd finally managed to cover themselves and now were glowering, but they hadn't burst into action to rip her head off, so maybe they'd recognized the woman for who she was without introduction.

"Plus," she added with a sideways grin, "I'm a succubus and I can smell desire from miles away. You'd summoned me to this world with your magic, but when I felt... this..." She splayed out her fingers and released a long sigh, "I couldn't resist. To feel the forming of your new bondmates is intoxicating. It reminds me of my first matches." Her gaze took on a faraway look as she smiled. "Jet, my dragon-shifter, was my favorite, but don't tell him that." She flicked her fingers, releasing a tuft of flame. "Little had I known at the time how compatible I really was with fire."

Curiosity ramped through me, fascinated that there were other magical bond-matches out in the world as strong as my own—even stronger perhaps with someone who was named the "Queen of Hell."

She clapped her hands. "Okay, so, clearly you don't need my help in the sex department. How else can I assist you?" Her grin grew. "Some hellfire, perhaps? Who needs killing? That bitch that got away last time? She's a real drag."

I cleared my throat, interrupting the woman who'd started babbling. "First," I stressed, "a shower, and then you and I are going to talk—alone."

WHEN I INSISTED I wouldn't call her the "Queen of Hell," the woman relinquished her name: Sonya.

She grinned at me as she crossed one naked leg over the other, her tight dress running up her thigh. She screamed of sensuality and lust, as well as danger. The faintest scent of ash clung to her, reminding me of who I was dealing with.

"Stop smiling at me like that," I said as I crossed my arms and leaned against the wall. We'd gone into Marcus' bedroom while the rest of the guys got cleaned up, or did whatever they were going to do. I shouldn't have felt humiliated, but I did. I'd used new magic against them to try and get my way and now I had a witness to my selfishness. Even if it was to save Cassidy's life, I knew it had been wrong of me to push them like that.

"I see so much of myself in you," Sonya said, tilting her head as she appraised me. She drew a line in the air as she outlined the profile of my curves. Even though she didn't touch me, I felt strangely violated. "You seem to have accepted your bondmates quite quickly. It even took me a bit more time to get all of mine in one place."

I narrowed my eyes. "Where are *your* bondmates?" I'd seen four men accompany her from the flames when I'd somehow summoned her from hell. If they were anything like my guys, they wouldn't be far and they'd only care about one thing: her protection. Damn anyone else who got in the way.

She shrugged. "They're close. I told them I needed some girl time."

I hadn't missed that hint that her protectors had also infiltrated the vampire stronghold. Stiffening, I reminded myself to keep breathing. My chest was getting so tight that my lungs fought to expand. "Is that a threat?" I managed to ask.

She grinned. "No, dear, it's not a threat. It's simply a reminder that I have allies, just as you do."

So, she didn't trust me. Fair enough. "I didn't mean to summon you," I admitted. "I just knew that Sarina was going to kill me and I had one chance to use my magic." The magic within me and that which had melded with my protectors was strong and it had a will of its own. It had decided to summon her. Based on what I'd seen in my lifetime, magic couldn't be trusted. Perhaps it had an alternate agenda for having summoned the Queen of Hell.

"You let the magic guide you," she said, her tone approving as she tilted her head back. "Going with your instincts is a wise choice. It'll bring you closer to your bondmates and show you your allies. You'll need that and more to face what's to come."

I shivered. "I know. Sarina is still coming after me. Taking Cassidy is just to lure me into a trap, but I can't abandon my best friend."

Sonya held up a hand to stop my rambling. "Sarina is the

least of your concerns. She heralds the Second Echo of Calamity. It is your fate to stop her, but there will no doubt be sacrifices along the way." Her gaze grew dark as if she'd experienced that firsthand.

"What did it feel like?" I asked, trying to change the topic. "When my magic summoned you, that is." I wanted to remind her that she'd been commanded—by me, and she'd obeyed.

Sonya smirked. "I felt the call of a sister, someone who deserved my help. Magic tugged at me and my bondmates and we could have ignored the call, but I would never turn my back on another who fights to keep those she loves alive. It is both the blessing and curse of being bonded to so many and have a heart big enough to care deeply for all of them."

In spite of my reservations about her, I felt my defenses falling. It was as if she was talking about me, but I knew that she was talking about herself, as well. We were kindred spirits and that's why my magic had called to her for aid. "Okay, then," I said, straightening. "Then if you are here to help me, I need to get into the Royal Covens and get my friend out."

Sonya's grin grew. She puffed her chest out, her impressive breasts straining against her bodice. A gentle red glow emanated from just underneath her skin and the room tinged with the scent of blood and power. "I have a better idea."

A TERRIBLE PLAN

"*N*o. Absolutely not," Quinn demanded as he slammed his palms against the table.

All of us sat in a large circle staring down at a map of the Royal Covens. I'd never realized that the estate was so large, and that just meant we had that much more ground to cover to find Cassidy. I was hoping that she'd be in the most obvious spot—the dungeons—but if Sarina was smart, she'd have found a better hiding place for the bait meant to lure me to her.

"I think it's a good idea," Marcus conceded, leaning back in his chair. His gaze had never left me ever since we'd gathered. Through our bond I could sense his memories replaying last night and today over in his mind, making me blush. He loved being so close to me and being a part of my bond. It turned him on to see me getting fucked by his friends. Even Bast was growing on him, and after seeing what Bast's cock made my body do, Marcus was all in for more fun.

I cleared my throat, trying to shove the enticing images out of my head. Marcus grinned with a hint of fang. "Sarina will be expecting a blatant attack," I said, hoping that I sounded confident and sure in the plan that Sonya and I had concocted. It was a brilliant plan, actually, and if we could get the magic to pull it off, I could do more than just save Cassidy. I could overthrow Sarina's power and stop the Second Echo of Calamity. Now that I knew what it was, the low, deep rumble like an approaching thunderstorm filled the horizon of my mind. Something was coming—something big, and it was my job to stop it.

"But," Quinn protested, looking stricken, "you want me to disguise myself as a *girl?*"

I tried to keep a straight face, but yes, this was a vital part of the plan for it to work. Even if we were disguised with different faces and bodies, one girl showing up with a bunch of guys would certainly give us away. As much as I hated Sarina, she wasn't stupid. However, if a mixed group showed up and blended in with the other witches striving for a place in the Royal Covens, we might just be able to pull this off.

"It's not like it'll be the first time," Tiros offered, leaning back into his chair and crossing his arms. He didn't hide how smug he was that he got to tell me the juicy gossip of Quinn's past. "Did you know, Lady Evelyn, that Quinn took your form in a past life before you bonded? Quite the little pervert."

"Tiros!" Quinn shouted, his face flushing with heat. It took a lot for a vampire to blush, but I could swear that a tinge of red overtook his features.

I snickered. "So, when I found you taking my form in the

Coven the first time we met..." My words drifted off as a smile stretched over my face.

Quinn buried his head in his hands. "I did it on purpose, and I could have changed back at any time," he admitted.

"Then it's settled," Marcus decided, "we move forward with this plan."

Sonya, the Queen of Hell, sat to my left and steadied her elbows on the table. She'd conjured her crown again and it gleamed with power that made it hard to look at her. "I wish I could help more, but I'm afraid I will need to return to Hell to battle the tainted demon-touched souls that Sarina has unleashed on us. They are spilling out into your world. The First Echo of Calamity had broken the barrier between Hell and Earth and I'd only managed to stop the worst of it." She glanced at me, her eyes glowing with internal flames. "It is my duty and my burden to maintain the fires of damnation from spreading to this world. It will be yours to stop Sarina and the force that drives her."

I didn't miss the edge to her words. She didn't see Sarina as the real threat, even though I knew what Sarina was really capable of. There was something working behind her, pushing her, giving her power that made her an even more terrifying force to deal with. "Do you know who her master is?" I asked.

Sonya sighed. "Unfortunately, this is not my battle, so I am very little help in this matter. I wish I could tell you what to do, or who your enemies are, but all I can say is that Sarina and the coming wave must be stopped or all the worlds will be consumed by death."

Consumed. It was the right word to describe how my

nightmares felt when that terrifying force would finally reach me. It was as if a thunderstorm edged the perimeter of my mind and it was only getting closer.

I cleared my throat. "So, we are in agreement then? We will infiltrate the Royal Covens tonight under the guise of the Pearl Coven witches and warlocks."

Sonya had helped me work out the whole thing. With a little bit of magic, Bast could return to his cat form. Of course he'd protested, especially given the heat still between us. If he reverted, he worried it might damage our bond, but it was a risk we would have to take. There was no way a glamour would hold on him. The best we could do is revert him to his black cat form and claim him as my familiar, which wouldn't be too farfetched. Many witches had black cat familiars.

As for the rest of my guys, Killian and Aaron would work together with Aaron staying permanently in his wolf form. With a glamour touch, his wolf would match a familiar's appearance. Killian didn't seem like the kind of guy who would still be nursing the connection to a familiar had he really been a warlock, but we all agreed that those two worked best together.

That left Quinn, who would take on a female form to give our group some texture and throw off Sarina, leaving Marcus, who could just take a different warlock's form.

"I will be joining you as well," Tiros said, standing from his seat.

Phoebe, the leader of the rogue witches, stood with him and frowned. "We don't have enough magic," she protested.

"I wouldn't have to change my appearance," he protested.

He bared his fangs. "I would only need a little help with this, and my eyes. I could pass as a warlock otherwise."

Phoebe frowned. "I know it's been a long time, Tiros, but Sarina could still remember you."

Marcus shook his head. "She wouldn't." He glanced at me and an emotion I couldn't read passed over his face.

Damnit. They were hiding something from me.

Regardless of any secrets Tiros might have had, I could think of more reasons than just a lack of magic to reject him coming with us. "Why the hell would you join?" I asked, slamming my palm onto the table. Everyone's gaze flashed to me. "You've been managing the stronghold while my protectors have been gone, am I right? Who will manage things if you leave as well?"

Sonya cleared her throat and raised a hand. "I could leave Xavier in charge," she offered. "He's the son of Hades and has managed the Underground in Venice for hundreds of years. He would be more than qualified."

Apparently everyone knew who Xavier was. Phoebe relaxed, as did her sister witches sitting between her and Sonya. Marcus nodded as if considering the idea and Tiros grinned. "Wonderful. It's settled then."

I balked. "I repeat, why the hell would you join?" It didn't make any sense to me why everyone seemed on board with the idea of Tiros joining us. That would be just one more male to add to the group and add to the suspicion.

Bast, the last person I expected to stand up for a vampire, leaned into my side. "I sense an abundance of untapped power in that vampire," he whispered so only I could hear. "Perhaps it is worth considering his offer."

I glowered at him. I didn't want everyone to be privy to our conversation so I tossed my thoughts at him through our bond. He flinched as I barreled into his head, but he didn't try to block me. *I thought you were afraid of our bond being in danger if you transformed back into a cat? Now you're all for this idea of bringing along a vampire I don't trust?*

He grinned, his sliced irises dancing with mischief. *Our bond can never be broken. That is not what I fear. I fear being unable to hold you and touch you like I can now. But even so, a vampire like Tiros offering to leave his stronghold after thousands of years is no small gesture. You mean more to him than he admits.*

Frowning, I glanced at Tiros who watched me with an unwavering gaze. I sensed that he knew I was talking with Bast in my mind, and about him, but I didn't care. If he had secrets, I'd get them out of him.

"Very well," I said, relenting. "Let's do this."

SACRIFICE AND TRANSFORMATION

*P*hoebe gathered her witches in an echo chamber that had me walking on my tiptoes. It reflected every single scrap of sound, even the faint whisper of breath carried back and forth until it amplified and slammed my ears. I covered them and squeezed one eye closed.

No one spoke, given the powerful reflection of the pure white chamber. It felt so sterile, yet mystical. The pearlescent walls gleamed with ancient power and Phoebe seemed at home, fluffing her robes and making me wince as it sent more sound tumbling around the chamber.

She joined hands with her sisters, all of them having opted out of their walking sticks once we'd gone inside the chamber. They wobbled into place, looking unsteady, but determined.

Phoebe started first with a low hum vibrating in her throat. When the resonance established, she nodded, and Bast came forward first. It was easy to forget how tall he was, but he towered over the woman, especially when he straightened and prepared for the spell that would turn him back into a cat. I knew that it wouldn't be permanent. Phoebe had assured me that when our mission was done, or my need for Bast was great enough, the spell would relinquish and turn him back into the man I had grown to love.

His sliced irises shifted to me. He didn't seem nervous, just sad. This was a sacrifice for me and I wouldn't forget it. The longing in his gaze told me how many unfinished caresses and kisses there were between us and I vowed to remedy that loss a hundredfold when this was all over.

Marcus squeezed my hand and I flinched, then pushed into the warmth of his chest, finding comfort in his embrace. I let the tears come and he didn't say anything, just swept them off of my cheek as he gently kissed the top of my head.

The hum intensified and sparks flicked around Bast's form, slowly digging underneath his skin and making him grind his teeth. He shifted faster than I had expected, his bones crunching and sounding impossibly loud as the sound echoed in the chamber. I whimpered and flinched deeper into Marcus' chest, smothering my voice as much as I could in his embrace. I didn't want to do anything to mess up the spell or make Bast regret his choice. If he could survive this, then so could I.

I sensed pain through our bond as the final transformation took hold, taking away his bulk and replacing his muscles with lean, graceful feline sinew. His coat gleamed black and emerald eyes blinked up at me, now unreadable to me as Bast always was.

I'm still here, he said, his voice a relief as it rolled through my mind.

Marcus raised an eyebrow at me and I realized that I'd sucked in a breath. I gently blew it out and smiled at him, letting him know that everything was going to be okay.

Tiros walked to the center of the circle and waited. After Bast's transformation, changing him should be a piece of cake. Magic shimmered over him and barely brushed his features. I thought perhaps it hadn't worked until he turned and glanced at me, making me suck in a breath. Striking blue eyes pinned me in place and held me captive until he finally released me, walking to the edge of the gathering to let Aaron go next.

Aaron shifted to his wolf first on his own, his bones cracking and making me wince. When he was an oversized beast with an impressive silver coat, he trotted up to the circle of weary-looking witches and sat on his haunches.

The hum intensified again, but this transformation wasn't as dramatic. Gentle motes drifted over him, changing his color to a deep midnight gleam and making his blue eyes gleam with magic. When they were done, he looked like a powerful familiar that would draw the envy of witches everywhere.

Killian and Marcus went next, accepting altered appearances, but I was surprised that they still felt like my bondmates to me. Their eyes, no longer a ruby red, still reflected their souls. It didn't matter what glamour magic made them wear, I would always know my bondmates. Even Killian, one of my protectors who'd kept his distance from me had an undeniable connection that screamed for me to repair. The blood rune on my arm hadn't come to life, not yet, but my skin tingled where his rune would appear. I looked forward to completing that bond, reuniting myself with my magic and a soul I had grown to love from a past life. Killian's glance told me that no matter how much he'd kept his distance from me, after what had happened between all of us today, he wouldn't be able to restrain himself much longer.

Quinn dragged his feet to the center of the semi-circle. He gave me a forlorn look before the hum grew louder and he transformed before my eyes. Quinn wasn't particularly feminine, but his face and body were gentler than the others. Where Killian was brute force and his movements as harsh as his blade, Quinn was wild, free, and in his own way, graceful. I watched, fascinated, as he transformed into a female form. The witches seemed to wither on this one as the last of the magic burrowed into Quinn's hair, lengthening it into lustrous auburn curls. His eyes stood out... now her, in a gorgeous green that made me blush as she looked at me with such intensity.

Quinn moved to me, nearly gliding across the floor, and instead of wanting to crack a joke or poke fun at him, I was enthralled. I had never seen such a beautiful creature in all my life and my blood rune hummed along with the magic in recognition that this was my mate, no matter what form Quinn took. She leaned in, brushing my lips lightly with a kiss, before swapping places with me and settling me into the center of the hum of magic.

Right, my turn.

Shaking off the confusing feelings that swept through me, I faced the witches who now barely seemed to be able to stand upright. They focused the last of their energies on me and my skin tingled as my features changed.

I had always been a bit coarse, and perhaps a little on the wild side like Quinn, but now I grew a little bit taller, my hair became sleeker, and my breasts grew to accommodate my new stature.

When it was done, we had all changed our appearance, and the rogue witches collapsed and the magic settled into dust along with them.

IT TOOK some getting used to, both with my own appearance having changed and that of my bondmates. Tiros was the only one of us who looked the same, except he'd lost his vampiric traits. Without his fangs and glowing red eyes, he looked very… handsome.

I don't know if he'd naturally had blue eyes before his turn into a vampire, but they pierced right through to my soul and I could hardly look at him without my heart stopping. He seemed fascinated with my own change, as were all my guys. Their gazes kept going to my chest and my face heated, this time having captured Quinn's attention. For some reason, with him in female form I just felt that much more violated.

Clearing my throat, Quinn finally glanced up at me with feminine, gorgeous green eyes accentuated by auburn curls. "So, what shall we call you now?" I asked, hoping to keep my voice light. Instead, I sounded irritated. Oh well.

Quinn smirked, the motion familiar and undoubtedly him

underneath all those curls. "I suppose it'll have to be a female name, won't it lass?"

I sucked in a breath. His accent was even more beautiful and smooth, putting my grouchy and scratchy words to shame. I almost didn't want to speak anymore and continue to embarrass myself in comparison.

Quinn is not a better female than you, Bast insisted in my head, our bond just as strong now as it had ever been. I sensed his longing to return to his human body, but he stretched and yawned, trying to adjust to his familiar feline form. It would be easier to protect me this way because he could stay with me. Had he not undergone the transformation, he would have had to wait here and watch me go without him. I knew that was something he never could have done.

I would hope not, I replied. *He's a fake female, although, I feel kind of fake with these enormous breasts and long legs that aren't natural to me, either.*

If Quinn could hear my thoughts through my bond, then he disagreed with me, because his gaze shamelessly swooped down, taking in the features that made me feel so uncomfortable.

"You shall take the name of the woman whose form you've borrowed, of course," Phoebe said, wobbling in on her cane. We all jumped to our feet and offered assistance, but she grumbled at us to sit down.

"And who might that be?" Marcus asked, leaning into his chair, seeming content with his transformation that only seemed to make him more refined than he already was, if that was even possible. His chocolate eyes made him seem innocent, even though I knew that was a big fat lie. The way he glanced at me, sending me suggestive winks, told me that he was eager to try out my new body. I squirmed and pressed my thighs together, trying to ignore him even though my body was inclined to agree to the experiment.

"Grace O'Malley was her name," Phoebe said, raising her chin as much as her hunched back would allow. "She was the daughter of an Irish Chieftain, and at the time, one of my closest friends. She had a wild spirit and an indomitable soul." The witch's eyes grew glassy and she swiped away unshed tears. "She was not a witch, but she had more magic than this world will ever know." She slammed the butt of her cane to the ground, making us all jump. "You wear her name proudly, boy, and do Grace justice. I do not give you this form lightly, but to benefit Evelyn." Her ancient eyes glanced at me. "You need magic now more than ever, my dear, and even if it's superstition, I'll make sure you can get all the magic the universe has to offer."

I had a feeling that Phoebe knew what I was really up against. Not just Sarina, but the mysterious force behind her, the Second Echo of Calamity that could destroy worlds if I didn't stop it.

Swallowing hard, I gave the witch a jerky nod. "Grace, then. In the presence of others, that is what Quinn shall be called."

With all of us transformed and packed, not that we had many things to bring, we readied ourselves for our departure in the transportation chamber.

I was surprised to see a small gathering of vampires come to see us off. Tiros spoke to them, raising his voice loud enough for the gathering to hear.

"I leave you all in capable hands," Tiros said, slapping another vampire on the back that I had only seen once before. "Xavier, son of Hades, Prince of Venice, will make sure to see to your needs while we are gone. I assure you, our venture is of vital importance and I do not leave you lightly."

A low hum swept over the crowd, although I wasn't sure if it was one of disapproval or disappointment. I would have thought the vampires eager to meet someone like Xavier, but it appeared that Tiros had earned more loyalty among his kind than I'd given him credit for.

Bast wound around my ankles, subtly feeding me doses of magic. I flinched against the sparks and bent to swat at him. "Not now, Bast. Tiros is talking." The cat nipped my fingers in retort, making me hiss and glare at him.

I wondered how the portal to the Royal Covens would open, being that the rogue witches had been entirely spent from their ordeal of giving us all powerful glamours that would hold for the duration of our mission. I had no idea how long we might be playing Sarina's games. She'd only just given out the call to warlocks and witches a few nights ago that she had resurrected an ancient and brutal trial—one that rivaled its risk in the reward.

Complete and utter command of the Royal Covens and the boon of magic that came with it. The Royal Covens had once had a Queen long before history even knew her name, but the collection of covens had always been the ones in charge, sharing power and decisions, making sure that all covens had a say in the way that magic was handled.

Now, though, Sarina wanted to change things. She wanted to claim power over the Royal Covens for herself, so I wasn't completely surprised that she'd resurrected the trials. It was the only way that she could wrangle control for herself without magic outright rejecting her.

My guys—and Quinn in a female's body—joined hands and surprised me by humming in tune. They didn't look like vampires anymore, but a powerful group of warlocks and one witch. When Marcus winked at me, then motioned for me to join them, I realized that we were the ones to cast the transportation spell.

Normally opening a portal to a place as secret and protected as the Royal Covens would be a feat of an entire collection of warlocks and witches working in tandem and led by a powerful Warlock. However, when I took Killian's and Marcus' hands in mine, joining my power into the circle, I realized that these were warlocks that were over a thousand years old. Their power rivaled my own—and thanks to my bond, was a part of my own magic and life-force. Magic swarmed through our touched hands and swept through us like a gleeful wave, splashing and dancing as it celebrated finally being used in a spell together.

I kept my eyes open during the spell, joining my voice with the others until power built. We didn't speak Latin, or ancient witch words, but simply let the power surge through us and understand our desire.

I pictured the Royal Covens courtyard where we'd entered the first time. I needed to get there and to set things right. So many had died already and if Sarina had her way, many more would follow. She'd hunt me down to the ends of the Earth— maybe even farther, and make sure my guys suffered long after they'd watched me die... again.

No, I would not let her win, not this time. With renewed focus, I surged my dose of power to the fold and the portal flashed into existence with a loud bang, sending my hair flying over my shoulders and a thud resounding in my chest.

Marcus grinned at me and Bast meowed with excitement.

It was time to beat a bitch at her own game.

A MAZE TO DIE FOR

$\mathcal{W}$e were through the portal and on the other side—deep in enemy territory—before I could blink and change my mind about my ridiculous plan.

Dread settled into my stomach when I saw how many witch and warlock hopefuls had heeded Sarina's call. The fresh initiates from that horrendous night were here, bright-eyed and dumb that they very well could be next on the sacrificial block.

Members of every coven dotted the glimmering courtyard and when I spotted Sarina sitting atop a throne that glided over the gathering, I clenched onto Quinn's hand—but then I remembered Quinn was actually Grace and the grip was gentle and soft. She squeezed my hand in return, a smile lighting her face.

"Fellow Covens," Sarina said, her voice barely above a whisper, but we all had no trouble hearing her as magic boomed her words out over the courtyard. The other

Anointed walked underneath her throne with plastered, fake smiles on their faces. All except Lenora, of course, my murdered Amethyst Coven's representative.

Willa seemed the most haggard of the group, her hair frizzed on the ends and her glasses still cracked where she'd been tossed like a doll on the remains of my Coven. I wanted to go to her and demand that she get ahold of herself, but Sarina had beaten them down. Warlocks escorted them, all of them with glowing red eyes that marked them as demon-touched.

Bast twined around my feet as we moved deeper into the crowd to blend in. We were supposed to be members of the Pearl Coven. I found our Anointed, Heather, walking deflated at the far back of the gathering of Anointed that escorted Sarina.

"You are the brave who have heeded my call," Sarina continued, smiling from ear to ear as she straightened in her throne. If I had been a fool, I would have said that she was proud of the warlocks and witches who had come to test themselves at the fatal series of trials. Instead, I knew to look deeper. I could see the disgusting glee in her eyes that there would be so much death for her to feast on in the next coming days. "The very first trial will begin in only a few short hours."

Excitement rippled through the crowd and all eyes were fixated on Sarina as she continued to drift, making sure everyone could see her blatant display of power. Levitation not only of herself, but of a heavy object like the throne she sat on was no small feat, even for an Anointed Witch of the Diamond coven.

Aaron whined, his wolf form distressed that his coven might have fallen so far to produce such a vile creature. Killian reached down and stroked his lush fur, calming the beast.

Dragging my attention away, I searched for other pearl witches, finding them huddled on the far clearing of blooms. They seemed content to crouch in the white blooms that matched their Anointed's gemstone, and we quickly scurried into the group without their notice. There were many Pearl Covens across the globe, so it was impossible for the warlocks and witches to know every face. One look at our conjured pearls at our necks and wrists and we were welcomed into the fold, completing our disguise.

I released a breath I hadn't realized I'd been holding and Tiros gave me a smirk, lowering his voice so that only I could hear him. He leaned into me, his rough chin grazing my cheek. "You'll give us all away with your nerves, little bird. Do you want some of my blood?" He flashed white teeth at my glower. "It's like a shot of whiskey and goes right to your head. It'll make you feel better, I promise."

When he slid out a blade and moved as if to slice himself, I squeaked and grabbed onto his arm. "Stop it! That's not funny!"

He chuckled, definitely way too amused by my protest as he put the blade away.

"Prepare yourselves!" Sarina said, her voice booming even louder so that there was no doubt that everyone would be paying attention. Her wild eyes scanned the crowd and no matter my glamour, I felt as if she'd see right through me and strike me down with a lightning bolt right there. Her gaze

369

matched mine, just for half a second, and I froze, but then she moved on. "The first trial begins."

THE GROUND RUMBLED as raw columns of stone jutted into the sky, transforming the once genteel and pristine courtyard into a jagged wound that bled stones and rock.

The crowd screamed, but the Pearl Coven crouched low, each of them whispering words of power to give them direction, clarity, and confidence. I was rather impressed by them and benefited from the cloud of magic that descended over the group, encasing all of us in the boon of power as the courtyard finished its transformation into the first trial: the Maze of the Lost.

Silence descended over the crowd, such a contrast to the screams and ripping of earth from just a moment before. Sarina grinned, watching, waiting, her throne having settled onto the ground. I made a note of that. The activation of the first trial had cost her in terms of magic and I didn't miss the sheen of sweat across her brow. But when I saw where she'd gained the majority of her magic, my fingernails bit into my palms as I made tight fists. Each Anointed had a terrible gash across their arm where they'd bled for the spell. Anointed blood was powerful, and a dose from each of them would make Sarina close to the Queen she wanted to be—but not close enough. She was weakened, forcing the magic when she had such unwilling participants. I realized now why she hadn't spelled them with Demon-touch to make them her thralls.

She couldn't use their magic if they were entirely under her control.

The first wave of witches and warlocks approached the entrance to the maze. By the look of glee on Sarina's face, I realized why the Pearl Coven hadn't made their move yet. That was the first trap. Within moments of reaching the entranceway, flames soared all the way to the clouds, engulfing the group before they could even scream. When the flames vanished, not even ash was left.

I swallowed the dry lump in my throat. Fuck, this was going to be a long ass day.

WE WAITED with the Pearl Coven while more brave souls tested out other ways to enter the maze. I hated to sit back and let others risk their lives, but by the way Marcus had a death grip on my arm, I wasn't going anywhere on his watch. The others had formed a protective circle around me. Aaron's big wolfy bulk blocked off my front half and his bright eyes watched for any threats. Even though familiars weren't uncommon, and there were a few among the Pearl Coven, most gave us a wide berth after Aaron's low growls.

To my sides were Quinn, Marcus, and Killian. Tiros pressed to my back and was so close that if I barely shifted I would run into his hard chest. I glowered at him over my shoulder. "We should be going in that maze," I snapped, not caring if I sounded bratty.

"No," Tiros said, the word final. "We wait."

"But the token," I pressed, reminding Tiros that we not

only had to survive these trials, but pass them. Sitting idly by and failing to procure what was no doubt a limited number of tokens was just as much of an assurance of death as running into the wall of flames.

His hands rested on my shoulders, pinning me against him. I tried to ignore the jolt of attraction that swept through me. Tiros wasn't a member of my bond. I shouldn't be attracted to him, but when his breath puffed against my neck, an unruly shiver ran through my treacherous body. "We... wait," he said, his voice low and dangerous.

I did as he wished, resisting the urge to put more of my weight against him as guilt ransacked my heart. No one else seemed even mildly interested in the attention Tiros was giving me. Even Marcus had his gaze pinned on Sarina while the others searched the stony edges for any hint of anyone who had managed to get in.

A scream sounded, making me flinch. Someone had found another trap and blood splattered across the wall. A girl stumbled away from the gore and cried out. Whoever had been the victim was already torn to pieces by the flash of teeth that had come from the wall, disappearing just as fast as it had devoured the warlock.

"There," Tiros said, pointing at the gore. "That's one of the monsters of the maze and our ticket in."

I balked at him. "The fuck? You want to approach that thing? I really—hey!"

Tiros jerked me along and the protective shield made of up the rest of my guys seemed to gravitate around me.

I stopped protesting when I realized that the rest of the

Pearl Coven was following suit. They'd spotted the trap as well. Did they mean to fight the monster and get past it?

The Pearl Coven was strong, but when the first member stepped foot on the bloodied ground, they were gone just as fast as the first victim. The crunch of bones and tearing of flesh made me cry out as hot blood splattered over us.

Marcus and the others were still vampires and their mouths parted as the droplets hit us, but they recovered quickly, shutting their jaws and glancing around to see if anyone had seen their moment of weakness.

Aaron, being a familiar, went unnoticed when he lapped up a puddle of blood from the ground. Killian kicked at him, chiding him openly for being a disgusting mutt. Realizing what he was doing, the wolf whined and stopped, his pristine fur red, matted and bloodied around his maw.

Quinn—Grace, squeezed my hand. "We'll need you and Marcus to use your time powers. See how fast it moves? We can get past it, but we'll need to pause time."

My eyes widened and Marcus took Grace's place, taking my hand in his. He lowered to my ear and pressed his lips to my cheek. "Are you ready for our first spell, my love?"

I blushed hotly, mostly because he'd never mentioned love to me before. I had no doubt that my bondmates loved me, but to hear it named aloud was a different story.

We took three steps and then Marcus raised my hand and began to chant. I listened to the words and then copied him, repeating the phrase over and over again. Roses and Jasmine burst to life and the mask on my hip begged for me to put it over my face so that I could inhale its scents even deeper, but I resisted the urge. It was already odd enough for me to be walking around with a masquerade mask on my hip, even if the glamour had altered its appearance to a white fru-fru set of feathers, just as it had changed the earrings that dangled against my neck to elegant dripping pearls on long chains.

Time around us shifted as the spell began to take hold. It was as if time was slippery water and we had tossed oil into the middle of it. Glimmers of it swarmed and fought against us, splintering into tiny bubbles and slipping out of our grasp. The spell would have been impossible on my own, but Marcus kept a tight grip on me, feeding me more and more power until I thought I might burst with it.

I was glad we had solidified our bond. I never would have been able to hold so much magic and partake in such a spell had I not been truly one with Marcus. His magic filled me to the brim until it overflowed and I swelled to make more room for it, continuing the spell and adding more oil to the waters of time.

Finally, we seemed to make a dent. The majority of our oil had gathered to the bloodied patch where the creature waited. I spotted how the loose leaves had stilled and droplets of crimson were now frozen in mid-air. Time would not move in our little bubble—but we could.

Already the spell was taking a toll on me and my fingertips went numb, but we only needed to take a few steps. I didn't dare let go of Marcus' grip and he seemed to know the importance that we didn't break our connection. We were what was holding the spell together and if it failed... we were monster meat.

The crowd hushed when we approached the bloodied

spot, then we walked through it and a collective gasp followed.

All of us stumbled inside and we hurried to avoid the stampede. A group of witches ran into me, breaking my hold on Marcus and I cried out in warning.

It was too late. Blood painted all of us as bodies exploded and massive rows of teeth sank into the remaining group still struggling to get inside the maze.

Panicked, I surveyed the faces, at first assuming the worst when I couldn't find my guys. Right... dumbass. Glamours.

I searched with my heart, with my bond, instead of my eyes, and instantly felt all of them with me. Bast still glued to my ankles, his eyes a little wider than usual and his voice echoing around in my head, although he didn't use any words I could understand just now, closer to the familiar I'd always known him to be. Marcus, Killian, Tiros, all safe. Aaron in his wolf form still with his bloodied maw gazed up at me with both distress and relief. Then finally Quinn—in the form of Grace—slipping her hand into mine and smiling. "Let's go get those tokens, shall we?"

PROCESS OF ELIMINATION

e moved as a group, and luckily quite the hoard of witches and warlocks had made it into the maze with us. The path parted into what seemed like a hundred different directions, all of them dark and shadowed except for one that was as bright as daylight, illuminated with a cheerful glow that made the cobbled path easy to see. Some witches opted for the lighted path, suggesting that the most obvious road was the correct one, but soon we heard screams and knew that they'd been wrong. Of course if anything seemed obvious in the maze, it was the wrong choice.

"We should split up," Killian offered and Aaron whined at his feet, although I wasn't sure if that was agreement or not.

"I think that's a terrible idea," Marcus countered. "If I remember this trial, then only one path will lead us to the tokens."

Killian frowned. "That's precisely why I suggest splitting

up. We don't all need to take the wrong path and die togeth-er." He gave me a hard look. "We leave Evelyn here and when one of us finds a safe path, we come back and guide her to the end."

"No fucking way," I growled through clenched teeth. "That is not why you are all here with me. No one is going to sacri-fice themselves for me."

Tiros cleared his throat. "No one will have to." He nudged me along one of the paths that a few warlocks had taken. I hadn't heard any screams come from that one yet, although it was one of the darker paths and even after only the warlocks had taken a few steps I couldn't see them anymore. Maybe their screams had been drowned by the weighty shadows. "I can feel the others who've gone before us. They're still alive. If something happens to them, I'll feel it, and then we'll turn around."

I gave him a raised brow. "You have magic?"

He grunted at me. "Your boyfriends aren't the only ones who weren't human before they turned."

Smirking, I followed in his footsteps. "Well you heard him. Tiros is leading the way."

And if he would be the first among us to die, I knew I shouldn't care. He wasn't a member of my bond.

Yet, the thought terrified me.

TIROS WAS RIGHT. He sensed death before us immediately and jutted out an arm to stop our progress. We backtracked as quickly as we could and tried the next path, failing two more times to find a safe route where death didn't proceed us until finally we seemed to be making progress.

"Did anyone else come this way?" I whispered, crouching and keeping one hand gripped tightly on Tiros' pants. His shirt would tear way too easily by the death grip I had on him, fear making me throw propriety to the wind, and I held onto his more sturdy pant pockets.

He reached out one hand to find my arm, then tugged me closer to him, nearly sweeping me off my feet. "I can smell fear ahead of us. There are others, and they've made it farther than anyone else so far. This must be the correct route."

We carried on in silence with only the popping of cobblestone beneath our feet to remind me that we were still in the land of the living. I'd lost any sense of sight hours ago and it felt like we walked on forever, every now and then running into a flat wall and forced into a turn. I wondered if we were perhaps being led in giant circles and this monster would be death by insanity.

Finally, however, my eyesight started working again and I spotted the two witches ahead of us clutching onto one another. They didn't even look back over their shoulders. Their gazes were locked onto the three pedestals up on a platform that held silver bowls.

One of them... would be the tokens and freedom to enter into the next trials.

The two girls contemplated the three pillars for a long time, arguing and shoving one another. Tiros pushed us back into the shadows just far enough that the witches couldn't see us. I almost suggested that we go out and try to help them until I spotted that they were Diamond Coven members. I didn't want to be prejudiced, but that was the Coven that had rejected Aaron for his shifter blood and had produced a monster like Sarina. I had a feeling that neither of those two witches could be trusted.

My suspicions were confirmed when one witch whispered a spell, sending her friend launching towards a pillar with a scream. She instantly hit an invisible wall and exploded into a thousand tiny pieces, her body instantly transforming into diamonds that scattered all over the marbled ground.

The girl who had cast the spell didn't break down into sobs. Instead, she cursed, and I guessed because she'd only been able to eliminate one of the trick pedestals. She drew in a long breath, approached one, backtracked, mumbled some more, then finally approached the one in the middle. Her hands shook as she reached to dip her fingers into the silver bowl, but then a serpent launched out of it and slithered around her body. She screamed, but then she couldn't take another breath in and the creature dragged her body behind the pillar, followed by sounds of crunching that made me cringe.

"That one," Tiros said.

"You're a genius," I muttered. "Watch out folks. He can count to three."

FIRST BALL

*A*fter we'd retrieved our tokens, a magic column of smoke wrapped around us and I'd been convinced that all of the pedestals had been traps and we'd gone the wrong route for sure. To my relief, the smoke dispersed, revealing that we were now inside the Royal Covens among the other survivors.

I craned my neck, taking in the surroundings of the very same ballroom where I'd stared Sarina down—and lost.

She walked in, her diamond shoes clinking against the ground. She didn't float around in her throne this time, but magic still clung to her. She definitely glowed with it. I hadn't realized one of the side effects of this terrible trial would have been sacrifice—the very power by which Sarina thrived. If I died... she'd get exactly what she'd been after, and she knew it.

Perhaps Sarina knew that I was disguised among the crowd. If she cared, she didn't show it. Surely I'd be dead soon enough if all the trials were this difficult. The crowd had been substantially thinned, but there must have been other correct paths. Groups of ten stood around the ballroom, weary and covered in the blood of other victims who hadn't been so lucky. By the multitude of vacant looks, not all Covens were as heartless as the Diamond Bitches and mourned their losses.

"Congratulations," Sarina said, her voice an irritating grating sound in my ears. "You've survived the first trial. It's time for a feast!"

THE LAST TIME I'd had a "feast" I'd nearly died. I had Outcast magic in my blood, and I didn't know what such a test would do to my bondmates or Tiros.

Luckily, Sarina didn't seem interested in weeding out any Coven that the Anointed would normally frown on. Chairs lined the walls and music started up. Servants with glowing red eyes came in with bowls of water and cloths for the witches and warlocks to clean the worst of the gore off of themselves. Finger-foods and drinks were served and I accepted them, knowing that I had to keep up my strength.

Finally the worst of the tensions eased and a quiet murmur joined in the cheerful music that filled the ballroom. Sarina announced that we all would be given rooms to rest and prepare for the next trial now that we'd celebrated our victory.

"You should find someone to feed on," I told Marcus in a whispered voice. When he glowered at me, I added, "You all should."

"We can't risk that," he insisted. "Our glamour will fall if anyone recognizes us for what we are and digging our invisible fangs into someone's neck will no doubt be obvious."

"Well, then what about the rooms?" I offered, even though a blush came to my cheeks. "You could feed on me."

Marcus glanced at me, need and desire clear in his eyes, but he shifted away. "Tiros would be in need most of all. He was the one who used his magic and that was without your aid."

"My aid?" I repeated.

Marcus nodded. "Like when we worked the time stalling spell, that was all you, sweetheart." He grinned, pride puffing his chest as he stole a quick kiss on my cheek. "Tiros, though, had to use his internal reserves. When it comes to a vampire like him, I'm afraid those reserves are blood, and he lost a lot of it today."

I glanced at Tiros, noting how he was definitely paler than usual and even his cheeks seemed to be slightly sunken in.

"Hmm," I hummed, both intrigued and horrified by the idea of letting Tiros feed on me. I glanced at Marcus. "Could you be there then, at least?"

Marcus drifted his knuckles across my cheek. "As much as I'd love to, that would only draw suspicion. I will make sure to find adjacent rooms and if you need me, simply tug on our bond and I'll be there."

I tested his promise, yanking on our bond in my mind and he grunted, stumbling closer to me. His breath puffed on my face as he chuckled. "Satisfied?"

I narrowed my eyes at him. "Not particularly, but at least I know it works."

TIROS

*W*e walked to the Pearl Coven's color-coded rooms as a group, then claimed the rooms in the far back so that none of the other Coven members would be able to hear us. I imagined that any room in the Royal Covens would be soundproof, but it made me feel better being on our own.

Walking alone with Tiros into the last room had the hairs along my arms standing on end. I'd never realized how tall and dangerous he felt. Even though he was a stranger to me, I felt like I knew him past the mask he wore to the world. His brilliant blue eyes glittered at me and I tried to remember that it was just part of his glamour that had me so fascinated.

He closed the door behind us and slipped past me, sitting onto the edge of the bed. He slumped with his elbows on his knees and his shoulders rolled down as if in defeat. "I'm sorry."

His dark strands covered his beautiful eyes and I wanted

to run my fingers through his hair and sweep it away. I stuffed my fingers into the hem of my pants to resist the urge. "For what?" I said, cringing at how high and squeaky my voice sounded. Damn, this guy had me nervous. "I don't mind the blood, if that's what you mean. After all you did for us today, it's the least I can do."

When I approached him, he tilted his head back and his tortured gaze made me halt in my tracks. "No, not for that. I mean... for lying to you for so long. For... failing you."

I blinked at him and something in his expression made me drift closer. I wanted to curse myself, and I looked down to see if Bast was still around my ankles and if he'd bite some sense into me, but he wasn't there. I glanced around the room, finding him curled up on a pile of fresh linens in the corner, having made himself a little nest and he was already sound asleep.

I swallowed hard, realizing that Tiros was someone even Bast trusted. That meant whatever he was about to tell me would be the truth. "Failing me, how?" I asked, reaching out to him and running my fingers through his hair, unable to resist the temptation any longer.

He shuddered under my touch. Even through the glamour I could see the whisper of his fangs extending as he reacted to the unspoken connection between us. "I don't know where to begin, Evelyn."

Moving slowly as if I might startle a deer, I worked my thighs around him until I straddled him. A voice inside me was screaming that I was betraying my bond, that I was a bitch, but... Bast was still asleep in the corner. Wouldn't he have stopped me by now if this was wrong?

"Then tell me in a few words what I need to know," I whispered, pressing myself lower and closer to him.

Tiros responded to me, his hands roaming over my hips and settling me atop him. His eyelids went hooded and it felt like we'd done this a hundred times, although I couldn't figure out why.

"Because," he whispered, his mouth going to my neck, eliciting a soft moan as he pressed his lips against my skin, "I was once in your bond."

I froze, and so did he, his hands still a hard grip on my hips and the now obvious erection showing his hard need between my thighs. "My bond?" I asked, forcing myself to soften. Even though my mind couldn't wrap around his words, my body screamed for me to listen to it. Heat broke out over my skin and tension made me so taut I thought I might snap from the pressure. My fingers roamed over his broad shoulders, then ran over his chest. When I felt the prick of his fangs, I closed my eyes, seeing him for what he was even if the glamour fought us.

Any other vampire would have buried his fangs into me, but Tiros wouldn't dare hurt me, even if I wanted him to, even if there was a distant memory so powerful that my body remembered him before I could.

He tasted my blood, sighing with relief as strength flooded back into him. It wasn't just the blood that rejuvenated him, but my magic and my power—my acceptance of our bond.

A new blood rune carved itself over my arm and I winced at the hot slice of pain, but that finalized all I needed to know. I ground myself lower, rubbing myself over his erection and suddenly wishing that there were no more clothes between us.

His hold on me grew more frantic, and he lapped at my tiny puncture wounds as his hips started to move. "Evelyn," he whispered my name.

Yes, I'd been here before, with him, hearing him say my name like that. My heart broke into a thousand pieces with the realization. "How could I have ever forgotten you?" I lurched back and took his face in my hands, glad that his glamour didn't take away his features.

He closed his eyes and focused on my touch and I knew that he didn't want to see my glamour where I was a different woman. He wanted to remember me, how I was, how I touched him. I eased off of his lap, the loss of contact excruciating but worth it for the effort it took to peel off my clothes.

Standing naked before him, I waited until he opened his eyes again. He raked his gaze over me, seemingly disbelieving of what was happening, but I remembered him. Somehow, I'd forgotten Tiros, one of the most beloved of my bond, most fearful, and most sacrificial.

All of my guys had turned to vampirism to save my soul, paying the price of imprisonment for a thousand years, but Tiros had paid it far worse. He'd already turned before he'd met any of us, which meant that he had to stay behind. He had to live in the vampire Underground and live each day alone, knowing that I was dead, knowing that his new brothers were trapped in a perpetual spell and would live their worst day over and over again. He felt responsible. He felt like he should have been there, but then who would have made sure there would have been a safe place for me to escape to once my protectors had awakened me, and I had awakened them? No, he'd had to wait out his days living each one with the brutal punishment of patience and grief.

A sob tore through me to realize what Tiros had done for me, that he'd pretended not to know me and that we'd been enemies.

He tore off his shirt and unzipped his pants, hunger blatant in his gaze. "I'm so sorry I lied to you," he repeated, and I knew what he meant. Our bond surged, stronger than it'd ever been with any of my guys and this was before he'd even taken my body. He needed to become one with me and the push of the bond to reunite was so strong that it left me panting.

"You let me think we were enemies," I whispered. Even when he'd seen me in the stronghold, he'd left me alone, thinking it better if I didn't know who he was, that he didn't deserve me, that I was better off without him. I growled, suddenly enraged that he would have been so stupid. "I could never live without you! You're such a fucking moron!" I slammed my fists into his chest and beat against him, crying and not caring if anyone heard me.

At some point the door opened, but it must have been Marcus checking on us, because it quickly closed again and Tiros held onto me tightly, shushing me until I crumpled into a broken ball and he covered me with kisses, trying every-thing he could to wash away all the terrible things that had happened to us.

I didn't want it to be like this. I crawled over him onto the bed and lowered myself until I pressed flush with his body and I crushed my mouth onto his, not caring if I hit fang or not. By an impressive measure of self-control, Tiros must have recalled his fangs, for he kissed me in return, his tongue invading my mouth and claiming me. His hands wound up to my breasts and squeezed, making a gasp escape me, and then I didn't want to wait anymore. I reached down and felt for him, the supple skin of his hard cock pulsing in my grip. I angled him, rubbing him along my clit and making myself wet with the harsh strokes. Tiros watched me as I pleasured myself with him, grinding over him and licking across his lips.

When I was wet enough, I angled him and lowered my hips, gasping when the full length of him filled me. I wasn't sure if I could lower all the way down, but he shifted, making me widen my legs and sink down until nothing but skin pressed against me from all around. He flipped me onto my back and began slow, deliberate thrusts. The bond between us burned to a fever pitch, begging for us to release and find harmony.

I felt his magic enter me with each thrust of his cock. It didn't have a scent like my other guys, but rather a deep feeling as if I was underwater and I might drown by sensation. He kept thrusting, again and again, rolling his weight over my clit and making me throw my head back and endure the sweet suffering of his cock. He kneaded my breasts, working me until he couldn't resist it any longer and lifted me, taking my neck again in a firm bite. This time his fangs sank deeper and hot blood trickled down my neck. A new kind of pleasure swarmed through me from his bite, giving me a taste of his magic he wanted to share with me.

Empathy. I could feel what he was feeling, and oh my gods, he was about to explode inside of me. Just the knowledge of it, of his heat and the swollen head of his cock zinging with sensations inside of my hot core made me clench around him with a scream. The orgasm hit fast and brutal, streaking through my body and leaving me at its mercy.

Tiros tried to hold back his pleasure. His magic allowed him to feel what I felt, which just made us an echo chamber of each other's ecstasy. He came into me—hard, and my world disintegrated into the drowning pleasure that only Tiros could bring.

DREAM TRIAL

*W*hen I woke, I was covered in sweat, semen, and my own blood, but I didn't care. I felt amazing. Everything hurt with delicious pleasure and I reached out to find Tiros, to show him how he made me feel through our bond... but he wasn't there.

I jerked upright when I sensed a desolate emptiness in my chest. My gaze flew to the pile of linens, but even Bast was gone. Fear gripped my heart so hard that I thought it might stop beating.

Jumping out of bed and gathering my clothes, I didn't even bother showering. I pushed open the door and was about to yank the shit out of my bond with Marcus when I realized even that wasn't there anymore.

"Tiros?" I cried out. "Marcus?" My voice grew frantic as I rattled off each name. Only silence greeted me in the eerie, empty corridor.

Heaving with panic threatening to choke me, I slammed the door and tried to calm myself.

That's when I remembered the next trial… and how it happened. I hadn't woken up. I was still asleep.

I was trapped in the dream trial… and shit was about to get real.

To Be Continued...

Oh yeah, this is a boxed set, so turn the page to keep reading!

CONSUMED: BOOK 3

This final trial is total bullshit.

I'm a Fate Witch, which qualifies me to become Queen of the Royal Covens, assuming I can survive the final trial. Sarina's dying breath took all of the men in my bond and cast them beyond time and space, trapping them in alternate worlds that only my power can cross. Their fate is in my hands and I'll have to tap into my power now more than ever to get them back into my arms where they belong.

Being my witch familiar, Bast is the only one of my guys who has managed to avoid this stupid trial. There's just one problem... he's stuck in his feline form. He can't hold me and comfort me like I want him to. Sarina cursed him to make sure I was alone. She thought the separation from my bond would crush me. Even in death, she still is a pain in my ass.

As if fixing Bast and crossing worlds to find my guys and

reunite our bond wasn't terrifying enough, I'm on the clock. If I fail the final trial before the Second Echo of Calamity arrives, Sarina will be resurrected and she'll will destroy our world as we know it.

Like I said, total bullshit.

CHAPTER 1

*T*iros. I still felt him on my lips... on my skin. To be deprived of one of my closest bondmates so soon after my memories of him had awakened rendered my soul apart. I gripped my chest and stifled the cry that wanted to come out and tried to ground myself. There was no time for pain or pity. Now was the time to fight.

The witch, Salina, thought she could mess with me. It didn't matter that she didn't know who I was; I could sense that she'd already taken a dislike to me even in my disguised form. No matter the face I wore, she and I would make quick enemies in any life. Nothing made that more apparent than the sense of dread and dark magic that wrapped around my ankles and threatened to topple me over.

This trial felt personal.

Her laughter echoed through the halls and swept away as if there was no end and no escape.

The moment I realized that I was trapped inside a dream trial, I could sense how everything around me felt *wrong*. Cold magic wrapped around my ankles and I shook it off before I began to walk.

I ran my fingers across the walls as I wandered the dimly

lit corridor. Numbing cold kissed my fingertips, but I didn't pull away. I needed to understand this place.

Each footstep echoed a muffled sound through the corridor and the faintest smell of death tinged my nose. I knew what the dream world was—a stepping stone between the world of the living and the spirit realm where the dead waited.

Good thing I had a lot of dead friends.

Those would be my first allies once I found my way out of the winding maze. The corridors weren't the same as when I'd come here during the night with the intent to give Tiros my blood. Something in me recognized him for who he was before I had any idea. He was a bondmate and someone I would always love, nourish, and cherish. Just because I couldn't sense him didn't mean he wasn't here. We'd been in bed together when the dream trial began, which meant that Tiros might be in trouble. The trial was meant for magic-wielders. Tiros was a vampire with no real magic of his own, no matter how ancient and powerful he might be. He wouldn't stand a chance alone in a dream trial.

A soft shout made me still and I crouched closer to the wall. Cold air clung to me, trying to strangle me again, but I ignored it. If I wandered into the center of the hall I could lose myself entirely to the tugging threads of power. The corridor hummed with magic with the walls alive. The walls were my only link to the world of the living. That's why the darkness wanted me to wander off out into the open. I squinted at the mist that came off of it and rubbed it between my fingers.

The shout came again and I turned around, trying to find

the source of the dull sound, but then I decided it was coming from inside the wall. I sucked my lower lip into my mouth and braced myself before pressing my ear against it.

Cold crawled over my neck and gave me an instant headache, but I ignored it and focused. I didn't move until I heard it again, the unmistakable sound of Tiros' voice.

Was he saying "rune?" or "rub?" I frowned. Neither of those made sense.

Then he shouted again, much closer this time.

"Run!"

The ground trembled and the walls instantly lost their icy touch, which was a relief until I realized that I'd lost all connection with the world of the living and I was now ass-deep in the world of the dead...

Angry spirits flooded the end of the corridor and came straight for me, arms outstretched, jaws unhinged, and white, unseeing eyes trained in my direction.

"Shit!" I jumped to my feet and did as Tiros demanded.

I ran.

My bare feet slapped against the tiles, the sound muffled in the heavy air that tried to slow me down. I cursed under my breath as I tried to fight my way through the invisible sludge. It was like all the nightmares I'd had before where I couldn't run. There was a logical reason for that. The spirit world has some damn thick atmosphere, except now I was trapped for real.

Fighting to suck in a breath, I dared a glance over my shoulder and regretted it immediately. The dead were gaining on me and I swear one of them had a grin on the shredded remains of his face.

Fuck, were spirits like zombies? I had no idea.

With no time to ponder if I was about to get ripped limb from limb in a gruesome display of a real-life zombie massacre, I relied on instinct and drew on the magic within me. My artifacts were still in the bedroom in the real world. I'd been dumb enough to take off my earrings and set aside my masquerade mask that contained the power that Quinn and Marcus had held for me for a thousand years. But, there was something else inside of me now... a power that relaxed me and allowed me to take in a long, deep breath that rejuvenated me. I focused on it and allowed it to grow. A warm tingling wrapped over my body and fought the numbing sensation of the spirit-world. Leather and horses came to mind as the comforting magic wrapped around me like a blanket.

Tiros... he'd kept my magic within himself all these years. No matter if he believed that he was a worthy member of my bondmates or not, he had safeguarded a piece of my soul and returned it to me without having even realized it.

Warmth flooded me and I skidded to a halt, swerving onto the coming hoard of spirits that were far closer than I'd realized. Their fingers outstretched and slimy, icy tendrils of their hunger grazed my skin. I let the magic overwhelm me until flames licked across my skin, growing in intensity until it jumped and latched onto the spirits.

Deafening screams filled the corridor as the spirits bucked back against the onslaught, but it was too late. They stretched out for me and cried out as they burned alive... or uh, un-alive?

The spirits disintegrated, leaving a pile of blue ash at my feet and I sniffed at it. "Serves you right," I murmured.

"That's my girl," came a sweet, amused voice.

I whirled only to find a beautiful woman covered in Amethyst jewels. She smiled, her eyes sparkling and triggering a sense of camaraderie.

She held out her hand and waited. "It's me, dear. I know I look different, but this is my soul's body. We get a new one on the other side." Her smile widened.

Aunt Sandra?

I blinked at her in shock before taking her hand. I flinched when her skin touched mine, expecting cold, but relaxed when I realized she was warm. "But, how…?"

"How am I not a zombie?" she asked, amusement bringing a blush to her cheeks. She looked so real, but a breeze resonated through her, making her seem translucent if I let my gaze wander.

"Well, yeah."

She laughed, the sound nothing like what I'd heard from my living Aunt Sandra who was always reserved and perhaps slightly irritated.

"Because I have a soul," she said, straightening proudly. When I continued to stare at her, she added, "The soulless dead came after you when they sensed you in the spirit world. You can thank Killian for that."

I glanced back over my shoulder. "Killian?"

She nodded. "Yes, he has a nasty little power that he abused when it first developed." She tilted her head and a small smile quirked at the edge of her mouth. "You know, I didn't even recognize him when I was alive. It's too bad. I was fond of him in my past life, as I was of all your bondmates."

I blinked at her, stunned. This was definitely not the same Aunt Sandra I'd known all my life. "You know about my bondmates?"

She opened her mouth to answer me, but a screech echoed down the corridor and the scent of more dead lingered on an invisible breeze. She grabbed my hand and tugged me towards her. "It's not safe to talk here. Let's get you to the gardens."

"Gardens?" I squeaked, feeling helpless as Sandra yanked me along with her as if I were a toddler who'd just walked into the middle of a busy street.

The spirit of my lost Aunt who'd always been a begrudging sort of parent to me took me through the winding maze with ease. I waited for the pit of my stomach to twist and tell me that this was all a trap, but the sense of cold and darkness eased the further along we made it through the maze. Finally, the walls spanned out and revealed a hazy wall of rainbow oil that separated us from the blur of a lively garden on the other side. Lavender sprouted along the edges, creating a natural fence of foliage that protected the delicate blooms spanning the world beyond.

"When I imagined the world of the dead, this was not it," I whispered.

Sandra, eyes glittering, tugged me through the veil and into a place of warmth and peace.

The dead appeared in the darkness where we'd just been and gathered, silent, deadly, waiting for me to venture out again. A shiver ran up my spine.

"Am I trapped here?" I wasn't dead. That much was clear by the tendril of golden light that was visible now that I'd crossed the strange veil into the gardens. The trail of light came from my chest and filtered through the darkness. I expected the dead to claw at it and try to devour its magic, but it was as if they couldn't see it. They walked by the strand of light, swaying, and their cracked eyes focused entirely on Sandra and me standing in the gardens.

"You'll be safe here," Sandra corrected me and squeezed my hand. "When the trial is over, you'll awake in your own body." A shadow passed over her eyes as she frowned. "Everyone will wake, but not everyone will still have their soul."

When I blinked at her, realization dawned on me, and I suddenly had the urge to find a mirror. If Aunt Sandra looked different here because this was the body of her immortal soul, and my flesh and blood body was still on the bed next to Tiros, then what body was I wearing now?

Loosening my hand from Sandra's grip, I hurried deeper into the gardens, passing by soft blooms that kissed my cheek and left glitter over my arms and fingers. I spotted a water fountain with still pools surrounding it and I ran to it as my breath came in short gasps.

Coming to a still pool of water, I bit the inside of my cheek and then leaned over it.

A gasp escaped me.

A beautiful creature looked back at me with fractured, multi-colored irises and silver skin that glittered with the golden dew of the spirit gardens. My hair came around my face in dark, wavy curls that was such a contrast to my pale skin and I ran a finger over my arched cheekbone.

"You don't remember who you are, even here, do you?" Sandra said, having silently approached me.

I tore myself away from my reflection and stared up at her. She sparkled from head-to-toe with Amethyst jewels that I realized glowed from within. A sentient magic made her seem so alive, even if her skin shimmered with translucence if I focused on her too closely. "I'm Evie," I said absently, knowing that to be true.

Sandra smiled and nodded. "Yes, that is who you are in this short mortal life, but eternally you are so much more, my dear." She knelt and trailed her fingers through the water, sending the ethereal image scattering. "Even if you can't remember, know that you are a Fate Witch, which puts you above all others in ways that only you can imagine."

Without a doubt I knew that I was looking at my own immortal body. I turned my hands over and examined the fine silver fingernails—the body of a Fate Witch. This might be my true form, but I didn't feel any different than I had just hours before when I'd made love to Tiros. Or before that when I'd begun my journey to understand Bast, Marcus, Quinn, and those I hadn't gotten to show my love yet. Killian and Aaron, they held pieces of my soul too.

I noticed the small fractures now that I knew where to look for them. As I ran my hands over my strange body I found grooves in my chest where pieces were missing.

"You'll find yourself again," Aunt Sandra promised. She opened her mouth to speak more, but then her gaze went distant and she closed it. "The others are here."

I turned and followed her gaze to find a silent gathering of witches and warlocks garbed in Amethyst jewels of power stepping into the garden's courtyard. This was an entire coven wiped out by Sarina and rage burned in my chest to see how many were here.

"It isn't right," I said through gritted teeth. "Sarina won't get away with this."

Sandra rested her hand on my arm and nodded. "I believe you, but first, you must survive this trial." She nodded for the rest of the coven to come and they approached without even the slightest crunch of leaves underfoot, making my skin crawl.

Hands reached out and touched me until I felt suffocated by my people, but I wasn't afraid. I sensed the warmth and hope that they pumped into me. Their coven had been wiped out by their enemy and I was the last Amethyst Witch left standing. It didn't matter to them that I was a Fate Witch, not anymore. Perhaps when they'd been alive they would have balked at the idea of embracing an outcast into their coven, but now in their immortal bodies they didn't fear me like they were taught to fear one of my kind in life. The living believed in fate and destiny and to take such powers into one's own control was viewed as arrogant and selfish. However, they weren't alive anymore, and they knew better now.

I wondered why the living were taught to fear and obey fate. The powers that governed time and space weren't all-knowing. Their grand mappings and designs were rarely the best path, which was why Fate Witches existed in the first place—a correction to the flaw of the main order of things.

The knowledge of what I was seeped into me like a lost, undeniable truth.

I was meant to sever chaos.

Embrace those who safeguarded my soul.

Stop death in its tracks.

I couldn't know if I could really correct fate, but anything had to be better than a world where Sarina was alive and wreaking havoc. The magic of an entire lost coven coursed into me like a flood and I threw my head back, allowing it to slip down my throat like wild nectar.

The dead waiting beyond the veil sensed the power and screeched, keening for just a taste, a drop of water in the desert, but I would leave nothing for them. This was why I had been taken in by the Amethyst Coven. This is why they all had to die. Without even knowing it, my life had changed their fate, and now they would help me change the world's.

"Evie," Tiros said so softly I almost didn't hear him. His touch ran over me with soft, gentle caresses. "Come back to me."

Reality seeped back into me like molasses seeping over my skin. The sensation of the dream world retreated, but the power I'd absorbed coursed through me with fresh, undeniable heat.

When I managed to open my eyes, I found Tiros hovering over me. He should have had his glamour active, but he looked just as he had when I first met him. Extended, dangerous fangs, shining ruby irises, and an intensity that had me swallowing the lump in my throat.

Then I remembered who he was to me—what he was. He was my bondmate and he'd safeguarded a piece of my soul for a thousand years. He would never do anything to harm me.

I ran my fingers over the arch of his cheekbone and let my touch run down his neck as my eyes trailed down his body. He wasn't wearing anything underneath the thin protection of the bedsheets. We were still in bed together, naked, and my cheeks warmed when I felt him harden against my thigh.

He reacted to me... just from a simple touch.

He smiled and banished any concerns that something might be wrong. "You made it out," he whispered, then nuzzled into my neck and kissed me. His cool fangs sent goosebumps spreading over my skin in a wave. "I was afraid you couldn't hear me."

I wrapped my arms around him and twined my fingers through his shaggy hair that was tousled after our night together. "You were my anchor," I said, knowing now that the lifeline back to my body had been strengthened because of him. He might not have warlock magic, but he was a powerful vampire who'd held a piece of a Fate Witch's soul for a thousand years. I didn't doubt for a moment that there was more than met the eye when it came to Tiros. "I've passed the dream trial," I said, more to myself than to him. I wasn't really sure what that meant for me, but it occurred to me that while I might have survived, others would not.

I straightened as my heart jumped into my throat and my eyes widened. "The others!" What if they'd been dragged into the dream trial, too? Marcus, Quinn, Aaron, Killian, and Bast all held pieces of my heart. If anything happened to them I'd lose my mind.

Tiros shushed me and pressed gently against my shoulders, leaning down to the soft, downy sheets once again. "Don't panic, my heart. You can feel them, can't you? They are all safe and well?"

I tried to still my rapid breathing but it felt like I'd just run a mile without stopping to rest. Tiros and Bast might not be warlocks, but the rest of my bondmates certainly were and they would have been subjected to the call of the dream trial just as much as anyone with coven blood on royal grounds. Sarina might have instigated the royal trials, but she did not create or control them. This was how warlocks and witches had proved themselves in the old days and anyone on the premises would be subject to its scrutiny.

Instead of listening to my panicked thoughts, I forced myself to close my eyes and focus. Tiros was right. I could at least feel Marcus and Quinn because of my bond to them that burned hot blood runes on my arm. I sensed the lingering beginnings of rekindled bonds with the others as well; Aaron and Killian were there in the back of my mind like forgotten memories that were just waiting for me to pick up again. Even Bast was out there in his feline form scouting the damage wrought by the dream trial. I sensed his determination and grim acceptance that he wasn't going to like what he'd find.

Bast was out there—not here, which meant that he'd trusted Tiros to pull me out. Bast had never shown that kind of trust with my other bondmates, so I wondered what made Tiros so special.

"Do you feel them?" Tiros asked. His fingers dug into my hip, making my eyelids flutter open.

I met his beautiful ruby gaze, full of blood magic and ancient danger. When I'd first met Tiros in the vampire stronghold I hadn't felt such an attraction to him. That was a testament to his power over deception and lies. He was able to hide something that came second nature to me now. I threaded my fingers through his as he pressed himself further against my side.

"Yes," I whispered, my words breathy with desire now that I knew the immediate danger had passed. My warlocks had survived the dream trial and everyone I cared about was safe —everyone except Cassidy.

Guilt tugged at me that I'd forget my best friend even for a single moment and I threw the bedsheets off.

"What is it then?" he asked, his voice lilting up with worry. "You should stay here, with me."

I couldn't miss the pleading undertones of his words. He wanted to explore me, to take me, and to rekindle a thousand years lost from a bond that should have never been broken.

Every part of me wanted to indulge him that desire. I felt it just as strongly. However I was here to save Cassidy and if my bondmates were in danger, it was because I'd brought them here. I needed to save Cassidy, stop Sarina, and get everyone out of here.

"I shouldn't be lying in bed," I said, trying to keep my words gentle with Tiros as I pulled open the dresser to find something to wear. I rummaged through oversized skirts and padded jackets, but wasn't happy with the selection. Witches liked their clothes sexy and it was a deliberate move on Sarina's part that everything looked so… frumpy.

Absently sweeping my touch over the masquerade mask at

the nightstand—although it didn't look like the mask Marcus had given me; it had been transformed to look more like a gentle accessory of white lace and feathers suitable for a witch of the Pearl Coven thanks to Phoebe and the rogue witches that had glamoured me and my bondmates. Thankfully, the glamour didn't change the functionality of my artifacts and my call sent a stream of magic over the clothes, transforming them into practical—yet flattering—sets of jeans, tanks, and cropped sleeves. A few of the dresses transformed into formalwear that Marcus would have approved of. He'd held onto my magic for so long that there was little I could do with the masquerade mask that didn't have his own magic along with it.

"Is that a good idea?" Tiros warned.

I rolled my eyes as I pulled on my clothes. "You sound like Bast." Even when Bast had just been my familiar, he'd always disapproved of frivolous magic, but there was no way I was going to walk around the Royal Covens looking like one of Sarina's pitiful house rats.

Tiros gave me a raised eyebrow as he propped himself up on his elbow. Gods, he looked sexy. "Not that I want to agree with the cocky cat-god, but sounds like he might have been on the right track." Tiros eyed the doorway and he tilted his head to the side. "Others are getting up. The survivors of the dream trial will be waking up and I expect Sarina will want everyone gathered to hear how great she is."

I opened my mouth to retort that I really didn't care what everyone else was doing when a shrill voice entered my mind, making me wince.

Attention, survivors. Congratulations on surviving the dream trial! You've walked the realm of the dead and returned unscathed, which means the next trial will be starting soon. You found your soul artifact, didn't you? Hope you woke up with it, because you'll want to guard it with your life.

I froze. Sarina was already telling us about the next trial, but some soul artifact? What was she going on about now?

Scanning the room, I looked for any clue of what she might be referring to. If I'd come out of my dream trial as planned by the ancient magic that ran the Royal Covens, then I would have had an artifact. I glanced at Tiros. "Didn't you pull me out?"

He shook his head. "No. I felt you tugging on our bond, so I helped you, but you got out on your own."

I narrowed my eyes and scanned the room—then I saw it.

A gentle rose rested on the nightstand and had I not been looking for it, I would have missed the ethereal glow that emanated across the gentle petals.

There it was. A piece of my soul the Royal Covens had ripped out of me. As if my soul wasn't splintered enough already.

DON'T TOUCH MY SOUL

"*H*ow will you protect it?" Tiros asked, eyeing the rose that I carefully turned over in my hands.

Sharp thorns protruded from the ends, but no matter how I handled the rose I seemed immune to the jagged edges. "I suppose I can't put it in a glass case protected by a beast," I mused dryly.

Tiros stared at me blankly. Okay. A thousand years and the guy never watched a single movie, seriously?

I gave him a hard stare in return. "What have you done with all your life?" I asked, meaning it to be rhetorical.

"Protecting the world from rogue witches and vampires gone insane," he answered honestly. He held out his hand. "Let me see it."

I rolled my eyes but obeyed and handed him the rose.

Tiros tried to pinch the delicate bloom carefully at the stem, but he instantly hissed and recoiled as the rose fell to the ground. "Damn, well, I guess that piece of your soul doesn't need much protection."

It hadn't occurred to me what Tiros might be trying to do, but then I remembered he'd actually held a piece of my soul within himself for a thousand years. Perhaps he believed he could protect this piece of my soul as well.

I plucked the rose from the floor, took note that the thorns did me no harm, and gently tucked the bloom behind my ear. If the rose bit Tiros like that, then I had no concern that anyone else wouldn't get the same treatment.

He gave me a wry smile. "You're confident."

I nodded, then tossed him some pants. "And you're still naked. We shouldn't be in here. We should be out there finding Cassidy."

He sighed and ran his fingers through his shaggy hair, making a deep, delicious part of me want to slip right out of my clothes again. "I admire your love for the human, really I do. But, they don't live long, you know, and—"

I turned on my heel and stormed right out the door before he could finish that sentence. I liked Tiros—I loved him. But it didn't mean I wanted to hear his lack of empathy for Cassidy just because she was human and didn't live for thousands of years. I didn't have the patience to explain to him right now that Cassidy meant just as much to me as he did. I loved her, maybe in a different way, but she was the only family I had and I wouldn't let Sarina hurt her.

The atmosphere itself seemed to change once I exited the comfort of the room I shared with Tiros. The halls were alive with groans, cries, and a few sadistic laughs. I followed the sounds and hunched my shoulders into myself as I walked. I felt like an outcast here, and even if I was used to that sensation, I was masquerading as a member of the pearl coven in a place where everyone was my enemy. The longer I stayed here, the more likely I'd be found out. I didn't like knowing that at any moment, something could happen to me or to one of my bondmates.

My stomach unclenched when I spotted Marcus and Quinn. Of course, Quinn still had the glamour of a female to not make our intrusion into the Royal Covens so painfully obvious. He glared over the crowd of warlocks and witches humming with his arms tucked underneath his borrowed body's breasts. He didn't just look the part—his appearance was illusion made flesh.

I approached him and offered a lopsided smile. "Glad to see you're okay."

He grunted in a sound that was definitely not feminine. "I still have breasts and... other, lacking amenities, so I'd say 'okay' would be relative, lass."

I decided that Quinn was definitely okay. Onto Marcus.

My refined bondmate towered over the gathering and watched with a pensive look on his face. I wasn't sure what time it was, but most of the witches and warlocks were dressed for a new day. I wasn't the only one who'd spelled the clothes for something more suitable. Many wore formalwear and flaunted their house jewels. Other chose to dress more practically and looked similar to me, and then there were a few that hadn't spelled the guest outfits and wore the drab, shaggy things while glancing around the halls as if unsure if they should spell the outfits right now.

Then there were some who still wore their pajamas, but

those were the ones with dazed eyes and ashen faces. I'd recognize that look anywhere.

Death.

"What's happened?" I asked, shoving through the gathering and ignoring Marcus who glared at me.

One of the ashen-faced witches grabbed onto my arms and her eyes went so wide that a solid ring of white surrounded her dilated pupils. "The dead—did you see them? They took her... they took..."

The witch collapsed and nearly took me down with her as her body racked her with fresh sobs.

The sadistic laugh I'd heard a few moments before sounded again. "Stupid Amber Coven witches," said a girl dripping in emeralds. Her Scottish accent would have been pretty had she not had a look in her eye that said she wanted to rip the wings off birds for fun. "Too sensitive and weak to handle the elimination of competition. This is a good thing, you dimwit!" The girl kicked the Amber Coven witch, her blow catching her in the rib.

"Hey!" I shouted and shoved myself between her and the grief-stricken girl. "What the fuck is your problem?"

I didn't know many Emerald Coven witches, but this one seemed like a real bitch. She sneered down at me over the perfect arch of her nose and flipped her red curls over her shoulder. "I don't know about you, Pearl Witch, but I'm here to win. It's not often that the Royal Covens has an opening and I'm going to celebrate for each and every competitor that falls over dead." She laughed behind her hand and glanced down at the witch cowering at my feet. "Or who falls *into* the dead—gods, isn't that funny? How clumsy are you Amber witches anyway?"

Before things could escalate further, a familiar brush of fur ran across my legs. I looked down to find Bast sending fresh waves of magic through my body—not that I needed it. My skin hummed with the gift of my dead coven and the magic that Bast added to my well of power felt like droplets in an ocean.

What is that? he asked, meowing up at me with confusion.

Not now, I hushed him in my mind.

The Emerald Witch frowned at me. "Should have known a pathetic Pearl witch would still have her familiar. I don't know how you survived the dream trial, but why don't you scurry off and quit wasting my time." She pulled out a pocket mirror and examined her overdone lipstick, using her pinky to smooth the edges.

I stared at the mirror. It was one of the most beautiful things I'd ever seen—then I realized why. It glowed from within with an ethereal aura. Stupid witch had found her soul artifact and flaunted it right in front of me.

I didn't have to be told what was the second trial was. I knew from history.

Be the last witch standing.

Even knowing what I had to do, I hesitated. I wasn't a murderer and I didn't know what it would do to destroy a soul artifact. Could a witch even properly move on? I rubbed my temple with my fingers. Gods, I couldn't believe I was even contemplating it.

"She's gone," the Amber witch cried, breaking my concentration. She hugged a teddy bear to her chest and choked on a sob.

The Emerald Witch rolled her eyes and bent as if perhaps she'd comfort the distraught girl. Instead she snatched up the teddy bear and throttled it in a tight grip. "You need to get your shit together or get out," she hissed, then ripped the head off the bear.

The crowd gasped as the Amber witch flung her head back at an awkward angle. Her mouth fell open on a silent scream and then a crack reverberated through her body, shattering her from the inside as if she were made of porcelain.

The Amber Witch was dead. I knew it before her body solidified and crumbled to our feet in a messy pile of glitter and ash.

"You need to get out of here," Quinn hissed in my ear.

I knew my bondmates would try to protect me, but what they wouldn't do is seek justice for the pointless death of an Amber Witch.

The Emerald Witch still held her artifact loosely from one hand while she stared dumbly at her handiwork. She hadn't realized that the teddy bear had been that girl's soul artifact, but when realization crossed her face, a sadistic smile made her grin from ear-to-ear. "Gods," she breathed. "That was fucking amazing."

That was all the encouragement I needed. I snatched up the pocket mirror and tossed it on the ground. She cried out, but I ground the delicate bauble under my heel before she could stop me.

"Bitch!" she shrieked as a sharp crack ran up her collarbone and split right through her face. She screeched with rage and magic colored green at her fingertips as she tried to start a spell, but it was too late. More cracks swept over her body and she crashed to her feet before disintegrating just like her victim.

A long silence drew out among the gathering of witches and each of them tucked small baubles to their chests, finally realizing the last trial meant protecting their very soul. The witches eyed each other with suspicion before the crowd scattered and retreated to their rooms, leaving me alone with Marcus, Quinn, and Bast.

Footsteps echoed throughout the hall and I turned to see Tiros joining us. A wry smile crossed his face and he raised an eyebrow at the pile of dust at my feet. "Already hard at work, I see," he said, then offered me a hand. "Come on. Let's go find your human."

I DIDN'T ASK Tiros what made him come around. It didn't matter to me if the entire collective of competing witches killed each other trying to win the Royal Covens final trial. It wouldn't be quick or easy, but now I knew that's why the trials were so taboo. The best and brightest of each coven would die here buried by greed and ambition to become the ultimate ruler. We'd had a council of witches to rule us for so long I couldn't even picture what a matriarchal witch society would even look like—all I knew was that Sarina could not be in charge.

"You know where Cassidy is?" I hissed at Tiros as he led me down a manicured garden path. Marcus, Quinn, and

Bast trailed behind us, giving me space to talk to the vampire.

It still baffled me that he didn't have his glamour, but he didn't seem very concerned about it. "I've known where she was this whole time," Tiros admitted.

I stopped in my tracks and curled my fingers into fists. "And you didn't think to tell me?"

He sighed. "Look, Evelyn, I think you should be focusing on Sarina." He glanced at the others. "But, it's been a long time since I've worked on a team. It isn't just about what I want, and I see that now."

I followed his gaze and found Marcus with his arms crossed watching me with a predator's focus. "I think we should get Cassidy out and then leave. We've already stayed here too long and put you in too much danger." He swept his gaze over my body. "Something happened to you during the dream trial and I don't like it. We need to get you back to the Palace."

I propped my hands on my hips and stared him down. "I'm not going to trade one problem for another. Sarina was able to get into the vampire stronghold and steal Cassidy from right under our noses, or have you forgotten already?" We couldn't just snatch her and run back to the Palace again and hope vampiric magic wouldn't fail us for a second time.

"We'll be better prepared," he insisted. "She won't get in again."

Not convinced, I decided this conversation would be best *after* we rescued Cassidy. "Enough. Tiros, lead the way." I gave him a raised brow. "And maybe put your glamour back on so you don't expose all of us."

An uncomfortable silence mixed with the gentle breeze that played with the blooms on the side of the path. The gardens were peaceful and beautiful, a conflicting image to the danger I knew we were in every second we remained in the Royal Covens.

"He does have his glamour on," Quinn said, his own glamour active in the form of a female voice that still held his familiar Irish accent. "Are you saying that you can see through it?"

I swallowed hard and continued to stare at Tiros just to make sure I wasn't seeing what I wanted to see. Ruby eyes glittered at me beneath that shaggy black hair. I'd forgotten how tall he was as he approached me, his mouth parting to reveal lengthening fangs he'd buried in my neck only the night before. I reached up to my collarbone and ran my fingers over the small grooves across my skin that assured me of our shared intimacy. "You mean to tell me you don't see him as a vampire?"

Marcus squeezed my arm. "As I said, the dream trial changed you somehow. You need to be careful."

Tiros shrugged. "Perhaps it's just the effect of our bonding." He flashed me a wicked grin. "My power, Evelyn, is to see through lies and deceit. I would never lie to you, and so you can see through my glamour."

"Then why can't I see through Marcus or Quinn's?" I asked.

Tiros surprised me by grabbing onto Quinn's breast and squeezing, making my bondmate yelp. Tiros grinned. "Perhaps this is their true nature?"

Quinn slapped the offending hand away. "You fucking bastard. Do that again and I'll—"

Tiros' grin widened, showing teeth. "You'll scream like a little girl for me again?"

"Guys," I said with a huff, "can we focus please?" I gave Tiros a shove. "Cassidy. Human. Save. Now." Perhaps if I used simple words then the vampire would stop fondling my other bondmates and help me save Cassidy.

He blew Quinn a kiss for good measure before complying. "All right, love, this way."

We followed Tiros through the gardens, leaving behind a hum of negative energy as the other witches and warlocks no doubt settled in for breakfast with Sarina. I didn't mind missing whatever speech she'd prepared for the countless lives that'd been lost due to the stupid dream trial. My absence wouldn't go unnoticed, I was sure, but that was a risk I had to take to find Cassidy and make sure she was all right.

I'd expected Tiros to take me to the dungeons where I'd been stuffed in before. Memory choked me as the suffocating sensations filtered over my mind. I'd barely survived that night and that was with the help of my bondmates and ancient magic to get me through it. If Cassidy was in such conditions again, she'd be dead by now without help.

Nope. Couldn't think about that.

Relief washed over me when Tiros swerved in the opposite direction, taking a path I wasn't familiar with deeper into the gardens that ran a border towards the maze we'd been trapped in just the other day. Had I been so close to her and hadn't even known it?

"There are human slaves being kept here," Tiros said, his

voice low and gentle. We reached a wall of vines and Tiros rolled up his sleeves before he reached through them. He grimaced as thorns sprouted from the vines and sank into his wrists.

"Tiros," I said, warning. "It knows we're not supposed to be here."

"It's just a defense mechanism," he said, continuing to reach through the angered foliage as he continued to search for something. "I don't remember them being this bad, but… there's a latch here somewhere. If I could just find it…"

My magic bubbled within me, but Marcus gripped my arm. "We can't use magic here. That'll trigger Sarina's automatic defenses."

With a sigh, I tried to calm the thunderstorm roiling inside of me. With each new bond I activated, each piece of my soul that I recovered, and new ally I made, new powers added to the tumult in my chest. Yet I had to watch, helpless, as blood trailed down Tiros's arms and dripped from his elbows.

I flinched when he hit the latch and an unsettling *click* thrummed through the door. "There," he said, smiling.

The vines instantly retreated and revealed a stairway that descended into darkness. I wasn't afraid of the dark, but I was afraid of underground prisons rigged with gods knew what. Sarina was all kinds of fucked up and I had no idea what we'd find down here.

Marcus offered Tiros one of his endless supply of handkerchiefs and Tiros accepted it, wiping off the blood from wounds that had already healed. I blinked, marveling at his smooth skin, as Quinn pushed by me. "Don't look so impressed," he grunted, lowering his voice as if trying to compensate for the feminine glamour. "All vampires heal fast."

"But not all vampires rock a set of knockers like that," Tiros countered without missing a beat, letting his gaze fall to admire Quinn's cleavage.

Instead of biting back, Quinn chose to ignore the comment. He lowered his voice and crouched. "I sense other vampires down there."

That made the hairs on the back of my neck stand on end. Vampires didn't just walk into the Royal Covens—not without witch assistance, anyway.

Before the conspiracy theories flying around in my head could get out of hand, Quinn grabbed my hand and dragged me down into the darkness. When we reached two shady forms illuminated by witch lights, my fears subsided.

Killian leaned against the wall and danced his switchblade across his fingers and Aaron relaxed at his feet, tongue out as he panted and seemed to embrace his wolf form. "Figured you'd bring her down here," Killian said as his blade continued to flash with the mesmerizing movements. "Aaron and I already checked it out. Cassidy is alive." His gaze fell on me. "And you're foolish for letting them bring you down here. Are you trying to blow your cover?"

I scoffed and propped a hand on my hip. "You're one to talk. You're wandering down here without even telling us where you were? What if you got caught?"

Aaron yawned, his wolfish maw showing off a line of dangerous teeth.

Killian chuckled. "Pretty sure it's anyone else we caught that would need to worry."

Tiros growled, showing teeth. "Evelyn is right. You two shouldn't be down here alone."

"You're one to talk," Killian said, shoving off the wall and sheathing his blade into a holster at his hip. "The only reason I know about this place is because Aaron followed you." He scoffed and pulled his hair back into a warrior's ponytail, securing it with a loop. "You've been on your own for far too long. You need to learn how to work as a team."

"That's exactly what I'm trying to do," Tiros growled through clenched teeth.

"Guys," I hissed and rested my hands on each of their biceps, pausing when I remembered how rock hard my bondmates were and the fact that Killian and I had not kindled our connection yet. A reminding blaze of heat ran over my left arm where his blood rune waited for the chance to break through my skin. "I want to see Cassidy. Is it possible to get her out?"

"No," Killian said flatly.

It was a marvel to me that my bondmates all seemed to know about the super secret slave dungeon, but they'd just left her here? Either they were douchebags or there was something strong enough to keep a group of powerful warlock vampires out.

I vote for both, Bast said in my mind, startling me. He had a way of slipping in and out of sight.

I frowned down at him. *For one, don't read my mind. That's intrusive. And two, where have you been?*

He stretched, sending his front claws raking into the

unforgiving floor with an irritating screech before winding around my legs.

"I need to see for myself," I said, crossing my arms and not hiding my irritation with... all of them.

Tiros sighed. "Come on. Last thing I want is Evelyn coming down here by herself when we least expect it. Let's show her."

Killian frowned and Aaron jumped to his feet with a pitiful whine, seeming to want to discourage me from going any further.

Whatever Cassidy was enduring, I could at least let her know that I was here, that I was trying to save her. I wasn't just going to turn around now that I'd come this far.

Stepping purposefully into the hall, I had a moment of confidence, then a feline screech made me tumble as I realized I'd stepped on Bast's tail.

Sorry...

WEAPONSMASTER

"*C*ass?" I hissed as we reached the prison cells.

There were people inside each cell, but they weren't moving. I knew they were awake because glassy eyes watched me as I moved, but they'd lost any sense of hope of rescue. Whoever I was might as well be a rat in their prison, another passerby that would only leave them with nightmares and disease.

I couldn't save everyone, but I tested the door locks anyway. A sting radiated through my hand and I lurched away.

"They're all spelled," Killian said. "I've already tried them." He nodded at Tiros. "What about you, any luck?"

Tiros frowned and reached out to the lock, only to be shocked even worse than I had. The flash of electricity sparked over him. He endured it, though, just for a moment before pulling away and glaring at Killian.

Gods. These competitive guys were going to be the death of me.

"Even though I don't have magic, whatever spelled this entrance reacts to any attempt to open it. Only the witch who made this spell can open the doors," Tiros said.

Marcus marched further down the hall and paused at one of the cells. "Here," he said, glancing at me.

I scampered over to him and leaned into his chest as I peered into the darkness. My eyes adjusted, revealing Cassidy asleep on a bed of straw and her hair a mess around her face. "Cass!" I whisper-shouted. When she didn't stir, I tried to touch the bars, wincing when it shocked me. "Wake up!"

She finally opened her eyes, but she didn't move. That's when I realized that the other humans hadn't just lost hope.

They were all paralyzed.

Her eyes pleaded with me, orbs of fire and rage as she ground her teeth together. Her body refused to move, but she groaned as she tried to anyway.

"Hey," I whispered, moving as close to the bars as I dared. "Don't use up your energy. We're going to get you out of here, okay? Just... I need to figure out..." I sighed with frustration, then whirled on my guys. "We have to take down Sarina in order to free Cassidy." That didn't change my agenda very much, but at least I knew Cassidy was alive.

Marcus frowned. "What if we mimicked her magic? It's possible."

"That's far too dangerous," Killian added, flipping out his switchblade, but he didn't dance it across his fingers. He jabbed the blade into the lock and sent sparks flying in all directions. He kept it up until a steady glow overtook

Cassidy's chamber and she groaned as if in pain, then he removed the blade. "If it senses tampering it'll kill whoever is inside. We can't risk it."

Marcus glowered, but didn't seem surprised by the caveat.

"You would risk Cassidy's life?" I snarled. When he refused to look at me, I huffed with disbelief. All of my bondmates were strong-willed and all of them thought they knew what was best for me, but no way was I going to put up with this kind of treatment. "Listen," I snapped, "all of you."

Killian put his blade away. Aaron sat on his haunches. Marcus and Quinn crossed their arms, and even Bast stopped cleaning himself long enough to pay attention.

I stuck up a finger as I pointed at them. Collective chastising. It always worked for Aunt Sandra. "No one is going to make decisions for me. No one is going to hide anything from me or do what you think is best just because I'm too mortal or naive to know any better. If you know something, you tell me. If you find something, you show me. I make my own decisions and none of you have the right to decide my life for me, is that straight?" Swerving my finger to point at Cassidy's cell, I continued. "That's my best friend in there. I don't care if she was once a human slave to my old coven—they're all dead now. And you know what? They gave me all their power for a reason. I never followed the old ways and I'm not going to start doing that now. Humans, witches, vampires, familiars—I gave a pointed look at Bast—even gods, we're all equal, all right? We all have our strengths and weaknesses."

Looking properly chastised, my bondmates gave a collective nod. "Okay, good. Glad that's clear. No more secrets. No more lies." I gave Tiros a glare for good measure. His power had kept the truth from me before and I was never going to be left in the dark again.

Well, except for now, in the slave dungeons where it was perpetually dark.

I went to the bars again, but didn't try to touch them. "Listen, Cass, if I break through these doors then the spell will kill you. I'm not going to risk your life like that, so I'm going to find Sarina and bring back whatever's left of her to make sure you're free. For now..." I let my magic hum inside of me. Cassidy's cheekbones stood out prominently on her pale face and her hair tangled with her eyelashes as she struggled to blink at me. The tattered remains of what she'd been wearing when she'd been taken clung to her, revealing sharp ribs. It'd only been a day, but the spell in this place was draining her reserves.

I thought of freedom, unlocking chains, movement and nourishment. Cassidy's fingers twitched in response and I smiled.

"Careful," Marcus warned, but I waved him away.

I kept the magic funneling through me like a steady faucet. Not too fast. Not too slow. My earrings and the mask at my hip supplied me with a portion of my power, but there was so much more underneath the surface. It crackled with delight, wanting to be used, and delighted after so long to be used for good. The magic of an entire coven glided through my veins and recognized me as its caretaker. I was a Fate Witch, and I was the last member of the Amethyst Coven still standing. It not only wanted to be used... it wanted revenge.

Sarina wanted to use Cassidy to make me feel defeated and helpless. She wasn't going to kill her, not yet, but she wanted to make sure that Cassidy was miserable and looked like death warmed over. I wasn't going to allow that.

With a slow exhale, I sent my power invading into the cell without breaking its bonds. I didn't have to undo it in order to manipulate the rules.

Cassidy shot to her feet just as a row of cheeseburgers appeared on silver plates. "Gods!" she shrieked, then dove for the first sandwich. "Oh, Evie I love you so much right now."

Relief swept through me as the magic settled, allowing Cassidy to move freely as she devoured the offering.

"How did you do that?" Killian marveled.

Tiros grinned. "Impressive, young witch. You didn't manipulate the spell, simply added to it. Trading paralytics of the occupants to the particles in the cell." He pointed at the dust motes that had frozen in mid-air.

I hadn't fully realized how I'd changed Sarina's spell to allow Cassidy to move, but I nodded along and tried to look confident by lifting my chin. "Yes, that was my intention." Totally on purpose.

You might fool them, but I can read your thoughts, Bast whispered in my mind a bit too smugly for my tastes.

I glanced down at him and glared. I can step on your tail again if you like.

He yawned and circled around my ankles again, needlessly feeding me magic. I knew it was just a habit, so I ignored him. He'd supplied me with enough magic to survive all my life. I didn't expect him to stop the practice now.

Footsteps broke us all from our moment of victory and even Cassidy froze mid-bite. "What was that?" she hissed around her food, sending particles flying into the nest of hay.

I mouthed at her "Pretend to be frozen!" and turned to face the source of the sound.

My guys all instantly stepped in front of me, making me roll my eyes. Had I not just proven that I was the most powerful person here? I conjured cheeseburgers for fuck's sake.

I was about to shove my guys out of the way and tell them to get behind me when a snarl sounded from behind us. I whirled only to find the dead from the dream trial dragging themselves over the concrete floor. Bones protruded at wrong angles and one of them had an eye loose from its socket. Gross...

Aaron snarled with warning and bit the first undead zombie thing on its arm. His vicious teeth went right through the rotting flesh and tore the arm off.

"There's a good puppy," I praised him, and he glanced up at me with disdain as he spit out the remains of the arm. I winced. "Ah, yeah, bet that doesn't taste too good."

Killian chuckled in my ear, the sound sending a chill up my spine. "He just doesn't like to be called 'puppy,' but I think it's cute."

"Enough flirting!" Quinn growled and grabbed me by the arm. "Exit. Now."

Aaron held off the zombies while the rest of us approached the unknown, running straight into a startled group of warlocks whose eyes widened when they saw us. "You're not supposed to be here!" one began, but then glanced over our shoulders and paled. "What in the seven hells is that?"

Taking advantage of the warlock's shock, I shoved past

him. "What, you didn't run into them during the dream trial?" I snapped. "Lucky."

"Hey!" another said, this one with a recognizable corsage glittering on his chest. His soul artifact. "You're not supposed to be down here. I'll tell Sarina—"

I snatched up the ethereal bloom, but didn't crush it. He froze. "You'll tell Sarina no such thing. I'm down here for my own reasons. What are you doing here?" I glared at him, then squeezed my grip just a fraction. He flinched at a minuscule crack formed over his collarbone. "Why are you stupid enough to wear your artifact where others could get to it?"

"Because those are the rules!" he shouted, panting as the crack breached his chin. "Sarina just told us that we all have to display our artifacts on our person. Makes the trial fairer." He seemed to finally recognize the rose I'd tucked behind my ear and he reached for it, flinching when my magic bit him and brought a droplet of blood to his fingertip. He popped it in his mouth. "Sarina said there were some easy pickings down here and we could get a head start..."

"Shit," I cursed. Sarina knew we were down here. This was just a fucking trap. "Come on." I grabbed my nearest bond-mate—which happened to be Killian, and dragged him through the crowd of stunned warlocks that were too busy gaping at the zombies to attack us. Good, at least the dead were useful for something.

I glanced once over my shoulder to see if Aaron was following us. No way was I going to leave anyone behind. Sickly black blood oozed from his muzzle, but his eyes sparked with excitement as he rammed through the warlocks and followed us towards the exit. At least someone was having a good time.

Once we breached the doorway to the outside, I realized that I was still holding the warlock's soul artifact. I wasn't going to play Sarina's stupid little game. As carefully as I could, I settled the bloom within the angry vines that lined the entranceway. They hungrily drew the object into their fold as if it were a long lost relative, but I was glad to see that it didn't harm the object. Instead, it kept it tucked safe. This was likely one warlock that wouldn't get his soul shattered in this stupid place.

"Okay, new plan," I said as the guys gathered around me. I winced when screams sounded from the halls below. Guess the dead found their warlocks. "Sarina is sending the survivors after us so we need to hide. I need to get to Sarina —alone."

None of my bondmates seemed amused by that idea.

"Are you thinking clearly?" Marcus asked, slipping his arm around my waist and reminding me what it felt like to be so close to him. "Sarina is powerful, dear. We've found out where Cassidy is and—"

"And nothing," I finished for him, managing to wriggle out of his grip even though I didn't really want to. I stared him down and let my defiance fill my senses. It was barely enough to overcome his intoxicating scent of roses and jasmine. Barely...

Marcus let out an exasperated sigh. "Look what you've done," he said to Tiros.

The vampire stared wordlessly at Marcus, then took a deep breath. "I'm not going to tell Evelyn what to do. If she wants to face off with Sarina, then I trust she knows what she's doing."

I clapped my hands. "Thank you!"

"You can't look for her right now," Killian said, lowering his voice as he glanced over the gardens. Even though it should have been morning, the gloom of dusk settled over the landscape. "She's called the dead after you, and from the sounds of it they're picking off the competition as well." He jerked his chin towards the greenery where the atmosphere didn't seem as thick. "The dead can't walk on holy ground. If the blueprints I saw in the Palace are still accurate, there's a patch this way."

I gaped at him, then glanced at Tiros. "Are you telling me you have intel on the Royal Covens and you didn't think to inform me?"

Tiros balled his hands into fists, his illusion of patience starting to crack as if I'd grabbed his soul artifact and squeezed—too bad he didn't have one for me to threaten him with.

"There is a thousand years of vampire history I haven't told you, not because it's a secret from you, but because you've only just come back into our lives and without any of your memories." Tiros crossed his arms and glowered down at me. "Have I not proven myself trustworthy? I showed you where Sarina was keeping Cassidy." He flung an arm back at the entranceway that was starting to growl louder with marching undead. I guess they figured out how to use stairs. "I let you walk in there knowing it was a trap, knowing that you wouldn't have cared either way."

"You knew this was a trap?" Marcus growled, shook his

head, then took me by the arm. "We have to get you out of here. I won't stand for you being put into this senseless danger any longer."

Wrenching myself free of his grasp, I slipped my fingers into Killian's and purposefully marched towards the one spot of the gardens that wasn't clouded over with fog. "Well, Killian trusts me enough to show me where I can be safe while this passes over. I'm not leaving, and I'm certainly not abandoning Cassidy."

"What would you have us do?" Quinn asked, sounding sincere.

I paused and turned to look at him. His glamour was starting to fade, or at least, I was getting strong enough to see through the spell. The feminine body he'd taken faded and his true self shone through like a brilliant ruby. Red, vibrant strands danced around his face and fangs protruded from his mouth, making me want to go to him and stroke one just to remind myself that he was a dangerous predator.

But he was my predator. They all were.

I squeezed Killian's hand, but didn't let go. Right now he was offering me an option none of the others were. A place to make plans and figure out how to stop Sarina without leaving the Royal Covens. If I left, I worried that I wouldn't be able to come back. This was my only shot and I had to do things right the first time. I wasn't like Marcus. I wasn't a Time Witch who could step through days, weeks, centuries, and find the perfect moment to make my move. I was a Fate Witch, which meant I lived in the present and altered the future in ways a Time Witch could never see coming.

"I need all of you to go back to the collective and excuse

my absence. Sarina doesn't know who I am yet, but she'll figure it out soon. I need a delay while I make a plan to stop her. Can you guys do that for me?"

My GUYS LEFT me with some reluctance, but we made a plan. I wasn't sure how any of us could think with the sounds of warlocks being torn apart by zombies in the secret dungeon Sarina had used as a trap, but a girl gets used to things in the paranormal world.

I didn't realize that I'd had a death grip on Killian's hand until he squeezed my fingers in return, letting me know that it was time to move. I'd watched my guys walk down the path, even Bast going with them, worrying if they'd be okay. They might not have soul artifacts on display, but I knew that they were more vulnerable here than they'd admit. Then my gaze went to the empty hall where the screams had gone silent.

"Cassidy is in the safest place she can be right now," Killian said, gently tugging me away.

I knew he was right. She was trapped inside an impenetrable magicked cell that even I couldn't break—and all the cheeseburgers she could eat. She'd be fine.

But would I survive?

"What is going on down there?" I wondered aloud. It was too quiet and it unsettled me.

Killian wrapped an arm around my waist and forced me to turn away, guiding me towards the small patch of holy ground. "They're probably feeding. We don't want to still be here when they're done."

I grimaced at the mental image. "Lovely."

He chuckled. "You're quite squeamish, for a witch."

"Shut up and get me to safety," I chided him.

His hand slipped lower and I nearly tripped over my own feet. He chuckled, the sound husky and expectant. I hadn't really seen this side of him before, but I suppose he'd always stayed in the shadows while I reunited with my other bond-mates. "I like it when you're bossy," he said, his face lighting up with a wicked grin.

My mouth opened, but no words came out. The tell-tale sign of heat building across a forgotten scar on my arm reminded me of a blood rune that was dangerously close to forming, as well as heat that built between my thighs that reacted to ancient memories of lifetimes ago where Killian did a lot more to me than let his hand slip to my ass.

"So, is this really holy ground?" I asked him, hating how my words came out nervous and shaky. I was never nervous. Assholes didn't do that to me, but Killian wasn't exactly an asshole, not like the others could be. I got the sense from him that he was actually quite shy and that made me care about what he thought of me.

Damn it, of all my bondmates, was Killian the sadistic weaponsmaster the one who really got to me? It took me off-guard how he made me feel and I realized I'd never really been alone with him. I wasn't sure how I felt about it.

He bit his lip, flashing fang at me without realizing it which made him even sexier. "You think I'm lying to you just to get you alone?" The question came off his lips playfully, encouraging me to call him out on it.

I glared at him, hoping that I looked serious. "If you think you're going to seduce me, you have shitty timing. I almost just got eaten by zombies and my best friend is trapped in a cell."

He lifted one finger as if to make a point. "Trapped with cheeseburgers." He shrugged. "I'd say she looked quite happy."

We walked together deeper into the gardens. It didn't feel like my life was in danger here or that everything was going to shit. If I didn't turn around and take in the darkening landscape, I could almost feel like I'd come to the Royal Covens at a time when it was good and pure, run by honorable witches—well, as honorable as Royal Covens witches could be.

Killian led the way and I took stride next to him, matching his leisurely pace and watching his fingers twitch. We were still holding hands, but I could tell that he wanted to go for his switchblade. "Am I making you nervous?"

He chuckled. "Actually, yeah. It's pretty lame of me to get nervous around you, isn't it? After what we were to each other, I was devastated to lose you, and then when I realized you were back in my life..." He let out a long sigh. "I don't know. This isn't how I expected to feel."

I knew exactly what he meant. Giving his fingers one last squeeze, I released him and scampered towards an oversized oak that seemed out of place in the pristine gardens. Its knobby bark flaked and the ground around it was peppered with needles, making the area look more natural and messy in a way that I decided I liked.

As I settled myself against the oak and tucked my knees to my chest, Killian gave me a raised brow. "How did you know this tree wasn't tainted?"

"Tainted?" I asked, my voice raising an octave. I cleared my throat and tried again. "What do you mean?"

He gave the gardens a once over before settling down next to me. He leaned back, stretching against the bark and moving slowly side-to-side to scratch his shoulder blades. "I mean that Sarina has her fingers in everything in this place, even a few spots on holy ground." He pointed at a particularly vibrant bush of daisies. "There."

I squinted at the flowers before recognizing the glimmer of magic that glistened across the petals. A soft gasp escaped me. "What is that?" It couldn't be a soul artifact. Sarina wouldn't be dumb enough to leave herself vulnerable like that.

He shifted closer to me and lowered his lips to my ear. "Have you ever heard of a witch 'seeding?'"

I turned to face him, but he didn't shift away, leaving me dangerously close to his fangs. I swallowed hard. "Not really, no."

Killian made my breath catch as he slipped his fingers through my hair and tucked a strand behind my ear. "She's drawing the magic out of this place. She leaves behind a spell and her weeds will suck up any power it touches, leaving a ripe harvest for when she returns." His hand slipped down my arm and settled onto my hip as he pushed me against the oak tree. "If you'd decided to take a nap in her trap, Sarina could drain you dry in a matter of hours."

A humorless laugh bubbled out of me. I couldn't decide if I was terrified by how easily Sarina could not only kill me, but take my powers without even me realizing it, or by the way Killian was making me feel right now. The hot patch of skin on my left arm burned, warning me that I was close to igniting a bond with Killian whether I was ready for it or not. His gaze fell to my lips and they parted for him. "I'm glad you're here to teach me, then."

He kept his attention on my mouth, his own jaw dropping in an aroused, vampiric hiss when I licked my lips. "There's so much you don't know about me, Evelyn. So much I am supposed to teach you." His ruby eyes finally lifted to match mine. "So much that you're not ready to learn."

He didn't get to say what I was ready for. My heart pounded in my chest and undeniable need thrummed between my thighs. My body knew who and what Killian was to me. It was time that I opened that locked box of memories he seemed so terrified for me to peek into.

I decided not to reply to him with words. I reached up and ran my fingers over his. He rewarded me with a smile. "I feel your power, Evelyn. You're getting stronger. Perhaps, strong enough..."

I didn't let him finish his sentence. His hesitation was because he thought he would hurt me. That was ridiculous. I pressed my mouth to his and his lips parted for me. I was familiar with the cool danger of fangs by now and I trusted him not to harm me. Grazing my tongue across his left me with an awakening thrill. He tasted of sea and salt and reminded me of freedom and a heart with such expanse that I'd never reach the horizon. He liked to scare others off with his weapons and threats, but he felt—and he felt deeply. That only turned me on more.

Growing bolder, Killian's hand on my hip pinned me as his other hand worked at my pants zipper. He paused after he'd pulled it down, leaving the fabric folded open as if he'd just opened a delicious gift. His gaze dropped and his fangs grew larger, but he didn't move as if he was going to change his mind.

"Don't tease me," I warned him. He belonged to me and I belonged to him. This was right. The blood rune across my forearm already burned to life, leaving droplets of blood to glide down my skin. "It's already begun."

Killian's gaze matched mine and I felt like his whole world opened up to me. When his magic came tumbling after, I realized why he was so worried about allowing our bond. He'd been a powerful warlock before his turn to vampirism, but now he was something more. "You almost died because of me," he admitted, his voice breaking as his fingers slipped between my legs at the same time. He stroked me so gently I almost didn't feel it. I arched into his touch, wanting more. "You must know how sorry I am, Evelyn. The only reason I took those souls in the first place was to protect you." He slipped my underwear aside and thrust a finger into me, making me gasp. He paused and allowed my feminine muscles to clench around him as he awakened new desires that felt so foreign even though I knew they were emerging memories. My past lives with my bondmates rarely came back to me as coherent thoughts, rather I remembered them with my heart and my body.

"I survived the dream trial," I assured him. My hips moved against him, encouraging him to release me from the sweet torture of the pressure of his fingers. I needed him to thrust and to take. I needed him to show me who we were to each other. An entire lifetime had been taken from me... A thousand years ago Sarina had won and I had died. She didn't get to win again. She didn't get to keep my bondmates separated from me.

Killian didn't obey my body's command. Instead, he spread his fingers, making me cry out as my need for him grew impossibly more. "You could have died," he insisted. He leaned over me without taking his fingers out of me. His fangs grazed my neck and I arched in him, wanting him to bite, to do everything to me that came naturally to a vampire.

"I will die if you don't put a part of you inside of me right now and give me what I need," I said through my panting breaths. I gripped his shirt and clung to him, riding my hips on his fingers and forcing him to give me sensation. "I need more, Killian. You want to torture yourself? Fine, but don't deny me."

His fangs tested my skin with warning. A low growl came from him as he removed his fingers. When I squirmed and tried to undo his pants, he grabbed my wrist. "No," he said, a command, a threat.

I froze and stared at him, but then I saw he wasn't going to deny me. He meant to deny himself.

"Don't move," he instructed as he tugged my jeans down over my hips along with my underwear, exposing my swollen flesh to the humid air. He kept his mouth open or else his fangs would pierce his lips, and when he raked his gaze over me I shivered with the sense that he wanted to bite.

"Killian?" I felt so exposed and vulnerable. I wanted to be in control, to take back the bond that had been broken, but he was determined to take this slow.

He settled between my thighs and spread the folds of my

skin, exposing my clit. I gasped when he ran his tongue over me and sent pleasure exploding up into my core. If he did that just a few more times... I wasn't going to last.

When I arched against him as he ran a second long lick over me, he grinned. "I said no moving."

Everything was too swollen, too crippled with need. I grappled at his arms as I tried to pull him over me. "I need you in me," I begged him, but he wasn't going to give me what I wanted, not yet. The mischief and endless horizon in his eyes told me that I was exactly where he wanted me.

He rammed two fingers inside of me without warning, making me cry out. He slammed into me a second time and covered my clit with his mouth. His fangs grazed my thighs and drew blood. The contrast of pleasure and pain sent me tipping over the edge and my back bowed as the onslaught of a powerful orgasm took control of my body.

Killian suckled me and spread his fingers, fighting against my contractions to lengthen my pleasure. I rode that high and forgot how to breathe until the burning need of the blood rune on my arm brought me back to awareness.

Killian felt it too. He sucked in a breath as the command to cement our bond rammed into both of us. "Now, Killian," I said, this time my words a command, not a plea.

He pulled his fingers out of my slickness and grabbed onto my hips, pulling me closer to him. I tore at his pants and freed his impressive erection. I didn't have time to admire him or return the favor. The compelling desire pouring into both of us demanded that we become one.

Killian's switchblade fell from his pocket when he rolled his girth over me, spreading my legs and lubricating himself with my slickness. I don't know why I did it, but I grabbed the blade and flicked it open, settling the edge against his throat. When he grinned, I realized that my body remembered something that my mind could not.

"There's my Evie," he whispered as he leaned into me, sliding his dick inside of me and filling me until he locked himself to the hilt. His body was a blade and I was his scabbard. "Draw blood," he commanded, then began a slow, agonizing rocking motion that made me groan.

I nicked him just enough to send a droplet of blood gliding over his skin. I wasn't a vampire. I didn't have fangs or want to drink blood, but my body was compelling me to take him into my mouth. He lowered, crushing me with his weight as he ground his hips into mine. When he arched his neck to me, I bit down and ran my tongue over the small cut.

His blood tasted like everything that was Killian, like salt and the sea and magic. I drank it in as he fucked me and something inside of me locked into place.

Need flooded my mind, but not my own. Killian's thoughts, desires, and a darkness that frightened me bore itself into my skull. He needed the pain. He needed the punishment to be cut and for me to take his lifeforce from him like he had done to so many others. In my past life, we'd been unhealthy for each other in a way. I pacified his need for punishment and he gave me sensations I wouldn't experience with any other bondmates. I wasn't really into hurting others for sexual pleasure, but when it came to Killian, I'd do anything to get him to stop denying himself pleasure. This was how he loosened up. This was how I had won him over to becoming my bondmate in the first place.

I took the blade and tried to still my shaking grip. I had to be precise.

Killian stilled, waiting to see what I'd do next. He watched me with such intensity that I shivered. "Do it," he said, begging me. All the command had seeped out of him and all that was left was his need.

He leaned back so that I could mark his chest, but he kept his dick inside of me. I would feel pleasure when I gave him what he needed and my heart fluttered, remembering times just like this one even though my mind wouldn't surface the memories that my soul kept hostage.

I drew a rune on his chest, one that I'd never seen in any textbook or ancient scroll. This was a rune that belonged between Killian and me. A weaponsmaster and his soul blade, a title given to any weapon he touched, had a witch's name. I drew the long circle and zig-zag marks across his chest, making sure to mark each line with intent. Blood seeped from his wound and as a vampire, should have been quick to heal, but he continued to bleed. This was a binding spell that named him for what he was and that gave me power over Killian. Power I would need to reclaim our bond and the piece of my soul he had safeguarded for a thousand years.

His dick swelled inside of me with each line I made. I pushed down the queasiness that came with the knowledge that Killian gained pleasure from pain, but this was what he needed from me, and this was what I needed from him. I needed to accept him, all of him, his darkness and his light.

A burst of magic glowed from his chest when I completed the rune. Invisible strands of power wrapped around us and bound us together. Killian resumed his thrusts and I pushed myself against the ground, bowing and arching into him so that he could go deeper. His fangs looked painfully long and swollen, needing to be inside of me. I turned my head to the side. "Take my blood."

This time he didn't hesitate. His eyes glowed with lust and he descended on me. When his fangs pierced me, I expected pain, but something else coursed through me instead. I didn't know if all vampires had the gift to make their bite sensual, but my bondmates seemed capable of it, and Killian more so than any of them. Perhaps it was his intimate relationship with pain that made him good at turning it into pleasure. Whatever the reason, it brought me to orgasm and I clenched around his dick as he thrust deep inside of me, piercing me as he took his fill.

Killian only took my blood when he could have taken so much more. We were linked in this state and he could have drained me dry. He was careful not to take my magic that he'd so painstakingly given back to me. He waited for my orgasm to crest and fall before turning me over. He shoved his hands under my shirt and squeezed my breasts. "You taste delicious," he whispered in my ear, voice husky and deep as he resumed a rocking motion that sent fresh waves of pleasure through me.

"I don't think I can take any more," I said, choking on the words through pants of pleasure. He kept his thrusts slow and deliberate, going all the way to the hilt and his thighs slapped against my ass before he pulled out again.

Still holding onto my breasts, he pinched my nipples, giving me a bite of pain with my pleasure that he was so good at mixing. "You can do anything," he assured me, then massaged the sweet hurt.

He only stopped when he grunted in pain, but he wouldn't let me turn to see what had caused it. He moved his hands to my shoulders and kept me pinned low with my ass in the air.

"Don't move, sweetheart," he said, coaxing me, not commanding.

"Are you okay?"

HE GRUNTED AGAIN, but his tight grip on me said that whatever was going on, I couldn't turn around. He didn't want me to see what had interrupted our bonding.

Then he lifted one hand from me. "Just, stay there. This'll only take a minute. No matter what, don't turn around."

I bit my lip and tried to obey him, but I couldn't help but twist to glance at him when a new groan escaped him, one most certainly filled with more pain than pleasure. I gasped when I saw why he'd stopped. The edge of a hilt stuck from his chest with a dagger impaled into his ribcage. He gripped it and slowly pulled it out.

"Killian, I—" I tried to tell him to stop, that removing a blade impaled in such a vital area would do more harm than good, but he slipped the blade free before I had a chance to stop him.

My stomach dropped when I spotted the white flash of bone just before his skin healed over, smoothing the rune that I'd drawn on him. He ran the sharp edge of the blade up my spine and grinned. "Don't recognize your own dagger?" he asked, all traces of pain gone and his dick hardening once again inside of me.

I didn't have time to examine the weapon, but my body recognized it. It was just like the earrings that Quinn had given me, or the Masquerade Mask that bore Marcus's gifts. This was my bond artifact with Killian, the item that housed all of my magic he'd kept safe for me. My mortal body was too weak to accept everything back into me, perhaps that's why my memories refused to resurface in anything more than sensations and instinct.

I wanted to take the blade, but Killian had resumed his thrusts with new vigor, no longer worried about hurting me —and I liked it.

Each thrust crested us both to new heights of our pleasure. I pushed back against him and dug my fingers into the soil, not caring that the grains got under my fingernails. The blood rune on my arm sang with pleasure and power. We were almost there. We were almost bonded again.

"Evie," Killian cried as he thrust into me harder, going so deep that my core clenched with the threat of a release so powerful it would take me under. "Evie, come with me."

I rolled my eyes back and allowed the sensations to take over. Killian kept the blade flat against my skin, allowing me to feel its danger and heat as well as the magic that funneled into me fueled by our passion. Yet I sensed that he needed pain to reach his climax—that was his curse—so he slid his hand over the blade just once and hot blood smeared across my back, making me sigh. There was just as much magic in his blood as there was in his soul and my vision speckled with stars as I struggled to contain it in my mortal frame.

Then he came into me, the heat of his blood on my back mixing with the heat of his seed inside of me. I cried out with him as my climax hit without warning or mercy, taking me under until there was only sensation, bliss, pain and pleasure that I never wanted to end.

When my vision cleared and I finally could sense the ground beneath my palms, I found myself collapsed in a heap with Killian panting beside me. He wrapped me in his arms and hugged me close, his fingers sweeping over the fresh blood rune that became a permanent scar from our bonding. "Thank you," he whispered, the words sounding reverent.

I chuckled. "You're welcome, my masochistic weapons-master." I twisted and tucked my head under his chin, not caring that we were both filthy, bloody, and in dire need of a shower.

I finally had Killian back. My memories might not want to return in their full glory, but I would never doubt how right it felt to be in his arms like this.

This was a new memory, one I would be keeping for good.

A NEW ME

*A*fter reigniting my bond with Killian, I thought I might feel different, and I did, but not in the way I expected. He thought that I'd shy away from his sexual tendencies and be disgusted by him. Perhaps if he'd been my first experience among my bondmates I wouldn't have been ready, but now that I had gained trust with my bonds and understanding of how deep those ties went, nothing was going to keep me from giving them all what they desired, and that was to be with me, and me to accept them for who they were.

My body thrummed with power and excitement. I was so close to awakening something lost within myself. I played with the dagger that Killian had given me and ran my fingertips over the sharp blade, wincing when I cut myself by accident.

Killian chuckled and took my finger, popping it into his

mouth. When I reclaimed my hand, he smirked. "Be careful. The weapon I safeguarded for you is as sharp as your magic, which seems to have amplified over the years." His gaze fell to the blade. "I was afraid..."

"You should never be afraid," I finished for him. Stroking my masquerade mask on my hip, I drew magic into myself and swept it over us to clean away the grime and blood. We didn't have time to seek out a shower in the dorms, assuming that was even safe, but I didn't want the other witches to put two and two together. Killian was still a vampire and if he was discovered, he'd be in even more danger than he was already was.

Killian adjusted his clothes as the magic did its work, even smoothing out the wrinkles from our love-making. "You shouldn't waste your power on me, or trivial things."

A laugh bubbled out of me. "You sound like Bast."

He wrinkled his nose. "Gods. I hope not." He leaned in and snapped his teeth, making me flinch with delight. "Cats scratch, but I bite."

"Yes, you do," I agreed and reluctantly got to my feet. I wanted to stay here all day with Killian and explore him again and again, memorizing every line and muscle that I'd lost. It was the silhouette of forms in the distance that warned me we wouldn't be alone for much longer, and that our brief interlude of exploring our bond was over, for now.

Killian followed my gaze and sighed. "It's just the others. I hope they bring good news."

Aaron, still in his wolf form, scampered ahead of the rest. He was the last bondmate that my runes called for me to complete, but he couldn't shift back to his human form, not here. It wasn't safe, but the sense of joy that wafted from him told me that he didn't care. He ran straight for me and tackled me right in the stomach, making all the breath go out of me as I crashed to the floor of soft soil and flowers.

"Aaron!" I squealed, laughing as he lapped at my face in eager greeting.

Killian grabbed him by the scruff and hauled the beast off of me. "What's wrong with you?" he growled, clearly not nearly as amused by the display of affection as I was.

Marcus chuckled when he reached us. "Someone's happy that they're going to be next." He gave me a raised brow, his gaze going to my arm. "You've accepted even our weapons-master, which means the beast thinks you're up for anything now." He roughed the beast up with a grin. "And he's happy that you're regaining your powers and your memories."

Killian scoffed. "She's not regaining her memories. It's her magic that recognizes us."

Quinn cleared his throat. He still thought that I'd actually regained my memories and he wasn't going to be deterred by Killian telling my dark truth. I couldn't remember them. Sure, something in me recognized them, my body responded to them and I knew there were memories there, but they were forbidden to me. My magic prevented me from doing harm to myself and I had a feeling if I truly regained everything from my past life then I wouldn't be the Evelyn that I was today anymore. I had no intention of becoming someone else. I liked who I was, flaws and all.

"We don't have time for this," Tiros said, crossing his arms and looking more like his rude, impatient self. He towered over the rest of us, which was a feat given how tall all of my bondmates were. "Sarina has called a meeting for those who have survived the first round of artifact hunting."

I rolled my eyes. "That's what she's calling it? 'Artifact Hunting?' She makes it sound like it's just all a game."

"I thought we were coming here to seek refuge on holy ground," Quinn said, then his gaze flicked to the disturbed bit of torn-up ground where Killian and I had cemented our bond. It looked more like a murder scene with the deep dark splotches of blood coloring the dirt and turning the green leaves that had survived our onslaught a shade of pink. He smirked. "Well, what used to be holy ground, anyway." He nudged Killian with his elbow, winning a glare from the weaponsmaster.

Bast wandered through the forest of legs, not seeming to care that he might get trampled. Even in the coven he'd been that way, always expecting special treatment because he was a familiar. Now I knew that his arrogance was top-notch because he was actually a god.

God of familiars or not, Bast was still one of my bond-mates and adorably cute in his feline form. I picked him up and gave him a snuggle. He glared at me, but didn't claw off my face, which was a testimony to how much he liked me. "We can't just hide from Sarina and let everyone kill each other in hopes to win her stupid game. She's not going to let someone else win these trials and take power away from her." I'd never worked out what she was up to when it came to restarting the trials, but with this much bloodshed I was starting to get an idea.

"Sacrifice," Marcus said, stroking his chin. "Her magic runs off of sacrifice."

I nodded and put Bast down who meowed his agreement. "That's right. She hopes all this death is going to give her enough power to come after me, and if we let this go on she might just get her way." I propped my hands on my hips and decided I wasn't going to be afraid of the witch. Even if she'd managed to kill me before, I wasn't going to stop trying to do the right thing. "Let's go to her little meeting and see who's left. Maybe we can convince them to turn on her."

Quinn ran his fingers through his fiery red hair that glowed with a healthy sheen in the magicked sunlight. His female glamour was almost entirely gone to me now. "I doubt that, lass. Sarina isn't the only power-hungry witch in all the covens. She just happens to be one of the only ones powerful enough to pull it off."

I waved away his concerns. I'd seen enough from the other covens to know that greed ran rampant in witches, but there was good there, too. Surely not everyone was a monster. "I have to try. I'm not going to just sit here trapped in the gardens and wait for her to come after me."

Tiros took a step closer to me, his comforting scent of leather and horses making me relax. "Then we're going with you."

I'd thought about proposing that my bondmates stay here, but one glimpse of the look in Tiros's eyes told me there was no way I was going to get them to let me face Sarina alone. "Are you sure?" I asked anyway.

"You know we all have different opinions when it comes to this matter," Tiros said, waving a hand to the rest of my bondmates. "Marcus thinks you should try and save Cassidy and make a run for it, but I am with you. You need to face Sarina and end her threat once and for all. Running didn't work for you before."

Marcus growled. "The last time she faced her she died, or have you forgotten so easily?"

Tiros didn't seem fazed by Marcus's anger. "I didn't endure a thousand years of penance the same as you, but in a way that made my punishment worse. While you were reliving the same moment over and over, I was forced to grieve Evelyn's death. Forced to know that I wouldn't see her again for so many years that I couldn't even wrap my mind around it without going mad." The haunting torment in his eyes broke my heart. He'd suffered, in some ways worse than any of my other bondmates had suffered and that only amplified my rage more. Sarina was the one responsible for all of this pain and she'd get her due.

"Enough," I said, the word final. Marching across the path that would take me out of the gardens, I glowered at the patch of daisies that represented one of Sarina's many traps. I pointed my dagger at it and a ray of magic pierced it, sending the weeds withering into nothing. "I'm going to face Sarina and this time she isn't going to win."

Aaron's wolf whined, scampering up to me and licking my hand.

Quinn caught up to me and gave the wolf a scratch behind his ear. "Aaron's right. What makes you so sure you're going to win?"

I didn't have to look at him to know that worry made his eyebrows scrunch together. I hated to be the cause for any of my bondmates to worry, but there was no helping it. I wasn't just going to hide from my problem.

I flashed him a grin. "Because this time I'm mortal, and mortals are scrappy as hell."

THE BLOOD DRAINED from my face when we entered the main spire of the Royal Covens and discovered how many witches and warlocks were actually left.

When we'd started the trials there'd been hundreds of witches, but now only a small group sat at the long tables that represented the various covens. A feast steamed on the table, untouched, enough to feed a single coven for a full month. None of us had any appetite after what we'd been through.

By the looks of everyone's haggard faces and rough appearance, I should have left the dirt and blood all over me. Only a few had managed to clean up for the dinner. Sarina was the only one who seemed untouched by the horror. She was the eye of the storm that turned the world around her upside down. She sat on her throne, which was a modified version of the Diamond Coven chair she used to sit in. It now was elevated, the other chairs completely removed and the rest of the coven leaders missing. I wondered if she'd killed them off already. The number of sacrifices going around would have given her more than enough power to kill off even immortal witches. The thought of it made me sick.

"Survivors, I'm so pleased to join you for this glorious evening," she said, her words ringing out over us.

I sat with the rest of my bondmates and one other Pearl

Coven survivor, a girl I recognized from my fight with the Emerald Witch I'd killed what seemed like forever ago. She glanced at me under her eyelashes. When I tried to meet her gaze, she grabbed a loaf of bread and put it on her empty plate and stared at it.

I sighed, returning my attention to Sarina's mindless drivel.

"Eat well, my fellow witches and warlocks, because I have a special task for you." She grinned at the remaining witches and warlocks. Most seemed underwhelmed by the idea of a new task and blankly stared at her. Others, however, the ones like the Emerald Witch I'd killed, cheered her on and toasted her with the blood-colored drinks that sloshed over onto the floor. Those few glowed with the power of stolen soul artifacts and I frowned at the madness in their eyes. Killian was one of the few warlocks who had the power to rip a soul from its body without going insane. It was part of his relationship with pain, but also his understanding and respect of it. He did not revel in hurting others, only did what he thought was right.

Killian nodded at me from across the table. Now that our bond was in place he could sense when I thought of him. He knew without a doubt that I understood him—the real him. He was nothing like these other lunatics.

"Please, enjoy your last dinner," Sarina said, emphasizing the words with a manic grin. "After you've eaten, please check underneath your chairs. If you've received a rose, then you may stay. I don't need everyone for this task." She leaned back in her throne that glittered with more diamonds than I could count, seeming quite pleased with herself.

Those who'd been reluctant to eat until now looked around the open chamber and pulled a bite or two onto their plate, nibbling at it thoughtfully. I watched to see if anyone was tempted to check under their chair right away, but no one did. These were the survivors of the past couple of trials for a reason. Even the ones who looked drained and shell-shocked were here to play by Sarina's rules.

I wasn't going to eat anything just out of spite, but Quinn pushed a plate under my nose and glared at me until I picked up a cooked vegetable and stuffed it in my mouth. I tried not to gag on it, wondering if the food was actually grown here among Sarina's weeds.

After everyone had eaten, Sarina gave a nod of permission and they checked under their seats. I reached under mine, only to find a sharp rose thorn that pricked my finger. I flinched, along with my bondmates, and pinched off the wound with my napkin.

I tried not to panic. None of the other witches or warlocks had gotten a thorn instead of a rose. They all held up a rose and looked for who hadn't gotten the same. Even the other Pearl witch at our table took her rose and scooted away, opting to sit at the empty section at the Amber table and put her back to us.

One glance up at Sarina made my skin crawl. Maybe she knew who I was. Maybe she just didn't like me whatever form I took, but her grin stretched out over her face and there was no doubting that she was up to something—something that involved plotting against me.

Easing to my feet, my guys all followed suit. Even Bast,

normally oblivious to tension, spiked his fur and growled. "Let's go," I said, and turned my back on Sarina.

The only sound that followed our footsteps was her slow, deliberate laugh that said more than words. She thought she'd already won.

TO BE WORSHIPPED

e returned to the dorms in silence and this time all of us packed into the same room. The sense of dread hung heavy on my shoulders and I didn't want to leave any of my bondmates out of my sight.

"What do you think all that was about?" Quinn asked, flopping onto an overstuffed chair and sinking into it.

Killian flipped out his switchblade and began working at a piece of wood that looked to be the bark of the oak tree where we'd made love. He sliced at it, sharpening one end. "Sarina must know who we are." His ruby eyes flashed to meet mine. "You can see through our glamour. Maybe she can too.

"That's impossible," Tiros said, seeming offended by the idea. "Phoebe and the other rebel witches gave the last of their power to glamour us and send us here. They wouldn't have given us a false sense of security." He glanced at me, giving me a once-over. His gaze settled at the new dagger I'd stuffed into my sock. "Evelyn is a powerful Fate Witch and close to regaining the magic that Sarina tried to strip from her.

Aaron surprised all of us by blasting us with a flash of light, shifting into his human form far faster than I'd ever seen him do. Normally his shift involved cracking bones and the slow, steady grating sound of shifting flesh that made me want to scream. Instead, he stood before all of us, naked, grinning at me. His blonde spiky hair had a single streak of silver down the side. It was the only evidence that his sudden shift had cost him magic he wasn't supposed to be able to use as a vampire. Yet, I wondered how many vampires were supposed to be able to shift into animal form at all.

"Evie," he said, his voice low and husky like an animal. "Sarina is plotting against you and the best way to fight her is to complete your last bond."

I glanced down at his impressive erection. He was definitely ready.

"By the gods, Aaron," Killian snapped, throwing a blanket at him. "She's not a bone you can gnaw on. Put your dick away."

The rest of my bondmates seemed amused by Aaron's eagerness. Even Bast jumped on top of the dresser and settled himself into a ball and started purring. He couldn't shift back to his human form, not without a little magical help, but he didn't seem to mind that my bondmates wanted to protect me —even if that meant fucking me. By the slitted look of his eyes, he had no problem with that either as long as he got to watch.

"Sick cat," I grumbled. I drew in a deep breath and then let it out. "Look, I know all of you are worried about me, but I'm not going to let Sarina scare me. If she really knew who I was do you think she'd let me live? She would have attacked me by now."

Marcus crossed his arms and leaned against the wall, looking like his broody, fine self that I was more accustomed to. "Perhaps she's learned her lesson. You've escaped her on multiple occasions now. What if this secret task she has for the others is to stage an attack on you?" He glared at the door. "We need to be ready for anything."

Aaron tossed the blanket on the ground, revealing his impressive dick again. I sucked in a breath when I spotted a glimmer and realized it was a piercing down... *there*. My mind filled with all sorts of unseemly thoughts of what kind of sensations that could introduce during a bonding...

"We don't know what's coming, which is exactly why we need to complete the circle," Aaron said, looking absolutely serious—as well as oblivious of where my mind had just gone.

He approached me and took both my hands in his. It would have been romantic if his dick hadn't prodded me in the hip.

Well, maybe he did know where my mind had gone.

"Evie, look, I'm sorry to be so forward, but you've mated with Killian, which means that you're ready. I'm ready. No matter how attached to you my wolf is, I know that Killian can keep me in line."

I gave him a raised brow. "And what does that mean?"

Tiros brushed dark strands from his eyes, but I caught him looking at Aaron's body. He wasn't turned on by this... was he? "Shifters, especially wolf shifters, tend to mate in packs. We aren't wolves, so Aaron's animal side shouldn't accept that you have other mates even if his human side does."

Killian nodded. "Yes, but wolves also respond to alphas, and Aaron's wolf sees me as the alpha of the mating pack. So, since you've mated with me..."

I drew in a deep breath. "His wolf will allow it," I finished. This was why Aaron had held himself back. I never would have guessed that all of my bondmates were so complicated, but they were. It made me want to understand each of them even deeper than I already did. I felt like I only knew them on the surface and that's not how it should be between all of us. I wanted to know them all the way down to their souls, and I wanted them to know me, every crevice and curve of me. No secrets. No holding back.

"Okay," I said, feeling breathless and excited all at the same time. This was not how I imagined my life would turn out that I would have sex with so many men, but these weren't just any men. These were my bondmates who'd sacrificed everything for me.

Aaron's blonde brows shot up on his forehead. "Okay?"

Marcus moved to the door. "We'll guard—"

"Don't you dare leave," I snapped at him, then a blush ran hot over my body. "I don't want any of you to leave."

They all looked at each other with bewilderment. Quinn was the first to give me a wicked grin. "And you guys said she didn't remember."

I wanted to ask what he meant by that, but he didn't allow me to ask questions. He ripped off his shirt and came up behind me, drawing in a deep breath at my neck and sighing.

"Do you remember when it used to be like this? All of us, together, loving you?"

A chill of excitement ran up my spine. I wished that I remembered, and even though my mind couldn't conjure up the memories, my body sang under Quinn's breath hot on my neck.

My hands lowered and wrapped Aaron's hardness in a loving stroke and he bucked against me, but didn't move to touch me, allowing me to explore him, to remember him.

"I think..." I began, trying to articulate how the memories came back to me, but there were no words to describe it, so I lowered to my knees and examined Aaron up close. I'd been wanting to do this with all of my guys. They were all so beautiful in every way, including their cocks. Aaron's stood rigid for me and two little silver studs stood out on the underside of his head, making me wonder what it would feel like when he was inside of me. I licked, liking the taste of him mixed with the metal. He bucked again, but the groan I heard didn't come from him.

"Damn, Evelyn," Tiros said, his eyes going heavy-lidded. "You sure know how to turn a guy on."

"Are you sure you're okay with this?" Marcus asked, putting himself between Tiros and me. Marcus, always my refined one, making sure that no one crossed a line. Aaron had been the one to transform into his human body and show me his erection, but I wasn't upset about that. In fact, I'm glad he was so eager to complete his bond with me. I was tired of my bondmates holding back, being afraid that I might not accept them for who they are.

To demonstrate my approval, I took one long stroke of my

tongue over Aaron's dick while keeping eye-contact with Marcus. His mouth parted at the action, fangs hinting and breaking through his glamour that couldn't hide his true self from me. I wanted to see fangs. I wanted to see desire and the truth of the impact I had on him.

"Evie," Quinn whispered from behind me, his voice pained. "I can't... not while..."

Oh, right. Quinn still had his glamour. I'd been so busy focusing on my guys that I forgot about that little hiccup.

Aaron had already dropped his façade and if my guys were right about one thing, it was that Sarina was coming after me. I felt it in my bones and there was no sense in hiding who we were from her anymore. We were already here and we'd face her—together.

It would take Tiros's magic to strip us all of the lies we showed Sarina. "Tiros," I said, breathing his name. He came to me and Marcus stepped aside, watching.

With Aaron still in my left hand, I licked my lips and let my gaze fall to Tiros's waist. He undid his pants without a word, giving me an eyeful to enjoy. Gods, they were all so beautiful.

I took him with my free hand, stroking him once and following the motion with my mouth. He tried to stay still, but his hips rolled with me, letting his dick go deeper into my throat with the smooth rocking that told me he wanted so much more. I would give him more, but first I needed his desire and his magic.

Reluctantly, I released Aaron and pulled the weapon from my sock. Tiros didn't flinch away even when I brought the blade up dangerously close to him. "I need some of your blood," I explained and poised the blade over his thigh. "Just a small cut."

Killian made a sound of protest. "You could use that blade on me, sweetheart," he offered, his ruby eyes blazing with the memories of what we'd done to each other just a few hours ago.

I grinned at him and made a shallow cut on Tiros's leg. "Later, Killian, I promise."

He chuckled. "Everyone hear that? She promised." He gave me a wink. "I'll hold you to that. I've got witnesses."

Pressing my mouth to the wound before it closed, I let Tiros's magic and lifeforce seep into me. He wrapped his fingers in my hair as I drank and his dick slid against my cheek leaving a musk of leather and desire. "Evelyn," he whispered, his voice so full of need that I took his dick and stroked him while I worked the spell.

It wouldn't take chanting or witch words. This was a dispersal of a spell that Phoebe had put into place. She'd left a loose strand for me to find if I wanted to remove everyone's glamour, like the edge of a great tapestry ready to unravel. I found the magical thread in my mind and tugged on it, using Tiros's magic to uncover truth and dispel the lies.

A sparkling glow overtook the chamber. Even Bast took on a golden hue, but while everyone else changed, he remained at the top of the dresser as a cat, flicking his tail with irritation. It seemed that something else was keeping him in his feline form.

I'm not going to change back yet, he told me, our words a secret between our minds from the others.

Why not?

His tail flicked again. *Because, your bondmates are right. Sarina is coming for you and we all need to be prepared to protect you. The Royal Covens is a place of magic. I can do more for you in this realm while in this body. As a familiar, I'm designed to be around witches.* His tail flicked again. *Enjoy them, my sweet Evie. Drink in the power they have to offer you. When the final fight comes, we'll all be ready, and when it is over, I will return to my true self to love you a hundredfold.*

Encouraged, I lapped at the small cut on Tiros's leg that was already starting to close, but I'd gotten enough blood to do what I needed. The strand of magic dangled in my mind's eye, already having begun to unravel the tapestry. I grabbed it again and pulled, making the entire room explode with light.

When the dust settled, each of my guys grinned at me, their true natures no longer hidden by the fine mist of glamour that I'd already been able to see through.

"Yes!" Quinn shouted, and ripped off the remains of his pants that had torn during his transformation. His dick stood proud and erect as he spread his stance and grinned at me. "You're going to be so glad you did that, lass. I'm going to—"

I squealed as Tiros grabbed me under my arms and tossed me onto the bed. He didn't dive over me like I know he wanted to. "This is Aaron's night," he said, every muscle in his body taut as he raked his gaze over me as if I was already naked. "He's right. We need to protect her, which means completing the bond and returning her power to her."

Aaron didn't need to be told twice. He moved in on me, fangs bared, and irises overtaking the vampiric red with the blue of his wolf. He hesitated as he reached for me, as if waiting to see if I would flinch away, but my breath caught, watching him, wanting him to rip my clothes off of me.

"If I do anything you don't like, stop me," he said, his words dead serious. "I'm a wolf, Evelyn." He crawled over me and tugged at the hem of my shirt, pulling it over my head. He brought me in for a hug as his hands worked at the clasp of my bra. "I'm a vampire, too. I'm a predator from two races and I will devour you, if you allow me."

"Is that a promise?" I asked, breathless. If he thought that he was going to scare me, then he didn't realize how much I wanted this.

All of my guys moved in on us, wanting to be closer to me. I wished that Bast could join us and I glanced at him up on the dresser. I saw his soul deep within those watchful eyes. He would memorize my every move and use it to torment me when he was himself again. Aaron peeled away my pants and I bucked against his touch, throwing my head back onto the soft mattress and giving myself over to the desire that rolled over me in waves.

"Take off your clothes, all of you," I demanded as Aaron took off my socks and underwear, leaving me naked. They all devoured me with their eyes and did as I asked with agonizingly slow movements, peeling away the layers and revealing taut muscle and deliciously erect dicks ready for my enjoyment. Me—and me alone. That realization made me shiver with desire.

Aaron moved over me, pulling me higher onto the bed, but he didn't fuck me, not yet. "I want to enjoy this," he said, his fangs brushing my breast as his fingers spread the swollen folds between my thighs. I gasped when he ran his touch over my clit. The final blood rune on my forearm blazed to life, ready to complete a spell I had woven on myself in another life. I had bound myself to these men, trusted them with pieces of my soul. I'd never had someone like that in my life, much less six someones.

When Aaron pushed a finger inside of me, I gasped and arched my back. My other bondmates couldn't take it anymore and moved onto the bed, their weight making it shift and sink. It wasn't large enough for all of us, so Marcus and Quinn pushed the adjacent bed closer to give us enough space for everyone to be close to me.

I loved that. I wanted to touch all of them and show them how much I loved them.

Quinn was the first to kneel next to me while Aaron worked me with his fingers. I took Quinn's dick in my hand and stroked him, letting him know that I had been the one to remove his glamour for this very reason. I needed him to give me everything.

"You have all of me," Quinn promised, his hips moving with the long strokes of my fingers.

I grinned, forgetting that Quinn and I shared thoughts when we were close. Not all of my bondmates and I had that sort of connection, which was what I loved about each of them. Their love brought something unique to our bond, each of them completing a part of the puzzle to make a new tapestry of magic. One where I was at the center and they were all a piece of my heart.

Aaron ran his fingers up my abdomen, leaving a line of slickness from where he'd awakened hot desire in me. He followed it with his tongue, making me arch again. He kept going up, his mouth finding my nipple and sucking it. He molded my breast to get a better grip on me and then his tongue flicked, his tongue piercing giving me new sensations. "Oh," I whimpered, the sound of surprise escaping me.

He grinned, flashing fang as he rubbed his dick over my slickness. "Are you ready for me, little witch?"

The sensation of his soft skin mixed with the hard piercing running over my clit made my eyelids flutter closed. He played with me, mounting my desire even higher. "Don't tease me," I warned him.

"Or what?" He rolled his dick over me, but avoided my clit this time, making me groan with frustration.

With Quinn still in my hand, I drew on his magic. I didn't need his blood for the simple spell that came from my burning desire. Honeysuckle scented the room as I pushed into Aaron's mind, Quinn's power over scrying giving me a loophole to torment one of my bonds. Perhaps if his mind hadn't been open to me it wouldn't have worked, but Aaron wanted me. I hadn't realized how badly he wanted me until I wrapped myself in his desires. With a wicked grin, I amplified them like turning up the volume.

Aaron's pupil's dilated and his dick went impossibly rigid against me. He groaned, pressing his weight on me before positioning himself. "That was... unwise," he warned me before thrusting inside of me—hard.

I cried out and threw my head back. I sensed all of my other bondmates reacting to my pleasure, but they kept their distance. Even Quinn had moved out of my reach, but the bed shifted with their weight. They would stay close until I completed my bond with Aaron. They would respect the intimacy required for us to reestablish what had been lost.

Aaron thrust again, merciless and rough, pulling out of me only far enough to slam back into me again. My entire body exploded with fulfillment as he gave me exactly what I wanted. He snarled as he pounded into me, his flesh slapping against mine as he hoisted my hips up to angle into me deeper.

"Gods," I breathed as his tempo increased. My whole body aligned with his rhythm and moved with him, wanting him to push me to the edge.

"Not the gods," he snapped back, his fangs dangerously long and sharp. He kept his mouth parted so that he wouldn't stab himself with them. His canines lengthened, showing me his mixture of vampire and shifter. He was going to devour me just as he promised.

He growled as he wrapped his hands under my ass, lifting me even higher so that he could thrust into me so deep that I cried out with the force of him. I could feel his piercing just as I'd imagined and the hard friction felt so good inside of me. He wasn't gentle and I liked that about him.

"You're mine," he said, his voice changing to a wolfish growl as his incessant thrusts increased in tempo. His eyes were entirely blue now and Killian lingered at the edges of my vision, ready to step in if his wolf took over and turned on my other bondmates. "You will come for me," Aaron growled, his words a harsh demand.

I was so close to the edge, but he was too rough. "I can't," I panted as he pounded into me, my world spinning as I surrendered myself to sensation.

Aaron surprised me, immediately slowing down and rocking my hips close to his, rolling his weight over my clit and making my eyes widen with the restraint in his muscles. His biceps flexed with the effort and I knew he wanted to pound into me until climax, but he needed my pleasure. "You will come for me," he said again, his voice still deep with the wolf but Aaron was in there too. "Close your eyes and give yourself over to me."

I did as he asked and allowed myself to enjoy the pressure of him inside of me and against my clit, and his hard chest rubbing against my erect nipples. Each new sensation built until I couldn't stand on the edge any longer. "Aaron, I'm going to... I'm going to..."

His fangs grazed my neck, the sharp danger making me suck in a breath, and then he bit, both with fangs and canines.

Killian had been the one to introduce me to pain mixed with pleasure. The force of his bite sent me over the edge and I cried out with an orgasm that took me under. I rode the waves of pleasure as Aaron fed on me. Our exchange wasn't like the rest of my bondmates. I sensed something deeper clicking into place and it felt right, like it was always meant to be like this between us. I always carried the weight of the world on my shoulders, but with Aaron I didn't have to worry. I could live in the present and forget about the past or the future. That's where my bondmates like Marcus lived, constantly jumping around in time and worrying about the long-reaching impact of our actions. It's what made me a Fate Witch. The strands of time were important and each knot and strand led to an important discovery, but there was a price that came with that kind of knowledge.

With Aaron, I didn't have to live in that constant state of flux and worry. I could just be me, right now, in this moment and enjoy what we had together.

Aaron released me and I felt like I drew in a breath for the first time in my life. He backed away, his eyes wide and blue with his shifter side almost completely taking over. Sprouts of fur swept over his skin just enough to give him his wolf's pattern. Then his nostrils flared and his pupils dilated as he seemed to notice my other bondmates around me.

"Not wolves," he growled, "not her mates."

Killian came out of nowhere and slammed into Aaron, sending him flying off of me. I screamed and reached into the empty air for them. The bond between Aaron and I had finalized and it physically hurt me to be parted from him so forcefully and suddenly.

Killian held up his switchblade to Aaron's throat. The beast in Aaron growled, not caring when the blade drew a line of blood across his skin. "You are not alpha," Killian reminded him. His voice thrummed with a growl of his own. It was as if he mimicked the way that Aaron talked so that they'd be on the same wavelength. Wolf to... master.

Aaron lifted his upper lip in a snarl, revealing fangs still red with my blood. They stared at each other for a long time before Aaron's eyes transitioned from the brilliant blue to the vampiric red. He relaxed and Killian backed off.

Aaron shook himself as if he'd just been dunked in cold water. When he saw me watching with wide eyes, he grinned. "Told you it was a good thing you mated Killian before me."

When I released a light chuckle of relief, my other bondmates took that as a cue to move in on me. They'd been stroking themselves as Aaron and I had cemented our bond. I marveled at their patience and the moment their hands touched my skin, my power blazed with fresh heat. They needed me... wanted me. For the first time in my mortal life, my bond with them was complete.

I closed my eyes and reveled as their hands explored me. I felt like a goddess being worshipped.

Quinn must have read my thoughts because he chuckled, his voice low and delicious. "You are a goddess," he assured me, his lips tracing the curves of my body and making me sigh, "and we intend to worship every inch of you tonight."

TRAPPED

I'd never slept so soundly or with as much
contentment as I did that night. Too bad it didn't
last very long. The best dreams never do.

I wasn't sure at first what woke me, but I opened my eyes
to a darkness with just enough light peering underneath the
door to reveal a tangle of arms and legs that cocooned me in
the bed. All the blankets had been kicked off except for just
the edge that had all but tumbled onto the floor. All of my
guys kept me warm and they were my blankets for the night. I
stretched as much as the tangle of limbs would allow to find
that a wolf was my pillow. Aaron had shifted sometime in the
night and I sensed his magic had doubled since our bonding—
as had mine. My entire body hummed with power and not
just what the Amethyst Coven had bestowed on me. I realized
now that I needed that power to be able to handle the influx
of magic that my bondmates had been holding onto for me
for a thousand years. Aaron didn't have an artifact to give me,

but when I realized my teeth felt sore, I ran my fingers over them and gasped with surprise. The slightest of canines elongated under my touch and pricked my fingertip. Amazing.

Even Bast was with us. His feline form slept in the crook of my arm and I smiled at him, running my thumb to smooth across his whiskers. "I'm sorry you couldn't join us last night," I whispered.

He didn't wake to my quiet apology. All of my guys were completely passed out and I chuckled. I really had worn them out. Every part of me felt sore in a deliciously good way, but I had to admit that they'd done most of the work. "Goddess worship," Quinn had called it.

Then I heard the sound again and the stupid smile I had on my face vanished as my heart jumped into my throat. Someone was in the hallway.

No, not someone. A lot of someones.

The only warning I had was the shifting of light underneath the door. A brilliant light flashed, blinding me and waking all of my bondmates who cried out in surprise. A hoard of witches and warlocks came flooding in wielding torches made of the same magicked firelight I'd seen in the dream trial.

This was Sarina's doing.

I'd fallen into her trap once again. She wanted me to feel like I was safe, that taking the time to complete my bond with my mates would give me the magic I needed to fight her. Perhaps that was true, but we weren't ready. I wasn't prepared for an onslaught of the entire remainder of the Royal Covens to come barreling through our bedroom door.

"Slut!" a witch cried. Her wild eyes flashed as she threw

the flame at me. I tore into my newfound magic and managed to throw up a shield. I would have given myself a pat on the back for such an incredible feat. Protection magic took years of practice and also usually required hours of preparation and chanting, as well as a whole slew of boring shit, but there was no time to get cocky about things.

Never mind the cocks that were flying everywhere. All my bondmates were still naked and jumped to their feet. The moment the threat of the flame extinguished, my protection shield fell down as if I hadn't conjured it at all and they attacked.

Killian was the first to land a blow. He jammed his switch-blade into a warlock's stomach, sending dark blood spraying all over his chest.

Tiros attacked next. He was impossibly fast when he wanted to be and he tore into a witch's neck. She didn't even have time to scream as his vicious fangs ripped muscle from bone. I stared like an idiot. Those same fangs had been used so delicately on me and I enjoyed his bite, but I'd never seen a vampire truly feed on human prey when it wasn't about love or sex. This was about survival and my guys weren't holding back.

Aaron snarled and nudged at my elbow, trying to get me to move. I was a prime target sitting on the bed and I knew it, but I couldn't help but watch the carnage unfold before my eyes. It was a warlock who came after me with a blade that made me move. I recognized the sheen of power over his weapon and the madness in his eyes that came with such power. Sarina must have gifted some of them with soul blades. Killian was the only warlock I knew that could handle such a burden without going insane.

I gripped my dagger that was on the edge of the bed and blocked the incoming blow. All of my soul artifacts were either close or still on me. Quinn's earrings dangled at my neck and I sensed my masquerade mask just a few feet away on the dresser. I needed to be at my full strength to fend off this hoard before one of my bondmates got stabbed with a weapon that could take them from me.

The fresh fear of losing them made me move faster. I sliced with my blade, catching the warlock across the cheek. That was enough when it came to my weapon. The wound festered with my magic and he cried out, clawing at his face as he tumbled away from me. If I had truly inherited Killian's gifts, then his body would move on to the afterlife without his soul. I wasn't sure if I could absorb his power, or if I even wanted to, but I wasn't going to stick around to find out.

I tumbled and dove for the dresser and grappled until I caught the masquerade mask in my hand. I didn't have any clothes on to secure it, so I pinned it to my hair and put it on my face.

All the witches and warlocks stopped in their tracks to momentarily stare at me. Marcus had a warlock pinned and was gnawing on the limp body. His bloodlust was the worst of my bondmates and he'd be trapped in a feeding frenzy if I didn't bring him back, but there wasn't time to help him right now.

My other bondmates had their own enemies to deal with. Aaron had a pair of witches cornered who taunted him with mocking snaps of their jaw as they yipped like dogs. Then there was Bast helping by clawing at a warlock's face that Quinn strangled.

There were still so many more and they continued to pour into the room. I didn't remember this many warlocks and witches surviving the trials, that or Sarina had found recruits once she'd figured out who I was. Maybe she'd known all along and this was all part of her plan.

Whatever Sarina's intentions, these warlocks and witches were all going to die and they knew it. Power swelled in me unlike anything I'd ever felt before.

"Do you really want to die?" I asked, my voice booming out, making me actually feel like the goddess that Quinn kept telling me that I was.

There was so much magic that it burned in me and illuminated the gruesome scene. I went weightless and my body lifted until my feet were no longer on the ground. I snarled with rage, hating that every good moment in my life seemed fated to end in destruction and carnage. Was this why I was a Fate Witch, to make sure not every blissful moment in my life ended so fucked? Because I wasn't going to just stand by and let this happen.

"You're not meant to even be alive!" a witch said, pointing at me with a snarl. "You're an abomination!"

I scoffed. "And Sarina, what is she?"

The witch straightened. "She is our Queen."

That hit me in the gut. The trials hadn't even been finished yet and this witch had decided Sarina was their Queen? What kind of mind-warping magic did the bitch have over these witches now?

It's not brainwashing, Bast said, his voice nervous in my

mind. He was never nervous. *Sarina has won these souls over with loyalty. Witches respect power.*

I narrowed my eyes. "Then they will respect me."

I let the power free from my body. I was just a conduit to the powers of Fate that I diverted like a steer working a great river. I let all of that magic flow through me, time, space, and everything that came in-between.

So, all good things end in destruction and carnage?

Yeah... this time it was me.

ANOINTED

When the light faded, there was nothing left.
And I mean nothing.

The room was entirely destroyed with everything in it turned to ash. I sensed the bodily remains of the witches and warlocks who'd come to kill me, but not my bondmates. I felt their absence like a knife to my chest.

Wait, not all of my bondmates.

Bast meowed at me and sank his claws into my leg. He didn't speak to me, which told me that he was truly disturbed by whatever I had done.

I swallowed hard and shifted through the ash of the room. When I walked outside I passed the entranceway mirrors to find that I was no longer naked. I still wore my masquerade mask, but it had elongated the elaborate purple and peacock feathers to give me a dress. My earrings glistened at my neck and the beautiful blade Killian had given me glowed with an aura of purple and blue magic in my grasp. Blue... for Aaron.

"Where are the others?" I urged Bast. I hadn't disintegrated them. My bond wouldn't have allowed me to harm them and even though I sensed that they were no longer physically near me, they weren't dead. My heart would have broken into a thousand pieces and destroyed me from the inside if that had truly happened.

When Bast didn't respond, I looked down at him and frowned. He blinked up at me as if he wanted to say something, but instead he stepped over my high-heeled toes and swept his tail across my ankles.

"What's the matter with you?" I whispered at him. "Cat got your tongue?"

Even that joke didn't seem to faze him, so I followed the only other remaining tug that had me feeling like something was very wrong.

Sarina.

I marched through the dorms and my heels clicked against the polished marble. I'd never been in a place that felt so eerily empty as if all the souls in the world had vanished all at once. It was possible, actually. The Royal Covens were in an alternate dimension underneath London and it didn't go on forever. It was a pocket realm where witches could practice magic without fear of discovery or having to hold themselves back.

Although, I certainly hadn't held back, and look what happened.

I returned to the largest spire of the Royal Covens where I felt the tug the strongest. Perhaps Sarina was waiting for me and this would complete some elaborate trap she'd set up for me, but I didn't care. I'd just demolished every witch and warlock she'd sent to kill me. Now that I had all of my magic back, I was confident I could face her and make it out on the other side alive. She might have killed me the last time I'd gone head-to-head with her, but I wasn't that same girl anymore. Sarina wasn't going to win this time.

I found the tug the strongest at a long length of spiral stairs that would take me up to the Anointed's chambers. It's where the wealthiest and most powerful witches spent the majority of their days after being awarded the coveted spot in the Royal Covens. Here, they lived like queens... like goddesses. In a way, the members of each coven worshiped their Anointed Witch. There was no one else more revered and respected.

When I reached the top of the staircase and wandered down the luxurious hall decorated with magical paintings that moved across the walls, I knew I was going to find something horrible. Dread knotted itself in my stomach and made it hard to swallow. I glanced down at my feet to make sure that Bast was still with me. His glistening, intelligent eyes looked up at me expectantly. He didn't traipse on ahead of me. This was my journey and he would stand by my side, but he would not lead the way. If I wanted to turn around right now and find a way to go home—wherever home may be—he would follow me without protest.

"No, Bast," I whispered, pausing to scratch behind his ear. I wasn't sure if he could hear my thoughts anymore and I needed to say it out loud anyway. "We're going to see what it is Sarina has done. We're going to face her, no matter what happens."

Bast meowed his encouragement, or what I hoped was

encouragement, and that gave me just enough strength to stand and continue down the velvet rug to the end of the hall where an ornate door waited. I frowned to find it slightly ajar. Finding my courage, I pushed it open and drew in a deep breath.

Sarina. She was Anointed all right—anointed in blood.

ANOTHER TIME, ANOTHER PLACE

"**W**ell don't just stand there," she snapped at me. "Finish what you've started!"

I stared numbly from the doorway as Bast gave her a hiss. Sarina hung precariously off the edge of her diamond throne as she watched me and paid the cat no mind. She seemed to materialize the throne wherever she went, but now it acted as a glorified crutch. Blood covered her entire body and blotted out what had once been a perfectly white dress encrusted with diamonds. Even her blonde hair matted against her face and left streaks of blood when she wiped it away.

I took my time soaking in the scene. Bodies were strewn behind her like haphazard dolls. Each an Anointed coven witch that should have been ripe with power had fought Sarina and died. They glimmered like the precious gems they represented: Sapphire, Emerald, Pearl, and Amber. The Amethyst Anointed Witch, Lenora, had already been killed by Sarina in a display of power, but it had cost her. She'd kept the others alive... well, I'd thought it had been because she simply didn't have enough power to kill them. What had changed?

"You killed so many for me today," Sarina said as she grinned at me. Blood stained her teeth pink and she chuckled. "Good little witch doing what I could not. Sacrifice..." She spread her fingers over her chest as if to reach for her heart, if only she had one. "True sacrifice comes from a death you do not wish. You didn't want to kill anyone, but you did, and you've given me exactly what I needed." Her grin widened and my stomach sank.

Yes, I'd instantly vaporized all the witches and warlocks who'd come to kill me and my bondmates. I'd had no choice... but... was Sarina right? Did I give her exactly what she needed?

"What are your plans?" I snapped, my panic quickly turning to rage. I took a deliberate step towards her and my foot sank into the blood-soaked carpet. "You've killed the other Anointed Witches. Do you think that automatically makes you Queen of the Royal Covens? Well, it doesn't work that way, you crazy bitch."

She barked out an unattractive laugh as if she'd truly lost her mind. "No, silly girl. I've no plans to become something as trivial as Queen of the Royal Covens. No..." She gripped the edge of her throne and managed to stand as her whole body shook with the effort. She raised her chin at me with defiance. "I want to become something so much more. The cost will be great, to others as well as to myself, but the ultimate reward comes with the ultimate price." She spread her arms and looked as if she might topple over. "Go on, then. Finish what you've started."

I didn't even remember pulling out my dagger, but it glistened in my hand and hummed with the need to kill. This was a soul blade weapon and even if Sarina was a monster who had already sold her soul, I could still destroy her body. She didn't have to plague this world any longer.

What made me hesitate was that she was asking me to kill her. I narrowed my eyes. "What if I just leave you like this?" I started to pace as I formed the plan. "The other witches of the world will see what you've done and put you on trial." There hadn't been a true witch trial for as long as I could remember. The Anointed kept things running and they ran a tight ship, but all the Anointed were dead save for Sarina. There was no way the other covens would let her live after her failed efforts to overthrow the Royal Covens.

A low chuckle rumbled in her throat. The inhuman sound mixed with energies that didn't belong to her. She still had an impossible amount of magic running through her body as if she was casting a spell right now. "Silly Evelyn. Let me live and you'll never see your precious vampires again." When I went rigid, she staggered her weight to keep from falling as she laughed again. "You think I didn't know who you were? You thought a simple glamour spell could hide you from me? Don't be naïve, girl. I knew exactly who you were the moment you stepped into my domain. And to bring all of your bondmates with you? Oh, that was too good a prize to pass up. They all own a piece of your soul, which allows me to extend my reach farther than I'd ever thought possible."

I didn't have time for her games or rambling anymore.

Marching up to her, I stepped over the slashed bodies and slammed my dagger into her chest right where her heart should have been. I wasn't sure if she really had one. She was a monster and a soulless husk of a creature, but she bled, which meant that she could die.

Sarina sucked in a deep breath of pain at the blow and her eyes snapped open wide. "Yes," she breathed.

A scream threatened to erupt out of me. "Are you insane?"

Her eyelids fluttered closed as she slumped into the bloodied throne. "Perhaps, but know this, little witch. With my death comes the Second Echo of Calamity and it will resurrect me as the goddess I deserve to be."

I twisted the knife, making Sarina gurgle on her own blood with a fresh cry of pain. "I don't want to hear your delusions. Where are my bondmates? Tell me!"

The light in her eyes flickered as life threatened to leave her. Bitch better not die before she told me what I wanted to know. "They're anchors in other worlds. You don't have the magic to reach them, little girl. Know that you helped me do what I never could have done on my own." She let out one long, last breath. "Keep the throne warm... until I return."

I wanted to stab her all over again, but Sarina was gone.

Ding, dong... the fucking witch is dead.

I DON'T KNOW how long I stood there. It could have been a few seconds or a few hours. Bast brought me back to reality as he nipped my ankles and meowed at me to leave the gruesome scene. Surrounded by death, dark prophecy, and an endless sense of dread, I definitely needed some fresh air.

He took the lead this time with his tail held high. I felt completely numb. All my bondmates were trapped in other worlds? I couldn't even wrap my mind around that idea. Then there was Bast who seemed completely incapable of talking to me. He wasn't just being quiet. Sarina had done something when she'd taken all of my bondmates from me. She wanted to break me. Even in death, she was in danger of winning.

Once outside I stopped and gawked up at the roiling dark sky. Sarina hadn't been kidding. The Second Echo of Calamity was real and every hair on my arm stood on end as I sensed the rolling wave of immeasurable power that could crush entire worlds without a second thought. My power as a Fate Witch helped me to see what I was really up against. A wall of black and blue made the very sky look bruised and battered, as if the gods had gotten into a fist-fight and this was all that remained.

"Bast," I said as I fell to my knees, hitting the street hard against my kneecaps but not caring. I couldn't feel the pain. "What am I going to do?"

Bast nipped at my wrist until I tore my gaze away from the otherworldly sky. He couldn't talk to me with words, but then I sensed he was trying to talk to me in the way that we used to do. No words, just emotion and intuition.

Your bondmates are connected to you... which means you are connected to them.

My eyes widened with the realization and one hand shot up to the masquerade mask still on my face. Marcus had given me this artifact that housed a piece of my soul, but it wasn't just my magic that it contained anymore. It smelled of roses and jasmine and was a piece of Marcus's heart.

"Marcus," I breathed, feeling the faint tug of his soul when I focused on the mask. He was out there... someplace I could reach if I focused hard enough.

Not just another place, but another time.

Before he was a vampire he was a Time Witch, so that didn't surprise me. What did surprise me was his haggard appearance. He seemed changed, almost aged somehow with lines across his face that hadn't been there before. His hair, usually elegant with every strand in place, tangled around his arched cheekbones as his ruby eyes stared at me through a foggy portal.

That's how strong our bond was. I just thought of him and a portal appeared. Sarina had underestimated me if she thought that I couldn't travel time and space to find the bond-mates she'd taken from me. Nothing could keep them away from me for long, not time, not fate, not even her no matter how many times she might come back to life.

I didn't miss the irony. I'd been reborn and Sarina saw my death and rebirth as a strength. In a way she'd copied me. She was always trying to use my strengths to her advantage. Well, my premature death in my past lives had created a bond so strong with those who loved me that it gave me the power I needed to find them. Love was a magic stronger than anything the universe had to offer and nothing would make Sarina understand that. That's why I was going to win.

"Evie?" Marcus croaked, his voice scratchy as if from screaming for too long. "What in the seven circles of hell are you doing here?"

I JUMPED through the portal without hesitation and Bast followed me. I should have known that my faithful familiar would follow me even through a portal created by my bond with another. Bast wasn't like my other bondmates. He'd loved me before he knew there were others who already had my heart, but he'd accepted that anyway. No matter what happened, he would stay by my side.

An icy chill ran over my body as I passed through the portal. Once on the other side, the atmosphere changed and a wave of humidity hit me in the face.

Earth.

Not only had I left the grounds of the Royal Covens, which definitely meant realm travel, I'd also traveled in time as well. I could sense it. Marcus had changed and stood before me with his jaw slack in shock.

"You're actually here."

I slammed into him as a smile overtook my face. "Marcus! Are you okay?" Hanging around his neck, I pulled him down for a kiss. He obeyed me and indulged in molding his mouth to mine as if he hadn't tasted me in years and I was a delicacy to be savored.

He held me so tightly to his chest I almost couldn't breathe. "I thought I'd never see you again."

Surprise made my eyes widen, then I twisted in his grasp to look at our surroundings. Desks lined the room and all faced us in a semi-circle. I peered over Marcus's shoulder to find an elaborate array of runes engraved on the stone floor.

"Is this... a classroom?" I asked. If it was, it was unlike any classroom I'd ever seen.

"Who the fuck let you out?" a woman's voice snapped like a whip from across the room.

Both of us jumped and I twisted, shoving Marcus behind me. I was going to destroy whoever had done this to Marcus. I'd never seen him look so worn down and beaten.

A college student started back at me and crossed her arms. She looked more like an innocent Barbie doll than my new nemesis. Sleek, blonde waves tumbled over her shoulders and pouty lips paired with a scowl too adorable to get mad at while she glared at me.

"Who let who out?" I asked as I straightened. I knew not to judge a threat by its exterior, but surely this girl couldn't do more than bitch slap.

She narrowed her eyes and pointed a manicured finger at Marcus. "Our time vampire-warlock! He's a one of a kind, you know. The dean will have your head if he finds out that you've broken him out of prison for a..." She grinned and gave me a once-over as if reevaluating me, "private lesson."

As if her anger had entirely dissipated, she shrugged and flipped her hair over her shoulder. "I'm not going to judge, sweetcheeks. Can't say I haven't thought about freeing one of the research projects here and there." She gave Marcus a wink. "Especially the hot ones."

Marcus shoved past me and I made an oomph as I struggled not to fall over. "You bitch!" he growled, his voice going all vampirey and inhuman.

I'd never seen Marcus lose his cool before. "Hey, she's just a girl."

Marcus whirled on me. "Just a girl? No, Evelyn. This is a

fucking monster. I've been trapped here inside a prison for gods know how long... It's been years, I just don't know how many." He laughed, the sound slightly manic, and tried to run his fingers through his tangled hair. "I'm a fucking time warlock and even I don't know how long I've been here. The irony."

"I'm not a girl, and I'm not a fucking monster," the college student corrected. She crossed her arms and made her uniform bunch around her impressive breasts. "My name is Lily and I'm a student of Fortune Academy with much more seniority than you." She narrowed her eyes at us. "I have the feeling that you two know each other." She waved a hand in dismissal. "No matter. I'll fix this. Step aside chicka and I'll put the vampire back where he belongs. You've had your thrill, but I will get blood duty for a millennium if I get caught with a research project on the loose, especially because I let a horny freshman get in the way."

Blood duty? I didn't want to know.

"You're not touching him," I said, stepping in front of Marcus and balling my fingers into fists. I still had my dagger in my sock, but I wasn't going to use it on a student. Magic hummed in me and begged to be used. I was a Fate Witch for gods' sake, there was an endless supply of possibilities of what I could do to this girl to get her out of my way. "What you are going to do is tell me who is responsible for putting my man into prison... again." I gave her a smirk. "I killed his last jailor, if that makes you feel any better."

Her eyes widened and her face paled. "Oh... you're... not a student. Are you?"

Ding ding ding. Barbie got it right for once.

NOT AS IT SEEMS

*T*urns out little miss Barbie was useful once she found out I was a witch. She grabbed both of my hands and grinned so hard I thought she was going to break her face. "You have no idea how long I've been waiting to meet one of you!" she squealed again and jumped up and down, making my whole body jostle with her movements as she clung to me like I was some sort of long-lost bestie. "A real witch!"

Marcus and I exchanged looks, then Bast decided to make his entrance. Gods knew where he'd been hiding all this time. He flew out of nowhere and all I saw was a flash of black fur, tiny teeth, and claws.

Lily screeched as Bast tackled her, leaving bloody streaks across her shoulder as he sliced right through her uniform.

"Bast!" I chided. Sure, the girl was kind of annoying, but there was no reason to draw blood.

Then I saw what Bast was trying to show me. Dark streaks of black oozed from her wound—not red.

My eyes widened. "What are you?"

"Something a vampire can't eat," Marcus growled, and now I understood why he looked so haggard and his eyes were a little crazed. He'd been here for a long time, yes, but they hadn't fed him. Or rather, he couldn't feed.

I instantly gave Marcus my wrist. "Feed."

His pupils dilated as he stared at the faint blue vein pulsing under my skin. "Not here, Evie. I can't..."

His nostrils flared when I shoved my arm underneath his nose. "You're not going to go into bloodlust. I won't let you, okay? Now feed before you drop over and faint on me."

Marcus hesitated as he glanced at Lily who was now giving us both dagger glares. He gently took my wrist and opened his mouth, fangs extended and ruby eyes shut closed as he bit down so delicately that I hardly even felt it. He groaned and leaned into me as he drank.

Lily shivered. "Wow, that's uh, hot." Bast hissed at her and she glared at him while she clamped a hand over her wounded shoulder. "Forgot witches had little gremlins. Won't be caught off-guard next time."

"He's not a gremlin," I said, surprised by myself that I'd be so offended, but Bast was my familiar and a god in his own right. He would not be insulted. "Now, tell me who imprisoned my man, because I very much doubt it was you."

Lily blinked at me for a few times before answering. "You're really not from around here, are you?"

"No," I snapped. "Now answer the question."

Lily sighed and straightened her uniform, her entire body relaxing as if she was no longer in pain. She wiped some of the inhuman blood away and I spotted smooth skin underneath the torn fabric. She'd already healed. "That would be our hunter. He collects projects and creatures for the academy." She shrugged. "He only goes after the bad ones, though. We didn't know this one already had a master. I'll let him know to be more careful next time."

"I'm not his master," I snapped, "and Marcus is not a monster."

She gave me a raised brow. "Oooookay, denial much." She pointed at the vampire feeding on my wrist. Pain lashed through me as he twisted and snarled. I would have to hit him with a blast of magic soon before he went into a complete feeding frenzy. "Do you not see the vampire tearing up your arm?" She leaned in as if she'd just spotted something. "Oh, your blood is red, guess that's a witch thing. Maybe that's why he likes it so much."

Having had enough of this conversation, I let magic course through my body, sending Marcus reeling off of me as he snarled. He blinked a few times and seemed to recover himself. "It's not a witch thing," I snapped. "It's a human thing, something you clearly are not."

Lily chuckled. "Of course I'm not human. The academy doesn't let humans in here. It either kills them outright or makes them go insane." She shrugged. "Security procedures and all. The dean is overprotective of us."

I marched towards the doorway. Nothing about this place felt right and I was ready to get out of here, but when I grabbed the handle an invisible force sent me flying back onto the floor.

Lily gave me a sympathetic frown. "Like I said, security defenses."

So, it turned out that Fortune Academy wasn't exactly on Earth like I'd thought. It was more like the Royal Covens, a realm nestled between Earth and a place of magic where only supernaturals could go. The Academy was designed for supernatural creatures, luckily in a broad sense, or I could have been obliterated the moment I stepped inside the portal.

I hadn't intended on meeting anyone in this place. I had my other bondmates to find and rescue, but I decided that I liked the dean. She kind of reminded me of an anti-Sarina. Tall, blonde, beautiful, and everything Sarina could have been had she had a kind smile and a warm heart.

I was a good judge of character and thanks to Tiros, I had a good idea of when I was being lied to. This woman didn't lie and everything about her was genuine—maybe a bit too genuine.

"I'm terribly sorry that we mistook your mate to be a rare monster," the dean said as she pushed her papers across her desk and gave me her full attention. I didn't go to public school, thanks to my coven's rules, but I'd seen it on TV. Everything about this place screamed "lucrative college" and I felt like I was underdressed to be talking to the head of the Academy.

She didn't seem perturbed at the unsightly splashes of blood across my clothes. Instead she clasped her hands and leaned onto the polished mahogany as her brows crinkled together with the deepest display of concern. I would have thought it overacted except none of my Tiros magic was going haywire and only confirmed that she truly did regret that they'd been keeping Marcus prisoner.

"I've been trying to tell you," Marcus growled, "that I wasn't a monster. Yet now when Evelyn forced you to release me, you see the error of your ways?" He crossed his arms. "I don't buy it."

Lily and the hunter—who she failed to mention was insanely handsome—sat in chairs against the wall looking properly chastised.

"What have you two to say to Marcus and our new guest?" the dean asked, straightening and giving off an air of authority that even had me wanting to apologize.

The hunter didn't look up from his knife that he picked at with his fingertips, reminding me of Killian. "How was I supposed to know it would be a problem?" he grumbled.

Lily thumped him in the ribs. "You're supposed to say you're sorry!"

The hunter sighed and lowered his knife before looking the dean in the eye. "I'm trained to find magical oddities. I found one. A vampire who still had his warlock powers. Vampires are monsters, right? Monsters are only good for two things." He pointed the dagger at Marcus. "For study, and for killing."

"Enough," the dean snapped, sending the ground trembling with an undeniable wave of power. If these people weren't witches, then I sure as hell wanted to know what they were. Talk about magical oddities. "You two have done enough damage. Apologize to our guest and then show her the way back to her home."

My mouth opened to protest. If they'd just let me concentrate I could find my next bondmate—gods knew what I'd find next. I needed to hurry and make sure there weren't any other academies who'd decided vampires were monsters.

"We're sorry," Lily said before I could get a word in. She jabbed the hunter again, hard enough that he grunted in response before giving what I assumed to be an apology as well.

Seeming satisfied, Lily turned her nose up at the hunter and then looped her arm through mine before dragging me out of the office. "All right. You from Earth, I hope? That's the only other place I know how to get to, so we're going there."

I murmured my agreement as Lily guided me through an endless set of halls. I craned my neck over my shoulder to see Marcus and Bast following me from a respective distance. They weren't afraid of the cute blonde... were they?

"Do you do this often?" I asked as Lily paused at a door and jiggled the lock.

She cursed and rummaged through her skirts until she produced a key. "Leave the Academy? Not really. Only for missions or assignment and stuff like that."

I gave her a raised brow. "Like hunting monsters?"

She flashed me an adorable grin. "Yes, like hunting. That's my favorite."

I decided to reevaluate her as she managed to get the door

open. I expected another classroom or training facility to be waiting for us on the other side, but I stared at... nothing.

Literally, nothing.

"Okay! In you go!" Lily said cheerfully and shoved me into the darkness.

You got to be fucking kidding me.

DARK TRUTH

*T*he darkness engulfed me and I stood as still as I could, which wasn't hard. The darkness was more like a thick type of sludge that infiltrated my nostrils and didn't even let me breathe. I thought that I might die there until a hand slipped through mine.

Marcus.

His confidence and firmness made me suck in a gulp of the sludge, which surprisingly worked. Oxygen, or something breathable like oxygen, gave me relief and I greedily sucked in more breaths.

Marcus didn't speak, or if he did I didn't hear him. A roar sounded in my ears that was a deafening kind of silence. I wasn't sure if it was the void of nothing that I was hearing or an endless echo of my own heartbeat reverberating around in my head. Instead of talking, he tugged at me and guided me through the darkness as if he knew where to go.

A brush of fur at my ankles told me that Bast had followed

us into the murky depths. I didn't sense any agitation or fear from him. In fact, I sensed relief as if my familiar had been in a place like this before. That gave me enough confidence to squeeze Marcus's hand and keep going.

A sticky film hit my face and Marcus tugged me through. The other side of the sludge felt surprisingly cold and I had the oddest sensation that I didn't want to leave this place. I was safe here. Time and space didn't pass between realms. I could live forever in a locked present moment with no worries that the Second Echo of Calamity would descend onto the world and destroy what was left of it. I wouldn't have to worry that everything was my fault or that Sarina would return from the dead only to finish what she'd begun. Marcus wouldn't have to die. He'd be safe.

As if he sensed my reluctance, Marcus shifted his grip up to my forearm and clamped down. He tugged me and refused to let go until I gave in and pushed myself through the veil.

Sunlight streamed down on my face and I blinked, trying to get rid of the sticky sensation of sleep that layered over my senses. It was strange that I'd felt like sunlight could have been cold compared to the nothingness between realms.

"It's addictive, the tunnels," Marcus said, his voice low and comforting. He knelt and brushed a strand of hair behind my ear. "Just give it a moment to pass. You'll shake it off."

Bast meowed at me cheerfully as if he'd been immune to the in-between realm's forces. In fact his coat was sleeker and shinier than it had been a moment before. His eyes gleamed with mischief and delight and the sensations of his happiness intruded on my thoughts without words.

I frowned, but ran my fingers through his fur just to

assure myself he was really there. He nuzzled against me and nipped my finger, making me laugh. "Glad to see you're perfectly fine.' I sighed and settled my hands onto my thighs as I knelt, trying to work out my senses. Hard slabs of stone rested warm underneath me and an open sky broke the horizon with a sharp line.

No, not the horizon, pillars.

I drew in a gasp when I realized I was back in the grave-yard where I'd released my bondmates from their prison. Old blood streaks still marked each pillar where I'd worked the spell to set them free without even knowing that's what I'd been doing at the time. I laughed at the irony now. Perhaps it was fate that I'd set them free, or perhaps I'd made my own fate.

"What are we doing here?" I asked as I struggled to my feet.

Marcus took me by the elbow and allowed me to lean into his side. "You're the one who stepped into the tunnel first, so you're the one who brought us here."

I frowned. "Why would I want to see this place again?"

Marcus pointed at a glimmer of silver in the center of the stage. "Maybe that has something to do with it?"

I recognized the beginnings of an unfinished rune from where we stood. "I'm not sure what spell that would be for," I admitted as I wandered closer to the blemish. "It has two long strokes and then it just stops like someone taped it off before painting it."

"That's not paint," Marcus said. He knelt and ran his finger over the mark. His skin came back glittering with tiny particles and he licked it. "It's diamond dust," he said, giving me a wary look. "This has something to do with Sarina."

Bast meowed at me, his aura sending me impatience that I figure this out already.

I glared at him. "If you know what's going on then why don't you speak up?"

Marcus adjusted his sleeve cuff. "Bast isn't talking to you anymore?"

The cat hissed at him as if insulted by the comment.

I shrugged. "I don't think he can. Sarina did something when..." I let my words drift off as my heart twisted. I might have saved Marcus, but the rest of my guys were out there in other worlds. What if I'd just gotten lucky with Marcus? What if I couldn't get anyone else back?

"Evelyn," Marcus said, his voice tinged with warning. "I sense your guilt. You have nothing to feel guilty about."

"Are you so sure about that?" I snapped and pointed to the bloody pillars. "Because of me, you were trapped for a thousand years reliving the worst moment of your life over and over again." I let my hand fall to my thigh with a slap. "And how long were you trapped in a new prison because of me? I released enough magic to kill all the warlocks and witches who came after me which gave Sarina exactly what she needed." My heart thundered in my chest as the futility of it all came crashing down on me. "I knew that her power worked off of sacrifice, and that's exactly what I gave her. Don't you see what a failure I am? Now Tiros, Killian, Aaron, and Quinn are trapped all in different worlds and only the gods know what's happening to them right now." I crumpled into a ball and tore the masquerade mask off my forehead. "I don't deserve these powers, Marcus. I don't deserve you."

The tears came, hot and unforgiving. I knew I was about to ugly cry because I was losing my shit, but I couldn't stop it. Every time I tried to stop something bad from happening I only seemed to make it worse. I couldn't keep doing this.

"Hey, Evie," Marcus said as he knelt and wrapped his arms around my shoulders. "You need to fall apart? Fine, that's allowed, but you will not blame yourself or say you don't deserve everything you want in life, because you deserve all of that and more." He pressed a firm kiss to my hairline. I knew that he was still battling his bloodlust and he should have taken the opportunity to strike while I was distracted. I leaned my head away from him and gave him access to my neck.

"You don't need to be nice to me," I said, biting off the bitter words. "All I'm good for is giving you blood, so take it. Take all of it for all I care."

Marcus hushed me and drew me in close to his chest. The sobs came then and instantly soaked the tattered remains of his shirt. My Marcus was refined and poised and always wore the finest of silk, but he'd been trapped in that vile place for gods knew how long because of me.

Bast was the one to snap me out of it. He bit my hand, this time hard enough to draw blood and I yelped in surprise. He glared at me and a flood of his projected emotions told me to stop behaving like a brat and pull myself together.

Why?

Because I had bondmates and an entire world to save.

Oh, and he wanted some fish.

"I AM NOT YOUR FUCKING CHEF," I chided Bast as I scooped tuna from a can.

He flicked his tail impatiently until I put the smelly stuff into a bowl and gave it to him.

There was only one place left for us to go in Belgium, so here we were, at old man Jordan's house raiding his kitchen. His wife wasn't home. "Visiting her mother," he said with a strained smile, but I knew the truth. He'd sent her away. After the destruction of the Amethyst Coven it wasn't safe here anymore.

"Why are you still here?" I asked him as Bast took his time inspecting the fishy meal. Once he decided it was up to his standards he took a delicate nibble.

Jordan sighed and rested on a stool. He looked like he needed a smoke and the kitchen had a faint tinge of an old smoker's habit coming back to life. Instead, he fingered the box of cigarettes in his shirt pocket without taking it out. "I belong here," he said as his gaze unfocused.

Fuck. I knew that look.

I rested a hand on his arm and leaned in closer. "Styles, did my Aunt Sandra put you under a thrall spell? Don't lie to me. I'm an Amethyst Coven witch and I'm asking you a direct question." If Aunt Sandra had put him under a spell that kept him under her control, it would take years before it wore off from the effect of her death.

His face went tight and he worked his jaw before responding. "That Aunt of yours did something, aye. But I asked for it.

I didn't even want the choice to abandon the coven. After all it has given me, I owe complete loyalty."

I sighed and leaned back. "There's no one left to be loyal to anymore, Mr. Styles. They're all dead. I'm the only one that's left from the Amethyst Coven."

Jordan Styles didn't seem surprised by this news and plucked the cigarette box out of his shirt. He popped it open, but didn't take out a cigarette. "I'm relieved to see you're alive, Miss Evelyn. I thought that all of the coven was gone after..." His gaze dropped to the ground and thanks to my powers of empathy from Tiros, I sensed a wave of frustration and guilt. He couldn't possibly feel that the downfall of an entire coven was his fault? "There's nothing but rubble, Miss Evelyn. I planned on starting to rebuild, because humans built that place you know. But, I didn't even know where to start. I'm just one old man."

My heart twisted. Jordan Styles was a good man and all he wanted to do was to help. I don't know what the coven could have possibly done to win that kind of loyalty, but they didn't deserve it. "Mr. Styles," I said, leaning closer. "Jordan. I declare you free from the thrall spell. You owe no allegiance or loyalty to the Amethyst Coven. Your life is your own and I command you to live the rest of it as you see fit."

Magic licked off my tongue as I spoke the words. I sensed Marcus watching me from the shadows. Had it been Quinn or Tiros or any of my other bondmates I would have been reprimanded for breaking a thrall spell on the only ally I had in the city, but I didn't do things because they benefited me. I did them because they were the right things to do.

Jordan blinked as the dust fell from his eyes. It took a long while and by the time the spell was completely broken a pile of spent magic glittered with purple motes around his wrinkled trousers. He looked down at it and stared. "Miss Evelyn, you didn't have to do that." He looked up at me with tears shining in his eyes. "This is why I took the thrall spell in the first place. You are worthy of my loyalty and when the coven took you in, I vowed to your mother I would always look after you. I am a man of my word. I don't need a thrall spell to be loyal to you." He lifted his lip as his mood changed. "But the rest of them, by the gods, I needed some help. They didn't deserve a speck of my loyalty. You did and you always will."

Okay, I'm not crying. Nope, not crying.

I hugged myself and straightened, waiting to make sure my lower lip wasn't trembling before I spoke. "You knew my mother?"

He nodded. "Aye, lovely woman. It wasn't right what happened to her and your father. Humans are always victims of the supernatural and the whims of those who live much longer than we do and ironically don't appreciate life for how precious it is. They wipe it out without a second thought." His gaze flicked to Marcus who should have been invisible, but old man Styles was no fool. He knew a vampire when he saw one. "I wasn't sure how I felt about your 'tutors,' but I see that they love you even more than I do, and that says something."

I sighed at the inevitable wave of depression that came when I thought of the death of my parents. I'd only been four years old so I hardly remembered anything, but a scene like that stayed with a young mind. All I remembered was blood strewn so far across the walls it looked like someone had taken a ketchup bottle and set it to explode.

"Demon-touched wolves came to Belgium around that time and the coven hadn't put in defenses yet," I said, both sad that my family was the one that had paid the price and glad that no one else had been a victim to the wolves after that. The coven had put up defenses to make sure those of magical heritage, discovered or not, wouldn't attract the wolves. That's why Jasmine surrounded the coven and had been installed all throughout the town. Humans had opted to call the blooms weeds, not knowing how it had protected them.

Jordan's features grew hard. "Now that the thrall spell is gone, I can't keep the truth from you anymore Miss Evelyn."

A chill ran through my entire body and I went rigid as if my muscles had suddenly seized. "What?"

He worked his jaw before continuing. "Your parents weren't killed by wolves. Yes, the wolves could have gotten to you, but your powers hadn't been awakened yet. They wouldn't have been able to sniff you out that fast." His hand started to shake and he put a cigarette into his mouth without lighting it. His grey eyes stared through me as if looking into the past. A darkness shadowed over him that put my whole body on edge. "It wasn't the wolves," he repeated.

I swallowed hard and turned to find Marcus had gravitated closer to me. I took his hand and squeezed it, allowing myself to curl into his chest to face an impossible truth that I wasn't ready for. I'd never be ready for this. "It was the coven," I whispered so softly I thought that maybe Jordan hadn't heard me.

"The coven," he confirmed. "They knew what you were from the very beginning. Not what kind of witch you were, but that you would win the trials to become Queen of the

Royal Covens." He lightly chewed on his cigarette before taking it out of his mouth and holding it between his fingers like someone familiar with the old habit. "You did win, didn't you?" He offered me a humorless chuckle. "It's a twisted sort of justice that the coven has been wiped out. I'm sorry, because I know they were your family, but they deserved what was coming to them."

Marcus squeezed me when I began to shake. Old man Jordan was right. The coven had been my family... but I had a new family now.

"Oh my gods," I said, my eyes going wide when I realized that my bondmates weren't the only ones missing. "Cassidy!"

WORST FRIEND EVER

I was the worst friend in the existence of friends. "I can't believe I forgot about Cassidy," I said for the billionth time.

Marcus tossed another pillow at my face. I wanted to run off into the nearest source of magic to create a portal and rescue her, but Marcus wasn't going to have any of that. "I had just assumed that you'd come to the same conclusion I had. She's fine. There's no one left alive to hurt her and with Sarina's death her imprisonment will be broken. The entire place is self-sustainable. There is a stream for water, gardens for food, and an entire royal pantry with human chefs that will no doubt be happy to help their fellow humans stay alive. They have no loyalty to Sarina." He clamped a hand on each of my shoulders and pushed me onto the bed. "You're no use to Cassidy or anyone else if you run yourself into the ground. You need rest."

Marcus ran his hands down my arms and began to take off my shoes.

I frowned. "I don't want to have sex right now," I complained. "You don't know that she's okay! I need to help her." I let out a long breath as Marcus finished tugging off my shoes and worked on my socks. "And the rest of my bond-mates! They could be anywhere. They could be dying!"

"Hush," Marcus chided. His ruby eyes glanced up at me and I realized that he looked as tired as I felt. He hadn't once complained that he'd been imprisoned all over again, for gods knew how long, and he hadn't even blamed me for any suffering he'd endured. "I'm not trying to have sex with you. I'm trying to take care of you and right now you need to sleep."

Bast meowed at me from his perch at the top of the bedroom's lone bookshelf that teetered haphazardly on one side.

"Don't agree with him," I said and crossed my arms. I allowed myself to fall back onto the soft bedding. Staring up at the speckled ceiling, I hated the feeling of being helpless. "Can't I just cast a spell and rejuvenate my energy? Do I really need a full night's rest?"

"You can't just magic your way out of every problem, and yes, you need a full night's rest, maybe even more." He took off his shoes and shirt and joined me, leaving his pants on. I frowned at him and he chuckled. "I promise, not trying to have sex with you."

Sighing, I finally gave in and peeled off my pants. He might be comfortable sleeping in the tattered remains of his silk trousers, but my jeans were definitely not comfortable enough to sleep in. "Good because I'm off the menu."

He gave me a raised brow. "Didn't you just ask me to drain all your blood earlier?"

I slapped him on the arm, which sounded like I'd slapped a brick wall. "Don't pick on me. I was feeling a little sorry for myself, okay? I'll get over it, especially when everyone I care about is safe and happy. I don't like wondering where everyone is and if they're alive or hurt." Tears pricked my eyes at the thought and I swiped them away before Marcus could see. "It just sucks."

I knew I was whining, but Marcus didn't seem to care. He chuckled and wrapped me in his arms. He was a vampire, so it wasn't exactly a warm embrace, but he gathered the blankets and tugged them over us and soon my own body heat helped to warm my chilled skin.

Bast must have sensed that I was cold, because he jumped onto the bed and curled up in the space between my neck and shoulder.

With my vampire holding me tight and my familiar purring right next to my ear, I somehow pushed away the guilt long enough to give in to sleep.

MARCUS WAS RIGHT, although I'd never tell him and his fat ego that he was right about anything. I really did need a good night's sleep and with the morning my pity-party was finally over and I felt more like myself—and ready to kick some serious ass.

"Hi-yah!" I screamed while slicing a karate chop through the air.

Unamused, Bast twitched his tail while I practiced my new moves. He'd found a good spot to watch the sparring session in the sun out on old Jordan's patio. Sadly the human wasn't here to watch my bitchin' moves. He'd gone into town to find us some more food to eat. Said something about "vampires going to drain you dry unless I feed you."

Marcus pinched the bridge of his nose and took in a deep breath. "When I asked you to show me your fighting skills, that's not what I had in mind."

Bending my knees and assuming a fighting stance like I'd seen in the movies, I did a good old fashioned "come here" motion. No such thing as overkill when it came to Martial Arts, especially the made-up kind. Maybe I could call it Eve-judo. "Don't knock it 'til you try it!" I shouted and dug my toes into the grass, trying to "root" myself, also a technique I'd picked up on TV. Aunt Sandra hadn't really believed in television, but we were permitted to watch some things so that humans weren't a total culture shock.

"I'm not going to try... that," Marcus said, wiggling his fingers at me. "We should find Killian first. He's the weapons-master." Marcus gave me a wink. "I'm a lover, not a fighter. But, you really need to learn how to defend yourself. When I was in the future I saw how many other realms there are out there and most of them are very... physical."

Marcus wasn't going to take me seriously unless I showed him that I wasn't just faking it. I'd been gathering magic within myself the whole time he'd been blabbing while I mined my brain for every Martial Arts movie I'd ever watched. All those fight sequences were real moves and the actors had been trained by real professionals. With a little bit of magic, I could recreate every move and technique and dissect it down to its core, how the actor had drawn his strength up from his legs and twisted that force into a punch or a kick. Mostly though, it was distraction and then attack, so I decided to test one of my moves on a thousand-year-old vampire who had a penchant for silk.

Moving so fast that the world around me blurred, I went for the soft corner of Marcus's handkerchief poking out from his vest pocket. He'd raided the clothes left in the guesthouse so that he looked more like his old self, complete with his magical endless supply of handkerchiefs.

Magic hummed in my veins and I marveled that Marcus's ruby eyes were still looking at the spot I'd been standing a moment before. Damn, this was going to work, wasn't it?

I reached out and plucked the first handkerchief from his pocket, only to find another one miraculously took its place, so I took that one too. I repeated the process until the ground littered with the things and my heart thundered in my ears from the effort to keep the spell active. The majority of my magic channeled through the masquerade mask at my hip, allowing me to manipulate time, and in this case slow it down. It didn't surprise me that Marcus's magic would come to me easiest given he'd spent the night with me. Even if we hadn't had sex, just being in his arms had rejuvenated me in ways I couldn't explain.

Finally, the spell weakened and Marcus's eyes tracked me

to his side, then widened. He glanced down at the mess I'd made of his handkerchiefs and then his lips spread in a large grin, flashing fang. "Well, Evie, seems I underestimated you."

Damn right, bitches. Marcus just got schooled in Eve-judo.

BIG CATS

I don't know if Bast was entirely convinced of my kick-ass awesomeness, but Marcus was satisfied enough with my display that he helped me to unlock the next realm.

It wasn't as easy as holding an artifact and trying to connect to my bondmate like I had with Marcus. It didn't stop me from trying, though. I held up Killian's dagger that glowed with his blue magic. I squinted at it and gave it a good shake. "Is this thing on? I don't feel Killian at all." I knew exactly what I should feel when my magic reached out for Killian. Excitement, that squeamish feeling that edged between pleasure and pain and the scent of salt and sea that filled my body in a way only he could.

Marcus offered his hand. "Give it here."

Frowning, I obeyed and gave him the dagger. Even though the magic wasn't meant for him, the blue sizzled across the blade and then spread up his forearm as he gripped the hilt.

He knelt and began slicing lines into the dirt. "You were able to find me because we share kindred magic. It takes more than a soul bond to travel to other realms. You need to know exactly where you're going."

I squatted and hugged my knees to my chest. Bast marched around the perimeter of grass while Marcus worked on what appeared to be an elaborate rune. "I didn't know where I was going when I found you," I protested. "All I knew was what I felt and I followed our connection."

Marcus paused to give me a measured stare. "You and I share magic over time and space. I still have a degree of my powers from when I was a warlock and they're not much unlike your own. The only difference between us is that you're able to bend time and space to your will, predict its patterns and form new ones to your advantage. I can only ride existing waves of time and space and observe, making small alterations to my path on what is already a predetermined tapestry."

That was way complicated, but I wasn't going to let Marcus know he was confusing me. "Right, we both have similar powers. Okay, so? Killian is a weaponsmaster and I showed you some Eve-judo. Doesn't that count for something?"

He smirked. "It shows me that maybe you're up for the challenge of a targeted spell to find him, yes."

I tried not to let the disappointment seep into my voice. "We have to do a spell?"

Marcus turned his attention back to the rune. If he was really working a spell then he had to get every line perfect. Even one wrong stroke could change the result entirely. I'd learned that one the hard way when I'd tried making a spell for "baseball mitt" and instead I'd made "baseball shit." Yeah, that wasn't very pretty.

"I had a lot of time before you freed me from Fortune Academy. At the very least, that place acted like a magnifier for my powers and I was able to locate where the others are. I might have been able to escape to one of the other realms, but I felt you traveling through time and space to get to me, so I stayed put until you arrived." He gave me a wink. "You over-shot your target by a few years, but we'll have to practice your time travel. It's not your fault you weren't trained."

I blanched. "A few years?"

He waved away my rising panic. "You forget, Evie, I'm over a thousand years old and I've been in worse prisons. The Academy studied me, and had they done a better job of feeding me it wouldn't have been so bad. The students kept me entertained and I knew that you were coming for me. I can be patient when I want to be."

Anger surged in my chest. "I'm going to go back to that fucking school and murder all of them."

"No, you won't," he said, then stood and appraised his handiwork before offering me the blade. Its magic had dimmed and now the rune on the ground glowed with a faint blue. "Are you ready to go after Killian? He's being held in the panther realm."

I stared at him for a long time. "Panthers." It wasn't a ques-tion, but a statement. Surely I hadn't heard him correctly.

He nodded. "Yes. Panthers."

I narrowed my eyes. "Like, big black cats? Just a whole realm of nothing but cats that'll eat me?"

Bast perked up at the mention of big cats and meowed with more enthusiasm than I'd heard from him since I got him a bowl of fish.

I glowered down at my familiar, desperately wishing I could change him back to his mortal form where he was just as irritating, but at least he made up for it in the sexy department. "Why are you excited about giant cats? You're a pipsqueak. They'll crunch you up and eat you as an appetizer."

Bast meowed again, sending me a flood of emotions that kindly reminded me he was the god of familiars, which meant god of anything feline, and he would rule an entire world of cats with his thumbnail that liked to scratch me when he jumped off my lap.

I rolled my eyes. "Okay, so, Bast is confident this is a good plan, but I'm still not sold. Why would Killian be in a world of cats?"

"It's a clan of panther shifters and they're part of the original family of the Onyx Coven Witches. Each Coven is descended from a different supernatural species, which is something the covens likely kept out of their educational systems."

My eyes widened. "Oh." Shifting uncomfortably, I edged around the perimeter of the rune that was now glowing in soft pulses and an undeniable tingling spread over my body. It felt more like an invasive set of fingers going through me, searching for my soul connection with Killian to establish the connection. Marcus was hella' powerful that he could work a spell like that without even uttering a single word of power.

"So, how are we going to get him out? Why do the panthers have him?"

"He's useful to them. They look for specialized supernaturals trained in the art of war. Panthers work in clans and they have their own natural enemies to deal with. Someone like Killian would be what I was to the students of Fortune Academy; a resource to study and learn from."

I swallowed hard. That meant that Killian was fighting, maybe even for his life, all so that some vicious panthers could learn his skills.

Decision made, I readied the dagger in my grip and took a deep breath. I'd been resisting the spell emanating from the rune on the ground, but now I let it claw into me and latch onto my heart. It hurt, making me wince as spikes dug into me and formed the brutal connection between this world and the one beyond where Killian waited.

I didn't panic when the pain reached a crescendo. Unlike Marcus who was all passion wrapped in silk, Killian and I had a different relationship. He had a unique relationship with pain, understood it on a level that no one else could know or appreciate, which made me different too. He embraced pain and used it for his magic, for his passion, and to feel alive. To feel no pain at all is to be dead, and that is one thing Killian fears most of all.

Sensing him and all of his dreams and fears, I released a shaky sigh as my body drew in all of the sensations and a portal formed across the expanse of the rune, devouring it and revealing a world on the other side.

I peered down into the portal that dropped out right in the middle of a thick patch of forest. I couldn't see any of the predators in the shadows, but I sensed them. The moment we stepped through we'd be walking into an ambush.

I shared a look with Marcus and he must have read the grim determination on my face. "I have your back," he assured me.

That was all I needed to hear. I pinched my nose as if I was about to jump into an icy pond and stepped into the portal.

TRAINING GROUNDS

A low growl emanated the moment my feet hit the soft soil of the forest floor. Musky scents enveloped me and humidity hit me in the face. This definitely wasn't a place I wanted to stay in very long, but if Killian could handle it so could I.

Orange eyes glowed in the darkness, blinking when Marcus and Bast came through the portal and landed on the ground after me. The panther wanted us to know it was watching. One false move and it would strike.

I decided to go for the non-violent approach first. Given that I could sense there were multiple cats in the forest, we were certainly outnumbered. If they attacked, I would use my magic to fend them off, but I didn't need to hurt them. I needed to know where Killian was, and then if he had been mistreated in any way—then I'd hurt them.

"I'm looking for my bondmate," I said, raising my voice loud enough to carry for any lurkers in the forest who might be watching. "He was sent here by mistake and I've come to bring him home."

Those orange eyes blinked at me again, slow and deliberate, then shifted to Bast who wound about my ankles and sent sparks flying as he fueled me with more magic than I needed.

I waved my hand at him. "Bast! Don't antagonize them. You know I don't need more magic." I had reunited with all of my bondmates and the god of familiars giving me a dose of his magic was just plain overkill.

The panther watching us was either offended, or intrigued, because the leaves moved and crunched. Then I realized it wasn't leaves crunching... but bones. I'd heard those same sounds when Aaron had shifted from his wolf form and I swallowed hard.

A naked woman stepped from the forest, surprising me enough to make my jaw fall slack. She was stunning. Brilliant green eyes with sliced through the irises and a long mane of sleek black hair that swayed all the way down to her waist made her look more mystical than human. She grinned, revealing pointed canines that gave her a dangerous look. I wondered if this was her true form, or if she had mastered her shift so well that she didn't change back into a human all the way. "You're a witch," she said, her words a statement. Her gaze shifted down to Bast again. "That is an unusual animal you've brought with you. May I see him?"

I glowered and tried to make my impression of this woman. No introduction. No shame to walk out in front of strangers completely naked. She'd completely ignored my request and was already asking me favors, but at least she was asking instead of taking what she wanted, that was a start.

"Sure," I decided and gave Bast a nudge with my foot. "Go on. You were so eager to meet the panthers. Looks like you've made a new friend."

Bast twitched his tail, the only sign that he wasn't amused with my rough treatment of him, before marching fearlessly to the panther woman with his tail held high.

To my surprise she knelt and stroked the feline and a soft purr rumbled in her throat. For some reason I didn't fucking like that one bit. "Bast is my familiar, but also my bondmate when he's in his mortal form, so don't get any funny ideas." I didn't know how kinky things got with the panthers, but I figured it was a good idea to lay out some ground rules.

The woman chuckled and stood, crossing her arms underneath her oversized breasts, making them perk up in a way that had me blushing. I turned to make sure Marcus wasn't staring and he seemed overly fascinated with refolding his handkerchief just right in his shirt pocket.

"We respect bondmates here, so don't worry, I was only saying hello." She brushed a long lock of her wavy hair from her shoulder. "About your other bondmate, does he by chance have a penchant for blades?"

My eyes narrowed. "Yes. Killian is a trained weaponsmaster. I want to see him immediately."

She clicked her tongue at me and four sets of orange eyes blinked in the darkness of the forest. "I'd watch your tone if I were you. You're not the only one with bondmates."

Marcus took me by the elbow and leaned in close to whisper in my ear. "Remember, Evie, we're in her world and we need to play by her rules."

I knew that Marcus wouldn't have let me come here had

he not believed that I could handle a pride of panthers, but I still swallowed the sour bile of fear at the idea of four big cats jumping out from the forest to pounce. Magic or not, the muscles lining the woman's body told me these creatures were fast and the glow in her eyes proved they had a bit of magic of their own.

Right, so I need to be charming. I'm totally charming.

I managed a weak grin and patted Marcus's arm. "Of course. I am only anxious to be reunited with all of my bond-mates. It's a long story, but they were all sent to different worlds and my weaponsmaster was sent here by mistake. I would be very grateful if you could permit me to see him."

She stared at me for a long time in the way that cats do. I wasn't sure if she was plotting my death or thinking about what she was going to have for dinner—probably both.

"Very well. You'll stay to the path and be escorted at all times." She glanced down at Bast and a smile flickered at her lips. "You're lucky that you have a god of felines with you, or else I would have eaten you outright."

I swallowed hard, but tried not to let the shock show on my face. "Thank you."

She shifted without warning, her bones twisting in opposite directions and her face elongating into the flat snout of a panther with long, silver whiskers. Only her eyes remained the same, those unwavering emerald irises that watched me with far more intelligence than she was letting on.

She swished her tail that had morphed from her hair and turned, expecting us to follow. She bellowed once. I'd never heard a panther call before, but it was a mix between the sound of a woman being murdered and a terrifying roar, followed by a series of chirps.

Echoing chirps came from the forest, but I didn't hear any movement of underbrush or leaves as the chirps followed us as we walked down the path.

"They're letting us know they could follow us silently if they wanted to," Marcus whispered. "Panther shifters are among the most stealthy and dangerous hunters in the universe. We must be careful."

Duh, he didn't have to tell me that. I squeezed his hand anyway and followed the panther sauntering in front of us. I wasn't sure how long we went on like that, but it felt like a million years. By the time we reached any evidence of civilization I was ready to throw up from the amount of tension splitting my stomach into two.

The panther shifted back into a woman as she stepped onto a stone path. A rack of robes sat at the ready and she grabbed one without even looking at it and wrapped it around herself. The other panthers that had been hidden from view emerged from the forest and I froze. Each of them appraised me with a sense of disdain, followed by bored glances at Marcus and Bast. They each shifted into lean, muscular men with eyes that held the same slitted irises as the woman's—and they were just as naked too.

I tried not to stare, but I mean, there were four penises swinging about with nothing to tie them down. Each man grabbed a robe and did a poor job of covering himself, making me feel rooted into place. They surrounded us in a semi-circle and waited.

"You're staring," Marcus hissed at me.

I know, double standards. He'd been good and avoided eye-fucking the woman when she'd met us in the woods, but I never said I was a very good bondmate.

Clearing my throat, I nodded. "Right, we follow her, got it."

The woman hadn't even stopped walking and I had to do a half-jog to catch up with her.

The path wound through a canopy of what looked like a kid's fort on steroids. It was an entire city of houses built in trees with nothing but tree limbs and pulley systems to ferry people and goods up and down. I spotted an elderly man grunting as he yanked on a rope and a bucket of water sloshed as it made its slow ascent to one of the treehouses.

"Don't spill it!" a woman cried down at him.

He grimaced and held onto the rope, his biceps bulging, before carefully trying again. Even the old dudes were ripped.

The sound of hushed village ongoings surrounded us as we made our way deeper into the settlement. No one paid us more than a curious glance or two before catching a glare from one of our escorts. The panthers watching over us must have been some scary dudes, because all of the villagers reacted by scrunching their shoulders and going back to whatever task they'd been doing before.

As we passed the last of what appeared to be village housing, we came upon long rows of trees in neat lines, definitely not naturally grown like the rest of the forest town. "These are the training grounds," the woman said, startling me with her crisp voice that she carelessly tossed over her shoulder. "Your weaponsmaster will be here training our cubs."

Training the cubs? That didn't sound too bad, I hoped.

"Why are the training grounds so deep within your compound? Wouldn't it be safer to have soldiers on the outside to protect the elderly?" I got the feeling that this world was a dangerous one. People in the middle of a dense forest full of treehouses weren't naturally this buff for no reason.

She scoffed at me. "The training grounds are for the cubs. You really should listen better."

As if that explained everything, she pushed past the first gates and a hum resonated in the air. She snapped her fingers and I spotted a flicker of magic echo over an enormous force-field that spanned from each tree strategically placed around the compound. "You can come in now, the field is down."

Marcus held out a hand when I moved to follow her. "I'll go first," he said, then stepped through the invisible barrier before I could protest. Sure, maybe he was a powerful vampire-warlock mix, but I was a Fate Witch and I was responsible for keeping him safe.

I glowered at him. "Pull another trick like that and I'll kick you in the balls."

The panther woman seemed immensely entertained by that comment and rewarded me with laughter that caressed my ears. "I think you'll fit in just fine around here."

I didn't intend on staying, but I flashed her a smile anyway. Trying to be charming and all. "Right, gotta keep those bondmates in line, am I right?"

Marcus rolled his eyes at me and motioned for me to step in front of him. "After you, your highness."

I glared at him because I knew he used that title on purpose. I wasn't the Queen of the Royal Covens, at least, I didn't think I was. Either way, I certainly didn't want to be queen of anything. I wanted to kick ass and go home and fuck all of my guys and have chocolate cake. In that order.

First, I had to get all of my bondmates out of their life-threatening alternate worlds and then we could decide where home was, preferably somewhere with lots of chocolate cake.

The clash of steel on steel echoed through the open air and I frowned. If there had been fighting going on I certainly hadn't heard it before.

I peered behind us to see the forcefield was much more visible on this side. It shimmered with rainbow-onyx waves that gave it a gorgeous oily sheen. Whatever that thing was, it didn't let soundwaves out of it, and probably not much else either.

"Do you think the forcefield is to protect the training grounds, or to keep whatever is inside of it from getting out?" I asked Marcus. Even though I kept my voice low, the panther woman and our manly escorts still heard me and chuckled.

"I don't know what kind of strays you're picking up, Isis, but this one catches on quick."

The female panther glared at the male. I wasn't sure if it was because he'd used her name in front of us or if she just didn't like him complimenting me. By the way she flashed me teeth, it was probably both. "Your bondmate isn't the only unique training relic we've acquired, so I'd be on guard if I were you."

Training relic? That made me bristle, but I kept my jaw screwed shut and curled my anger into my fists as I balled them at my side.

Another forcefield hit us without warning. My ears

popped and once I'd passed through, an explosion of panthers and half-naked fighters came into view out on a large open field filled with obstacles. It looked like something out of a paranormal bootcamp with nets, poles, and mud pits complete with various groups of fighters.

I spotted Killian immediately among the clash of weapons and claws. "Killian!" I screamed.

He jerked his bloodied face up at my voice, which gave his panther opponent the opportunity to pin him and go for his throat. Blood splashed over dirt that had once been white, but now was stained permanently pink from the constant onslaught of brutality.

"Killian!" I screeched again as panic gripped my heart. No way I'd come across entire worlds, braved a bitchy panther shifter and her escort of bondmates just to see Killian mauled to death before my very eyes because I'd been stupid enough to distract him.

I relaxed when the panther slid off of Killian's body, revealing that the blood wasn't his. He plucked out a dagger from the creature's hide and wiped it on his pants.

Isis didn't seem very happy that Killian had just murdered one of her own, but to be fair, he was outnumbered and looked as if he'd been fighting for quite some time. Three more panthers circled him and growled, lifting their lips to show teeth red with blood.

"What kind of fucking training is this?" I asked, my voice's pitch going up into "only dogs and cats can hear this range" mode, but Isis was part cat, she'd figure it out.

She sauntered past me and didn't seem to notice that her robe was running loose around her voluptuous breasts that seemed to be more of a hindrance than a benefit for someone who acted as if she was the warrior woman of this town. She brushed her fingers over the fallen panther and a metallic taste of strong magic ran across my tongue before the dead panther stirred.

My eyes widened. So, mystical training grounds where death wasn't permanent. Good to know.

"Time for a break," she snapped and all of the fighting stopped minus a few disappointed growls. She glared until the remaining panthers shifted and sauntered off, grabbing robes that immediately soaked up blood from large gashes, although none of the shifters seemed to mind the wounds.

Isis approached Killian who still knelt on the ground gripping his switchblade so hard that his knuckles were white. She offered him a hand, which surprised me. Killian looked as if he'd sooner cut her hand off at the wrist than accept her help.

Putting away his switchblade, he placed his fingers in hers just long enough as was appropriate as he stood and then shoved his hands into his pockets. "Glad to see you're okay, Evie," he said, trying to give me a smile but all I could see was how tired he was, both physically and of putting up a show for the panthers.

Gods, how long had he been here? Did time move differently in other realms? My heart twisted and I ran to Killian and wrapped my arms around my neck. I kissed him all over and didn't care about any of the dirt or blood I got on my face. "I'm so sorry I didn't come sooner," I said and then squeezed him as tight as I could. I was never going to let him out of my sight again.

He chuckled and the sound made fresh shivers go through my body. "I'm fine, Evie, really. The panthers have been good for me. Keeps my skills sharp with all this non-stop training."

I held him at arm's length and frowned. "Are you just saying that to make me feel better?"

He gave me a sideways nod that I couldn't decide was a yes or no. "Let's just say I'm glad to see you and leave it at that, hmm?"

Marcus joined us and clapped Killian on the back, making my weaponsmaster wince. No telling what kind of cuts and bruises he had all over his body, but he gave the vampire a warm grin. "Hey, Marcus. Hope you've been taking care of our girl."

Marcus took one of his handkerchiefs and offered it to Killian who used it to wipe his face. "She's a handful, but I've managed to keep her in one piece."

Bast meowed at my feet impatiently. "Yes, Bast, we'll get you some food soon."

Isis clapped her hands twice. "The cat god is hungry, so we feast. To the commons, everyone."

To my surprise, those who'd remained behind to watch us obeyed and moved towards the main structure in the center of the forcefield.

Isis gave me a toothy grin. "Don't look so surprised, darling. If there's one thing I love more than watching bloody men fight, it's eating a good meal."

LUCKILY PANTHERS ENJOYED MORE than just fish, but Bast had

a prime spot at the table and there was no shortage of delicacies for him to feast on, scales and all.

I'd seen feasting halls, but never one quite like this. Everyone except for a select few looked to be around my age, maybe a little younger, and cheerfully talked with one another while they ate even though they were all covered in cuts and bruises. There was a wash basin at the entrance to the feast hall with massive buckets of water and towels, enough to clean off the worst of the blood from any open wounds. There wasn't enough water and soap in the world for this crew in my opinion.

I'd been seated at what looked like a spot of honor, or maybe it was a spot of dishonor, I wasn't sure. Our table consisted of Isis and the male shifters I believed were her bondmates by the way they protectively kept watching over her. I was glad to have Marcus on my left and Killian on my right. I didn't like Bast having a propped up stool next to Isis, but he seemed content as he ate his fish. Isis took what looked like an entire turkey leg and slashed at it with her teeth. After she swallowed the bite, she grinned at me. "Please, eat. If traveling between realms is anything like hunting in the forest, you're surely famished."

I glanced down at my untouched plate filled with nothing but meat. Blood oozed from the half-cooked bones and I dabbed at my mouth with one of the wash towels I'd grabbed for a napkin to cover my grimace. "I apologize, Isis, but I'm not that hungry. I have other realms to travel to and other bondmates to bring back to my world where they belong."

Isis took another thoughtful bite and then addressed

Killian. "Weaponsmaster, are you ready to leave us? You said that you'd stay until your skills were honed."

I blinked at him. Was he actually with the panthers... voluntarily?

Killian worked on a rib with his switchblade and didn't seem bothered by the layer of fat running through it as he brought a bite to his mouth. After taking his time chewing and swallowing, he answered Isis. "Your cubs are doing well." He nodded at one of the male panthers. "I believe that Jason can pick up where I left off. He's been paying the most attention."

The panther named Jason straightened and gave Killian a cat-like grin, canines and all.

Isis nodded. "Very well. Tonight, you all rest here, then I will personally donate my magic to send you on your way. A deal's a deal."

I glanced at Killian, but he shook his head. Whatever deal he'd made, he'd tell me when we were alone.

I kicked him under the table to make sure he didn't forget it, but I'd forgotten he actually liked pain and he gave me the most wicked grin I'd seen on him all day.

This was going to be one hell of a night.

A NIGHT TO REMEMBER

"*There's* no way I'm going to be able to sleep like this," I said, still catching my breath from climbing the billion tree limbs to the "guest quarters" as Isis had called it. One small hammock hung outside—yes, outside—a window several stories above ground.

"We'll put furs out on the ground," Killian said, dismissing the deathtrap in the window. "I don't expect you to sleep in the hammock." He grabbed a bounty of furs from the closet and waggled his brows. "It's about time we spent a night together."

Marcus snaked an arm around my waist and pulled me against him as he grinned. "Only if you're willing to share, weaponsmaster. I think I've earned a night with our witch just as much as you have." He leaned over me, surprising me by brushing his lips gently against mine. "What do you say, Evie, can you handle both of us?"

I don't know if it was because of all the cats or heights, but my men were all sorts of horny and I gave them a raised brow. Even Bast seemed put off by the overt manliness as he decided to brave the windowsill and curl up in what was left of the day's sunlight. He gave me a slitted glare before closing his eyes completely, as if to say, *yep, I'm still a cat. If anyone can figure out how to turn me back into my mortal form, it's a realm full of cat shifters, but no rush. Go have a good fuck with two of your bondmates. I'll just wait right here on the windowsill.*

"What about Bast?" I asked, then squirmed out of Marcus's grasp. "Or Quinn? Or Tiros? Or Aaron?" Anger mixed with fear flushed my cheeks. "I'm not even tired. We should go now and look for them."

"We can't go anywhere, not yet," Killian interjected as he spread the furs out on the floor. He wadded up a few to make pillows. "Aaron is in this realm, well, not exactly, but he's here. We won't be able to get to him until morning. It's why I've been keeping an eye on the panthers to make sure Aaron didn't get himself killed."

"What?" I screeched, my voice in danger of going high range again. "What do you mean? If you knew where Aaron was why aren't you with him?"

Killian scoffed. "Do you know how long it took me to get the panthers not to kill me permanently. I proved myself valuable to their training program after they captured me. Then when I gave them intel on the wolves they're at war against, they decided I was an ally. I promised them I'd stay until I was satisfied that I could go after the wolves myself." He shrugged. "I never told them I was going after one particular wolf and that I had no intention of killing him."

I really needed to sit down, and as much as I wanted to

punish Killian and slam a door in his face, there were no doors in the man-child hunting lodge that was our premium guest quarters in panther city. So, without having a more dignified way to digest all that information, I grabbed a wad of furs from Killian and hugged them to my chest and plopped down onto the cushiest spot I could find, even if I did wind up hoarding most of the furs to myself.

Marcus didn't say a word and sat cross-legged at my side with one hand on my thigh. His touch was comforting and I drew on his calm reserves. "Killian, it would help us if you told us how long you've been here. Evelyn performed time-travel magic to retrieve me from the prison that Sarina's spell sent me to. I tried to return us to the proper timeline, but it was difficult to tell when our method of travel was... unique." He left it at that. Unique was an understatement. Fortune Academy mixed with a Fate Witch and time-traveling warlock turned vampire definitely could make a trip go wonky.

Killian fumbled with his switchblade like he wanted to argue, then thought better of it. He glanced at us with those pensive ruby eyes that held so much pain and mystery. "I've been here for six months, which is a blink of an eye compared to the thousand years we were imprisoned in the reincarnation spell."

Six months. Just trying to wrap my mind around that span of time made me queasy. Killian had not only been stuck with battle-hardened panther shifters, but forced to fight in an arena where training meant dying and reviving over and over again.

"Killian, I am so sorry," I said, hugging the bunch of furs tighter to my chest. "I didn't know."

Instead of making me feel worse like I deserved, he smirked and edged closer to me. He brushed a kiss across my cheek, sending flutters spiraling through my stomach. Killian wasn't the type to be gentle, but he would be gentle with me when I needed it. "None of this is your fault, babe."

My lip quirked up on the side. "Did you just call me 'babe?'"

Marcus's hand was still on my thigh and he squeezed, reminding me that he was still there, and that his touch had edged ever so slightly higher on my leg, inciting warmth between my thighs. "Do you like that? We can call you babe if that turns you on."

Killian nuzzled into my neck. "Dibs. I called her babe first and she liked it."

"I never said I liked it," I protested, failing in my mission when a light moan escaped me as Killian began short, sweet nibbles up to my ear. "Okay, maybe a little bit."

With both Marcus and Killian's hands on me, I allowed myself to tumble back into the embrace of warm furs. The nest Killian had made for us was more comfortable than I would have imagined and I found myself closing my eyes, just indulging in the sensation of loving hands wandering over my body and tugging at my shoes, then my pants, and running the tangles out of my hair. They'd left my underwear and shirt on, which meant they weren't going to pressure me into sex even though I could feel their need through our bond growing with tension.

I reached out and found Marcus closest to my face, so I

pulled him in close for a tender kiss. He indulged me, running his tongue over mine as he began to massage my breast through my clothes that were starting to feel too constricting.

"Marcus," I breathed against this mouth, suddenly wanting more, needing more.

My guilt weighed heavy on me, but each touch and caress told me that I didn't need to be so hard on myself. I was loved.

I was worshipped.

Quinn would have read that thought and made fun of me for it, but I didn't think that Marcus or Killian had that kind of connection with me. Instead they made my thoughts come true and whispered in each ear how beautiful I was, how much I turned them on, and how much they needed to explore every inch of me.

When I found the strength to open my eyes, I found that Marcus had migrated down to my hips and grinned at me before licking gently at my underwear and rolling pressure over my swollen sex. I clenched against the sudden wave of pleasure.

Killian wasn't going to be outdone. He gently lifted my shirt to expose my bra. I had dressed for combat, which meant I was wearing a sports bra that held my breasts tightly to my chest, leaving my nipples no forgiveness against Killian's tongue when he mimicked Marcus's movements on my sensitive areas.

They were worshipping me... with their mouths.

"I... guys..." I tried to speak, but that only seemed to encourage them more as they teased around sensitive skin with only a thin layer of cloth a barrier between them and the most intimate parts of me.

Killian was the first to tip me over the edge as he gently teased my bra with his thumb, finally pushing it up to reveal my swollen breasts. His fangs lengthened as he let his gaze soak in my reddened nipples hard from his attention. "I want to bite," he said, his ruby gaze glancing at me almost shyly.

A blush rose in my cheeks. We'd already had sex, but to be intimate with him the same time as Marcus gave me a thrill that would never get old. I glanced down at the vampire who had paused to watch us. He grinned and ran his finger under the elastic band of my underwear, sliding it aside as I squirmed and his breath puffed against my pussy, but he didn't taste. "Let Killian bite you, and I'll reward you," Marcus said, his mischievous grin growing as my heart pumped faster.

I knew that both of them could hear the embarrassing effect they had on my heart rate, but in the moment I didn't care. My need outweighed any sense of propriety I might have had in me and I arched as if in pain when Marcus continued to be so close to my sex but not give me what I desired.

"Bite," I told Killian, knowing that he needed pain with his pleasure and that could work both ways. He could feel what I felt, which meant that biting me would not only give him my blood, but give him the sensation that would make him rock hard.

Killian took his time as he molded my breast to his hand and opened his mouth to reveal swollen fangs. I'd never actually seen the magic that gave pleasure with a vampire's bite, but this time a light poisonous layer glimmered. He waited until the layer reached the tips of his fangs before he slowly sank his teeth into my upper breast.

The magic hit my bloodstream with the force of a train. I felt as if both Marcus and Killian had rammed their dicks into me and my body reacted, arching with the force of the wave of pain mixed with pleasure that made an orgasm hit hard.

Marcus must have known what was coming, because he clamped his mouth onto my clit and rammed two fingers inside of me, giving me both sensation and the force of his fingers to clench around as the force of climax made me cry out.

I rode the waves of pleasure and treated this new sensation as I would pain, absorbing it, accepting it, and letting it spread through me thoroughly and completely until I knew nothing else.

Killian released me and lapped at the two small wounds with his tongue, his saliva working new magic to close up the skin until there were only two pink marks to prove that he'd bitten me at all.

I sighed into the lasting echoes of sensation as Marcus finally released me from his relentless attack as well. He kissed my thigh and grazed his fangs over my skin, but didn't bite, as he gently massaged me from the inside.

Killian grinned. "Are you back to the world of the living?"

I released a light laugh and shook my head. My sweat made my hair stick to my forehead and I swiped it away. "I don't know what the fuck that was, but you'd better do it again."

His grin widened. "Vampires can give pleasure with their

bite, but what I've figured out is how to control the levels of pleasure delivered with a bite. I can make you come whenever I want to."

I swallowed hard and glanced at Marcus who didn't seem surprised by the development. "Killian is an expert of pain. It would make sense that he was an expert of pleasure, as well." He twisted his fingers and spread them apart, making me gasp. "But I won't be outshined just because Killian has a good bite. Sometimes it takes a smooth touch to show you how much we want you."

I licked my lips, glancing from Marcus to Killian and back again. "I want both of you."

Marcus lapped at my swollen sex, winning a buck out of me. "You mean, both of us inside of you at the same time?"

The sane voice inside of me screamed that there was no way I was ready to handle that sort of sensation, but the words that came out of my mouth didn't align with my brain. "That's exactly what I want."

Killian flipped me over and grabbed at my breasts, holding me in place. Marcus slipped around us and stripped in front of me, revealing a hard cock and a beautiful body that made my mouth water.

I wanted to taste him, but he stroked himself once for my benefit and then laid onto the furs on his back. Killian nibbled at my ear. "You want to fuck Marcus, don't you?"

They were teasing me and I knew it, but I didn't care. Marcus watched me with such intensity that my sex clenched, wanting to feel him inside of me again. I squirmed in Killian's grasp. "Yes."

He bit me, but not hard enough to break the skin. "I didn't hear you."

"Yes, I want to fuck Marcus," I said, probably loud enough that the other panthers were starting to stuff fur into their ears. Nobody had climbed the height of the guest quarters to shut us up though, so I wasn't going to even attempt to be quiet for this.

Killian pushed my legs apart and put me on top of Marcus, forcing the vampire's dick to press against my clit and make me gasp. "Inside," I begged, even though the pressure felt orgasmically good.

Marcus gripped my hips and settled me on top of him before slowly, agonizingly slowly, lowering me onto the full length of him.

I groaned when he had buried himself to the hilt inside of me. He panted with the effort not to move and I knew that his efforts to tease me were finally starting to backfire. I wanted to provoke him, make him break his calm exterior that he always showed the world, so I grabbed Killian's hands and worked his fingers over my breasts, massaging myself in front of him. "I need you inside of me too, Killian," I said, breathless. I didn't break eye contact with Marcus who tried to pretend he wasn't affected by any of this, but his cock hardened impossibly more inside of me.

Killian released me and I eased over Marcus, putting my breasts in his face and exposing my ass to Killian. I swallowed hard. I'd never done anal before. My mind might be ready, but my body surely wasn't.

"Try to relax," Killian coaxed as he wet a finger and rolled small circles around my delicate skin.

At first I froze and clenched with Marcus's dick still inside of me. I wanted to move and fuck him, but Killian's fingers worked at a spot I'd never considered feeling sensations before.

Marcus ran his fingers through the roots of my hair and gripped me, bringing me closer and kissing me until I relaxed enough for Killian to push a finger inside. I gasped, but Marcus wouldn't let me go and continued to roll his tongue over mine.

Killian was so in-tune with my body that he never pushed me past the boundary of discomfort to pain, although he rode that line as closely as I could bear. No one else could have the insight or patience to help me do this, but Killian could.

When he'd begun new massages that I realized were different, it was too late, his dick nudged at my back entrance and I froze when my mind caught up with what he was doing.

Marcus was still hard inside of me and the slow rocking had only made me more swollen against him. He gripped my hair and twisted me just enough so that he could graze his fangs over my neck.

"No, don't bite yet," I told him. I knew what he wanted to do. A vampire's bite overrode pain and if I was in discomfort, he could mask the negative sensations with his bite, but I wanted to do this. I wanted to feel Killian and Marcus both inside of me and absorb every single second of it.

Killian pushed inside of me slower than I would have thought possible. He paused every half inch just to give me time to adjust. When I relaxed, he pushed just a little bit more until finally he was all the way inside of me.

"You're full," Marcus whispered to me, making goosebumps spread over my body. "You're full with two of your bondmates."

A sense of victory made me smile. If I could do this, then I could experience everything my connection with my bond-mates had to offer. I wanted the others here so badly, Quinn and Aaron with their dicks in each of my hands and Tiros with his cock in my mouth, but that fantasy would have to wait. I would give myself completely to all of my bondmates as soon as I could, but for now, I would give all of myself to Marcus and Killian. I would never allow them to feel like they were alone again.

The slow rocking escalated and sensations exploded inside of me. I lost any sense of time or presence and I was only the sensation. Marcus's hands on my breasts while Killian gripped my hips as he thrust in and out of me, sending me rolling across Marcus until the friction made me feel like I was going to go insane.

Marcus growled with frustration and I realized he needed to bite me. He hadn't fed for so long and what little blood I'd given him likely wasn't even close to enough.

"Bite," I told him, and knocked my head back, exposing my throat.

He sank his fangs into me without any warning, making me gasp as hot blood gave him the nourishment he craved. He wasn't going to allow me to feel the pain thought and he pumped me with pleasure from his bite. It wasn't the same force as Killian's, but it was enough to push me over the edge when both his dick and Killian's were inside of me, moving and thrusting and I clenched hard as the climax hit.

The most beautiful sound in the world is a man in the

throes of pleasure. I almost couldn't hear them when they came into me, but it spiraled bliss through my body as their hot seed came into me and their delicious cries filled my ears.

Finally, all of us spent, we collapsed onto each other and I never wanted that moment to end.

OH THE CALAMITY

$\mathcal{I}$’m not sure how much sleep I managed to get, but I was so exhausted that I fell asleep in the tangle of arms and legs of my bondmates until I woke to a warm sun kissing my cheek. The bliss of the night left with the moon and the far too cheery light of day reminded me how much work there was left to do.

Killian, Marcus and I had somehow found the energy to clean up using water from the thankfully large basin and the surplus of towels. The panthers were a hygienic species, so I'd tried to leave the place in decent shape, but even after an hour of picking up and scrubbing I felt a little ashamed with how much of a mess we'd made. I held up one of the bedding furs with a wrinkled nose. "Yep, definitely needs to be burned."

Aaron was with a clan of wolf shifters right now. Killian had made it sound like he was in danger, but a little voice deep inside made me wonder if Aaron really would want to leave once we got to him. He'd been denied his wolf all his life, much less been with any others of his kind. What if he felt like he found the family he'd been missing and he didn't want to come back with us?

"Why do you look like you're worrying," Marcus asked as he handed me an apple.

I was so grateful to see food other than meat that I clasped it with both hands and sighed before taking a deliberate bite. "Oh, fruit, how I've missed you," I murmured as I chewed.

Bast meowed unhelpfully from his perch. My cheeks warmed as I wondered if he'd been a spectator to the entire session last night, or if he would be angry with me that I hadn't worked harder to find a way to return him to his human form so that he could have loved me too.

His irritated meow told me that if I was worrying about last night, I shouldn't be. He was of more use to me as a familiar until all my bondmates were returned to me.

I wasn't sure what he meant by that. As my familiar, Bast could feed me with magic, but in his human form I hadn't explored all of what he was capable of. Other than getting me insanely horny by pushing me into heat, maybe there wasn't a whole lot else he was good at doing.

One more irritated meow, to tell me that I'd better be getting my mind out of the gutter and focusing on the task at hand. Right.

Killian chuckled as he lathered one of the furs in the basin in the hopeless attempt to save it. "I've never seen anyone enjoy fruit so much. You sure we didn't literally fuck your brains out last night?" His mischievous grin said that he thought he was enormously funny.

"Ha ha," I said with mock laughter. "I'm just hungry and

I've had my share of meat." I smirked at the pun. "Anyway, tell me more about Aaron. How are we going to get to him?"

Killian looked at the fur forlornly then set it onto the windowsill to dry, offending Bast enough to remove him from his perch. "The wolves do raids twice a week. They're consistent because they want to make sure the panthers understand the new territory the wolves have claimed ever since their worlds merged."

I raised an eyebrow. "What does that mean exactly?"

Marcus piped in. "I think I can answer this one. Sarina's spell sent all of us to different worlds, and in my case, to a different time. Because of that, it disrupted the time-space continuum."

I gave him a slow nod. "Okay. Time and space got disrupted, what does that have to do with wolf and panther shifters?"

Marcus brought five more apples from the bag.

"Where have you been hiding those?" I shrieked.

Marcus shushed me and organized the apples in a circle. "We don't know exactly how many realms there are, but for now we know of at least five." He pointed to the apple in my hand. "That's Earth. Place it in the center of the circle."

I took one more bite so only the core remained and then did as I was told. "Okay, half-eaten Earth realm, check. And these are the others where you and the others were trapped?"

He nodded. "Precisely. Sarina's spell had two objectives. One, to separate you from your sources of power, or so she believed. She thinks without us that you can be killed and that you won't be able to stop the Second Echo of Calamity. That was the second objective, one that we need to stop."

I buried my face in my hands and groaned. "This end of the world stuff is way too much pressure."

Killian chuckled and sat next to me. He bumped into my shoulder and grinned. "Don't fall apart just yet. Marcus is giving a lesson." He rolled his hand and gave Marcus a mock-bow as much as his seated position would permit. "Continue, professor."

Marcus frowned. After spending so much time at an academy for supernaturals where he was a research project, he likely didn't like being called a professor, even if it was a joke.

But Killian didn't know what Marcus had gone through and I had a feeling that Marcus would keep our experience between us unless I wanted the others to know. He ignored the comment and continued as he pointed at each apple. "These are the realms that we know have been impacted by Sarina's spell. When supernaturals from the center point were sent out to the others, it created a bridge." He pushed each apple until it touched the core in the center. "Now, they're all merging onto one another."

My eyes widened. "That doesn't sound good."

His features went tense. "It's not. If we don't do something, then the realms will continue to progress and overlap each other until they're all destroyed. If this was Sarina's plan, then it explains why she didn't mind dying. Whatever world comes next she didn't need to stick around to be a part of it. Remember, her power works off of sacrifice. What is a bigger sacrifice than multiple worlds destroying one another? If that happens, I have a feeling that her spell will come to fruition and she'll be reincarnated in the new world of her own choosing."

A violent shiver went through my entire body. "That sounds terrifying."

"The Second Echo of Calamity," Killian said, flicking his switchblade over his knuckles. "Everyone knows the prophecies, but no one really knew what they'd look like in reality. It's more fucked up than anybody realized."

I'd heard the prophecy, but the end of the world wasn't something I really paid attention to. It was far too outlandish and unbelievable, but now the end of the world was here on my doorstep and it was time to catch up. "How many echoes are there?" The end of our world as it merged with multiple others sounded as bad as it could get.

Killian pointed his blade at Marcus. "Ask the time warlock. He's seen past and futures."

Marcus shook his head. "Quinn has probably seen more than me." Marcus flashed me an encouraging grin. "When we rescue him from heaven we can ask him what other Echoes of Calamity we have to worry about."

I flattened both hands in a "hold it" motion. "Wait, heaven? Quinn is in heaven? Like, the heaven?" I didn't voice the rest of my question which was, doesn't that mean he's dead?

"Yes," Marcus said matter-of-factly. "Quinn is in heaven and Tiros is in hell." He grimaced. "It doesn't mean they're dead, if that's what that tortured look on your face is about."

"Aaron first," Killian said as he flipped his switchblade closed and shoved it into his pocket. "We'll worry about what other realms we need to travel to after we get our wolf back."

A NEW PACK

*G*etting out of the panther stronghold was a lot easier than getting in. I was sore, tired, and my apple had been poor nourishment for what we had planned. I was starting to understand why the panthers lived on meat.

Sunlight peeked through the filter of treetops and illuminated the quiet village. Bast trotted ahead of us with his tail held high. Apparently he was happy to be moving forward with our quest. The sooner we rescued all of my bondmates, the sooner he would get his mortal form back. Although, I think he was worried about the guys too, even if he wasn't going to admit it.

I would have expected more guards, snarling, and growls if we tried to walk out of the panther's den without an escort. However, getting out of the training grounds and working our way through the compound had been easy thanks to a rune Isis had given Killian in return for his services. Force-fields blinked open a doorway for us when it grazed his skin and the few members of the village awake gave us a wide berth, letting us pass. It was no surprise that panthers were night creatures, but I did expect more of them to give us a hard time leaving, even if it was earlier in the day. "You must have made quite an impression on the panthers," I said once we were past the sleepy village and watchful eyes of those on morning duty.

"Yeah, I can be a charmer when I want to be. But maybe I was too charming." Killian scratched at the paw print on his neck. I hadn't seen it appear on his skin until we'd breached the forcefield. "Hope this thing fades. I don't like being marked by another woman." He gave me a wink. "You, on the other hand, can mark me any time."

Jealousy spiked along with the throbbing reminder in my body of what he'd done to me last night—he and Marcus both. "How'd she give you that mark?" I asked, trying to sound aloof. Instead my voice did this weird pitch thing at the end and I cleared my throat.

Killian chuckled. "She had one of her burly man-cats tattoo it on me and she blessed it with her magic. Don't worry, I would never do anything sexual with another woman, even if it meant getting a free ticket out of cat hell."

"Where do they think we're going?" I asked once we were out of earshot of the village. The humidity of the forest pressed in on us and Killian veered off the path, to my dismay. Marcus took up the rear and I tried to avoid getting slapped in the face with sharp ferns every two feet.

"The rune Isis gave me has enough magic in it to get us back to Earth, but she doesn't know you have the power to travel worlds all on your own." He gave me a grin. "Especially with the dose of bondmate power we gave you last night."

I raised one eyebrow. It was true, I did feel a particular humming of magical energy since I woke up, but I'd chalked it up to nerves. I hadn't considered that sleeping with my bond-mates would strengthen the powers they'd already given me.

I hummed and ventured closer to Killian. His footsteps gave me a safer path through the tangle of underbrush of the forest so I lengthened my steps to match his strides as I placed each foot carefully in the grooves he left behind. "If you only had sex with me so that I'd have enough magic to get us home, then that's not cool."

He chuckled. "Oh, that was a happy bonus. I'll take you anytime, anywhere, any which way you want, magic or not."

Marcus cleared his throat. "Tell us about the wolves. If you're not using the paw-print rune to get us home, then what will we need it for?"

Killian brought out his switchblade and it lengthened into a sword. I'd never seen him use magic on his weapon, but I guess that we'd never been in a situation where he needed to use it. He slashed at the dense foliage, carving a path for us deeper into the forest. "Even though the panther and shifter realms are similar and now merging onto one another, they are still distinctly different realms. It'll take magic to cross the boundary once we get there. I know where we need to go because I've been on spy raids with the panthers a few times, but the problem is that the wolves keep gaining more and more territory. Their world has overlapped onto this one and the magic to invade the panther's world isn't as intense as it is to get back to the wolves, so they're infiltrating and taking more and more ground each day."

I decided that I didn't like the wolves very much. "This isn't their world. I'd say the panthers have every right to be pissed off."

He shrugged. "Yeah, well, you don't know the whole story."

As much as I wanted to hear more, the dense forest abruptly broke, revealing a sheer crest of stone and soil that broke onto dead trees as if a slab of earth had just been dropped from the heavens.

I grabbed onto Killian's shoulder and peered around him as I pressed to his back. "What the hell?"

We stepped out of the brush and Killian ran his fingers across the rough layers of stone that looked like someone had cut up a piece of layered cake and oversized it. The paw-print rune on his neck lit up and he pulled his hand away. "This is it."

"The Diamond Realm," Marcus said with a sense of foreshadowing.

I frowned at him. Nothing about this looked like diamonds at all, but then I remembered that Aaron originated from the Diamond Coven. My eyes widened. "Are you so sure that Aaron will want to leave?" The question just popped out of my mouth before I had time to filter it.

Killian gave me a raised brow. "Why wouldn't he want to leave?"

I ran my fingers over my face. Gods, my bondmates could be so dense sometimes. "This is what the Diamond Coven was supposed to be for Aaron. He can be himself here, his wolf, and maybe he feels like he's finally found... I don't know, his family."

Marcus squeezed my shoulder. "Maybe that would have been true had he never met you, Evelyn, but I know that Aaron loves you just as much as I love you and that means that you are his family." He glanced at Killian. "We all are."

I wasn't sure how I felt about that. A wolf mated for life, so in a way I had accidentally trapped Aaron. What if I'd used my voodoo Fate Magic on him without even knowing it? What if it had always been his fate to return to his own kind but I'd messed it up by bonding with him?

Bast startled me by jumping into my arms and swatting at my face, but he kept his claws retracted so the soft pads of his paws brushed against my cheek. His emerald eyes bore into mine with determination. I shouldn't worry about things that are already done. First, get to Aaron, and then I can question the meaning of life later.

I gave Bast a weak smile and scratched him behind the ear, then smoothed the ruffled fur. "You're right. I tend to get ahead of myself."

Killian gave me a raised brow, but didn't comment that I was conversing with a cat. "Okay then, are you ready?"

Fuck no. I'd already traveled between two worlds, was told that after this we'd have to go to heaven and hell itself and that terrified me almost as much as it did facing Aaron who might be furious at me for trapping him with my web of fate.

So, of course, I gave Killian my brightest smile and took his outstretched hand while I shifted Bast's weight into the crook of my arm. "Lead the way."

WITH BAST IN MY ARMS, and Killian holding onto me, he scaled the wall and my feet lifted from the ground. A squeak of surprise escaped me as he used only his switchblade and his feet to ascend a vertical wall. Damn, my bondmates were strong.

Marcus climbed below us and followed the breach of magical waves that Killian left behind as he worked his way between worlds. I could sense the shift, as well as the atmosphere and scents adjusting. What had once been a humid forest changed to something with more musk and quiet wildlife.

When we breached the cliff, Killian pulled me over the edge and I drew in a much more serene forest and less of a jungle that we'd just escaped from. If the wolves were waiting for us, they were even quieter than the panthers had been. I didn't sense anyone at all.

"They'll be getting ready for their raid," Killian told me as he helped Marcus over the edge.

Bast jumped from my arms and trotted closer to the trees with his nostrils flaring. "Do you sense anyone nearby?" I asked my familiar.

His tail twitched and a gentle nudge of his magic told me that Killian was right, we were alone.

Trees swayed with a gentle breeze and to my dismay, I decided that I quite liked it here. That probably meant that Aaron would too.

"Would you wipe that look off your face?" Marcus chided as he looped a hand around my waist and pulled me in for a quick, reassuring kiss. "I told you that you have nothing to worry about. We're going to find Aaron and get him out of here and he will *want* to leave, okay?"

I wanted to believe him, but that was something that Aaron was going to have to tell me. To appease Marcus, I gave him a shaky nod. "Yep, okay. Let's just get going."

Killian marched into the forest. "The wolves' den will be this way. I don't have a rune to get inside, so we'll just have to hope they bring Aaron out once they see we're not panthers." He frowned at Bast. "Maybe he shouldn't be with us."

"Bast is one of us," I reminded him with more bite to my word than I intended.

My familiar meowed his agreement that the wolves would not take kindly to seeing a feline familiar, so he'd be nearby, but out of sight and he'd make sure to stay downwind so they didn't pick up his scent.

I didn't like it, but I watched Bast disappear into the forest instead of running after him and snatching him into my arms again. When he was out of sight, I reached out to him with our bond and I felt a reassuring tug in return as if he was saying: *Don't worry, I'm still here. I'll always be here.*

We walked in silence with only twigs and leaves crunching underfoot for what felt like hours. I was still sore from last night, but I also wasn't used to walking for long stretches at a time. I preferred lazing about with my journal or sitting and chatting with Cassidy who was also on my conscience. All the more reason to find Aaron, and whether he decided to come with us or not, I would make sure he was safe, and then I would move onto the next piece of my heart.

The wolves didn't try to hide the entrance to their den like the panthers. No forcefields, no special guards, just a surprisingly modern array of buildings that looked more out of a scene of a wealthy Earthly community than a place where humans shifted into wolves and planned domination of other worlds.

The first thing I noticed was that everyone here was blonde-haired and blue-eyed and that made me uncomfortable. Maybe it was the distinct lack of diversity that bred intolerance in their society, which was perhaps why the panthers and wolves had always been destined to war against one another.

A group of tall, handsome men loitered around the entrance gates of the community, although they didn't look like they were particularly guarding the place, just keeping an eye on things. They spoke to each other in a language I didn't understand, but their tones had changed from relaxed to stern and hurried. One of the younger males of the group only wearing a faded set of jeans broke free from the pack and ran down the paved streets with impressive speed.

The rest approached us, not in a particularly menacing way, but their body language said that if we made one wrong move they'd show us what wolves were capable of. The tallest of the men stepped forward and offered me a smile. I noticed like the panthers, his eyes also looked a bit unnatural, although wolves didn't have recognizable slitted irises like cats did, so it was hard to be sure. His teeth, though, were definitely pointed enough to show his bite could be deadly. "Hello, you must be Evelyn," he said, surprising me in both speaking my language and knowing my name. "Aaron said you'd be coming."

To Killian's surprise, we were all welcomed into the community of wolves, although everything was a bit too smooth for me to really buy it. The wolves had an agenda with us they weren't letting on about, but for now, I could play along.

We were taken through the streets and walked past progressively larger homes. I never would have expected wolves to be so civilized, but the wolf who guided us called himself "Silver," which was appropriate given the streak of grey coming from his temples that left an attractive striped pattern through his hair. He looked like he couldn't have been older than thirty and his muscular body cut through his thin shirt promised he got plenty of exercise. However, there was an ancient sense of knowledge and past pain in his eyes that had me captivated. I'd met a few immortals here and there, so I knew how to spot true age when I saw it. My bondmates might be over a thousand years old, but only Tiros had truly lived all of those years and carried the burden of time that came with it. I saw the same kind of ancient wisdom in Bast when he wasn't being a snarky ass, but I was pretty sure godhood eliminated him from my comparison.

"Aaron joined us about six months ago," he said, straightening proudly as if it had been his idea to snatch Aaron from my world and bring him to his own. "We nearly killed him on sight, luckily he has all the traits of a wolf shifter that made it pretty clear he wasn't a panther who'd somehow managed to get into our world." He wrinkled his nose. "Uncivilized beasts are impossible to deal with. If it weren't for Aaron though, we would have wiped them all out by now." He shrugged. "Anyway, I'm sure he's eager to see you. This is his house."

I stared up at the mansion that Silver had called a "house."

"He'll want to leave," Killian said under his breath, although I think it was more to assure himself of the sentiment that Aaron was still our family.

We stepped up to the polished doors and Silver rang the bell. A camera swiveled to us and a screen popped on with Aaron's face suddenly appearing. His eyes nearly bugged out of his face. "Fucking hell, you didn't tell me Evie was here! And Killian, and Marcus! Oh gods, you guys are okay!"

Silver produced a key and unlocked the door. So, ringing the bell had just been a courtesy.

I wanted to ask if all the wolves had keys to each others' homes, but I chose to leave it be. We entered the mansion only to be greeted with finery that rivaled the Royal Covens itself. A striking chandelier sparkled over an entranceway that led to an immediate sitting area.

Aaron bound down the stairs that spiraled on the side, reminding me of the Amethyst Coven. Except he wasn't nearly as patient and refined as the warlocks of my destroyed home and he took the stairs two at a time before barreling into me and choking the life out of me with a sweet embrace.

Instantly the magical scents of forest and burnt wood tinged my nostrils and made tears come to my eyes. This was my bondmate and my body sang under his touch. His rough stubble lightly scratched my cheek as he pulled away from the embrace. He moved in to kiss me, then hesitated. "What's wrong?"

I tried to hide my emotions, but the world around me felt

like it was about to implode from everything I wanted to say to him. My heart thundered in my ears and I tried to ease my breaths. "I'm... uh, I'm fine." I wiped the sweat from my brow. "Do you think I could sit down?"

Silver watched us as Aaron guided me to what looked like a fainting couch... appropriate.

Marcus and Killian followed, but kept their distance. I didn't like how Killian kept his hands low, which meant he was keeping his fingers in reach of his switchblade should he need to use it. Marcus also pretended to be aloof, but he had a tell. He slicked back his hair for the third time since we'd entered the mansion. The faint scent of roses and jasmine wafted from him and I wondered if our wolf friend could smell it. The only evidence that he noticed anything was the slight flare of his nostrils.

Yeah, they wouldn't have their eldest wolf watching us for nothing. He probably knew exactly what was going on. We didn't trust him and rightfully so. They were hiding something from us.

"Aaron, can I ask you something?" I asked as he handed me a glass of ice water.

He smiled at me and I hadn't seen him at ease like this in a long time... maybe ever. "Of course. You can ask me anything." He took my hand in his and kissed my knuckles. "I'm your bondmate, Evie. We never hide anything from each other, so ask your questions and then we'll talk some more with Silver, yeah?"

I glanced up at the wolf who lingered over us like an unwanted chaperone. "Right, okay. Well, uh, does Silver have to be here? I'd feel better if we could have some privacy."

Aaron's brows scrunched together, then he whispered a silent "Oh."

I glowered. Of course he thought I meant sex. I gripped his hand harder and closed my eyes for a brief moment as I swept my bond connection through him. When it bounced back I got all the information I needed.

Aaron was under a spell.

SILVER'S ATTACK came out of nowhere. Maybe I didn't see it coming because he didn't actually have a weapon, but he didn't need one.

He *was* a weapon.

A shifter as ancient as Silver had impeccable control over his magic. The fact that all the shifters we had encountered so far looked so inhuman was either a testament to the strength of the shifting magic in their blood, or a result of their age. Being saturated in constant shifts meant someone like silver could say, only shift his claws and his teeth while keeping the rest of him in his strong human form that could barrel down two vampires to get to an unsuspecting witch about to utilize a fainting couch.

Luckily, that's exactly the image I wanted Silver to see and for him to show his cards first.

The world around me blurred as I dove into my magic that came as easy as breathing, especially after the boost I'd gotten from Killian and Marcus and now the brief embrace from Aaron that awakened the blood runes on my arm.

I moved fast, but I knew that I was only utilizing my skills as a Fate Witch. Bending time and space meant that while the world around me stilled, I could move through it, even if it was only briefly. Luckily, brevity was all I needed.

I glowered at the half-shifted wolf that had his claws extended, his canines pointed as he snarled. He'd seemed so genteel and friendly just a moment before, but that had been a mask. The face before me now was one of pure rage.

I didn't know why he blamed me for whatever he was going through. Maybe he had a right to. Sarina wouldn't have been able to bring the realms together if it hadn't been for me, but I was done beating myself up over something that wasn't my fault. If I hadn't been alive, then Sarina would have no one to stop her and the Second Echo of Calamity would have found a way to come to fruition.

I took my glass and splashed the water into the air. It froze on its trip to land on the wolf. "Cool," I murmured, then smashed the glass on his head, making sure to fuel a powerful sleep spell behind it.

The world caught up with me and the wolf's eyes flashed with surprise before he fell to the floor in an unconscious heap. He landed, soaked with my ice water while blood dripped from his hairline. Served him right.

That seemed to snap Aaron from whatever spell he'd been under and he jolted to his feet. He looked between Marcus, Killian and me and blinked a few times. "What just happened?" he asked, seeming dazed, then he looked down at the wolf on the floor. At first I thought he might be upset that I just decked his wolf mentor, or whatever the hell he was, but he snarled and kicked the unconscious man. "Bastard!" he roared. "You're not my alpha and I told you that a hundred fucking times! I already have an alpha!"

Aaron marched over to Killian who'd drawn his switch-blade, but didn't seem like he knew what to do with it. That made me grin. That's right, bitches, Eve-judo strikes again.

Aaron smacked Killian on the back. "You're my alpha, Killian. Not even a spell can make me forget that."

I wanted to remind him that he'd looked pretty enthralled to me just a few minutes ago, but instead I breathed a sigh of relief. The wolves had been trying to force Aaron to join their pack, but his love for me, for all of my bondmates, flooded into me and left no room for debate.

The only place Aaron wanted to be was right by my side. We were family. All of us.

HOME

*B*ast made a miraculous appearance. He must have been hiding in plain sight, or had the power to go invisible, and if so I made a mental note to always assume Bast was watching me. Although that was a sentiment I'd grown used to throughout my life. Bast was never far from my side even if I couldn't see him, privacy be damned.

We needed to get out of this realm and we needed to do it fast, which meant we couldn't go straight to my other bond-mates. Quinn was in heaven and Tiros was in hell, neither of which were places I felt like I could just waltz into willy-nilly.

Bast interrupted my thoughts with a swat at my ankles. Was he reading my mind again? *If so, yes, Bast, I'm the kind of girl who says willy-nilly, and I'll also kick anyone's ass who stands in my way. Get over it.*

There was only one place we could go that wasn't too far a stretch for my powers. If we returned to Earth, I'd be wiped out and I just didn't have time for that, but the Royal Covens was a place in-between realms, a halfway point where I could catch my breath while we figured out what to do next.

It also meant I could make sure Cassidy was okay.

Of course, I should have known better than to worry about her. When we entered into the portal room, a human with a slave marking was waiting. She smiled and waved before scurrying off down the hall.

I wondered if I should prepare for some latent trap from Sarina, but that girl with the slave marking had actually smiled and it had been genuine. Slaves did not voluntarily smile.

"You should stand behind us," Killian said, flipping out his switchblade as Aaron crouched into a fighting stance. Marcus took my flank and straightened his handkerchief in his shirt pocket. No occasion too dire to excuse an imperfect hand-kerchief.

"No, wait," I said, then a patter of footsteps sounded down the hall.

The girl entered the portal room, which was essentially a room with no windows and marble walls. She had Cassidy in tow and a weight I hadn't even realized was on my shoulders immediately lifted. "Cass," I said as tears blurred my vision.

She looked nothing like the starved prisoner I'd left behind. She wore a knee-length dress that covered her slave tattoo on her thigh and I don't think I've ever seen her in modest clothing before. A halter-top style strap made her look shapely and her hair pinned up with jewels told me that whatever she'd gone through while I was gone, she'd defi-nitely made it out on top.

She barreled into me and gave me a tight hug. "I'm so glad

you're okay, Eves. You won't believe what's happened since you've been gone!"

Stunned, I held onto her and tried to absorb that this was all good news. Cassidy was alive, healthy, and well. No matter what happened now, I wouldn't have to live with the guilt that she'd died alone in a prison cell with nothing but cheeseburgers.

"You have to tell me everything," I murmured into her neck.

She laughed and put me at arm's length. "It's a hell of a story... literally."

A CACKLE SOUNDED in the room, making Cassidy and I freeze. My mates moved closer to me and snarled, glancing around for the source of the sound.

"Fools," came a feminine drawl I'd recognize anywhere.

Sarina.

Cassidy squealed when I shoved her behind me. "Show yourself!" I shouted as the room darkened and the temperature dropped.

We weren't alone.

"Evie," Marcus said, his tone sharp. "Take my hand before—"

His voice cut off as if a wall had shut around me. I swirled as the room crashed into darkness and all connection to my mates vanished. I turned, unable to find Cassidy either.

My breath caught in short gasps. Sarina was dead... wasn't she?

How was she doing this?

She materialized with a greenish, translucent form just out of my reach. She grinned, although she was still covered in blood and looked exactly as I'd seen her when I'd killed her.

"You shouldn't have come back here," she said as she took slow, deliberate steps around me, although she floated, the movement of her feet more for show.

This was her spirit. How did she still have one?

I mirrored her movements, keeping my dagger ready. It took a moment for me to find it, but I spotted the lingering string that wrapped around her ankle, forming a chain as it disappeared into the floor.

Oh, she didn't still own her soul. She was tethered to the demon who owned her.

But that demon had permitted her to come here... why?

"What do you want?" I snapped as I continued to pace.

She chuckled, the sound scraping against my ears. She swept out her hands and the atmosphere around us changed, revealing different scenes.

"These are the worlds that must be sacrificed," she began, showing different scenes, some of which I recognized. The lush forests of the Panther Shifters strained under the weight of the Wolf's domain, crushing under a fissure that groaned with its weight. A bright scene swirled from above, moving downward, followed by a red heat coming from blow. They orbited a smaller orb that hummed with light.

Sarina ran her ghostly fingers through the scenes, sighing. "They should have merged by now," she lamented. "My death began the Second Echo of Calamity, but it won't complete its cycle." She ground her teeth, glaring at me. "My master gave me the power to create a new world, one that will never come to fruition if your kind continues to interfere, *Fate Witch.*"

My kind?

There were more like me?

I moved in a step closer, gripping my dagger as tingles ran up my spine. Something was very wrong about this spirit. I didn't sense Sarina's maliciousness was alone, anymore. Someone else was at play here.

Something... else.

"And you expect me to feel sorry for you?" I asked with a rough laugh. "Well, I'm not. I'm glad that all the realms in the universe can't destroy one another to build your supposed utopia. You know what I think? I think your master lied to you. When the realms die... that's it. There is no world for you to rule anymore because it'll all be gone."

She hummed, as if in agreement, making me hesitate. "I'm afraid I agree with you, now that I've viewed Calamity from this realm." She ran a finger over her chest, revealing a red glowing symbol I didn't recognize. Her eyes met mine, flashing with heat. "I will burn, witch. I'll burn for all eternity for my failure, which is why I have a new proposal for you."

I leaned in, not trusting her one bit. "And what would that be?"

She spread her arms and lifted her chin. "Kill my spirit. Release me from this torment."

Was she for real?

I stepped in closer and poised my dagger over the symbol at her chest where her heart should have been. "How do I know this isn't a trick?" I considered her for a moment, then stepped away. "Maybe eternal torment is what you deserve, even if you're serious."

Her face twisted with rage. "You would deny my request? After I have come to you so willingly?"

I considered her for a moment, recalled how many lives she had taken, how much suffering she had caused. Plus, Quinn and Tiros were still trapped in other realms. If I killed her now, I didn't know what that would do to them. "That's correct," I stated, deciding it was too much of a risk.

She roared and the chain around her ankle jerked. Massive bat-like wings spread from her back and her teeth elongated into a terrifying smile.

"Shit," I cursed, turning on my heel and running as Sarina's spirit transformed into the likeness of the demon that bound her soul.

Heat billowed all around me and a screech followed my footsteps. A thunder of wings sounded as Sarina took flight. I turned just in time to see the transformed spirit swooping down with her arms changed into talons.

I screeched, shoving up with my dagger as the only thing to protect myself.

Sarina released a cry and tumbled into me. A sharp sting radiated across my cheek as one of the talons along her wings grazed me. We both went down, a tangle of arms and legs as she snapped at my throat.

I didn't have a choice. I thrust my dagger into the glowing symbol at her chest.

A surge of power went through me as Sarina threw her head back and roared. I bucked at the lurch of heat, and I knew that if I didn't have the power of all my bondmates, as well as the remnants of my coven, I wouldn't have survived it.

Sarina twisted and screeched as her body took on a deep red glow. My dagger grew hot and I cried out as the sweeping heat of hellfire ran up my arm, but I didn't let go.

The shimmer of realms all around me spun, crushing in on one another another fraction as Sarina's spell struggled to complete its cycle, but she'd made a crucial mistake. She'd sent my mates to other worlds in an effort to separate me from the power they offered.

Instead, she'd only cemented my grip on those realms, giving me a foothold to keep them from crushing one another entirely.

She burst into ash a moment later, showering me with embers that burned my skin as the spell vanished and I panted. The darkness around me melted away, leaving me staring up at a tall, beautiful woman with kind eyes.

"Well, that was quite the entrance," she said, giving me a smile as she offered me her hand. "I'm Renee... Fellow Fate Witch. It's wonderful to meet you."

RENEE.

Fellow Fate Witch.

Cassidy held onto me, determined not to let me go after the spectacle of taking out Sarina's spirit. My mates growled with similar disapproval, but they kept their distance. I expected they didn't like being unable to follow when a demonic spirit trapped me in another realm, a place where the Royal Covens had merged with Hell, but I'd survived because of them.

Cassidy took us to the audience chamber where I had so many bad memories, but maybe it was time to make some good ones.

She told me how after Sarina's first death, another Fate Witch had made an appearance, although Renee said she didn't care for the title.

Fate Witches had many names over the years. Seer. Psychic. Keymaster. While other witches could see into the past and future, a Fate Witch could make adjustments to the path fate had planned.

Renee Fortune, daughter of a powerful Fate Witch before her, stood before me with her bondmates at her side... plus my own that they had rescued from heaven and hell.

"How did you..." My words drifted off as I stared at Quinn and Tiros, both unscathed for the most part, although Quinn had a bit of a golden glow around his head and Tiros's eyes were far more of a ruby blaze than I was used to, as if an inferno had awakened inside of him.

Renee smiled and introduced her bondmates, who were, of course, angels. That was a dead giveaway with their wings they kept tight to their backs. "This is Edwin. He is an angel of heaven and he returned to rescue your bondmate, Quinn. I hadn't understood why my angels had to leave me so shortly after the First Echo of Calamity, but now I understand. They needed to help you stop the next wave."

The angel with gorgeous white wings bowed his head. "I am pleased to meet you, Evelyn. You're famous where I come from."

I blinked at him a few times and then opened my mouth, but no words came out.

"And this is Devon," Renee continued, "he's an angel of hell, if you hadn't figured that out yet. Was it difficult to rescue Tiros?"

Devon smirked at me in a way that made a thrill go through my body. I wasn't attracted to him, but I could appreciate a devilish smile when I saw one. "It isn't the first time I've busted someone out of hell. Let's just say I'm picking up some tricks."

Renee chuckled. "Ah, then, that leaves just one left to prevent the Second Echo of Calamity from completing its work." She looked around the audience chamber. "Jeffery? Where are you?"

A rustle sounded from behind a row of elegant sofas and a vampire popped up holding Bast. My familiar growled and squirmed, hissing at the offending vampire for good measure.

"Got him!" the vampire said and moved so fast he blurred, then he sat Bast down between all of us gathered in a circle.

Two angels, four vampire-warlocks, two purebred vampires, and two Fate Witches stared down at the feline who was really a god in disguise. Meanwhile Cassidy and the other freed human slaves watched from the edges of the audience chamber and nibbled on finger foods as if this was some kind of elaborate play.

Yeah, this wasn't awkward at all.

Renee held out her hands. "Okay, everyone, join hands. Together we can break the final spell Sarina put in place."

I clasped hands with Quinn and Tiros, both of which gave me a jolt of sexual tension and desire just by touching them.

Quinn leaned down and his breath tickled my ear. "Later, lass. We'll rekindle everything later."

With that promise in mind, I swallowed hard, and then Renee began to chant.

A witch as powerful as Renee didn't need to chant, not for most spells, anyway, so I braced myself for what came next. A wave of power snapped between all of us like lightning, sending a wave of power illuminating all of us as if we'd caught on fire. The flames started out purple, a testament to how much of the Amethyst Coven's power and legacy I still had inside of me, followed by bursts of blue.

Bast meowed as if in pain, but he didn't move outside of the circle. Instead all of his fur stood on end as he growled and took the energy into himself. Renee continued to chant, her words growling louder until the magic amplified each word of power so much it resonated in my bones.

Bast transformed, his feline body growing and shifting until a muscular man with tabby stripes and a tail stood before me. Of course, he was naked, but my entire face blossomed with heat and I looked down only to see my own tabby markings had appeared across my chest.

Bast grinned at me and it rivaled the wickedness I'd seen in the fallen angel's smile. "I'm back, sweetheart, and we have some catching up to do."

THERE WAS nothing more I wanted than to rekindle my connection with all of my bondmates, but first I had to speak to Renee.

We sat at a table intended for the Anointed. Elaborate and glimmering thrones marked each empty seat where a witch had died because of Sarina's greed and ambition.

I stared at the empty Amethyst Coven's chair. Renee had insisted that I sit on the higher throne at the end of the table that consisted of all the gems, even those of the outcast covens such as Onyx, Opal, and Ruby. After meeting the origin ancestors of the Onyx, I knew the panthers would have detested anything like this. They'd probably declared themselves outcasts just to get out of the Royal Covens.

"You're the Queen of the Royal Covens now," Renee told me with a sweet smile, as if she'd told me I'd won a free year of ice cream.

She'd said that a few times now, but I hadn't quite digested it yet. I put my face in my hands. "What does that even mean?"

She chuckled. "It means that only you could have stopped Sarina. When you made the ultimate sacrifice and put your bondmates ahead of yourself, then you opened a loophole where I could intervene. The Second Echo of Calamity is designed to build a new world, and that's exactly what we've done, just not in the way that Sarina had planned it."

She'd said that a few times too, but no way was I able to believe that all the worlds had actually merged. Humanity wasn't ready for the supernatural, they never had been.

"Vampires have already come out into the human world, even if the Male muses have been working to try and keep supernaturals a secret, they won't be able to maintain secrecy for much longer. Vampires aren't the only ones causing trouble, there are a few other supernatural creatures such as the female muses, demonspawn, and mermaids, just to name a few, that are starting to get restless," Renee continued, then took a sip of her tea.

She sat in a plain brown chair, claiming that she had no coven affiliation and didn't plan on staying longer than she needed to. She wanted to reunite with her bondmates and that was something to which I could relate.

I sighed. "So you're telling me that heaven, hell, panther shifters, and wolf shifters are all going to infiltrate Earth? That'll just mean war. Humans have never reacted well to the supernatural. Just look at what's going on with the vampires."

It was a mess. The male muses were the supernatural creatures that kept our world a secret from the humans and they had their hands full trying to keep the massive vampire battles in explainable terms, but if wild shifters, as well as angels and demons, started pouring out onto the streets, then it was just a matter of time before too many humans found out for the secret to be kept. Witches had tried exposing themselves once before and it did not end well.

"So what do we do?" I asked, feeling hopeless.

A sparkle glittered in Renee's eyes. "We start a school, we can call it Fortune Academy and it'll be in the pocket realm right underneath my psychic shop in New York. Think of it as a miniature Royal Covens where all supernaturals will be welcome." She bobbed her head. "Well, there will have to be some exceptions. No life-sucking supernaturals allowed, such as succubi or the vampires." She leaned in close and wrinkled her nose. "Don't tell Sonya or Jeffery about that, okay? They'll just get super pissed off at me."

Sonya, the Queen of Hell, was on a first-name basis with

Renee, the all-powerful Fate Witch that was playing chicken with the Echoes of Calamity. Yeah, I shouldn't be surprised.

I gave her a weak nod. "Right, secret is safe with me." I wrung my hands together as I built up the courage to press her on the issue. After all, most of my bondmates were vampires too. "Why is that, though, if I may ask?"

She spread her hand out for me to see. "So, see this line right here?" She followed one of the creases across her palm. "That shows me how much I've altered fate. If this line goes all the way to my wrist, then I will die and I won't be able to stop all of the echoes that come next, you see."

"Okay," I said, leaning over to see her hand. I was a Fate Witch, not a palm reader, but she had this expectation about her that I was like her, so I tried to see where she was going with this. "So, by helping me for example and freeing Quinn and Tiros, as well as breaking Sarina's magic on Bast and the rest of the Royal Covens, you've altered fate, probably quite a bit."

She nodded. "Yes, and the Academy will prevent chaos, but I can't be at the head of it, and neither can anyone dangerous be allowed to join its ranks. Think of the Academy as the training grounds for the Third Echo. We will need an army for what comes next." She swallowed and traced the line on her palm again. "I've seen enough to know that the Third Echo will involve a creature that uses lifeforce as magic, which could be a numerous amount of creatures, and I hate to eliminate so many who might need help, but the vampires know how to take care of their own on Earth, they don't need special care. The succubi and incubi as well have been on Earth since the beginning of time and won't be upset by the realm shift. It's the others I'm worried about. The shifters and the divine. They need guidance or they'll go down a dark path that could ruin us all."

"Okay," I agreed, "so, we will begin Fortune Academy and all supernatural creatures impacted by the realm shift will be welcome."

Renee beamed. "Yes, exactly. Wonderful, isn't it? The realms have already merged and portals will be popping up all over the place. I recommend you make recruitment teams to start right away and guide the poor lost souls either to the Royal Covens or to the Academy."

"Does that mean that the realms won't separate? We're stuck like this?" It horrified me that Sarina had changed the world so much that we couldn't put it right again.

Renee shrugged as if it wasn't that big of a deal. "I don't see a path that allows the realms to be separated without further destruction. The best we can do is mend the damage that's been done and control the aftermath."

I went silent as I pondered the ramifications. I was now the Queen of the Royal Covens and responsible for not only the witches, but the successful integration of four different realms with my own. My head was starting to spin at the thought.

Luckily Bast interrupted the heavy conversation. He'd found some clothes to wear, although it was only a pair of pants and his gorgeous chest was on full display. He clasped his hands behind his back while his tail swished back and forth. "I apologize, however Marcus insisted that I come save you from the 'suspicious witch,' as he called her." He bowed his head to Renee. "No offense, Keymaster."

Renee chuckled at Bast's honesty. "None taken, God of Familiars. I believe Evelyn and I have come to a conclusion anyway." She pushed her chair back and stood. "When you're ready, meet me at my psychic shop in New York, it's on Fortune Street and you can't miss it." She gave me a wink. "We'll begin after we've both had a chance to rebuild our magical reserves."

A blush crept over me and I didn't dare look down. I knew my tabby markings were showing again. I desperately missed Bast in his mortal form and my body reacted to him, going into heat. I was careful not to touch Renee when we left the chamber, knowing my heat was probably infectious even to a powerful witch.

Feeling dizzy, I watched Renee turn around the corner, leaving me alone with Bast. He offered his arm and grinned. "You heard the witch. It's time to rebuild those reserves of yours."

EPILOGUE

I would have thought that I'd be nervous to reunite with all six of my bondmates, but nothing felt more natural or more right.

We took what would become my new bedroom, a royal suite prepared by Renee in her generous foresight that I would need a proper chamber and a proper bed with so many mates. I stared at what looked like three king-sized beds pushed together and I wondered if she'd actually found a store with that bed, or if she'd conjured it by magic. There wasn't a crease to suggest multiple mattresses were pushed together and as each of my bondmates began to disrobe, I swallowed hard.

Bast's effect on me made everything amplified a hundred-fold. I marched to the end of the bed and sat down, then waited. I wanted to watch them all strip for me, just take it all in, and they seemed to understand that. They took their clothes off slowly, even though I knew they wanted to hurry and get *me* undressed.

Killian pulled his shirt over his head and pulled out his switchblade before unbuttoning his pants. An attractive "V" disappeared into his waistline and I couldn't look away from the enticing image. I wanted to follow those lines with my tongue and explore what was underneath the straining fabric.

His blade changed to a short dagger, one that matched my own and he flipped it in his grip to hand it to me. "Make sure you use that on me," he said with a wicked grin.

I nodded my promise as my gaze tore away from him, forced to pay attention to Quinn as he peeled away his clothes. He still had a glimmer of heaven in him that made his skin glow from underneath as if he'd swallowed a piece of the sun. He moved in-between my legs and took my face in his hands.

"You're... warm," I marveled. It was the first time any of my vampires had felt warm to the touch.

He chuckled. "If you think I'm warm, then Tiros is going to blow your mind."

The vampire appeared at my side and slipped onto the bed with me. He nibbled my neck and made me gasp. His breath was hot as if he'd swallowed fire. When he pulled away his eyes glimmered with power. "Let's just say that hell gave me a few new tricks I want to try on you."

Marcus chuckled. "Look how beautiful our Fate Witch is." He squeezed in and pressed a long kiss to my cheek. The innocent gesture turned me on most of all.

I allowed Bast to sneak up from behind me. I sensed him

prowling and I knew he wanted to play with me. I squeaked when he wrapped his hands around my body to cup my breasts and give them a firm squeeze. He hauled me up so that my back leaned against his chest as he bit down on my ear. "I remember what Killian did to you," he whispered, making my stomach leap, "and I remember what you fantasized that night. Do you want it to be real?"

My world swam as I realized that Bast had been able to read my mind the entire time he'd been a cat. Damn, that wasn't fair, but if he could make my fantasy come true, then I was about to have the night of my life.

"Yes," I whispered. Even though my body trembled with both the fear of being overwhelmed and the excitement of it, I wanted this. I wanted to be as close to all of my bondmates as possible and let them know that I loved them all equally.

One word of acceptance was all it took and the guys shredded my clothes with teeth, claws, and maybe a dagger was involved. Before I knew it I was naked. Anyone who still had pants on ripped them off, revealing so many cocks standing to attention all for me that I forgot to breathe. Bast hauled me onto the center of the bed and flipped me around to face him before he laid down on his back. He massaged my breasts while Quinn spread my legs, my butt feeling ridiculously high and on display while exposing my wet folds to the air. I tried to twist a glance over my shoulder to see what he was going to do, but Bast grabbed my face and pushed his tongue into my mouth. I'd forgotten how it felt to kiss him. His rough tongue gave me new sensations that distracted me long enough for Quinn to work his own magic with his tongue.

I gasped when Quinn lapped at me, then he moved and I knew one of my other bondmates was taking a turn. This one softer, gentle… Marcus.

A blush crept over my face. "Bast, tell them to stop," I begged. This wasn't my fantasy, but gods, was I turned on.

He grinned at me in a way that said I wasn't going anywhere. "Let them taste you first," he coaxed. "Can't you feel how much we want to pleasure you before we pleasure ourselves?"

I'd never thought of it that way. It gave me pleasure to see them happy, but when I twisted enough to see Marcus and Quinn and made room for my other mates, allowing Tiros and Aaron to disappear behind my thighs, and I gasped. Both of them kissed my sex, which meant that they were close to kissing each other. I'd seen the way Tiros had looked at Aaron and the ramifications of that made me clench.

"I think she liked that," Tiros whispered, his breath a sweet agony against my folds.

Aaron rumbled a growl that vibrated through his tongue and into my body. I took that as agreement.

Just when I was about to reach an agonizing cliff, Bast grabbed my hips and pulled me over him, positioning me above his throbbing need. I wasn't sure if I was ready for it, but he waited for my whimper that begged him to take me before he rammed me down onto his dick, making me cry out and clench around him as the powerful climax hit without warning. He ground his hips against me, prolonging my pleasure until I collapsed against him.

Killian came up behind me. I knew it was him because the cool kiss of a blade ran down my spine before he worked his wet fingers over my swollen flesh. Bast was still inside of me, but Killian wanted to be in my other opening.

"I'm not ready," I protested.

"You just need to relax," Marcus whispered, running kisses down my neck and his gentle fingers slipping between Bast and I to massage my breasts.

Bast began to rock his hips and reawakened nerves that had gone numb with the force of my pleasure. He held me up so that I rode him while Killian massaged me from behind. Tiros knelt at my left paired with Marcus and Aaron at my right while Quinn stood stepped over Bast.

So many cocks, all for me.

The desperation on their faces twisted my heart and I suckled Quinn's dick into my mouth, making him buck. If his ass was in Bast's face, the God of Familiars didn't complain and continued to hold my weight as he slowly fucked me.

I took Aaron's dick in one hand, then Tiros in the other. I had no hands left and gave Marcus a panicked look, but he grinned and stroked himself for me, showing me what to do. I copied him with the dicks in my hand, stroking them both firmly at the same time and was rewarded with their groans.

Killian eased himself inside of my ass that was far too tight for him and his magic immediately took away the inevitable pain that came from his entry. I knew that the pain had to go somewhere, so it meant that he was feeling it himself, and that was pretty hot. He panted as he shoved deeper into me, making the sensations soar higher.

When Killian sheathed himself in me, a new sort of bond snapped into place. I had established bonds with all of my mates, but not one like this, one that united us all together as one. I took turns taking Quinn in my mouth and then Marcus until each of them looked ready to explode. With every rocking movement I gave them all pleasure and they pleasured me. Magic burst in my chest and spread out through my limbs, singing the air like fire and traveling into my bondmates. The impact tripled our pleasure of one another and connected us all together. Their thoughts flooded my mind and I gasped with the force of their love for me. This wasn't just sex to them. This was the ultimate worship of their witch, the meaning of their existence. I had no idea how much I meant to them and that they would die right now if it meant I would live.

They'd do anything for me.

I rode them all harder, stroking my hands up and down, swallowing Quinn's dick as much as my throat would allow, then taking Marcus next, and I worked my hips to fuck Bast and Killian at the same time. I fueled them with my own inner desires. They needed to know that I would do anything for them too, that I loved them more than life itself.

My magic amplified the pleasure and we all reached the cliff together. I cried out first when the powerful climax hit. Every muscle in my body clenched and every part of me was filled with my bondmates. They exploded into me, onto me, and their hot seed and ecstasy completed a bond that could never be broken.

For the first time, I knew I had found my family and my home.

The End

Next in the Blood Stone Series: Fortune Academy

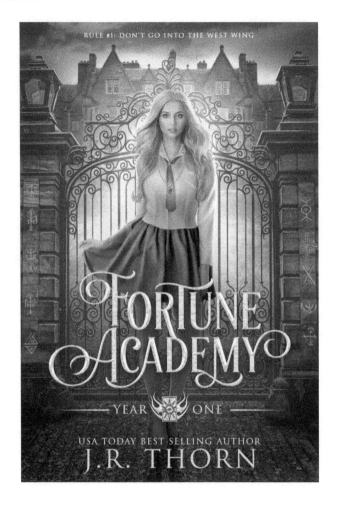

NOTE FROM THE AUTHOR

Thank you for reading all the way to the end of Evelyn's story! I hope you enjoyed it and will leave a review!

Royal Covens has been such an exciting series to write! I feel like I took everything you guys loved about Seven Sins and made it even better with this series, and of course who doesn't love a good dollop of sexy times with vampires! Bast was actually a complete surprise and totally unplanned. He turned out to be one of my favorite additions to Evie's harem and I love it when characters surprise me!

If you haven't guessed, the next series is a reverse harem academy that takes place in Fortune Academy itself! You already briefly met Lily in this series, and if you recognize that name from Seven Sins then kudos! You just figured out a big mystery that even Lily herself doesn't know (yet)!

I recommend reading Seven Sins before moving onto Fortune Academy. Although definitely not required, it will help you understand Lily's past and ultimately why she's exactly what Fortune Academy needs to dispel a deep-seated corruption.

I hope you'll continue on this journey as the Echoes of Calamity continue to ravage the merging realms. Together, we can unite the bondmates who will stop the end of the world coming to fruition while finding love and acceptance in the process!

Next in the Blood Stone Universe: Fortune Academy

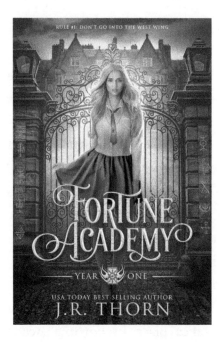

RECOMMENDED READING ORDER

All Books are Standalone Series listed by their sequential order of events

Elemental Fae Universe Reading List

Elemental Fae Academy: Books 1-3 (Co-Authored)

Midnight Fae Academy (Lexi C. Foss)

Fortune Fae Academy (J.R. Thorn)

Blood Stone Series Universe Reading List

• Chasing Fate (USA Today Bestselling Book)

Seven Sins

• Book 1: Succubus Sins

• Book 2: Siren Sins

• Book 3: Vampire Sins

Royal Covens

• Book 1: Captivated

• Book 2: Compelled

- *Book 3: Consumed*

Fortune Academy

- *Year One*

- *Year Two*

- *Year Three*

Non-RH Books (J.R. Thorn writing as Jennifer Thorn)

Noir Reformatory Universe Reading List

Noir Reformatory: The Beginning

Noir Reformatory: First Offense

Sins of the Fae King Universe Reading List

(Book 1) Captured by the Fae King

Learn More at www.AuthorJRThorn.com

Lightning Source UK Ltd.
Milton Keynes UK
UKHW011958010223
416337UK00018B/243/J